A Question of Loyalty

Property Of
Darlene Ryan Port robinson
Community Centre
Lending Library

Tony Vandermaas

A Question of Loyalty

Second Edition

iUniverse, Inc.
Bloomington

A Question of Loyalty
Second Edition

Copyright © 2007, 2011 by Tony Vandermaas

All rights reserved. No part of this book may be used or reproduced by any means, graphic, electronic, or mechanical, including photocopying, recording, taping or by any information storage retrieval system without the written permission of the publisher except in the case of brief quotations embodied in critical articles and reviews.

Certain characters in this work are historical figures, and certain events portrayed did take place. However, this is a work of fiction. All of the other characters, names, and events as well as all places, incidents, organizations, and dialogue in this novel are either the products of the author's imagination or are used fictitiously.

iUniverse books may be ordered through booksellers or by contacting:

iUniverse
1663 Liberty Drive
Bloomington, IN 47403
www.iuniverse.com
1-800-Authors (1-800-288-4677)

Because of the dynamic nature of the Internet, any web addresses or links contained in this book may have changed since publication and may no longer be valid. The views expressed in this work are solely those of the author and do not necessarily reflect the views of the publisher, and the publisher hereby disclaims any responsibility for them.

ISBN: 978-1-4620-7120-3 (sc)
ISBN: 978-1-4620-7121-0 (e)

Printed in the United States of America

iUniverse rev. date: 12/2/2011

For my wife, Penny

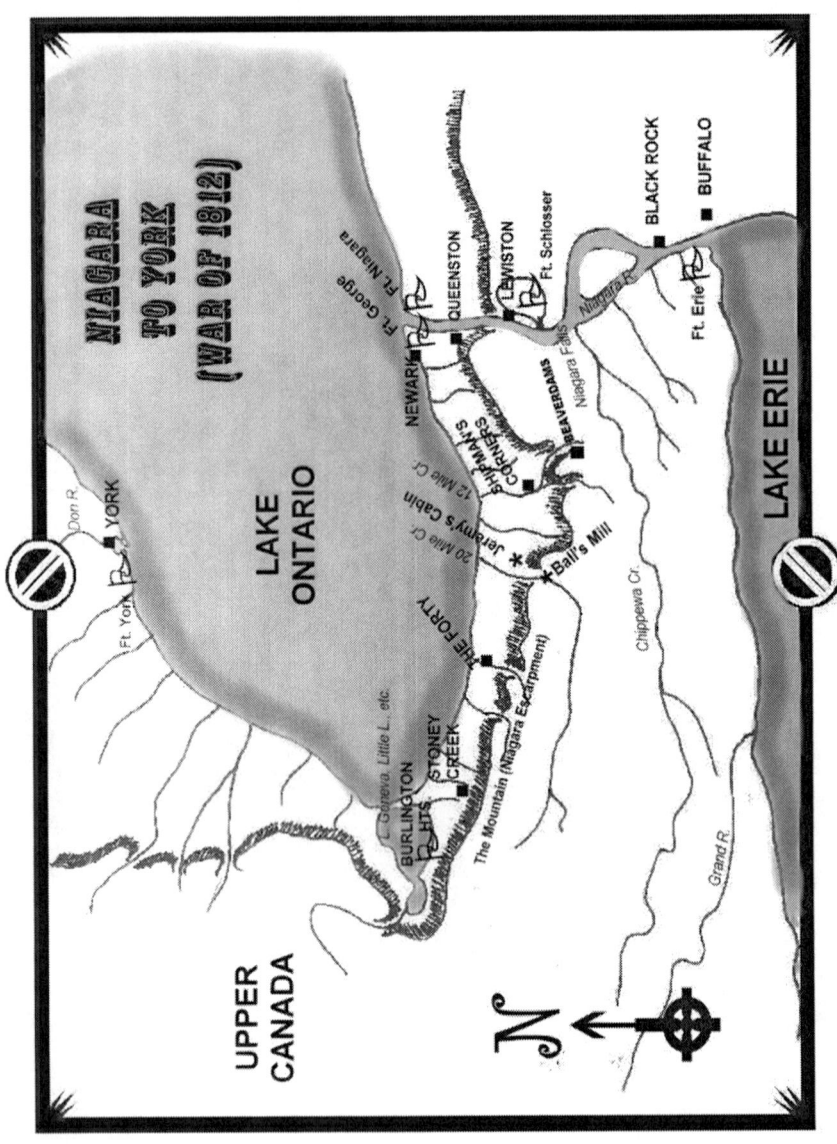

The Cast of Characters

The Battle of Beaverdams was a historical event, but the details of what happened, why and exactly where will likely be debated well after the War of 1812 becomes a vague memory.

Historical Characters (in alphabetical order):

British:
- Bisshop, Lieutenant-Colonel Cecil – commander of the forward post at Shipman's Corners
- Brock, Major-General Sir Isaac – commander of all British troops in the Canadas
- DeCou, Captain John – Beaverdams miller and militia captain whose home is used as a supply depot for the British in Niagara
- De Haren, Major Peter – commander of the forward post at the mouth of the Twelve Mile Creek
- Ducharme, Captain Dominique – commander of the Caughnawaga Indians Fitzgibbon, Lieutenant James – "The Green Tiger", leader of the irregulars officially called "The Green Tigers", better known as "The Bloody Boys"
- Merritt, Captain William Hamilton – leader of irregulars known as the Provincial Dragoons, future builder of the Welland Canal

Canadian:
- Ball, John and Charles – millers and entrepreneurs at the top of the Twenty Mile Creek

American:
- Boerstler, Lieutenant-Colonel Charles – commander of the attack at Beaverdams
- Boyd, Brigadier-General John – Dearborn's second in command at the start of 1813
- Dearborn, Major-General Henry – former Secretary of Defence and commander of the U.S. Army in Niagara
- Scott, Colonel Winfield - Dearborn's second in command at the end of 1813 and effective commander

The Renegades:
- Chapin, Dr. Cyrenius – leader of American "irregulars"
- Mallory, Benajah – Willcocks' second in command
- Willcocks, James – leader of the group of mostly traitors known as the "Canadian Volunteers" – former politician, newspaper editor, etc.

Fictional Characters (in alphabetical order):

Canadian/British:
- Carstairs, Second Lieutenant - soldier at DeCou's house
- DeForce, Sergeant - soldier at DeCou's house
- Dixon, Lieutenant Robert – soldier at DeCou's house
- DuLac, Josef – Caughnawaga Indian and friend of Jeremy
- Rhodes, Elizabeth – Jeremy's love interest
- Van Hijser, Jeremy – trapper, hunter, farmer and hero of this story who lives near Beaverdams
- Van Hijser, Sarah – Jeremy's wife
- Zimbauer, Ensign - soldier at DeCou's house

American/Renegade:
- Smythe, Captain Seymour – captain of the guard at Fort George
- Williamson, Dorian – one of Willcocks' "platoon" leaders

Also fictional are the incidental characters that appear in this story, including all of Williamson's men, all of Smythe's men, the minister and his wife, all the farmers and landholders, and assorted bad guys not listed as factual.

The Places

All of the towns and villages mentioned in this book are or were real places. Some have changed their names, some have been amalgamated into towns that didn't even exist then, and some still thrive under their original names.

Beaverdams – now a part of the City of Thorold
Chippewa – now a part of the City of Niagara Falls
Fort George – still exists as an historical site in Niagara-on-the-Lake
Newark – former capital of Upper Canada, now the Town of Niagara-on-the-Lake
Queenston – still known by that name, but now part of the Town of Niagara-on-the-Lake
Shipman's Corners – also known at the time as The Twelve, became the City of St. Catharines
Stoney Creek – still known by this name, although it has been amalgamated into the City of Hamilton
The Forty – now the Town of Grimsby
The Twenty – became the Village of Jordan, now part of the Town of Lincoln
York - capital of Upper Canada after Newark, now the City of Toronto

Prelude

Jeremy was near exhaustion, yet couldn't imagine the fatigue and pain his wife must be experiencing at that point in time. Exactly what point that might be, Jeremy couldn't possibly know, for timepieces were dear, luxuries the meagre earnings of a farmer could not in all conscience purchase. He knew only that it was well after dark, and their trial had begun when the sun had not yet broken the horizon that morning. He brushed his long dirty-blond bangs from before his eyes, an exercise in futility since the thick, straight, chin-length hair just returned to its position.

Sarah had awakened him with a whisper that morning. "It's time", she muttered from between clenched teeth. "Go for Mrs. Dobson."

Sarah was in labour, and Mrs. Dobson the local midwife. It would not normally be expected for a midwife to attend all births, but Sarah had already lost one baby in childbirth and they believed that the attentions of such a skilled woman could increase their chances at delivering a healthy child this time.

Into the crisp October air Jeremy stumbled, hitching up his braces and pulling on his coat as he headed, on foot, across the frosty fields in the general direction of the Dobson property some four and a half miles away. All of twenty years old, Jeremy was yet in good health, the ravages of a hard farm life not in his fate for some years to come, and he loped easily once he reached the dirt path that served as the main road for this concession.

An hour later, he and Mrs. Dobson had arrived back at the

cabin he shared with Sarah to find her lying on the floor, moaning and breathing labouredly.

"Sarah!" Jeremy had cried in alarm, rushing to his wife's side. "What happened? How did you end up here on the floor?"

Mrs. Dobson quickly took charge of the situation. "Never mind that!" she snapped, brushing the worried husband aside with practiced ease. There were times that she believed it would be much better if the nervous Nellies weren't present at these times. Too bad, she thought, that they could be so helpful in fetching and carrying when necessary. "Did you hurt yourself in the fall?" she asked of Sarah, who could only shake her head. "Jeremy, pick Sarah up and put her back on the bed", she ordered.

Jeremy had lifted his wife's slight frame from the floor with ease and she had settled back onto the thin stuffed mattress, groaning in unison with the dry slats that held it. He brushed her long dark, sweat-soaked tresses from her face, which was normally pretty in a plain way, but now appeared red and bathed in perspiration. Jeremy was at a loss for an explanation, for the last birth hadn't been nearly so strenuous, nor had any of the births of own siblings that he had experienced as a youngster.

Now the entire day had passed by and night had fallen once more, but there was still little sign that the ordeal would end soon. There were moments all day wherein Sarah relaxed some and she and Jeremy exchanged whispers of their hopes and dreams for the future and their child, while Mrs. Dobson sat quietly sewing on one of the only two chairs they owned. But then the labour would begin in earnest yet again. Now Sarah was fatigued beyond crying out, and Jeremy feared for her health.

"Will this child ever come into the light?" Jeremy asked desperately of Mrs. Dobson, who had come over to the bed to check on her patient. While ever maintaining a passive expression, the stern woman was beginning to show signs of concern in the frequency of her ministrations, now wiping Sarah's face, now moving in close, ostensibly to tuck in Sarah's blanket but appearing to be feeling for Sarah's breath.

"Only God knows the answer to that, Mr. van Hijser", she answered sternly. "Every birth is different, even for the same woman, and we can but wait for the outcome."

"But surely she has become too tired to deliver the child", Jeremy insisted. "Will she lose this one as well?"

Mrs. Dobson stepped up to within inches of Jeremy's face. "Mister van Hijser", she breathed, pronouncing his name "van Hizer", with a long "i", as did all who knew the family, "it is as I've said. Only God knows when and if this child will be born and I can give you no better answer than that. I've been trained only to assist in this miracle, but the answer truly lies within your wife's body and the good graces of Our Lord." With that, Mrs. Dobson retired once again to her chair and needlework.

Sarah turned her head and her pained, exhausted eyes met Jeremy's. She blinked as if focusing upon her husband, almost as if to ascertain that it was indeed he. "Care for our child", she whispered, almost a throaty sigh that seemed spent before it was completely past her lips.

Jeremy was confused. "Of course we shall", he whispered back, reaching once again for his young wife's hand. "Together we shall raise a child the whole township will envy."

Sarah's fatigued body seemed to go rigid, her hips rising momentarily in yet another spasm, held for what seemed an eternity and then relaxed, settling back onto the bed. Her hand feebly rose a short distance from Jeremy's own, as if to point to her breast and then dropped, her breath becoming ragged and strained.

"My God! What's happening?" Jeremy cried out desperately to the midwife, who now looked up from her needlework, showing a look of concern she could no longer mask. "Sarah?" he pleaded hoarsely, but received no reply, the expectant mother's face seeming frozen in a mask of pain. "Sarah!" he repeated, more loudly and wit a note of stridency that he hadn't intended, the panic rising to his breast from deep within the core of his being.

Mrs. Dobson, who had rushed immediately forward, now pushed the distraught husband out of the way. "Go outside, Mister van Hijser", she commanded quietly but firmly. "I'll see to Sarah." Against Jeremy's protests, she shoved him firmly out the door into the cold night air. He would be of no help here, she thought, for she now doubted that even she would.

Feeling quite helpless and useless, Jeremy paced about in an ever-tightening ellipse just outside of the door to the upgraded log cabin that served as their home. A seeming eternity had passed and he could stand the stillness no longer. Surely now that he'd calmed himself down and found his head he could now go back inside and resume his watch.

As he opened the door, however, he saw Mrs. Dobson step soundlessly away from the bed. Sarah lay still, her visage now peaceful and serene.

"Has the child been delivered?" he asked of the midwife, ever hopeful against all the evidence that things would come to pass as they should. Then he saw her brush the tears from her eyes before she could turn quickly away.

"No", Jeremy muttered the softness of the sound unable to mask the tortured soul that issued it, the awful truth breaking over his confusion like a massive wave, destroying all hopes and dreams in its path. "The child then?" he whimpered, grasping at the last straw available to him, but the midwife did not reply, merely stared at him, a look of profound pain in her eyes, both at the death of both her patients and at the unenviable task of dealing with the distraught husband and father.

"No! No! No!" Jeremy shouted, each repetition louder than the one before, the crack of hysteria in his voice.

"Mister van Hijser", the midwife's stern, disciplined voice crept past the young man's sorrows. "Jeremy", she added, her voice softening, "Sarah has gone to her reward, and her child is there in her arms, mother and child together." She looked at a loss for something else to say, and then added lamely, "It was God's will."

Something inside of Jeremy snapped at the sound of that final platitude. "God's will", he muttered. "God's will", he repeated, this time louder. "How can this be God's will?" he demanded of the now stoic older woman before him. "I though that it was God's will that we bring children into this world. How can it now be God's will that our first was stillborn and now this second one has been taken, this time with Sarah as well?"

He turned away from Mrs. Dobson, his heart feeling as it might be about to burst, the initial panic of being alone in his life tearing at the fabric of his being, and looked upon the still body of his wife.

"If this be the will of your God", he muttered through clenched teeth, his mind gone cold through the pain. "If this be the will of your God, then I turn my back upon Him even as He has done to me and my family."

Mrs. Dobson took Jeremy by the shoulders and shook him vigorously, now a righteous fear showing in her eyes. "Don't say such things", she demanded. "That is only the Devil speaking through your pain. I suggest you get some rest and then ask God for His forgiveness in the morning, when you can think more clearly."

She gathered up her needlework and her shawl and proceeded to the door. "I shall return to attend to your wife's earthly remains in the morning", she offered quickly as she hastily fled what she felt must surely be the coming wrath of God at the words spoken this night.

Jeremy sat down on the chair next to the bed and looked quietly at what remained of his wife, his partner in this farm, in life itself. Sarah's face had relaxed and there was no sign left in it of the suffering she had endured for the past day. Jeremy thought that, in spite of the requisite aging that came of carving out a life of farming in Niagara, even with the newer conveniences available at the beginning of the nineteenth century, Sarah still looked as beautiful at the age of nineteen as she had when he had met her, a woman of sixteen.

His mind rushed with ebbing and flowing images from their hard but satisfying life together on this small but self-supporting farm, of the quietly rewarding times they had shared, and he broke down in great wracking sobs there in the chair beside her bed. He cried, he railed, he pleaded for her to come back, he cursed God and all the angels in Heaven, until finally spent, he fell asleep, draped across the bed, holding the hand of his soul mate.

And, in the morning, when he awoke, he set out with a heavy heart, to prepare a grave for Sarah, in the back yard by her vegetable garden, and near the grave of their first stillborn child. He no longer knew if there was a God to look over them, but at least they had each other.

Chapter One

Jeremy moved cautiously forward, attempting to manage the tricky balancing act of using the trees to keep a screen between himself and his quarry without losing sight of it. The numerous dead branches that lay strewn about because of last evening's storm further complicated this delicate task, also threatening to compromise the imperative of stealth. Just to add more roadblocks to the task, the late spring sun had warmed up the wet earth, making a day moderate in temperature seem close and uncomfortable.

Despite his caution, he could not avoid the rustling sound he created as he pushed through the leafy vegetation that proliferated here near the forest's edge. It was a sibilant whisper that seemed to him as loud as the brass band he had heard in Newark two summers previous. He had been painstakingly stalking his prey for hours, as the skittish animal used any stimulus as an excuse to bolt to the next clearing. Any sound now that might suggest a predator and he would be starting the hunt all over, a most unappealing prospect.

He was now only two months shy of twenty-six years of age, almost middle-aged by the standards of a hard frontier life. Despite the pain he had endured and the hard earlier life as a farmer, his face still held the boyish good looks that had so attracted Sarah when they met at a local church social, her mother in tow.

Jeremy had now taken mostly to hunting and trapping for a living, farming only at a subsistence level. The few animals that now remained on the largely neglected property took care mostly of themselves, and were thought of by the young man more as pets, or perhaps even friends, than livestock. When Sarah had passed on, he had lost any further desire to be a respected citizen, knowing full well that the righteous Mrs. Dobson had passed the word of his conversion by the Devil, instead chose this less reputable vocation.

The young buck now stood unsuspecting at the boundary between the trees and a small natural meadow, his concentration fully occupied by the task of stripping all vegetation within easy reach, occasionally stepping gingerly forward to avail himself of more. From time to time he would raise his head and scan about the territory looking for obvious signs of danger. It was at these times that Jeremy would stop almost at the same instant, his mind strangely attuned to that of this magnificent animal. Once his game resumed with his preoccupation, Jeremy manoeuvred continuously to keep himself down wind and out of sight, at times seemingly impossible to manage simultaneously.

When Jeremy reached a point a mere fifty feet from the unsuspecting game, he braced himself against a tree and raised his firearm to his shoulder. A European gunsmith's masterpiece, it had been won in a card game from a hard-drinking German gentleman he had guided on a hunting trip near Niagara Falls. Forty-seven inches from butt to sight, the German flintlock, an over/under rifle/scattergun was, to Jeremy at any rate, a rare find. It was reasonably accurate for its day, firing a thirteen-millimetre slug from the rifle or a scattered fourteen-millimetre gun load, and this treasured weapon was the envy of all who saw it.

Just at the moment that Jeremy sighted the Teutonic marvel on his quarry, the deer raised his head, neck muscles tensed, the sinews in his haunches prepared to spring away at a moment's notice. He appeared to look directly at the hunter, as though he had sensed the man's presence and wished to face his nemesis head-on. Jeremy's finger pulled, flint struck steel, the primer powder ignited, in turn setting off the main charge. With a roar more powerful than the shot itself, the charge and what remained of the wadding flew from the muzzle in a cloud of smoke.

For a moment, it was difficult to determine whether the shot had indeed done its job. Through the clearing smoke, Jeremy could see that the deer was still standing. Without conscious thought, he began the process of recharging his weapon, with a speed and accuracy to be envied by many soldiers. Then the deer wavered and weakly sagged onto the knees of its front legs, all the time making no sound discernable to Jeremy who admittedly yet had the roar of his rifle ringing in his ears.

As the deer fell over onto its side into the meadow, Jeremy leaped forward, hunting knife in hand, to ensure that the magnificent animal would suffer no more if still alive, and to prepare his kill for travel. He knew he must move quickly, for the sound of his rifle must have carried for some distance through the forest, and there were many in these trying times who would fight and even kill him for this day's work.

It was late May of 1813, and the Americans were in control of the forts and fortified outposts along the Niagara River; Fort George, Fort Erie, and Chippewa. Although their sheer numbers practically guaranteed dominion over this territory, they rarely left the protection of these camps for fear of ambush by Indians or isolated rear-guard actions by British or militia. The real danger to the British and their loyal subjects, and even those who stated no preference in the war's outcome, was from two groups that would in later times be referred to as terrorists. These men used the American occupation to rob settlers, raze farms and generally bully all those they came across.

One of these was a Buffalo surgeon named Dr. Cyrenius Chapin who operated with a band of mounted American volunteers that was only loosely under the command of the regulars at the fort. Their specialty was night raids and pillaging to supply the fort, an activity to which the American commander, General Henry Dearborn, would not have admitted any knowledge. He was, after all, an honourable soldier, and actions against helpless, unarmed civilians were not to be publicly condoned.

The other was a turncoat named Joseph Willcocks, the son a wealthy and landed British Irishman, and a neighbour of the very people he victimized. A member of the Upper Canada's House of Assembly, he served the previous year under General Isaac Brock and was the man sent by that officer to convince the Mohawk warriors to fight on behalf of the British. The man had once been a pillar of the community both as a politician and the editor of the local newspaper, although he was known more for his opportunism than his place as a gentleman.

His reasons for his actions during this contest and those of his sidekick, Benajah Mallory, had nothing to do with loyalty to either side. It was rather, a personal vendetta against all those neighbours who had ever criticized him, not to mention a chance for wealth for himself and his men. "The Canadian Volunteers", at times numbering somewhere between two hundred and three hundred men, mostly Americans who had recently settled in Niagara, laid waste to all against whom they bore a personal grudge.

The Mississauga Indians near Chippewa were of concern to Jeremy because they were always an unknown quantity. Although they were technically allies of the British, Jeremy was in territory held by the Americans and the Indians could not always discriminate between them. Just one of the many unfortunate circumstances created in a war between people who spoke the same language, dressed the same, and were often related. Although Jeremy knew some of the Indians through his travels in the area, they were but a few, and one could not be careful enough when hunting near their land.

Finally, there was the danger that he would be discovered by one of the infrequent American patrols sent out from the grandly named Fort Chippewa to reconnoitre. If they found him here, if they didn't charge him with espionage, they would probably confiscate his deer and, much worse, his treasured firearm. For a man who made his living primarily from hunting and selling and trading the hides and meat he did not need for himself, such an event would have been an unmitigated disaster.

The day's work now complete, it would be a long walk back to his land near Beaverdams but he had been gone for several weeks now, hunting and scouting both sides of the Niagara River as he went. He was one of many, from both counties, who roamed the border areas, carrying on as they had before the war but for a sharpened eye to the positions and strengths of the enemy. They often passed each other in their endeavours and even shared fires in the colder seasons, where they discussed the war only in passing, never divulging their allegiances except by accident. Instead, they dwelt heavily upon the factors of their trade, including their weapons, game signs, and the availability of different types of game they might be hunting. There was often no shortage of gossip the men had encountered en route, most of it of little value but quite entertaining after a generous portion of whatever spirits were available. They also traded among themselves for their necessities and swapped furs for the kinds in demand back in their own home areas.

Men such as these were generally ignored by the soldiers on either side of the war, except to pump them for information and hire them to hunt food for the troops. The former led to a booming business in disinformation on both sides, and an officer had to develop a keen eye for the truth among those who would freely offer information, although the less scrupulous among them would certainly offer up their tidbits to either side for money.

Jeremy continuously collected information for the British and it was under such circumstances that he had come to pass on his observations to Lieutenant James Fitzgibbon the previous day. "The Green Tiger", as he was known, spent much of his time during the occupation scouting about the eastern end of the peninsula with his "Green Tigers", testing American troop strengths and positions and trying to capture Joseph Willcocks. They were semi-officially so-named because of their uniform, which consisted mainly of a green coverall, but "Bloody Boys" was the name they preferred and indeed the name used by most.

The two had met up just outside of Chippewa, where the two exchanged pleasantries over a shot of rum, along with Jeremy's information and the war stories of both men. All this had occurred right on the Americans' doorstep. This was what made Jeremy nervous at this time for, if someone who harboured sympathies for the Americans had seen him, being found here by them might be to his great disadvantage.

Having stripped the buck of all he could pack, including the hide and choicer cuts of meat, Jeremy loaded it all onto a hastily constructed travois. With his rifle slung across his back, he shouldered the longer two poles of the contraption onto his shoulders and set out toward home along the boundary between the meadow and the woods, using the confusing shadows of this transition area to keep from sight.

Taking into account the load Jeremy was dragging he estimated that, barring major impediments, he could be home by nightfall, a goal he savoured with much anticipation. The way would have been greatly eased by using well-travelled Lundy's Lane, but this was too dangerous with his cargo, for the thoroughfare was popular with troops and all manner of brigand as well as local folk. For this reason, he followed an Indian trail that shadowed the main thoroughfare from mere yards into the woods. And fortunate it was that he had decided to do so.

Less than half of the distance toward his home, Jeremy heard the sound of hoof-beats approaching from the west along Lundy's Lane. It was the lazy pace of a number of horses being ridden close together and generally being allowed their own heads. Caching his load in a thicket beside the path he'd been using, he stepped cautiously and stealthily through the thick cover toward the road, careful to remain hidden at all times.

Jeremy saw the riders draw closer. They seemed to be in no particular hurry, as if on a Sunday outing, looking about at their surroundings with a sleepy curiosity as they approached. Only one displayed subtle signs of tension, as if he were searching his environs for something specific. Initially, the young hunter just eyed them curiously, feeling nothing was unusual about these men. Groups of riders passed along Lundy's Lane on a regular basis, for many reasons but, as Jeremy turned to retrieve his goods, one of these men caught his attention.

Upon closer scrutiny, Jeremy recognized the traitor Dorian Williamson, one of the lieutenants of Joseph Willcocks, in the fore of the riders. Willcocks' Canadian Volunteers numbered anywhere between two hundred and three hundred men at peak times, allegiances being what they where during that war. Barring major raids or skirmishes, however, his men would often split into smaller "platoons" to carry on some independent bullying and raiding. And Jeremy was well aware that this group was one of the worst.

For a long moment in time, Jeremy felt that Williamson looked directly at him, but he then looked away again without any sign that he had seen anything. This would have been an unlikely result if Williamson had noticed, for he and Jeremy had crossed tomahawks once before. To Jeremy's intense relief, the band of scoundrels continued on past with hardly a word spoken except to each other, and nothing of great import at that. He breathed a controlled sigh, allowing the tension to slowly escape, as it seemed Jeremy would be safe this time.

Then, as fate would have it, one of the men near rear dropped back and dismounted his horse, which Jeremy recognized as having belonged to a neighbour who lived just outside of Shipman's Corners on the Twelve. He walked to a spot only a few feet from where Jeremy hid and, to ribald jest from his companions, began to unbutton the fly to his trousers, the intent obvious. Jeremy held his breath, in part to avoid the man's urine, which he could actually smell on this warm afternoon, and in part because he feared the man would be able to hear his breathing.

The man completed his task, rebuttoned his fly and let out an exaggerated sigh of relief as he turned to mount his horse and rejoin the others, who had long since lost interest. At the last moment, his eye thought he had caught a glimpse of something nearby. He took a step closer to make sure that he wasn't suffering from some form of post-alcoholic hallucination. Jeremy decided he had no choice but to act, for this man would immediately call for backup once he confirmed the reliability of his eyesight.

Jeremy reached out, grabbed the man by the neck and pulled him suddenly through the bushes in which he had been concealed. His victim didn't even have the time to cry out in surprise as the young man's strong hands closed more tightly about his windpipe, making any attempt to do so quite impossible. The man wouldn't surrender as easily as that, however, lashing out with his fist and catching Jeremy squarely in the stomach, catching him off-guard and driving the wind out of him.

Jeremy could not afford to let go even for a moment for, if he did, there was no doubt that an immediate cry for help would issue from the lips so cruelly snarling mere inches from his own. He groaned as quietly as he could once again, ever conscious of this man's companions just down the road, as his adversary landed another punch. This time the blow landed on the right side of his rib cage, and Jeremy could feel his normally considerable strength wavering. There was nothing for it, he decided. Although he had hoped to avoid doing the man serious harm, his options were rapidly fading. While yet holding onto the man's throat with all his remaining strength, Jeremy reached over his shoulder and grabbed hold of the handle of the tomahawk that hung there from a specialized loop.

With a sickening crack, he brought the weapon down upon the crown of his foe's head, separating skin, muscle, bone, and brain halfway along the depth of the tomahawk blade. With barely a sound, the man's eyes first opened wide in surprise at this unexpected turn of events, and then glazed over as his brain ceased to function.

Jeremy sat back on the ground as his body was released of the tension it required to survive the situation, and he allowed his opponent to drop limply beside him. It was not the first man he had killed in battle, but the victory did not leave him with the feeling of power that some were afforded. He swallowed hard as nausea welled up in his gut and he felt completely drained, as if a part of his essence had departed along with that of his victim. No glory here, he thought. What a terrible soldier I would make.

There was no time for contemplation, however, as he heard the sound of hoof beats hesitantly approaching the spot where his adversary's horse stood waiting for the rider that would not be appearing.

"Where'd you vanish to, Jake?" the man called out, a lack of certainty apparent in his voice. "Did you decide to take a nap somewhere? You know Williamson ain't gonna be happy about the time we're losin' here. You know he doesn't want to get caught out in the open after dark." His question seemed to fall upon deaf ears, as indeed it had. Hearing no reply, this second man dismounted and began to walk cautiously toward the spot where he thought he had last seen his companion.

Jeremy knew there was a distinct possibility of discovery if he did not think quickly. There was no way he could hide the body nor run away quietly without being noticed. If these men should decide to come after him, they would certainly capture him. He had no horse and there were nearly a dozen of them to chase him down even if he managed to take advantage of the forest's tangle and the horse-crippling terrain.

Just as all options seemed hopeless, the ghost of a plan began to formulate itself in the trapper's mind. He would need somehow to frighten them away, perhaps using the one fear that seemed to be common to those on the American side in this war. Deciding the course of action to be his only hope, Jeremy lifted the bloody body of his enemy off the ground with one great heave. The corpse crashed loudly out of the bushes onto the road, its bloody visage facing upward for all to see, and he began simultaneously to whoop wildly in a poor approximation of a Native war cry.

The man who had almost discovered Jeremy took one quick glance at the cracked open skull of his companion and bolted back to his mount, screaming in terror as he almost ran past the skittish animal. "Indians!" he cried. "Indians! They got Jake! Must be a hundred of them!" With that he bounded up onto his already galloping horse and streaked off past the other riders. They whirled their horses about in uncertainty of action while Williamson yelled at them to hold their positions.

Jeremy watched the men who rode away in panic, regardless of Williamson's orders to his men to regroup, that he commanded it, and that they should turn and face their enemy. But they would have none of it, and rode on in such a panic that they were leaving their leader behind. Williamson was no coward, but as the already-old saying went, discretion is the better part of valour and, all said and done, he was no more certain than they of the strength of their enemy.

After a few more war whoops for good measure, Jeremy slumped against a tree, exhausted by the effort and the pain in his stomach and ribs from opponent's punches. All these things were, of course, in turn exacerbated by his overwhelming desire to laugh at the spectacle of those men and horses flying in terror down Lundy's Lane. It would be fine with him if he never saw that gang of cutthroats again in his lifetime. In this small world in which Jeremy and Williamson both travelled, however, this was a futile hope.

After a rest of only a few moments, Jeremy looked down upon the body of his adversary. He certainly could not leave the corpse here to rot, he thought. An enemy he may have been, but he was a man all the same, and it was only proper that he receive some sort of burial. So, digging a hole with his knife and his hands, he dug down a couple of feet through the soft forest soil, just deep enough that the body would be covered, and dragged the body into it. Saying a few funereal words that he could remember from past experience, he quickly carved a marker reading "Jake", that being all he knew of the man, and headed back to his cache.

Jeremy was exhausted beyond any attempt at description. Only a few times in his lifetime had he been as tired as today, but he knew that he could not remain here and rest. Even more, and much to his chagrin, it would now be suicide to continue to use his travois much longer. He was merely an hour from Beaverdams and less than that from his own home near the Niagara Escarpment's edge. Even a blind man would be able to follow the furrows created by the wooden poles directly to his home if he continued much longer. With a deep sigh, he decided he would continue on for maybe another half hour with his travois, until a point near where his path diverged from Lundy's Lane. From that point, barely able to remain erect with his load, he headed northward toward home.

In a near sleepwalking state, he finally reached the edge of his overgrown fields, dragging one foot behind the other, stumbling often over minor obstacles such as roots and stones. On his back now was the full weight of the deer hide and venison, carried for several miles in this fashion overland and along the edges the marshes of the area known as the Beaverdams, namesake for the village that squatted at their edge.

He burst through the door of his house and fell upon his bed, leaving his burden where it landed upon the floor, to be considered at a time of awakening. He thought that, perhaps by then, he'd be able to lift his arms once more. That was the last thought he entertained, as he fell into a deep, dreamless sleep almost instantaneously, continuing through the supper hour and well past the first light of morning.

Chapter Two

When Jeremy finally awoke, he set to work at the more mundane tasks of his life on the farm, even if he was no longer a practicing farmer. It may have been that he no longer tended his farm to any degree, but he still cultivated a garden at the back of his house to sustain him through the year. Heavily planted in root crops, which he could easily store in his cold cellar, even over the sometimes-dreadful months of winter, he also had staples such as cabbage, peppers, the plant that some called maize but he knew as corn. He even grew a small plot of tobacco, mostly for personal use during those long, cold winter nights before the fireplace, when he'd have naught but his thoughts to keep him company. Those were sometimes the most unbearable moments of his existence, when the memories of his previous life would creep in and leave him aching for those times.

Jeremy collected the deer remains he had dropped so unceremoniously to the floor the previous evening. The hide was taken to the barn, where he had a special place set aside for such work. Laying it out carefully on a drying rack, he covered the inside of the hide well with several pounds of salt. This he'd leave here for perhaps a week, when he'd take it, along with any others he may have, to the tannery below the escarpment. He was well aware that he stood to gain more if he did the tanning himself, but it was a painstaking process and he'd much sooner spend his time and effort hunting and travelling.

The venison he took to the small smoke house behind his home, hanging strips of the meat on drying racks and lighting a smoky hickory fire. It was the easiest way he knew of to keep the venison until he had sufficient to bring to the British Army's supply depot for sale.

The deer now taken care of, he headed to the garden to see to his young garden, seeing that the new plants had water and picking off the occasional insect that had taken a liking to his future food supply. Those chores satisfied, Jeremy set about the more physically taxing work of drawing water and chopping firewood, finding it necessary to travel a half-mile into the woods to find green hickory to use in the smoke house.

Though the list of chores seemed short, by the time he was done, the morning had slipped by and the day had passed well into afternoon. It had not helped, of course, that he had slept to the ungodly hour of eight o'clock that morning. A regular man of leisure, he chuckled to himself.

The truth was, Jeremy had much more free time than the regular farmers who were his neighbours. His hunting, trapping and trading lifestyle allowed him much more freedom than they had, and the fact that he had no family to support made him something of an enigma in his time. He had heard from others on occasion that his neighbours did in fact think of him as something of a vagrant who did not recognize the virtues of large families and regular, backbreaking work from sunup to sundown every day but the Sabbath.

From time to time, some neighbouring woman would attempt to arrange a match for him, an act that was no doubt well meaning but no less annoying for all that. He felt no desire to remarry at this stage of his life, the pain of his double loss six years earlier still burned in his soul, a commodity he was not altogether certain he even possessed.

Jeremy also was not bound to working the land, as were the others in his area. Many, if not most, of his neighbours were United Empire Loyalists or more recent American immigrants and they had been granted free land on the condition that they clear the property and derive an income from it in order to keep it. His case was different, his property having been purchased with cash his great-grandfather had obtained as prize money in the capture of

French territories during the French and Indian Wars of the mid-1760s.

The van Hijser family had originally been among the settlers of New Amsterdam in what had become, under British and American rule, New York. They had prospered in that colony, becoming a shipping concern first with their Indian Dutch and later with the British. They had at one time owned a great deal of land in the future State of New York in a manner contingent with that of the land barons back in their ancestral home.

That had all vanished during the French and Indians Wars. The van Hijser patriarch died at the early age of forty-two of an influenza outbreak and his only son had bought an army commission, marching off to war and glory and leaving the family business to suffer in the hands of an incompetent manager. By the time the war was over, the van Hijser fortune had been reduced to the level of the middle merchant class and the family home forfeit to creditors.

But Colonel Jacob van Hijser was not overly distraught at the loss of the status and wealth his family had enjoyed. While serving in the eastern theatre in the war against the French, he had discovered the region that would be known as Niagara. He was drawn by the apparently more moderate winters of the area between Lakes Erie and Ontario, the view from the escarpment (or Mountain, as the few settlers referred to it) and the plentiful streams and undeveloped land. He would retire from the army and, under the rules of the time, pay a pittance for the land he had picked out on the edge of the escarpment not far eastward of the Twelve Mile Creek.

By the time the Empire Loyalists began to pour into Niagara, the van Hijser farm was already a going concern, but not under the strictures governing the new farmers. At the time that the van Hijsers bought their land, the Crown's only interest was in moving large numbers of English-speaking, protestant settlers into the Canadas, loyal to King and Country. The Loyalists, however, found themselves bound by a rule to actually clear and develop a large part of the land they were granted, as the Crown had by that time discovered an interest in the productivity of those under their rule.

It was for these reasons that Jeremy now felt little concern about his lack of attention to his land, beyond the occasional lecture from neighbours. He was sufficiently even tempered that he could withstand their prejudices, smiling and nodding politely in the face of the latest lecture or criticism. He was quite content with his new lifestyle, travelling about meeting people, hunting and learning the ways of the land.

Dorian Williamson was in a black mood, and the other members of his platoon kept their distance for fear of what might happen should they attract the man's attention while he was of such a disposition. Williamson was a crack shot with a rifle, although he preferred the wide scatter of shot from a musket, and he was without equal in this camp when it came to fighting with a blade or a tomahawk. More than one man had been seen to feel the bite of his steel when saying the wrong thing at the wrong moment, and many more unwitnessed victims were rumoured than were known.

The most fearsome aspect of Williamson's fighting was that he gave no quarter. All fights with this man were fights to the death and the pure and unbridled rage that issued forth from the man when he felt slighted denoted a slim likelihood that the death would come to Williamson. Even when ordered to bring in a person as a prisoner, there was a great chance that the subsequent battle to subdue that person would result in a captured corpse should he be the one to carry out the task. Such prisoners were much easier to handle as far as he was concerned.

Now, however, Williamson was irascible to a level even greater than was normal for him. Ever since the band had returned from their raid along the Mountain, at the same time trying to obtain fresh intelligence for the U.S. Army, he had been the model of an insane man. He took swipes at those who came within reach, broke furniture, all the things that might be expected of a madman, which he was, at least temporarily.

His own men felt little but fear and contempt for the large, plain-looking man, and would long have deserted him but that many of them were like-minded and the booty from their raids was rewarding to say the least. Many of the members of his gang ranged from local farmers who had come to Niagara for the free land, mostly from the U.S., and had no real loyalty to the country they lived in. This group had no real loyalty to anything or anyone, in fact, and frequently disappeared to tend to other business, which conveniently and frequently occurred when a battle broke out. Most of the rest were at best described as adventurers, at worst as murders and thieves, as unwelcome in the U.S. as here. In fact, for all his own reputation for ruthlessness toward those he disliked, even their overall leader, Joseph Willcocks, was leery of them.

"If you women ever turn and run like that again, I'll shoot you myself", he growled when finally calmed down some. "Those Indians have little enough respect for us white men, as is our due, especially we Americans. Allowing them to see us turn tail like that will give them lots to laugh about around their fire tonight."

"Maybe you have little value for your scalp", John Newsome growled back. "But I'd like to keep mine well attached for some years to come." Newsome was one of the very few who had no fear of their leader, although he did have a healthy respect for Williamson's abilities. Standing almost six feet and three inches tall, a massive man of solid muscle from his years working the portage around Niagara Falls on the American side, John had little fear of any white man. He was, however, filled with the typically American, sometimes irrational fear of Indians, largely due to tales from the less settled areas of the U.S.

Williamson looked Newsome in the eyes. His anger rose rapidly to the surface once again, and only his bloodlust and skill kept the slight trembling of rage from showing. He sighed heavily, as though about to deal with a recalcitrant child, and stood up from his seat slowly and deliberately.

Newsome's eyes followed him, his eyes never leaving the other's. Dorian took several slow steps in John's direction, unsheathing and brandishing his knife. Newsome, seeming just as casual, reached for his as well. Several times they circled the fire, which was now dying due to neglect, and the other men in their group nearly tripped all over themselves trying to get out of the way. As the incredible tension of the seemingly inevitable battle rose to a crescendo, none wished to look away, for their own blood lust was running high, in part a reaction to the mortification they had felt at their cowardly display that afternoon.

Geoffrey Smith, a tall but gaunt member of the team, was Williamson's deputy and the keeper of the wilder man's sanity... or tried to be. Whenever there were flares of temper such as this, Geoffrey would attempt to intercede, trying to keep the peace in the camp. There was no percentage in a platoon riding or walking about bound with bandages and leaning on crutches, and Smith had the uncanny ability, under normal circumstance, to smooth over "misunderstandings" such as these.

Of course, this was no minor disagreement. The fury between these two men was caused and fuelled by the shame brought on by the events on Lundy's lane. To add fuel to this fire, Newsome's words were a challenge to Williamson's authority, something he would not allow under any circumstances. Smith had his diplomatic job cut out for him on this evening, for all were in a murderous humour.

"Get out of the way, Smith", Williamson growled. "If you interfere this time, there'll be two bodies lying aside this fire tonight."

Geoffrey shrugged and retreated to the edge of the clearing. There was no doubt this time that his talents would be unappreciated and interference unhealthy for him this night. He would clearly hold no sway in this matter, and it was best if he move well out of the way, for it would certainly fall to him to clean up the mess when the matter was settled.

Now the two men circled slowly around and around and around the fire, using the flames as a shield until each could take the measure of the other. They watched each other's faces warily; each aware that any move to attack would be betrayed first by the eyes. A sweat had broken out on both men's faces, a testament more to the tension than to the heat of the fire.

Williamson was the first to move, feigning a lunge and withdrawing. Then Newsome followed suit, testing Williamson's reflexes but not yet ready to commit to full battle. The manoeuvres were repeated, this time each man's blade coming closer to the other, but still with great caution. Neither man felt sufficient confidence in his position to attack just yet.

Finally, Newsome believed he saw the opening he needed to strike, as Williamson's eyes momentarily left his to glance at one of the men who had shifted his position. The blade flashed across the open space between the men, catching the top of Williamson's left hand and drawing first blood.

Williamson's eyes narrowed as his attention was refocused upon his enemy. With a roar not unlike that of an angered bull, he rushed in toward the completely unsuspecting Newsome. He stabbed viciously, catching his insubordinate subordinate in the side, ripping Newsome's shirt and causing blood to flow from him as well. Now both men had been blooded and, contrary to the expectations of the spectators, both settled down once more, their concentration even more focused than it had been originally.

As the dance continued between the two men, another of Williamson's thugs, David Mills, a slight man prone to gambling on most anything, began to take bets on the fight. As the heat of the event reached its apex, Mills began to call out the odds to the others, attempting to goad the others into placing ever-larger bets.

"Five will give you six, that Newsome will take the fight", he called out.

Williamson stopped in his tracks, scarcely believing his ears, and glared at the little man. Abandoning his fight with Newsome and showing no concern of the possible consequences, he stalked over to Mills, grabbing him solidly by the collar of his shirt. The small man trembled, seeing the rage in the leader's eyes and realizing the foolishness of his actions too late.

Enveloped by the rage in Williamson's eyes, he became mesmerized with the ferocity he saw there, and he did not see the large knife come up from the big man's waist. The blade bit hard and buried itself deep into the slight man's chest, surprise displayed in the saucers that his eyes had become at the unexpected turn of events. He barely had the time to whimper as he felt the momentary searing pain before his heart, neatly cloven in two, stopped beating.

Williamson threw the offending man's body to the ground with no more care or respect than as though it were a dirty rag.

His eyes glared all about the circle at the now-silent crowd of men, soundlessly daring anyone to say a word.

"So", he bellowed, "anyone else want to place a bet against me?" He started to pace slowly and deliberately about the fire as each man backed off from his rage. "I thought as much", he sneered contemptuously. "Now, drag this wretched body off away from this camp. And be sure to take his scalp so they'll think it was the work of the Indians he ran away from today, shaking like a frightened schoolgirl." He paced about even more quickly, his anger not yet spent; almost hoping someone else would challenge his authority. "Just like the rest of you."

No one moved, the terror of the moment and the distaste for the command apparent among the men, rooting them to the ground they occupied.

"Now!" Williamson roared. "I don't care who does it, but if this corpse isn't moving by the time I count ten, it won't be alone!"

Three men rushed forward and took hold of the hapless victim's body. With as much speed as they could muster, they dragged their load into the woods, puffing with the combination of exertion and the fear that had motivated them into action. Once clear of the camp and out of sight of the madman, however, they dropped the body, ignoring Williamson's instructions concerning the scalping. They scattered off into the bush in separate directions to put as much distance as possible between him and themselves before he should decide to see what had become of them.

The British Army had just found three new recruits.

This interlude seemed to reduce the excitement and tension brought by the original fight, and by the witnessing of the cold-blooded murder. The two initial combatants once again took their places at the fire, their enmity apparently spent if not forgotten. But before they could become quite comfortable once more, a lone rider tore into the clearing.

The man, one of Willcocks' riders, dismounted and ran up to Dorian Williamson, saluting as he stopped before the sweating, bloodstained leader. The act would have appeared ludicrous if there had been any hint of a sense of humour left in the camp that night. In fact, the act was a vain attempt by Joseph Willcocks to give his ragtag band of cutthroats a legitimacy and military air they didn't deserve.

"Sir", the man began, gulping for air, clearly exhausted. "Lieutenant Willcocks requests the pleasure of your company at Fort George in Newark." Williamson noticed with some annoyance that the man had used Willcocks' self-designated rank, an affectation that reflected the man's almost obsessive desire for legitimacy and official titles.

"I know where Fort George is", Dorian growled. "What is the purpose of this summons?"

The messenger hesitated in answering, knowing of Williamson's legendary instability. "I'm afraid I don't know sir. Mr. Willcocks sent me riding several hours ago to gather together all of his forces at Fort George and that's all he confided in me." The man cringed as though expecting a blow for his trouble.

Williamson looked about the fire at his band. "What say, gentlemen?" he asked rhetorically. "Mount up and let's be on our way. Perhaps there's a chance here for glory." Then, a wicked grin appeared on his countenance. "But, most important, perhaps there'll some prospect for booty."

The men jumped to their feet as one, happy for a way out of the evening's stresses and, picking up their saddles and effects, ran for their horses, whooping and yelling, cheering at the prospect of robbing more defenceless settlers of what little money they might have, as well as their often-meagre family heirlooms. The thought of riding from Lundy's Lane to Fort George on the dark Niagara roads was not greatly appealing, but on they rode from a mixture of greed, fear and the pleasure bullies often feel at the thought of tormenting the vulnerable, not to mention their fear of Williamson.

Chapter Three

A week had passed since the incident on Lundy's Lane. Jeremy had not ventured out at all since then, tending to repairs about the property and generally just enjoying the summer's start. When he had finally reached a level of ennui with the domestic life that he wanted to venture off again, the rain had come, and stayed for several days. The resulting sodden conditions would have been quite troublesome for the packing of significant weights, as would be necessary if he bagged game on the trail.

He had managed to shoot a deer near his property although, with the comings and goings of British troops, Fitzgibbon's Bloody Boys, militia, brigands, and Caughnawaga Indians through the area, it was more than he had honestly expected. But the hides now hung in his shed, waiting to be brought to the tannery in the village of St. Johns, located in part of what was locally known as the Short Hills, the origin of the Twelve Mile Creek.

Today was much warmer and, thankfully, also much drier. Jeremy checked over the condition of his home, made such repairs as were immediately necessary, and headed out to make his fortune, such as it might be, once more. With his trusty over/under, his grandfather's knife, the Mississauga tomahawk, and the bayonet rescued from the road where some careless soldier had dropped it, Jeremy set off. He had decided that he would travel westward along the top of the Niagara Escarpment and hunt the creeks and streams that had created waterfalls, which carved countless ravines through the multiple layers of the escarpments rock over the millennia since the glaciers had scoured the Mountain's face.

He made his way along the well-worn forest trail that had been used by animals, natives and white men alike over the years. He revelled as always in nature's creations, getting a pleasure from the incredible diversity of life that abounded everywhere. His was an almost romantic regard for all the differing varieties of flora and fauna. But he always held a special place in his heart, a special delight that he couldn't have explained, for one of his favourite areas, one that would come up soon after leaving home – the incredible wetlands of the Beaverdams.

Jeremy felt an overwhelming attraction to the wetlands that fed the Beaverdams Creek, at least in part. Although many thought the swamps a nuisance, he believed there must be a purpose to it, and he knew that an amazing variety of wildlife claimed as home this small sea of rushes, reeds, grasses, and small islands of higher ground covered in flowering plants and the occasional tree. Birds of all descriptions hovered, flew, swam, and dived through this lush land, feasting on the abundant insect population, which could, on occasion, be an annoyance to humans and livestock. Deer grazed along the edges, where they had a broad field of vision and a plentiful supply of food, and yet a cover of trees to vanish into if they feared an intruder.

Numerous other species inhabited this bountiful habitat. Frogs, turtles, and toads all made their homes and/or laid their eggs in the very waters, while salamanders of several varieties benefited from the dampness that was wicked up from the marsh. Mice and voles scampered erratically through the high grasses that fringed the edges while foxes lay in wait for them at night. Raccoons and skunks foraged along the shores and streams, living variously on aquatic life or insects, and muskrats dove from the grasses into the water as Jeremy passed. Wolves hunted about the fringes, carefully avoiding man, their only major enemy, occasionally glancing furtively and longingly at the creatures that lived outside their reach, knowing from experience and instinct that it was likely only a matter of time before one would make a fatal error.

Birds, too, took full advantage of the diversity, animal and vegetable, of these wetlands. Perched several feet out into the softer ground, holding seemingly effortlessly onto a swaying cattail, a red-winged blackbird eyed Jeremy suspiciously. At a distance, Jeremy could see the distinctive white spots of the loon, just before it disappeared under the water, no doubt having found some small fish to spear. And there seemed to be regular flights of Mallard and Black ducks and Canada geese setting down in or taking off, often scattering flocks of the seemingly ubiquitous gulls that cruised the air overhead in search of opportunities.

Once known for its large quantity of beavers, many had by now been trapped out, prized for the felting qualities of their pelts back on the Continent. But even these few were in danger, not so much from trappers as from the farmers of the area that were taking up ever larger tracts of land and draining the streams and ponds, using the water for irrigation and the newly uncovered land for fields.

That was not to say there were none left. On the contrary, even as Jeremy traversed the familiar territory, he now found that he was forced to retrace his steps to find another way across this particular stretch. Where once he had found dry, solid ground, he was now confronted with a large pond. And the cause of this change was a dam that was yet under construction, a fact he realized when his approach provoked a soft splash from the seemingly haphazard collection of brushwood, mud and leaves.

As he looked closely into the amazingly clear waters, he caught the shape of a fairly large animal, plump with brown-black fur that bore an oily appearance. Even had Jeremy not known what this animal was, the flat tail would have betrayed it as being a beaver. His eyes followed the surprisingly agile animal's trajectory and spotted its home. The beaver had constructed a lodge, a roundish pile of essentially the same material as the dam, wedged between a clump of trees that stood on what had previously been dry land. The beaver would access by way of an underwater passage, leaving it safe from all but those animals that could dive there, or those that would take the time and effort necessary to dig down through the layers of debris.

Jeremy thought little of matters such as the extinction of these animals, for there seemed to be plenty of them still around. He had never been a beaver trapper, a viciously wasteful enterprise

A Question of Loyalty

in his opinion, hunting an animal for only its skin. He certainly knew of no other good use for the animals, unless one considered the especially foul-tasting castor oil that the doctor insisted would prevent many diseases and cure the rest. He was also no conservationist, development of the lands yet considered a necessary part of civilization. His interest was merely in the here and now, the beauty around him and feelings that it engendered in his soul.

On he walked for about two and one-half miles, following the weaving path along the higher points of the marsh, on solid ground where he would not wet his feet. Although he enjoyed his environs, he could not help but think that he would be happy when a proper road was built in the direction of his house and straightening the way. By constantly weaving throughout, looking for dry places to step, and switching back because of new ponds, he was covering a great deal of extra distance in this manner.

Jeremy forded or simply jumped several small streams and then followed the north ridge of the ravine carved out by the Beaverdams Creek, now on the Mountain Road, which led to DeCou's property. His progress was interrupted often by neighbours who wished to hear of his latest exploits, or to tell him of theirs. But, around mid-morning, he finally arrived at the miller's house, now used by the British army as a supply depot for operations in the Niagara Peninsula. John DeCou was, himself, a captain in the army and he hailed Jeremy now from the front porch of his house.

"Mr. van Hijser", he called out, the smile on his face belying the sternness of his voice. "Could I have a moment of your time?"

"Surely", Jeremy replied, and headed for the house. "How may I be of assistance?"

The captain looked at the young trapper as if taking his measure, almost uncertain as to whether he should continue. He had known Jeremy for some time now and knew how he felt about military service of any type. "Might I ask where you would be headed?" he queried.

"I'm just heading along the top of the Mountain. I hope to find some game to fill out my stock of hides before I bring them to the tanner's, and explore some while I'm at it", Jeremy replied. "If I'm lucky, I may be able to sell some of the meat of my kill along the way and lay up some money for future needs."

"And what needs might a man such as yourself have in future?" the captain goaded him. "There are no taxes to be paid here, you have no wife or family, and you seem to take care of all your other requirements yourself."

"Ah, but maybe some day, when you are no longer a rich man, I should be tempted to buy your mill from you, John, and settle down. Surely you wouldn't be thinking of giving it away, then?" Jeremy could not help the friendly dig in return, the reference to his marital status hardly having gone unnoticed.

DeCou snorted in mock derision. "And what makes you think that I would be willing to sell my mill just because you might someday be thinking of becoming an honest gentlemen, should that be at all possible? Anyways, if you wish to earn some money, hunt around here and sell your game to the King's Army."

Jeremy let loose with a loud, bellowing and exaggerated laugh. "I already have enough of the King's credits to buy your mill twice over", he returned. "That is, if I should ever see any of the money that goes with these credits."

With that, Captain DeCou, officer in the King's Army, drew himself up in pretending great indignation on behalf of the Crown. "Why, sir, do you question the integrity of the King?" he demanded haughtily.

"No sir, I would not. I merely question the integrity of his credit."

Jeremy and John DeCou were accustomed to this sort of banter, living in the same area and encountering each other quite often. Neither took offence with the other's familiarities, a kind of friendship having developed over time between the two men; as strong a friendship as could be built between a man who worked long hours at his mill and an itinerant trader/trapper. John had long suspected that Jeremy's wanderings were in search of more than a mere living, that the latter was searching for his place in the world since the loss of his family.

"I'm afraid I have something to ask of you, Jeremy", John said, becoming serious and the tone of his voice suddenly more businesslike.

"What do you need?" Jeremy replied, concerned by his friend's sudden change of demeanour.

"If you should happen across Lieutenant Fitzgibbon on your travels, please pass along the word that there is a rumour of Willcocks and his so-called Canadian Volunteers or what have you, making headquarters somewhere along the Twenty. The good lieutenant and his men have been out looking for the damned cowards since the battle at Stoney Creek." DeCou's face appeared troubled. "We simply must do something to stop them. Morale among the settlers, especially below the Mountain, is reaching a dreadful low because of the bastards, and we fear that they might join the enemy if we cannot guarantee their protection."

Jeremy allowed the comment to sink in, then replied. "I'll surely pass along the news", he said. "I've had my own run-in with some of the worst of the blackguard's men." Knowing he would not be allowed to let it stand there, he proceeded to tell DeCou of his brush with Dorian Williamson's men near Chippewa.

"Well, our intelligence has it that Williamson has rejoined with Willcocks and the two are wreaking havoc with the lives of those who would but scratch out a life from the soil of Upper Canada", John told him, exaggerating to an extent. Willcocks and his men tended to prey upon the more affluent of the country folk, due to their conflicting views of the political world. It wasn't unheard of that they might victimize those who "but scratched a life out of the soil", but they were generally left alone; they were neither political enough to be foes, nor affluent enough to fill Willcocks' coffers.

"I'll keep my eyes open for Fitzgibbon and his men", Jeremy promised. "And I'll be sure to pass on your information. You know, though, that it will take me some time to work my way along the Mountain, and I don't know how good your intelligence will be by then."

"There's another issue at stake as well", DeCou confided. "Fitzgibbon is also trying to find a spy that has been reported in Niagara of late. Rumour has it that he's been headed this way, but we don't know who he is."

Jeremy may have appeared somewhat puzzled, for he certainly felt it. "What's the concern with spies all of a sudden? There are spies about all the time."

"This one, it seems, is a military man", the captain answered. "A British military man. If that's true, he must be stopped. So while you're about, could you keep your eyes and ears open for sign or word of someone of military bearing who might be asking questions in the wrong places?"

"Certainly."

John nodded gravely. Then, suddenly, he brightened visibly and, with a slight grin, he barked, "Well, Mr. van Hijser, the message isn't getting any newer while you stand here."

Jeremy smiled at his old friend and held out his hand. DeCou accepted it and shook it heartily, a serious look once more overcoming his visage. "Just take care", he warned. "We can only guess where that bunch of traitors might be, and it would not do you well to be caught alone by them. They just might consider that you might be some kind of spy."

Jeremy smiled wryly, for he knew that nearly anything was possible in these days. Without another word, he once again shouldered his meagre load and continued on along the dusty road. He cut back into the forest before reaching the point where the way dipped down through the valley of the Short Hills to lower Niagara.

Try as he might to focus on tracking and hunting, Jeremy could think only about DeCou's parting words, words that struck home because of his personal experience with Williamson. He would, indeed, stay alert for any sign of trouble. And he could but hope that he could find Fitzgibbon in time to help him find their common enemy, although the task was daunting in light of the fact that DeCou hadn't known where to find the man.

By nightfall, after searching gullies and waterways where his intended prey might feed and water, Jeremy had reached a point only two miles short of the Twenty Mile Creek. All day, since he had left DeCou's House near Beaverdams, he had crossed paths with no one in his travels. This was not completely surprising, since most who wished to travel any distance tended to use the road that ran along the base of the Mountain, if one could call it a road. Truth be told, it was more like a well-worn Indian path enlarged and flattened by the horses and carts of settlers, soldiers, and all others who had business along the way.

Jeremy had made his way down through the mixed forest before nightfall, to a broad plateau that ran for some distance along this part of the escarpment. As he reached the southern boundary of this large shelf, he scouted out an excellent location for the night's campsite not far from the edge. Still surrounded by trees, there was a natural rocky depression where a crevasse had opened due to some unknown geological force, and then had been partially filled once again by rocks that wore from the edges and had fallen into the opening. Sitting in this sheltered space, he discovered that anyone passing by this way could fall unsuspectingly into the opening, long before Jeremy himself would be discovered.

To make the campsite more appealing and comfortable, he cut some branches from nearby cedars in such a way that they would not be readily noticeable to the casual eye. He then laid them in the bottom of the former crevasse to fashion a bed. In one of a number of natural niches in the walls of his temporary home, he built a small fire, enough to cook the rabbit he had caught, yet not enough to alert any who might be below of his presence.

Deciding that his hideout met his standards as a campsite, Jeremy headed to a small outcropping, which jutted out over the plain below. He could see mainly forest from where he sat, but here and there were signs of civilization, in the forms of domiciles of various types, depending upon the wealth of the settler and the age of the plot. One thing they had in common in that time of war and occupation was a lonely and defenceless appearance, open to the ravages of whoever should wish them harm. He could fairly feel their insecurity as he looked across to the ravine that marked the Twenty Mile Creek, starting at the lake and disappearing into the bend created by its own cut into the side of the escarpment.

Somewhere down there, among the trees, rocks, farms, and occasional road or pathway, was Lieutenant Fitzgibbon, he thought. Also occupying the space below, although he had little idea where it might be, was that animal Williamson and his master, Willcocks. Although he strained, however, Jeremy could see no sign of either, the trees of the vast lower plain hiding many secrets both good and evil.

With the sun coming down to rest upon the very crowns of the trees to the west, setting the striated clouds in the sky above into a veritable blaze of brilliant pinks, reds and oranges. He watched this amazing display for as long as he could and then, when the sun threatened to cast him into darkness for his walk back to his camp, rose from his lookout and headed reluctantly back. A supper whose entrée consisted of a stew of boiled preserved venison and some locally picked wild greens, and then to sleep, he thought, settling into the tear in the earth that he would call his home for this night. And, on the morrow, well, the only thing that he knew with reasonable certainty, would come the morrow.

Chapter Four

The next morning, Jeremy awoke hungry and somewhat stiff, still hidden in his small redoubt. He wasn't sure what had awakened him, but something had drawn his attention sufficiently to summon him from the slumber that had finally overtaken him in the wee hours. With a slight groan and a great stretch, he climbed from his hiding place and shuffled slowly to a spot where he could see past the trees and brush to look out toward Lake Ontario.

He panned slowly across the trees and fields below, not sure what he was looking for, or even if there was anything to be looking for. All appeared sleepy down below, no sign yet of any activity in the sparsely populated area below. Nothing but the odd wisps of smoke escaping from what must have been chimneys, signalling the first meal of the day.

"I must have been imagining things", he muttered to himself sleepily as he started to turn away from the pastoral scene below.

At that moment, he heard a sound coming from below, no dream this time, indistinguishable but infinitely more identifiable. It was the sound of a number of people shouting and yelling in alarm although, from this distance, it was impossible to determine what it might be. He scanned down below again, more slowly this time, trying to pinpoint the source of the confused noise, the echo created by the stone of the escarpment making it extremely difficult. But then, movement caught his eye and he saw riders not far off down below his position, trotting casually along the road, seemingly in no great hurry.

Jeremy wondered if this troop might be Fitzgibbon and his men but he realized upon closer inspection that none wore the telltale green coveralls that marked the Bloody Boys. Although there were a number of other possibilities, his mind latched onto only one, the idea lancing through his being with a surge of adrenalin. The Canadian Volunteers, he thought! He'd probably stumbled upon Willcocks and his gang! Now, if only he could quickly find and arouse Fitzgibbon to set him on their trail...

But Jeremy was distracted from this thought as he caught another slight movement out of the corner of his right eye. A thin column of smoke drifted skyward in the direction the men below had come from, a column too thick for a breakfast fire to be the source. He turned to look, as the smoke rapidly gained in volume and became darker, heralding only two likely possibilities in this area and in the circumstances of these times. It could be that a forest fire was building, an unlikely prospect since the season had not yet grown particularly dry for non-lightning occurrences. More likely, however, in light of unconcerned men he had just seen riding from that location, someone's property had been set ablaze!

Jeremy ran back to collect his belongings from his previous night's lodgings and returned quickly to the ledge where he had been standing. His eyes darted furiously, scouring the slope for any trace of an established pathway. Seeing none he threw all caution to the wind and scrambled down as rapidly as possible, almost losing his handhold on the rocks and then slid down the leafy, still damp incline toward the bottom. He tried to remain upright as he hastened down, using trees to brake and then swing, jumping deftly over fallen logs and rocks, barely aware of the scrapes and bruises he collected in the process.

Finally nearing the bottom, Jeremy slid down a muddy embankment and lost his balance, spinning hard into a large maple tree, which stood directly in his path. He fairly bounced as he struck and then lost his balance as the impact destroyed his sense of balance. He lay there for a moment, the wind knocked out of him and the pain from his minor injuries catching up to him. Momentarily forgetting the reason for his condition, he was initially happy just to have reached the bottom and lay there fighting to collect his wits. But then a cry from off to his right re-galvanized him and he jumped to his feet once again, leaving the slope to run down the road toward the now well-defined black plume of smoke billowing above the treetops not more than a couple of hundred yards away.

As he approached the stricken property, he saw that some neighbours had also taken notice and responded to this farmer's plight, some running like Jeremy, others arriving on horseback, but almost all carrying pails and shovels. He sprinted the final hundred or so feet of the farm's laneway and turned the corner about the trees that lined both sides of it. He now could plainly see the conflagration that was every settler's worst nightmare. The barn fire was well along by now, the dry boards, along with the straw inside and the stiff breeze blowing down from the north-northwest, coming together to create the perfect conditions for the fire.

Jeremy found a place to cache his gun and other personal items and grabbed a well-used, well-dented pail from a man who was already handing them out to anyone who would take one. He joined the other men in a line from the stream that ran behind the farmhouse not far distant and began to pass buckets of water forward, where the man in front would toss it futilely at the roaring blaze that was once a barn. There weren't enough men and the line was stretched so far that some of the members of the bucket brigade had to run to pass on the buckets.

"Never mind the barn!" someone cried, through the haze of the smoke and the din created by the shouting voices of the volunteers. "It's gone. Let's keep the house wetted down so it doesn't go too!"

As quickly as the anonymous man gave the order, the line shifted to pass the water toward the house. Since it was much closer to the stream than the barn was, a few men were freed up to climb ladders to the roof, where some of the buckets were passed to wet down the tinder-dry shakes that constituted shingles. And not a moment too soon, as the fire soon began to rain sparks on the surrounding area, endangering everything flammable.

The women and children that had now arrived on the scene wetted down burlap sacks, and went about beating the sparks and the occasional small fires that broke out, the women with an anger borne of empathy for the plight of these neighbours. The children ran about helter-skelter, also beating out the embers, but with that spirit of youth that allows them to take an event such as this and turn it into a game.

For several hours, this drama dragged on, sapping the strength and will of all involved. Muscles strained to lift yet another pail of water, to swing the wet and heavy burlap sack yet one more time, to pull a bucket yet again up the ladder. Men cursed and groaned, women prayed and groaned, children cried and complained they were hungry, skin burned both from the sun and from errant sparks, and finally the fire began to diminish. The timbers had long ago fallen in on themselves, showering all with a storm of embers and sending up a renewed frenzy of pail passing and sack swinging, but now the fire had almost burned itself out, reduced to low flames and an occasional shower of sparks as the few remaining timbers surrendered to their fate and collapsed. It was not much longer before the recently proud barn was gone, replaced by a glowing, crackling pile of embers and wisps of smoke that drifted off with the afternoon breeze.

Even as the immediate emergency was abated people continued to arrive, no doubt from farther away. They knew they would be too late to be of any assistance in fighting the fire but, all living the same lifestyle, they brought what would be needed. These newcomers brought food for the weary fire fighters, food that was wolfed down by some, nibbled at in exhaustion by others. The neighbours dropped where they stood to enjoy the respite and nutrition, some falling immediately asleep, while those who had just arrived took a fire watch on the embers and kept an eye on the roof of the house. The worst now over, they approached the ruins and began to shovel dirt onto the ashes at the edges, slowly working inward and occasionally throwing on additional buckets of water where warranted.

Jeremy, now exhausted to a point he had never before in his life experienced, lay up against an old oak tree in the shade of its mighty branches. He was too tired to be hungry, but he had graciously accepted some bread and preserves from a lady that was bringing the food around. He drank heavily from the water drawn from the farm well, suffering from dehydration at least as much as any of the others here.

As he looked about the grounds, he watched the exhausted people who had arrived with him, the newcomers who had thought to feed the crowd, and even the children who had already found their second wind. These were indeed neighbours and, looking about, he was hard-pressed to determine who the residents of this property were. For all were equally tired, all were equally distressed at the damage caused by the fire, and all were equally thankful to the others who had helped that day.

That thought brought another to mind. "Who is the landholder here?" he asked tiredly.

"You mean you don't know, sir?" came the reply of one man, who peered at him in curiosity and then realized this man was a newcomer to this community. "I've not seen you here before", he said, a twinge of suspicion in his voice, and more than a twinge in his eye.

"George!" a woman's voice rang out, and George received a wet burlap sack across the shoulders for his obvious attitude. "This man has been helping here with the rest of us since the start. We saw him come running off the Mountain to help, so you just keep your suspicious thoughts to yourself."

George appeared sufficiently contrite, so the woman who was so obviously his wife offered Jeremy a handshake, an offer tiredly taken up by the man. She was probably in her forties, although Jeremy always had a hard time discerning such things, especially among farm folk, many of whom had lived difficult lives carving their places out of the wilderness. There was no doubt she had been an attractive woman in her day, and he could not help but wonder at the union with George, who was a strong but small man, of no handsome appearance and obviously of no great charm.

"Pay no attention to him", his wife smiled from behind heavy eyes. "By the way, we are George and Priscilla Morris. Our farm is just a half mile up and a quarter mile over."

"Pleased to meet you both", Jeremy answered. "I can't fault George's suspicions, madam. If something like this had happened to one of my neighbours up at my place near Beaverdams, and some stranger just happened to appear just then, I think I might be wondering a little myself. These are trying times for us all, and one never knows whether the stranger riding by might be friend or foe."

Priscilla smiled in a manner that seemed to Jeremy to contain a flirtatious shadow to it, and then answered him. "That's true, that's regrettably so true. And, as for coming and saving you from the odd ideas of my husband, not at all Mr...."

"...van Hijser", the younger man replied. "I'm terribly sorry, I should have introduced myself sooner. I shall blame it on fatigue, Mrs. Morris, having no better excuse. The full name is Jeremy van Hijser."

"Well, Mr. van Hijser", Priscilla continued. "To answer your question, the man who lives here is Walter Davis." She craned her head about, as if searching. "Ah, there he is, over on the porch steps. I'm afraid he has no wife though. Died two winters ago of the ague, you know. He now runs the farm by himself, since they had no surviving children." She looked self-consciously at the ruined buildings. "I don't know what the poor man'll do now.

"I'm sorry to hear that", Jeremy answered, looking over at the man, slumped on the steps beside his house, his shoulders collapsed in an attitude of utter defeat. "If you'll excuse me, I wish to ask Mr. Davis a question about what happened here." Without awaiting any further discussion, Jeremy got up and walked over to where Walter Davis sat, head in hand.

"Mr. Davis?" Jeremy opened tentatively, and then introduced himself. "Were those Willcocks' men I saw riding away from here?" he asked with the niceties out of the way. When the farmer nodded, he continued. "Can you tell me why Willcocks and his men would wish to burn your barn in this manner?"

Davis looked up at Jeremy, exhaustion well beyond the physical written deeply in the lines of his face, and slowly shook his head. "There's no answer to that, young man", he started. "They appeared here two nights ago and just took the place over. They drank my liquor, ate my food and generally feasted upon my property for the better part of two days. Then, last night, they loaded up all the things that my dear Emily loved so much, God bless her." The farmer choked back a tear and continued, "emptied my cellar of the last of my supplies, and ate my chickens and my pig. This morning, and without a word, they mounted up and, just before

A Question of Loyalty

they set off, the man the others called Williamson suddenly lit up a firebrand and tossed it into the barn. No reason, no explanation, no accusations..."

With this, Davis broke into great wracking sobs. "Now there's nothing", he moaned. "There's absolutely nothing left but the house and a pile of ashes."

"Oh, I don't know about that", Jeremy reassured him. "You have a great lot of neighbours here. And I'm certain they wouldn't think twice about helping you to get started again."

Davis looked about the yard at the people milling about, many now catching their second winds and going about helping with the cleanup of the fire. "You're right about that, Jeremy. They are a lovely bunch of people and that's for certain. I couldn't want for better neighbours living around me."

Jeremy politely waited for a moment, and then cautiously asked, "Mr. Davis, do you have any idea where they may have been headed after they left here?"

Davis initially shook his head, but then suddenly looked up. "Wait a minute. Now that you ask, I heard them saying something last night about heading up the Mountain by the road that follows the Twenty up", he said. "But that's all. The fellows that were doing the talking noticed I heard and shut right up."

"Thank you, Mr. Davis", Jeremy said softly.

"You don't intend to go after them all by yourself, do you?" the older man asked, dumbfounded. "You can't hope to take them on by yourself. They're on horseback and so I doubt you'll ever even catch them, but even if you did, you won't be able to do a thing about it."

Jeremy looked up toward the gap where the Twenty Mile Creek had been cutting its way into the side of the escarpment for centuries, thoughtfully stroking his beard stubble. "No, you're right", he said, retrieving his gun and other gear that he had collected from their safe keeping. "But, with a little luck, I may just be able to find a man who can."

Chapter Five

An hour later, Jeremy trudged tiredly uphill just above the Twenty Mile Creek, the heat of the day thankfully dulled by the shade of the mixed forest that climbed the escarpment ahead of him. The Mountain access "road" was little more than a dirt trail, rutted from wagon traffic and full of rocks and tree roots. Among the other hardships associated with a climb up a steep hill, it was a trial in itself and wound about considerably to take advantage of the terrain in such a way that a wagon might be hauled up it, making the trip much longer than should be necessary. Added to these things was the ankle-wrenching unevenness caused by horse traffic in muddy, wet conditions, and Jeremy was beginning to wonder at the wisdom of taking this "civilized" way to his destination.

The climb was beginning to take its toll on him and he was beginning to think that he should have given in to the overwhelming urge to rest before setting out on what was surely an exercise in futility. While it wasn't that far to the summit in absolute terms, the morning's exertion and the now heavy, humid air conspired to sap his remaining strength before he should reach his goal. The fact was that Mr. Davis had been correct – there was no way he was going to catch up to the gang and, even supposing that he should, what would he then do with them? He was hardly in any position to take on more than a hundred mounted men.

Nearing a point almost three-quarters of the way to the top, Jeremy decided to climb down the creek valley to quench his thirst and rest, giving him a chance to consider his dilemma and his options before he found himself in an even more impossible situation. Partly walking, partly sliding down the slope to the rocky creek bed, it did not take him long to reach his goal and he sat heavily on a small, fallen tree in the shade of a large slab of fallen rock.

He reached down and dipped his hands into the stream of running water and tasted of the liquid borne of the previous days' rains up top in the in the creek's watershed. He then let it run freely across his hands, revelling in the feel of this nectar of life itself slipping between his fingers before scooping another double handful and splashing it over his head. The coolness of the running water felt at once comforting and invigorating, lifting much of the fog of fatigue that had been dogging him since the fire.

Leaning back against the large slab, which had no doubt at one time been a solid part of the ridge along the top of the escarpment, still high above Jeremy's head. It was the result of the incredible power of water as it seeped into cracks, freezing and thawing until, inch by inch, the cracks widened while the rains washed the softer rock and soil out from underneath it. All that remained was for gravity to take over when the process reached the point where the overhang could no longer be supported, sending this chunk sliding and crashing down the hillside, probably leaving a trail of downed trees and crushed undergrowth, long since grown back.

Half asleep, pondering the incredible natural powers of the world he inhabited, he was barely aware of a sound nearby, a sound barely discernable from the sounds of the stream rushing and swirling between the smoothed stones of its bed. But aware he was, and his subconscious immediately brought Jeremy to a state of full alert. Peering cautiously around the rock that formed his backrest, he scanned the bank, looking for the source of the unidentified anomaly.

Almost immediately, Jeremy heard another sound from the creek's left bank, upstream from his position, and two men appeared, stumbling dangerously on the natural obstacles of the escarpment's sloped forest floor.

"Hey, Will!" one man called out, in a voice somewhat slurred and angry, much louder than necessary for the distance between them.

"Wha-what?" the other replied as he tripped over a tree root and fell heavily down a slope until halted by bushes growing along the top of the creek embankment. "Damn, Seth, see now what you've done? Help me back up now."

Jeremy rolled over quietly and picked up his rifle, which he had placed high and dry, just within his reach, on another rock. He rolled back just as quietly, considered priming his gun, and then deciding that it would probably create more noise than Jeremy would like. While he was far from sure, there was every possibility that these men might be from Joseph Willcocks' contingent, and a gun report might alert them to his presence. After all, it was highly unlikely that they would all be as drunk as these two.

"Slow down, fool!" the Seth man called out, in what was surely intended to be a command, but was distinctly lacking in authority. "We're to stick together, or Williamson will have our necks. He always says that it takes two men or more to make a patrol."

"Cert-tainly", Will answered. "After all, Williamson knows everything." He stopped for a moment, appearing thoughtful, then began to giggle. "But he doesn't know we're drunk."

With that, both men began to laugh uproariously, their peels of hilarity echoing freely up and down the close confines of the narrow gorge, obviously greatly amused by the witty nature of their comment, until the Seth put his finger to his face and shushed his companion.

"You hear something?" asked Will, suddenly paranoid.

The other man looked annoyed. "No, idiot", he answered. "But it echoes here and we don't want Williamson to hear."

With that warning, the two men began to giggle again, this time self-consciously. The bigger man put the whiskey bottle to his lips, took a long pull, and then passed it to his companion, who tipped the bottle back, arching his back in an attempt to find some of their precious liquid there. Being unsuccessful, he scowled at the offending container, cursed, and smashed it dramatically against the rocks.

"It's empty", he whined. "You drank the last of it."

His friend laughed, the effort causing him to lose his balance and slide into his companion. "It's a good thing, then, that I have another", he announced, triumphantly pulling a second bottle from his clothing, obviously proud and thinking himself the day's saviour.

Will stood up, grabbed at the bottle, missed, lost his balance, and fell into the creek with a splash. Laughing uncontrollably, his friend also got up and walked down to the water, offered his hand in assistance, and promptly fell in with his sodden cohort. The two sat there for a moment, sputtering and laughing and cursing, and then, finding the bottle yet in good condition, began to drink once again. They were by now so intoxicated that they seemed no longer to notice that they were sitting in cold water.

Jeremy could not help but smile at the antics of these two drunken fools. They obviously posed no danger to him, as long as he did not show himself to them. Quietly, he picked up his gun and started to climb up the loose soil of the embankment, intending to skirt the drunken clowns and continuing his journey upward along the creek's bank. As he was almost past the two drunken front guard below him, however, all his attention focused on the ridiculous pair, he felt a stone give way underfoot. Before he had time to react, he had lost his balance and slid, still standing on his feet, to a point directly behind and to the right of the two men.

"Wh-what was th-that?" the drunker of the two asked, his peripheral vision just barely catching the movement.

Jeremy acted before either of them could any further gather their wits about them, if that was at all possible. Taking a long stride through the water, he stepped up to the backs of the two men who had not yet moved, their reflexes almost nonexistent due to their high alcohol blood level. With his hands, he scooped the heads of the confused men, which were only about a foot part as they had been partially leaning on each other when the distraction arose. Then, with a swift push, he smacked their heads together, creating a loud, wet thud.

Neither man made a sound as consciousness, which had not been fully present anyways, faded and they sank down into the creek bed under the gentle guidance of Jeremy's hands which were still in place against their heads. Seth ended up on his back on a rock, but the one named Will had sagged to his knees and flopped, face down, into the stream. Although Jeremy felt a temptation to leave them in that position, he could not allow a man with as few wits as this one displayed, drown in an alcoholic stupor in some shallow creek.

He left Seth lying on the rock, the whiskey bottle still cradled in his left arm. The other, he pulled from the water and dropped him onto Seth. Satisfied that he had done the right thing or, at least all that he could, Jeremy erased all signs of his slide in the soil and his presence here, and then headed back up the slope, careful to step only on stones so he would not leave any evidence of a third person at the site.

The two men awoke groggily, heads throbbing mercilessly, to the sound of laughter coming from the bank of the creek. Will saw to his horror that he was lying on top of his friend in a most compromising position and shakily rose to his feet with all the speed he could muster under the circumstances. The other man remained as he was and merely glared with bloodshot eyes at those having all the fun at his expense.

"What's so funny?" Seth barked, wincing as he realized the sudden increased pain in his head as he raised his voice.

"Absolutely nothing", a voice sounded from behind the men, and they rapidly parted to let the author of the reply go through.

A shudder of fear shot through both men as they realized they had been found in this compromising position by their commanding officer, or so he insisted upon being called. Joseph Willcocks stepped closer to the embankment and, giving a shove to the men on either side of him, sent them flying down toward his wayward guards.

"Get those sorry excuses for men on their feet", he growled. As the still-prone man was hoisted to his feet, the whiskey bottle smashed onto the creek rocks. "Drunk?" he bellowed, as though shocked. "I thought so. Bring them up here that we might take their measure, which I suspect will not take much."

A nervous laugh rippled through the approximately two dozen men who had been in the company of their leader when the search for these two had finally borne fruit. When Joseph Willcocks was angry, there was no telling what might happen, or to whom.

A Question of Loyalty

When finally the miscreants stood before the leader, shaking with fear, he looked them up and down as he paced slowly and deliberately around them, stopping behind them for effect, that being to instil terror in their very hearts. Then he continued his circuit and stopped again, stopping mere inches from their faces.

"I sent you two out this afternoon to scout and guard against an incursion by the enemy", he said softly, the tone anything but reassuring. "When you didn't come back, Mr. Williamson sent out searchers to retrieve you." Once more the man who insisted they refer to him as "lieutenant" paced around behind them. "And what did they find?" he demanded in steady crescendo, frightening even the onlookers.

"But, Sir", protested Will. "We was attacked. A whole lot of them came upon us and we tried to fight them off, but in the end, they bested us." He could not, however, look his commander in the face as he sputtered out this fanciful explanation.

"Um-hmm", Willcocks muttered thoughtfully, once more continuing his pacing. "You must indeed be valiant fighters", he continued mockingly. Then, with a roar, he shouted directly into Will's ear. "Because I see you managed to save the whiskey despite all the odds!"

Will almost collapsed from dread, but Seth broke in valiantly, trying to back up his friend, and hoping to save the both of them. "I can show you where they hit me, Sir", he said, parting the hair from the tender area that was the source of the throbbing in his head.

"Me too", Will enjoined eagerly, trying to bolster their case, and he began to separate his hair as well.

"Yes, I see that", Willcocks muttered, losing patience with these proceedings. "Stand side by each, gentlemen", he ordered.

The two men complied, unsure of what was coming next. Suddenly and without warning, Willcocks slammed their heads together, eliciting howls of pain and protest from both men as their injuries were aggravated by the demonstration.

"Ow-w-w", Will whined. "And just on the spot where I'd been hit before." No sooner had the words left his mouth than he realized the implications. "They...they must have snuck up behind us and banged our heads together just so", he offered hopefully, trying to dig himself out of the hole he'd begun, but only making matters worse.

"What?" barked Willcocks, making both men visibly jump. "Perhaps. Perhaps some of the assailants snuck up behind you and, while you were busy fighting off the rest, making sure you didn't let go the whiskey bottle, smashed your heads together to end the battle." By this point, the angry sarcasm fairly dripped from the man's tongue, his patience at an end.

"Let me paint you another scenario", the "lieutenant" began, his voice as cold as a viper's hiss. "You idiots got drunk and came down here to hide while you did it." With a menacing wave of his hand, he silenced a protest from Seth before the latter could open his mouth. "Then, vying for the drink, you slipped down this embankment, banging heads as you did so. Could that be a more accurate telling of the tale?"

Seth and Will could not find the courage to answer this charge, in part because it may have been the truth and in part because they really did not know the truth. Neither man had ever been completely aware of Jeremy's presence. He had been but a smudge in the periphery and the rattle of loose gravel and, for all they could remember, the story may indeed have been just as Willcocks had related it. The result was that they stood silently, unable to look their commander in the eye and glancing at each other only sideways, afraid to turn their heads.

Suddenly, the large form of Dorian Williamson appeared, pushing through the crowd of men, which had by now expanded as more searchers came upon the proceedings.

"If I may speak, Sir?" the man requested, a snarling smirk on his face.

"Go ahead, Sergeant", Willcocks acknowledged, allowing this man a rank which he also did not merit.

"Well, Sir", he began, the smirk growing more cruel. "I think they must have done quite some job fighting off the enemy." He pulled two muskets from behind his back, where he had been dragging them out of sight for dramatic effect. "And they did it without these."

Chapter Six

With a self-satisfied laugh, Williamson stepped back while Willcocks looked at the two muskets. There was nothing unusual about these guns – just the standard British-issue long musket that, in some circles, and for reasons unsure, was referred to as the "Brown Bess". These guns were common to soldiers and others from both sides of the border, and one looked much the same as any other, but the two men had carved identifying figures into the stocks, that they would not be stolen.

Willcocks gave the muskets back to Williamson and, turning his back on the two men, began to walk away. "Bring them along", he ordered. "This type of behaviour must not go unpunished."

Now completely sober, the hearts and minds of both men were seized of a gut-wrenching terror as their hands were tied behind their backs and pushed, none too gently, to follow in the direction Willcocks and Williamson had taken. They knew their leader was capable of meting out just about any sort of punishment he felt befit any untoward behaviour and there was no doubt that, in any army, theirs would be considered to be serious indeed. Unceremoniously up toward the road, through the woods they were marched, often stumbling on the roots and rocks, scraping and bruising themselves until their legs and arms ached and bled. But neither dared complain. They were in enough trouble already.

At the road, Willcocks, Williamson and Joseph Willcocks' right hand man, Benajah Mallory stood waiting for them, all three serious, their arms clasped behind their backs. As the two men were herded into their presence, they noticed that now nearly all of the Canadian Volunteers had formed up behind these leaders, in rank, waiting for the punishment. By now, the sun had begun creeping lower in the late afternoon sky, casting long shadows across the road, seemingly multiplying their numbers.

"Where would you like them, Sir?" one of the escorts inquired, as they stepped out onto the road.

"Just where you are", came the reply.

Now Willcocks turned around, his back to the two men, and addressed those assembled. "Gentlemen", he began officiously. "You have been brought here to witness the service of justice on these two men, William Forne and Seth Garnet, charged with the serious crime of drunkenness and dereliction of duty while on guard detail in a war zone."

He now turned to the men who had followed him, accompanying the prisoners and who had been present when the two men were found. "As you know, I believe in proper justice. After all, that is why we have joined the Americans in this fight. Therefore, I will not make this judgment on my own. To that end, I ask you now, gentlemen, you have heard the evidence given at the scene of the crimes, and of these crimes, how say you? Guilty or not guilty?"

Not one man present dared plead or declare the innocence of these two wretched creatures they had ridden with for months now, fearing the consequences of Willcocks' temper. Those who weren't already standing jumped to their feet and yelled, "Guilty, aye, sir!"

Willcocks sauntered slowly to where prisoners stood quivering, wondering desperately at their fate. "Prisoners", he said, in a forceful but even tone. "You have been found guilty of the charges as stated." He paced slowly across in front of them, stopping directly midway between the two, and spat on the ground at their feet. "You sorry excuse for soldiers."

Of course, neither man was in reality a soldier. In fact, none in this crowd could be called a soldier in any sense of the word. Whatever their original reasons for joining up with this group, by now they had all degraded to simple opportunists, bullies, and thieves. To attach a military title to any was laughable, and to date no American officer would even consider doing so. They were convenient to the U.S. military because they kept the heads of the British down while they waited endlessly and in vain at Fort George, in Newark, for support from the U.S. Navy, their commander afraid to venture forth lest their supply line be cut off by a British Lake Ontario fleet that was never to come. But they knew only too well what these men were, and kept their distance from them.

Now, Willcocks pulled himself up to his full height, a reasonably handsome man by the standard of the time, looking dashing in his way, dressed in a fashionable suit. He looked Will and Seth directly in their filthy, perspiring and tear-stained faces and delivered their sentence. "Gentlemen, and I use the term advisedly." At this, a nervous laugh broke out in the ranks. "For the crimes stated here this day, and within the penalties militarily proscribed for these crimes, I hereby sentence you to hang by the neck until you are dead. And may the Good Lord have mercy upon your souls."

He turned to the several men he had coached to step forward at the pronouncement of the sentence, who now did just that. "Gentlemen, the ropes."

The four men walked up to two nearby trees and tossed two ropes, already complete with traditional hangman's nooses, over suitably high, stout tree branches there at the side of the road. The other ends of the ropes were tied to the bases of the trees, and the prisoners were marched, none too lightly, to where the nooses hung, three feet above their heads. No scaffold had been prepared, of course, so the same men who had strung the ropes raised the prisoners to the nooses, which were then slipped over their heads. They were allowed no hoods, for Willcocks had decreed that all the men present look at the prisoners' faces as they died.

At a signal from Williamson, Will and Seth were dropped. The fall was not sufficiently precipitous to break their necks, so the gathered crowd watched in horror as the condemned men's faces turned bright red and then purple as they kicked and struggled to breathe at the ends of their respective ropes. When their struggling visibly slowed, Williamson once again nodded at the executioners, who walked solemnly to where the ropes were anchored and pulled the ends of the slipknots.

Will and Seth crashed to the ground like sacks of wet sand, striking the uneven surface of the road with a dull thud. Both immediately began retching and gagging while trying desperately to gasp in mouthfuls of air into their tortured lungs. A growing dark spot appeared on Will's breeches as he wet himself. Seth tried to rise to his feet, an effort rewarded by Williamson's application of a boot to his side.

"If I were you, I'd stay down there and kiss the ground in thanks that you're not under it", the big man growled. "If I had my way, it'd be otherwise."

Willcocks stepped forward once again and faced his men, who had not yet recovered from the shock of either the hanging or of its surprise termination. "This display was necessary to remind you that dereliction of duty will not be countenanced by myself or the other officers here", he announced sternly. "Next time, the ropes will not be released."

With that proclamation, he stalked off through the crowd; back to the site they had chosen as their daytime rest stop, not far from where Jeremy had slept the previous night. They had only marshalled at this location because it was an excellent vantage point from which they could spot any organized attempt at reprisal for the damage done to the Davis property. From here they would also be forewarned if any military units were close, that might have been drawn by the heavy smoke.

"Bring those two along and dump them on their horses. It'll be dark in a couple of hours, and we need to find someone who will offer us their hospitality for the night."

Willcocks thought that remark quite humorous and he laughed aloud, a dark but hearty laugh that was quickly taken up by his men as if on cue. They understood the humour of the statement. While they occasionally stayed with sympathizers, there were many men on this trip, and many mouths to feed. Rather than trouble those who saw things their way, it was much easier to simply take over the homes of those against whom Willcocks held a personal grudge. That way, they could strip the homestead of all food and other supplies without inconveniencing friends and supporters, who might raise an issue with American authorities concerning the behaviour of some of his men on the likely chance that some of them might become intoxicated and get out of line.

As Joseph Willcocks and his Canadian Volunteers were only

A Question of Loyalty

on this escarpment shelf to regroup and check for signs that they had been found by one of the groups looking for them, Willcocks stood on a rock outcropping with his navy glass and scanned the land below. He saw no sign of pursuit or ambush so, within an hour, the group had struck camp and headed back down the Mountain. At the bottom, they headed back toward Newark, not wishing to come too close to the British soldiers who, since the battle of Stoney Creek, had once again moved eastward to the Forty. After riding for a half hour along the lower road, they came upon a farm nestled in a fertile creek valley.

This would be their home for this night.

Jeremy made his way along the Twenty Mile Creek clambering over rocks and trees, both live and dead, unaware of the drama unfolding behind him. He could not help but admire his surroundings as he headed ever upward along the embankment. The bed of the creek itself was a collection of pieces of rock, some still angular but most worn smooth by the stream that often raced along, swirling and crashing over and around all obstacles on its way toward the distant lake. But it was looking at the top of the narrow gorge that always took Jeremy's breath away, and he marvelled at the amount of soil, rock and other debris the creek must had to move out of its way in carving it. Up above the various types of soil and rock and clinging trees, layer upon layer of sedimentary rock hung precariously over the creek like a partial roof.

The cliffs that comprised these overhangs soon became the reason for Jeremy's forced crossing to the opposite side of the creek. At a turn in the gorge that almost comprised almost a right angle, the slopes created by the inexorable wear to the walls became too precipitous for walking any further. He had to clamber over huge slabs of rock piled in the curve, all in various stages of wear, probably all fallen from the cliffs on the inside of this turn, where already a new overhang was forming high above.

The roar of the water rushing over the rocks and crashing against the banks became more pronounced now, increasing almost with every step Jeremy took, an ever-rising crescendo matched by nothing man-made that he knew of. As he approached the final bend before the falls, which he could now recognize as the

Twenty's precipitous drop from its upper limit to its lower, the barely pronounced trail that he was now following began to leave the shore of the creek, gaining altitude rapidly. Perspiration from the humidity of the air, combined with the lack of air motion in the confines of the gorge soaked his hair and shirt as he continued upward. The long, strenuous day was taking its toll, and he muttered a low thank you to no one in particular when he saw the top of the ridge was in reach.

Now having past the slope's mixture of clay and lighter soils, he knew he had finally reached the crest, the several yards of layered sedimentary rock that capped the escarpment. With a final burst of energy, Jeremy threaded his way through the most climbable spaces, as it was obvious others had before him, and finally threw himself onto blessedly flat ground at the top.

As he lay there regaining his breath, he became aware of a structure nearby that had not been there the last time he had travelled this route. Although he had, on that previous occasion several years before, travelled by way of the road, he was certain he would have noticed this. For at the edge of the cliff and adjacent to the falls, stood what apparently was a newly built mill and, judging by the noises coming from within, a gristmill at that. He'd heard rumours that the Ball brothers might be attempting such an enterprise, but he'd never heard the outcome. Apparently, the brothers had succeeded.

He forced his aching body one last time into motion and walked toward the front of the mill, marvelling at the construction and keeping his eyes open for the owners. It had been some time since he had seen the Balls so they might not recognize him, and he had no desire to be shot for his troubles.

As Jeremy approached the large front doors, a man appeared at the doorway, using his sleeve to wipe his face of the dust, grain and flour that had combined with his sweat to create a sickly paste. He blinked several times in the unaccustomed sunlight, trying to overcome the glare while clearing his eyes. Jeremy greeted him, the unexpected sound of a male human voice so startling the man that he almost visibly jumped.

"What is your business here?" the man asked, still blinking as he tried to size up the situation, seeing no wagon for the items of his trade. "Why do you skulk about in front of my mill in such a fashion?"

"My name is Jeremy van Hijser", came the reply. "I'm here because I'm scouring the peninsula looking for Lieutenant Fitzgibbon."

"Well, Jeremy, it's been some time since we've seen you here", the man said, looking closer. "I must apologize that I hadn't recognized you. All the same, this is an odd place to be looking for James Fitzgibbon", the man continued. "Wouldn't he be down below, raising the Devil in the name of the British Empire?"

Jeremy laughed heartily, his fatigue forgotten, for the moment anyways. "Well, sir, I wasn't really looking for him here. In truth, I was following Joseph Willcocks and his band after they burned down the Davis place. But the exercise went awry, I found I had to escape his guards, and this is where I ended up."

The man looked truly concerned when he heard mention of Joseph Willcocks. "You haven't brought that band of thieves to my front door, now have you?" he demanded.

"No, I don't believe they really knew I was there", Jeremy assured him, proceeding to tell the miller his story.

When the tale was finished, the man could not help but laugh at the imagined sight of the two drunks in the creek. His concern had not been totally abated, however. "Well, Jeremy, my name is John Ball, and I bid you welcome to our mill. But you'll have to excuse me if I yet have some concerns about the arrival of those brigands to my home and business. My brother and I just completed it not four years ago and it would break our hearts should it be sacked and burned by the likes of Willcocks and his ilk."

"I fully understand, John. If you like, I'll scout back down along the road and look for any sign of their approach."

John scratched his chin thoughtfully and then nodded slowly. "It would set my heart greatly at rest if I knew they weren't coming", he said. "If they aren't on their way now, I suspect it's safe to assume they're not coming."

Without another word, Jeremy trotted out along the road to look for any sign of approach by a large group of men. When he reached the point where the road sloped off down the Mountain, he made his way to a rock ledge, from which he hoped to spy the camp of the Canadian Volunteers so that he could determine their intentions. There was no sign of an encampment on the shelf anywhere near the Mountain road, and he had about resigned himself to going down to have a closer look when he noticed a large column of men moving away along the road far below. Since their demeanour was anything but military, Jeremy realized that this must be Willcocks' gang, surprised as he was to see them moving away so soon after setting up camp.

The small army of thugs would not be a problem to either himself or the Balls, at least not this day.

Jeremy ran back to the Ball mill to apprise the miller of his discovery. He was about to leave when John's wife appeared and invited him to stay for supper, even if it was but "a common stew and fresh made bread." As the sun sank below the treetops, Jeremy enjoyed his first complete home-cooked meal in weeks, he generally availing himself of whatever was at hand while fending for himself.

After eating, he thanked Mrs. Ball heartily for her hospitality and the two men repaired to the porch to smoke. It was in this domestic setting that John Ball brought up the Battle at Stoney Creek, not long past. He seemed to know all the details of the battle, but his enthusiasm truly soared when telling of a young man who played a key role in the battle. "Have you heard about the young lad they call Scout Billy Green?" he asked eagerly.

"No, sir, can't say that I have", responded Jeremy, his curiosity peaked.

John Ball proceeded to tell Jeremy of the part the young Billy Green played in the battle. "Apparently this nineteen-year-old young man, who lives in Stoney Creek, found out the countersign for the pickets from his brother-in-law, or some such, and I'm not sure how. But he takes the information to the troops at Burlington and leads them back to the American camp and gets them through the guards with the countersign. With that piece of information, that young fellow may have changed the whole course of the war."

"And this young fellow is a scout for the British Army?" Jeremy asked.

"No", John replied. "But I understand the commanding officer gave him a corporal's sword before the battle, with which he actually ran through the guard they gave the countersign. And, when the battle was over, he went back home to the family land with tales of war adventures to tell all who would listen." The miller's voice held a hint of envy at young Billy's exploits and fame.

As the evening deepened, Jeremy was offered shelter in the mill for the night, for the sky threatened of rain. "Don't be thinking of this as charity, now", warned John with a smile. "I'll be needing some help in the morning, since my brother's away, so I want you to be well rested."

Thankfully, Jeremy accepted the offer and bedded down on the sacks of grain stacked on the top floor, where the dust from milling had at least settled downward. There he lay, listening to the approaching thunder of a summer storm, and caught sight of the sky lighting up in great flashes. He was infinitely more comfortable than he had been the previous night, he thought just before fatigue overtook him and he slipped into a deep sleep bordering on unconsciousness.

Chapter Seven

Jeremy opened his eyes, but did not move. It took some time for him to realize where he was, and his muscles ached from the previous day's unaccustomed labour. While he was in good physical condition, well muscled with barely an ounce of fat on him, his lifestyle did not normally entail hard physical labour. So he lay there for a time on the sacks of grain, staring at the sunlight filtering through the planks that made up the mill's walls.

But his inertia was soon cured by the noise of the mill machinery being set in motion, a bone-rattling cacophony consisting of the rush of water through the sluice, the creaking of the water wheel picking up speed as it overcame an inertia of its own, and the groan of the great grinding wheel, all accompanied by the squeak of gears and leather belts throughout the structure. He felt more than heard the pounding of feet coming up the stairs from the level below, just before John Ball's head poked up through the floor.

"I hope I didn't wake you", he yelled, a grin belying the words. "It's nearing six o'clock and I simply cannot wait all day to get my work started."

Jeremy grinned back and headed for the stairs, following his host to the main floor, where the latter had been readying the enterprise for the day's milling. "This is quite the mill you have here", he said, keeping his voice above the level of sound. "I meant to ask you, where is your brother, Charles?"

"Off shirking his duties while I toil here", John laughed. "No, in truth, he had to travel to York to attend to some business of the mill. He should be back in a couple of days."

The miller showed Jeremy the operation of the gristmill, starting inside with the enormous gears that turned the rotation of the waterwheel outside into the slow but inexorable power that operated the rest. Then they went back to the main floor, where the great grinding wheel itself turned ever so slowly, awaiting some grain from the floor above, where Jeremy had been sleeping. He had noticed the bin across the floor from where he lay, into which would be dumped the sacks of grain that had made up his bed. From there, the grain would travel down a pipe to the hopper, which would feed it between the stones and be ground into the product required by the customer. Stones of different sizes were stacked on the floor, each with its own pattern, which would determine the coarseness of that end product.

The inside tour complete, John and Jeremy headed outside to look at the dam that controlled the creek level, in an attempt to ensure a steady supply of water for the sluice to carry to the wheel. The excess water simply flowed over the dam and the waterfall to continue its journey below. Jeremy was suitably impressed by it all, always fascinated by the intricacies of modern technology.

"It's still early in the summer", John said. "The water in the creek is yet fairly high, but there will be a time, maybe two or three weeks at the height, that there won't be enough rainfall to keep the wheel turning."

"What do you do then?"

"We work on improving the mill and any other tasks that await us", John replied. "For instance, we hope to build a sawmill in connection with this mill, and we have our eyes on another mill site farther upstream. Well, Jeremy, I hate to be a poor host, but we'll need to get working if I'm to pay for it all."

"What is it I'm to help you with?" asked Jeremy. "Do you need help loading grain?"

"As much as I can always use help with that, I'd need to keep you here, chained to the hoist", quipped the miller. "No, my problem is more technical in nature." Seeing that Jeremy was about to protest his innocence as he regarded the mechanics of the mill, he added,

"Not to worry. I'll do the thinking, but I need you to help me with the heavy lifting."

Ball headed into the barn and, with the throw of a lever, closed the gate that controlled the water flow to the sluice, thereby bringing the entire works to a slow halt. "I only started it up to wake you", joked Ball. "And to let you see how it works. Now, see that large gear there in the corner?" The miller pointed to a collection of parts, one of which was a new looking wheel with teeth. "It's the same as that one there", he said, now directing Jeremy's attention to an identical piece of machinery atop the shaft that rose from the grinding stone.

"That's the crown gear", he continued. "It turns the gear that runs the hoist to the floor above."

Jeremy followed the miller's explanations closely, fascinated with "the mechanics" as his host had called it. The machinery involved in these water-driven mills were like a miracle as far the formally uneducated trapper was concerned. He marvelled at the intelligence that must surely have been required to produce such technical wizardry.

Ball turned to Jeremy. "The crown gear is what I wanted your help with", he explained. "You and I will have to get down the one that's up there and replace it with the new one. I'd hoped it would do until my brother returned, but it'll not wait any longer. I'm afraid it'll damage some of the other equipment soon."

The two men set to changing the enormous gears, using a set of pulleys and ropes that Ball had arranged, tied to beams overhead. The strain was enormous as, even with the help of the ropes, the old gear had to be worked off the post and the new gear needed to be rolled to the site, positioned for tying, and finally, positioned and lowered by the swinging ropes into the place of the original. Their backs ached and arm muscles fairly screamed from the exertion but before lunch, the mill's water wheel had begun to turn once again.

John and Jeremy sat catching their breaths on the porch of the house, listening as the mill settled into its belts, gears and wheels once again.

"Well, Jeremy, once again, I'm afraid I've not been the best host", Ball said at last. "I believe I've somewhat taken advantage of you. But you've done me a great service getting this mill operating efficiently again."

"No, sir, you've been as hospitable as any I've met", Jeremy answered sincerely. "The education I've received from this will easily offset the work." He got to his feet, stretching. "Well, I'd best be on my way and let you get on with your trade. I'll get my things from the bin floor, and thank you for your kindness."

John smiled. "Of course, if you would want to stay and work the mill..." he said, half in jest.

"No thank you", came the answer, Jeremy putting out his hand as if waving off the offer. "I'm not accustomed to this industrial lifestyle. Part of the education I've received is that what you do is hard work. I'm afraid I was just cut out to be a trader and a hunter in this life."

"Well, that's a shame", John said. "But before you go, my wife has a bit of breakfast left for you. A man can't travel and fight traitors on an empty stomach", he added, with an amused gleam in his eye.

A half hour later, with a hearty meal weighing on his belly and fond farewells from his friends, Jeremy set off up the rise that led back to the road. It was fast approaching the heat of the day and he allowed himself some measure of enjoyment as he stepped down the road, his gun slung over his shoulder.

The roadway seemed like a tunnel in places, walled in by forest on both sides and sheltered by a leafy canopy overhead, as the old growth trees easily spanned the narrow way. All about him, Jeremy could hear the sounds of the Niagara wilderness; the rustling of leaves moving in the gentle breeze, the calls of birds as they vied for territory or announced some find of food, the scamper of squirrels and chipmunks through the undergrowth, at times seeming to shadow him as he went. For a man who made his living in part from hunting, he had little desire in tracking and killing anything this morning. After yesterday's dramas, life just seemed too relaxed today, since the work had been completed.

When he rounded the final bend, at the bottom of the Mountain, Jeremy turned right onto the main road, heading back toward home. As far as he was concerned, he had made a reasonable attempt to

Tony Vandermaas

locate Lieutenant Fitzgibbon, to no avail, nor had anyone he spoke to even an inkling of where the man might be. If the Bloody Boys were looking for Willcocks, he knew where they should have been looking, as near-fatal experience had shown. It had become very dangerous in the Niagara Peninsula these days, and he still needed to make a living. It was time to get back to his own enterprises.

As he walked, he passed very few homes, at least that he could see from the road. However, after about a half hour of walking, he came upon what he guessed to be a two-room log cabin set back possibly a hundred feet from the road, at the top of a small laneway that meandered up the hill. He saw a lone figure, a man by all appearances, working in a garden at the front of the cabin, so Jeremy waved his hat, shouting a friendly hello. The man looked up and saw him, and waved back uncertainly, but then seemed to decide to stop Jeremy.

"I wouldn't be sticking to the road if you're headed much farther in that direction", the inhabitant warned.

Upon hearing the voice, Jeremy was caught off guard. This was not a man after all. Hidden in the farmer's clothing and the slouch hat was a young woman, in perhaps her early twenties. Although Jeremy could not clearly make out her features because of the baggy accoutrements, he had the impression she might be quite attractive, although he found that it mattered little to him.

"And why would that be, er, ma'am?" he asked, once the surprise abated.

"Ma'am it is, sir", she replied, with just a hint of an uncertain smile. "But the reason I came down to warn you is that, last evening, I saw that scoundrel, Joseph Willcocks, and his men ride by here."

"I sincerely hope they have done you and your family no harm, ma'am", Jeremy offered, truly concerned. This was not a good time to live in so isolated an area.

Her smile faded. "I have no family, sir. My husband was killed at Queenston Heights last year and I have been eking out a living on our meagre spread by myself ever since." Immediately, she wondered why she had shared information of her vulnerability with this stranger, who could well be anyone.

Jeremy was momentarily at a loss for words. "Are you sure you should be out here all alone?" he asked, unaccustomed to seeing a young woman living alone without an apparent support system. "Have you no other family to return to?"

The woman's eyes seemed to flash with a momentary fire, as if angry, but then she answered, "And why should I run home to the safety of my parents when I have this place to sustain me?" Her voice began to rise, as the fire once again returned. "Do you think that a woman cannot do for herself?"

"Pardon me, ma'am", Jeremy looked for safe ground in this discussion. He had heard before of some women who wished to live men's lives and claimed they could do the same things as men. He knew from the stories that they could become quite agitated if challenged. "I meant no offence. I was merely concerned about you."

"Well, save your concern for those who require it!" she snapped.

Jeremy knew not which way to look. This was a discussion he felt could only become worse for him, so he decided retreat was the best option.

"Yes, ma'am, and thank you for the warning", he muttered, turning to face the road once again. "But perhaps Willcocks and his men continued on back to Newark, so I think I'll continue on this way."

"I think not", the woman said, a stern tone to her voice.

Jeremy turned around. "Pardon me, madam? Did you mean to tell me I could not continue this way?" he asked incredulously.

The young woman started to laugh, relaxing her manner in such a way that Jeremy could not help but find appealing. "No, sir. I meant that Willcocks did not go on to Newark last night", she said. "In fact, they stopped but a short distance down the road, at the Jenkins place, down in the creek valley." Her voice was sober once again. "In fact, I ventured near there this morning, after hearing noise for the better part of the night, and the blackguards are still there."

Jeremy looked at her and then down the road, in the direction he was heading. "Perhaps I should be thanking you most profusely", he finally said. "As long as I should manage to do so without offending you", he added with a mischievous grin.

"I think a simple thank you should suffice, sir, and there is no reason to do so profusely", the smile returned to her face as well. "And, you are most welcome, sir."

"I think before you 'sir' me one more time, I should tell you my name", Jeremy offered. And that would be Jeremy van Hijser, ma'am."

"Pleased to meet you, Mr. van Hijser", the young woman said, with a mock curtsey, a move appearing all the more humorous since it was done with baggy trousers.

"Jeremy, please", he said. "Mister is barely better than sir."

"Very well, Jeremy", she responded. "And my name is Elizabeth Rhodes. Elizabeth, if you please." As Jeremy bowed slightly, she added, as if suddenly remembering, "Were you not at the Davis fire yesterday? The gentleman from Beaverdams?"

"That I was", Jeremy answered. "I was looking for Willcocks to report on his whereabouts and, unfortunately, came upon an unfortunate circumstance in finding him. By the way", he said. "How is Mr. Davis? Was he better later in the day? I heard his good neighbours offering him comfort and assistance, and thought that might lift his spirits somewhat." He looked away, as an old sadness crept in upon him. "I know it helped me somewhat when I suffered a great loss. Friends can be such a comfort to the soul."

Elizabeth felt for this man, who was yet practically a stranger to her, and one from places unknown at that. "Did you lose your farm, too?"

"No", Jeremy answered, his voice and his gaze both distant. "Not a farm." His voice had lowered now to almost a whisper.

"I'm sorry", Elizabeth said softly. "I didn't mean to pry. I'm a stranger to you, and here I am, asking you personal questions."

Jeremy looked up into her soft blue eyes, and had the unexpected but not entirely unpleasant sensation of falling upward into them. "It's alright", he said softly. "It seems almost a lifetime ago. In fact, it was, for that was a life that no longer exists." For several long moments, not a word passed between them. "My wife, Sarah, died six years ago while giving birth to our child", he whispered.

"And the child?" Elizabeth asked, tears now welling up in her eyes.

"Gone, as well."

A Question of Loyalty

Again a long silence. Then Jeremy pulled himself together, sighed deeply and turned to be once more on his way. "Well, once again, thank you for the warning about Willcocks", he said, forcing the strength back into his voice. "And, all suggestions of ability aside, please keep yourself safe. You have been very kind and I should hate to hear the news someday, that you were harmed in any way."

"Before you go, would you like a drink of water?" Elizabeth offered, suddenly finding she enjoyed this stranger's company. "And perhaps something to eat? It is a long way to Beaverdams, I understand, and you may find yourself thirsty and hungry if you don't have something before you press on."

In truth, Jeremy was not hungry in the least, having enjoyed a hearty breakfast at the Ball house, but he was strangely drawn to this young lady who reminded him of Sarah, in ways he did not quite understand. Perhaps he had merely been alone too long and subconsciously wanted for the company of a woman, if only for an hour. Perhaps Elizabeth was indeed something special. Whatever the case, he accepted the gracious offer and sat with Elizabeth on a bench in front of the house, eating bread still warm from baking and enjoying the proffered water as he was sure he had never enjoyed water before.

Elizabeth inexplicably found herself explaining that the reason for her attire was to keep from drawing unwanted attention from passers-by. She had affected her manner of dress when she realized, soon after her husband's death, that many used this highway, and that not all the wayfarers were of good intent. So she now dressed in her husband's clothes and tried to keep from sight as much as possible, usually going inside if she heard the approach of horses or wagons. She had been out front tending to her garden when Jeremy passed by quite simply because he'd made no noise as he approached.

But as the afternoon drew on, Jeremy knew he must be on his way lest he not make it back to DeCou's house before sunset. Once again, he thanked Elizabeth for her hospitality and the warning and prepared to set off. As he bid her farewell, he lifted her right hand by the fingertips, surprised that the skin should be so soft on a woman who had to perform all her household's chores. Then he softly brushed his lips against her fingers, intending it to be an act of gallantry, but finding the experience most sensual. He mentally shook off the thoughts, feeling shame at his reaction in regard to such a wonderful lady. Angry with himself, he pulled his hat roughly onto his head and, without a further word, started off up a path that began at Elizabeth's hilly south field, and headed to the trail that led along the escarpment, to return the way he had come.

Elizabeth watched him go, a whirlwind of emotions overtaking her. Inexplicably, she had wanted Jeremy to take her into his arms and kiss her, but she knew he was too much of a gentleman to do that. The very thought made her blush, bringing her to think that the young man would certainly think her wanton if he guessed at her thoughts. But she hoped that he would chance to use this road again in the not-too-distant future so that she might see him again. The truth be told, she rather missed having the strength and comfort of a man at her side, her protestations of independence not withstanding.

Jeremy grunted with the effort as he crested the Mountain, pulling himself over the last bit of rock before the top, the path having veered away from the summit and back towards the road at the last moment. He turned and looked back in the direction he had come, spotting the Rhodes homestead with ease from this vantage point. He shrugged his gear back into place and, just before he turned away, a smile played upon his lips. He'd find an excuse before long to come by this way again.

Chapter Eight

As Jeremy made his way eastward along the edge of the Mountain, the wind picked up, changing to a southwesterly direction, and the sky began to fill with heavy mid-grey clouds, darkening the afternoon prematurely. Any other time, he might have expected that maybe the weather would pass but, although he could never quite explain it, he could somehow always tell if it was truly going to rain by the smell of the air. Whatever the explanation for this phenomenon, his nose now told him that he did not have long before he would need to find shelter or face a soaking.

He kept his eyes peeled for overhangs or any other possible protection should the expected rain begin to fall, with little luck. Only twenty minutes later, he was chagrined to find that he'd been correct. In the space of a few moments, the sky went from grey to black, and the fast-approaching rumbles of thunder and flashes of light lent final credence to his instincts. He was resigned to walking the rest of the way home soaked to the bone, for once he was drenched there would be little point in stopping.

It was then that Providence led him by a hastily constructed lean-to, no doubt leaky, but no doubt a great improvement over his present situation. Jeremy managed to duck inside just as the first enormous drops of rain struck his back. He was grateful for the unexpected fortune that brought him to the shelter, although he did not know who the recipient of these thanks should be. He looked quickly about, sizing up the construction and discovered it to be better built than he had expected. No child's fort this, he thought, unless that child was extremely precocious.

Holding the entire structure together was a sturdy ridgepole that ran between the crotches of two young two trees, which grew directly beside a low rock outcropping, giving it a height of approximately four feet. Upon this pole leaned a number of thick staves, firmly embedded in the ground, and covered by overlapping sections of bark. As Jeremy approached, he'd thought that the evergreen boughs placed upon the outside were the fabric of the roof, but he now realized that they were probably placed there to provide camouflage. And to keep the small shelter from flooding in a rain, a trench was dug along the bottom of the rock face to drain away any leakage from the cracks in the stone. Someone had gone through a great deal of thought and labour to build a structure that was normally intended to be quite temporary.

By now, visibility was decreasing steadily as the intensity of the storm heralded its full arrival. The rain hammered on the roof of the lean-to and the previously stiff wind built to a fury, forcing Jeremy to back away from the entrance. He began to consider whether even this construction would hold up in this weather. In fact, he wondered if there was any building that was well enough constructed for this storm, for Jeremy felt particularly small and vulnerable in these tiny, cramped quarters.

On and on the storm raged, lightning flashes so frequent it seemed the sky was perpetually lit, and thunder peals so close upon each other's heels that the ground trembled with one extended shudder and the noise seemed endless. The wind lashed at the forest around him, and Jeremy spied an old tree crashing to the ground not fifty feet away. He heard no sound, however. There was no competing with the deafening level of the storm. In spite of his vast wilderness experience, he began to know a fear that he could not remember ever feeling in the presence of natural phenomena.

After what seemed like an eternity, the storm finally abated. The rain stopped as suddenly as it had started, the wind was reduced to a stiff breeze, the thunder rumbled off down the peninsula, and the lightning was no longer visible as the sky brightened up once more. Jeremy peeked out through the doorway of the lean-to, just in time to see a doe run out from the dubious protection of a copse of cedars and bound from sight. And, amid the sounds of heavy drops yet falling from the trees overhead, the sounds of birds calling to each other brought life to the forest once more.

Jeremy crawled forth to leave the shelter, anticipating being free of the confines of this shelter, as fortuitous as it had been. He pulled his belongings toward him and began to back from the lean-to only to find, to his shock and annoyance, that his way was barred. Two men stood dripping near the entrance, scowling fiercely at him.

"What are you doing here uninvited?" one asked, spitting something dark from his mouth in the direction of the shelter's roof.

Jeremy studied the men before answering, attempting to ascertain his level of danger from these two. The one who spoke to be rather short, perhaps just over five feet tall, although it was difficult to judge from his perspective. He wore an old set of woollen clothes; grey in colour, and none the cleaner for the soaking they had obviously received in the rain. In his arm, he cradled an old musket of a brand not familiar to Jeremy and a long hunting knife was inserted between the strands of the rope that secured his trousers. His face was no tidier than his clothes, and his sodden hair hung down shoulder-length in uneven strands.

His companion was oddly dressed, quite out of the ordinary in the middle of a forest. Although he was certainly no cleaner than his companion, this man sported a pair of grey cotton trousers, mid-shin in length. Tucked into their waistband were the remnants of a white shirt, all topped with a green knee-length suit jacket. At his side was an officer's sword, its clean and apparently well-kept appearance out of step with his overall tattered look. Jeremy almost expected to see a tricorn on the man's head, but his hair, which appeared to have been trimmed raggedly with his own sword, was covered with what looked like a lady's bonnet. There was a mad gleam to his eyes, which never rested, darting back and forth and seemingly focusing on nothing in particular.

"Well", the first man growled impatiently. "We aren't accustomed to being kept waiting when we ask a question, isn't that so, Cedric?"

The man who was no doubt Cedric glanced quickly at his companion and then looked away again, at an apparent loss to understand his companion's comment. "Ask him why he's here, Tom", he suggested, his voice sounding as absent as his eyes appeared.

"I meant no harm", Jeremy answered, his left hand moving cautiously toward his bayonet. At the same time, his right hand reached as though scratching, over his head as he readied to pull the tomahawk from its place behind his shoulders. "I saw the storm was coming and this great shelter you built beckoned me."

"Do you not understand the meaning of private property?" Tom demanded. "Do you always help yourself to things belonging to others just because these things 'beckon you' as you say?"

Jeremy could see that reason would not be an effective tool in dealing with these men. He slowly crawled from the lean-to, hoping to get out and upright before one or both of them decided to take advantage of his vulnerable position. "I can assure you gentlemen that when I came upon it, I thought that it was just some hunter's temporary shelter, and realized no different until I had gotten inside."

Tom watched Jeremy carefully, his hands tightening on his gun, the knuckles going white with the tension. Jeremy knew it would be but a matter of time before he swung it around to take a shot, unless he could misdirect them somehow. He knew he could probably kill both before they could react, but he felt that should only be a last resort, as they obviously had problems of some kind.

"What's the matter with your friend?" Jeremy asked. "What did you call him? Cedric?"

Tom eyed him suspiciously. "What makes you think there's anything the matter with Cedric?" he challenged, anger evident in his voice. "He's a little different from some, but he's a good friend and I'll thank you not to insult him"

Careful, Jeremy thought to himself. It seems Tom is very protective of his friend. "I meant no offence by the question. It just seems his attention wavers somewhat."

Tom studied the trapper for a moment, apparently trying to decide whether to tell this stranger anything. "Cedric is an officer in the United States Army, isn't that right, Cedric?"

At the words "United States Army", Cedric's attention was immediately captured. "U.S. Army", he said proudly, coming to attention. "Lieutenant Cedric Johnson at your service." Then his eyes glazed over once again and he began to look about as before, seemingly watching for something, edgily expecting something to happen.

"Cedric was at Frenchtown, on the Raisin River", Tom continued. "Do you know where that is?" When Jeremy shook his head in the negative, the man spit on the ground and continued. "That's south of Detroit, I think. Doesn't matter. It's that way in general, and Tom was fighting there along with the Kentuckians, whatever they may be, against the British and the Indians." A cloud crossed over his face as the next part came to him. "There are times when he's normal, and that's when he told me the story, although he seems to get a little confused at times. Anyway, they lost the fight and the British Army disarmed them and promised to protect the Americans from the Indians."

Once again, Tom looks quite upset. "And here's the part I hope he's wrong about. He says the British pulled back that night to return to Amherstberg and left the unarmed prisoners to the mercy of the Indians. And he says Tecumseh's Indians didn't show any. Mercy that is."

Tom looked about, apparently trying to come to grips with what he had just said. "Cedric, here, he was one of the few to escape from the massacre, and he wandered around in the woods, lost, until some British soldiers found him. They then took him back to Amherstberg and sent him east to join other officers that were prisoners of war. He escaped just a few months ago and lived off the land until I found him. He's been living with me ever since. But he's always looking around like that, for what I don't know, and he only sleeps during the day, because every little sound at night frightens him so." He finished his tale looking at Cedric, and one could see the empathy in the derelict's eyes.

"By the way", Jeremy said, changing the subject. "My name is Jeremy."

"It makes little difference what your name is", Tom growled. "You trespassed in our house, and trespassers die. It makes no difference who a dead man is."

"I thought we were becoming quite well acquainted", Jeremy

answered smoothly, his mind racing to find a peaceful solution to this situation, one he thought he had found only moments before.

Without another word, Tom tapped Cedric on the shoulder and pointed at Jeremy. "This man's a British officer!" he shouted.

"What?" Jeremy replied, startled by this odd turn of events. But the intent quickly became obvious.

Cedric smoothly pulled his sword from its sheath and pointed it menacingly at this newfound enemy. "Tippecanoe and Tyler too!" he screamed without warning and lunged at Jeremy's midsection with the razor-sharp weapon with a motion that denoted some expertise with the blade.

Reflexively, Jeremy pulled his bayonet from the loop on his belt and swung it across in front of his body, and the two steel blades met just inches away. The bayonet parried the longer blade with sufficient force to send the lunge wide of his body and, with his free arm he lashed out, his fist catching Cedric roundly on the chin.

When Tom saw his companion collapse from the sudden blow, he sprang into action, and tried to bring his musket to bear, intending to aim it at his foe. Before Jeremy could react to this new threat, the man pointed the weapon at Jeremy's waist and pulled the trigger. The hammer struck down on the flint, making a spark, but nothing happened.

Cedric, sitting up now, shook his head in disgust at his friend. "You let your powder get wet, soldier!" he barked, and slowly pulled himself to his feet with the aid of a young maple sapling. With, a roar, he renewed his attack, this time slashing rapidly at Jeremy, creating a deadly scything action that the latter would be hard pressed to counter. The soldier pressed his advantage, seeing his opponent back away to avoid the blizzard of flashing steel.

Jeremy tried to find an answer to this renewed attack, especially since Tom was also now fumbling with his knife to rejoin the attack. The best he could do for the moment was to try to keep trees between himself and his attacker, but he had been forced back into what was mostly clearing, and Tom was attempting to outflank him. In desperation, he pulled his tomahawk from the loop behind his head and, holding it so it was evident to the American, he brandished it and, not actually knowing any Aboriginal languages, loudly let out an approximation of a war cry.

Cedric's sword stopped in mid-swing. A terrified expression overcame his features as the memories he had previously shared with his camp mate washed over him in all their gory horror. Once again, he found himself in Frenchtown, twilight falling over the settlement, and the whooping of the Indians from the forest. Try as he might, he could not see the Indians through the fog of his fear, only heard the blood curdling war cries and saw the flash rifle muzzles and blur of tomahawks as the unarmed men all around him were slaughtered. Petrified with terror, he began to tremble uncontrollably, and the sword fell useless onto the ground.

"British officer!" Tom cried, trying to bring Cedric back around, to no avail. "British officer! British officer!" His voice rose in pitch as it dawned upon him that he was now effectively alone with an enemy of his own making.

"You'll have to fight me yourself", Jeremy said evenly, his voice low and menacing. "Raise your knife, sir."

Tom held his blade level with his waist, in a classic fighting position and slowly circled, waiting for an opening to attack. Jeremy had replaced his tomahawk and Tom now faced a sharpened bayonet. He lunged suddenly, and his blade caught part of Jeremy's sleeve, ripping his shirt from elbow almost to wrist. The man jumped back and laughed maniacally. "Next time it'll be more than your clothes", he taunted.

Jeremy did not flinch. The attack had done no harm and, while it had come uncomfortably close, he had been in enough knife fights to keep his concentration about him. A moment's inattention could give your opponent an advantage from which you might not ever recover. As they began to slowly circle each other once again, Jeremy noticed that his opponent was investing all his attention in Jeremy's weapon hand rather than his eyes. This, he knew, could be used to Jeremy's advantage. It was much easier to get a good read of the other's intentions by watching the eyes than the hand.

Jeremy shifted the bayonet ever so slightly in his hand and Tom, thinking that Jeremy was making a move, opened up his arms to try to avoid the weapon. Seeing this, Jeremy moved suddenly forward and buried the bayonet to the hilt into the man's abdomen, and then drove the blade upward into his chest.

Only a squeak of surprise escaped across Tom's lips as he

looked in amazement at the bayonet protruding from his body. His raised his eyes unsteadily until he found the cold eyes of his opponent, and the rolled back as he gurgled his last breath, pink foam bubbling to his lips. Almost in slow motion, he slumped to the ground and rested in a kneeling position against a rock, legs tucked under him.

Jeremy stood looking at his vanquished foe, a mixture of emotions in play. There was no time to come to terms with them, however, for just then he heard the telltale sound of a ball being rammed into a muzzle and the lock being pulled back. Without a thought, he swung about, automatically pulling out his tomahawk once again and letting it fly in the direction of the sound. With unerring accuracy, it flew through the air and the blade struck Cedric solidly in the forehead.

With his hands no longer controlled by the brain, the musket swerved off its aim as all command was relinquished to the reflexes and the dying man's finger tightened the hold on the trigger, firing the ball harmlessly into the ground. Cedric fell where he had stood, with his final words barely breathed from his dying lips, "No, no, no! Watch out, men! More damned Indians!"

Jeremy looked down on the demented man as he retrieved his tomahawk. Whatever else he may have thought about the poor soul, at least he would no longer be reliving the terror at Frenchtown.

Chapter Nine

Dorian Williamson seemed in a foul mood again this morning, in spite of the fine weather, although, truth be told, it was not always an easy thing to determine. His men knew to stay well clear as he ranted and swore. He kicked violently at anything that he found in his path, often hurting himself in the process, which in turn brought on a renewed bout of swearing. This seemingly endless cycle continued to build as he made his way from the Jenkins house, across the yard toward the barn.

Willcocks was the reason for Williamson's frustration. The "lieutenant" had decamped the previous day, heading for Newark with new information they had obtained from an informer close to the Fitzgibbon unit. According to this spy, the Bloody Boys had returned to DeCou's house near Beaverdams to set up a headquarters and supply depot. According to the little information that Willcocks was willing to share, Fitzgibbon was planning, along with Merritt's Provincial Dragoons and others, an effort for an even more concerted harassment of the American troops at Fort George. Willcocks saw this as a possible precursor to an assault to remove the Americans from the former capital of Upper Canada, and he felt that he should deliver this news personally to Major General Dearborn. No doubt another grasp at that army commission he had been campaigning for.

Williamson was not privy to the identity of traitor within the British midst, and this made him angrier, feeling this a stain upon his honour since their leader obviously felt he and his men beneath him. In fact, Willcocks had come right out and said so on a number of occasions, but Williamson tended to try to put the best light on it.

The real snub came, however, when he and his men were told they were not accompany Willcocks to Newark, but must remain behind to provide a rear guard. Williamson knew they needed no rear guard, although there are a number of British and allied units in the area to harass them. Not one of these groups of harassers posed a real threat to Willcocks' Volunteers, whose numbers alone made them a formidable opponent. Willcocks merely wished to keep his platoon out of sight of the American brass. Good enough to fight for them, but apparently not good enough to be seen with them!

Williamson was not actually quite as frustrated as he seemed, though the anger directed at his commander was genuine enough. What Willcocks, and even his own men, did not yet know was that Dorian now felt he might have an edge of his own.

When he reached the barn, Williamson shouted for his second in command, Geoffrey Smith. Geoffrey, it was readily known, had been sleeping here in the hay rather than face the wrath of his boss the night before. Smith moaned an unintelligible response, and then his head appeared finally over the edge of the loft.

"Get your lazy carcass down here!" Willcocks roared from below. "It's been hours since the cock crowed and yet I find you here still asleep! What manner of trash have I associated myself with, sleeping away the daylight hours while there's so much work to be done?" he bellowed.

Smith knew better than to answer. To do so would be to invite a beating or worse for insubordination. He scampered down the ladder to the ground, fumbling with his suspenders as he did. "What's it to be today, Mr. Williamson?" he asked, in an appropriately chastened manner. "Will we be riding to another farm?"

"No", growled Williamson pensively, rubbing his hand over the heavy stubble on his jaw. "I think it's time we beat Willcocks at his own game and did a little contributing to the war effort ourselves. Maybe we can beat him to that commission and teach him to look down on us."

"And just how do you propose we do that?" Smith asked, the

incredulity just a hair too evident in his voice. "Willcocks has an insider to give him information. Where are we to get solid military intelligence like that?"

Williamson stopped rubbing his face and glared at his adjutant, then suddenly lashed out with his large fist, catching the taller but slighter man squarely in the midsection. The bully was entertained by a satisfying expulsion of air followed by an equally rewarding moan as the other doubled over in pain.

"Don't ever mock me", he growled. "Now pick up whatever things you have here and meet me in the house. Time for a council of war."

Smith gazed at him carefully from his bent-over position, the hatred of his leader barely disguised. "Yes, sir", he groaned, wishing it were in his power to get even. "I'll be right there. My things are still in the loft."

"Be right quick about it!" Dorian snapped, and stalked off toward the frame farmhouse that, until recently, was the home of the Jenkins family.

Willcocks and Williamson had never truly grown to like or even respect each other. The reasons for the enmity between them came down mainly to matters of social class. The former was basically an aristocrat by birth, well educated and versed in all aspects of social respectability, even if he did not always follow the social mores. Williamson, on the other hand, was a third-generation stonecutter, whose family had worked at the quarries above Queenston, cutting the stone for houses built for the likes of Willcocks. Barely able to read and write, he often needed Smith to read more complex documents for him.

Williamson's entertainment was simply anything that involved becoming inebriated and causing others pain. On the other hand, his leader, attended fine dinners and teas, at least in the days before he turned on the Newark gentry. Willcocks had a gift for debating and convincing others of the rightness of his opinions, but Williamson's main verbal gifts were cursing and lying.

But the two needed each other, maintaining their association as a symbiotic necessity to continuing on with their present lifestyles. Willcocks needed the gruffer man's sheer bullying ability at times, and Williamson would likely be hunted down and shot by either side without the legitimacy his boss gave to his actions.

When Geoffrey had finally collected his things, after taking a generous pull from the bottle of rum he had hidden in the loft, he entered the house's kitchen, where Williamson was sitting at the homemade, rough-hewn dinner table with another man, a man he had not met before. The newcomer was of average height and build, but his distinguished mode of dress was out of place in these Niagara backwaters. He sat in his chair with a relaxed air, and his devil-may-care attitude made it seem he was not at all concerned about where he was, or with whom.

"Hullo", Smith greeted the man tentatively, taking a chair at the wall, well away from the table. This positioning was intended for self-defence purposes more than a dislike of strangers, since Dorian was known to attack unsuspecting companions under the table with little or no provocation.

The man looked curiously over at Smith, thoughtfully stroking his goatee, and then addressed Williamson. "Doesn't he sit with us?" he asked, suspicious of the adjutant's behaviour. "He wouldn't be sitting over there so that he can attack me unawares, would he?" The stranger smiled in a cold, reptilian manner, sending shivers along Smith's back. Suddenly, Williamson no longer seemed the most dangerous man in the room.

Williamson answered with a loud guffaw. "No, you needn't worry about him", he chuckled. "Geoffrey just knows where it's safest."

"From me?" the man asked, his eyebrows raised in surprise. "Why? Does he know who I am?"

"No, no. So far, he knows nothing", Williamson laughed. "But he is well acquainted with me."

The laughter died as quickly as it had started, and uncomfortable tension pervaded the meeting, as none of the three men spoke. Each seemed to be taking the others' measures, appraising the risks and the opportunities.

In the end, the new man spoke up first. "Well, Dorian, if it's all the same, there's no need to be telling Smith who I am if he doesn't already know", he suggested rather darkly. "After all, what he doesn't know won't hurt me." He laughed at his own joke and banged his fist on the table. "Now, then", he said abruptly. "Let's get on with the business at hand, shall we?"

"This gentleman here", Williamson began, addressing Smith while gesturing at the new man with his open hand. "This man is - how shall we put it? He's a purveyor of information. Yes, yes, that's good", he said, quite proud his wording. The man smiled coldly and nodded. "That's really all you need to know about him."

"But you should know that he has some information we might use to put that popinjay, Willcocks, in his place", he continued, stopping suddenly as he lost his train of thought to the dark anger which was once again interfering. "Anyways", he said, giving his head a slight shake. "Mr. Jones, shall we call him?" He looked at the stranger, who nodded ever so shallowly. "Mr. Jones says he knows where the British are hiding the supplies for those men such as Fitzgibbon, Merritt, and Ducharme, the leader of the Caughnawagas."

"And we're going to lead the Americans right to them", Smith chimed in knowingly.

"No, you idiot!" Williamson bellowed. "We're going to capture the stores and the few men guarding them ourselves, and then ride triumphantly into Newark with all the glory, the fate accomplished, as the French say."

The stranger sat quietly listening to all of this, wincing at Williamson's murder of a language the boor obviously did not at all understand. Far be it for him to correct the man, though. After all, Williamson was going to pay him good money for the information. More the fool he, "Jones" thought. Paying a man he could not identify for information he could not verify. This was to be a good month for him and as soon as he was paid, he was going to get well clear of this God-forsaken battle zone and make his way back to Montreal. There, he could finally realize his dream of outfitting his own northern traders. Ah, well, first things first, he thought.

"It should be quite easy", the man called Jones explained. "All the supplies for all the British raiders operating in Niagara are kept at the stagecoach stop known as Shipman's Corners, in the tavern at the crossroads there, above the Twelve Mile Creek." He stopped momentarily, making sure his audience was still with him. "It's kept in that very tavern, lightly guarded, since they feel no one would ever expect it of being there. If you attack at mid-day, the guards will be somewhat relaxed, shall we say, from their usual liquid lunch, military discipline not being much at that location." He leaned in on the table, noticing that Williamson did the same, and that Smith was resting forward with his forearms on his knees.

I have them now, "Jones" thought to himself. It was all he could do to keep his stern expression on his face, wanting to laugh out loud at the two fools in the room with him. "With the men you have here, you should be able to walk right in and take the tavern, supplies and all, with a small handful of drunken prisoners to ice the cake, as they say.

"I heard tell that the supplies are at Beaverdams", Williamson broke in, suddenly suspicious of the information. That much of Willcocks' information had been divulged.

The information peddler's face seemed to show no change in expression as far as the others could tell, and that in spite of Williamson's close scrutiny. Inside, his heart was galloping like a runaway horse as he struggled to recover from this momentary setback. "It's at Shipman's Tavern right now but, as you know, in war nothing's for long", he said in a matter-of-fact manner, no sign of hesitation evident as he covered for his error. "But you'd better hurry, because I understand it's to be moved very shortly.

Williamson leaned back in his chair and turned to look at his second in command. "What do you think?" he asked, although his mind was all made up, pictures of the glory of riding triumphantly into Newark as vivid as the faces of the men in this room. He could picture the livid face of Willcocks as he bested him in front of the U.S. officers and handed the prisoners over, maybe even being awarded the commission his leader wanted so badly.

Smith, however, was not quite as easily convinced. "It all sounds rather too good, if you ask me", he opined.

Williamson fairly exploded from his chair, shot across the room and knocked Smith from his chair with one swipe of his meaty hand. "We need nothing of any Doubting Thomas in this room!" he bellowed. "I can quite see the British, in their arrogance, thinking we'd be too stupid to see through their ruse!" He bounced back into his chair, his enthusiasm building. "I can finally show the damned Americans who the mastermind in this organization is." Suddenly, his voice lowered menacingly. "Then we'll see who gets a military commission first."

"Jones" watched the childish display with barely disguised contempt. Fortunately for him, contempt was the correct expression for his character to be wearing, being known far and wide as a murderous spy in the employ of the U.S. Army. He was not actually certain whether such a person existed, although tales of this man had been circulating for over six months now. But no one seemed to know what he looked like, so the part seemed perfect for this man when he stumbled across these fools, who took him prisoner on the road. Quick thinking had made him jump into this identity and a chance to obtain the money he needed to fulfil his lifelong dream.

"Well", he said with finality. "I think it's time for me to get on the road. I've been sent to check on the British troop strengths in Burlington." He arose from his chair, pulling on his jacket as he did so. "If you gentlemen don't mind, I'll take my payment now, in gold coin as we agreed." A dangerous smile played across his lips. "One never knows how the fortunes of war will turn, now does one?"

Williamson rose from his own seat, offering "Jones" his hand. "It was good doing business with you", he said.

As the spy took his hand, Williamson yanked him up close just as his other hand darted in between their bodies. The knife he had kept hidden there sank to its hilt in the stranger's gut, driven to its hilt by the impact of the two men colliding. "Jones" looked directly into Williamson's face, his eyes wide with the shock of the turn of events, his face contorted with pain and disbelief.

"You're absolutely right, Mr. Jones", Dorian breathed, his voice almost a hiss, the cruel laughter in his eyes betraying the twisted pleasure he took from the other man's death. "One never knows how things will turn out during a war." He laughed aloud, now, sending a shiver down the back of even Geoffrey Smith, who should by now have been accustomed to his boss's cruelty. "And now that I have the information", he muttered to the man's dying eyes, "it would be best if you were to disappear. After all, we wouldn't want it getting out somehow that I bribed one of my own commander's spies."

Williamson let the agent's body slip off his knife and collapse to the floor. He stood there, strangely revelling in the feeling of the other man's blood dripping from his hand. Then he reached down and wiped both the hand and the knife on the spy's jacket.

"Smith!" he barked, and his adjutant fairly launched to his feet. "Clean this up", he ordered. "Then, come on back in here. We need to discuss how to best use the information this gentleman was good enough to provide us with so we can get to our just reward at Newark."

Geoffrey took firm hold of the dead man's feet and dragged him roughly out of the door into the yard, muttering obscenities under his breath the entire time. Then, after delegating the task given him by Williamson to the first men he saw, he headed back inside. He was rather anxious himself to help plan this attack on the British stores. They had been too long without any real action, and the idleness was taking a toll. Drunkenness and fighting were rife in the camp and, if the men were not soon provided with a solid distraction, the injuries and desertions threatened to tear the band apart. Not that he was completely certain that it would necessarily be a bad thing, but he feared for his own life should such a fate befall the command of the madman inside the house.

Smith had considered desertion in the middle of the night more than once, to get as far away from this insanity as possible. But should he leave, he would be forced to collect his family, now staying in Buffalo, away from neighbours who now probably hated him enough to take things out on them, and hide them and himself, perhaps for the rest of their lives. All things taken into consideration, his best hope was that Williamson would be killed on one of these raids. Then he could get back to his farm and pick his life back up, hopefully where he'd left it before the war.

His initial error had been in becoming involved in the idealism of North American politics. At the outset, he had espoused the republican rantings of Joseph Willcocks, feeling an American-style government would be best for Upper Canada as well, but the cost of these thoughts was running much too high. Although he was not educated in the higher sense, he was an avid reader and seemed to have a talent for analysis of various kinds.

His second mistake had been in allowing himself to be seconded to the platoon of this madman. Now he wished it would just be over, whatever the political outcome. His idealism had been completely crushed and those things just did not seem to matter any longer.

As he stepped back into the house, he saw Williamson once more seated at the table, his hands clasped before him as in prayer, his brows furrowed in thought. Smith approached carefully, sure to clear his throat so Dorian would know he was there. The brute was never so dangerous as he was when surprised, much like a vicious dog. He took a place at the table once more and Williamson looked up at him through raised eyebrows, the recent exertion apparently tiring him so much he could no longer raise his head. But Smith knew this was deceiving, as Dorian was not that predictable.

"Well", Williamson's voice boomed through the stillness of the kitchen. "How do you see this?"

Smith was well aware that Williamson was not asking this question as a matter of collaboration. The truth was that Dorian rarely made his own plans – he simply was not in possession of that level of depth. Plans were Smith's job. Then his boss would pretend to mull it over before changing the wording slightly, and then claiming the ideas as his own. Thus it had been when Geoffrey signed on, and thus it would be until one of them sighed his final breath.

Geoffrey sighed in resignation of his place in the hierarchy and offered his initial thoughts. "Well, Dorian, if we ride very early tomorrow, we can probably catch everyone at the tavern asleep."

Dorian interrupted Smith's narrative, sounding rather surprised. "You mean you don't think we should attack at noon, as Jones suggested?" It would have been much easier for him to simply follow the spy's plans as laid out, but he had the makings of a good politician, if not a tactician, and he recovered immediately. "So, you didn't completely trust him either, eh?" he asked cannily.

Jones smiled ironically, and continued. "If they are indeed lax in their discipline, the soldiers should yet be too drunk to respond in the wee hours of the morning", he said. "And, if Jones was exaggerating somewhat, as we both suspect", Geoffrey threw in, glancing up to see if his boss noticed the paean to his ego. "If that's the case, they still won't be terribly alert that early, and I doubt they would post more than one guard under the circumstances. After all, they don't think anyone knows about their secret cache."

Williamson nodded sagely, as if Geoffrey's thoughts had been his own, although he had never even considered the idea of such a fallback position. "Keep going", he commanded. "Let's see how good you've been at figuring out the rest."

By now, Smith was an expert at swallowing his pride and allowing his boss to take the credit for his thoughts. He controlled a smirk that fought to get out and continued. "Well", he offered tentatively. "I thought maybe we should rush into the building through both the front and side doors at the same time and take them before they can react." He looked up, as if seeking Williamson's approval. "Then we'll send any militia there packing under the rules of parole and tie up the officers and any regulars that might be there and load then in a wagon. From Shipman's Corners, it's not a long or dangerous ride to the fort."

Williamson mulled over what his second-in-command had offered and then, straightening himself up, he looked at Geoffrey. "Not bad, Smith", he said. "But I think we should go into the side door slightly sooner, the better to catch those sleeping in the back. And we make the officers ride their own mounts into the fort. Much more demoralizing." Thus having made his superficial changes to Smith's plan, he sat back once again, the glow of self-satisfaction evident upon his face.

Smith groaned inwardly, but was relieved that the charade of this particular planning exercise had passed so quickly. There would be more to the plan, of course, such as advance scouting, what weapons were to be carried, how many men to send to each entrance, how many to post outside to watch for unexpected turns in the tide of battle and, probably of greatest importance to this group, how the booty from the tavern itself were to be shared. All of these matters Smith would attend to on his own as always, he thought. Sometimes these sessions had been known to drag on for hours, particularly if the boss were in a foul mood, but Williamson seemed pleased with the input he had allowed himself to believe he had, and Smith should now thankfully be able to get on with it.

"Well, what are you waiting for?" Williamson bellowed suddenly, startling his assistant. "Get the men ready! We ride tonight!"

Obviously the big man was impatient, Smith thought, hiding an ironic grin by turning away. "Yes, sir!" he cried convincingly and darted from the room, before something else should strike Williamson's fancy. Besides, he had much work to accomplish if they were to ride for Shipman's that night.

Chapter Ten

Just as Jeremy had planned, he travelled directly on toward John DeCou's house. The morning already passed, and slowed by the topography because of a reticence to get caught by Willcocks' men on the open road, he made his way slowly, once again careful to stay close to the edge of the escarpment. Between Elizabeth's home and DeCou's, Jeremy encountered numerous creeks and streams. This left him with the choice of either going some distance around, or climbing down one slope of the ravine and back up the other, neither method bearing a great advantage in time or energy.

The journey itself was not entirely unpleasant in itself. Jeremy had long been a lover of the Niagara Escarpment – The Mountain, as those who dwelt here knew it. He had an abiding love for the ravines such as these, for the rocky outcroppings, the layers of rock that made up the cliffs, and the boulders strewn about the creek beds like so many marbles used by the children of the farms in the area.

The vegetation was a wonder to behold as well. In one of those quirks of geography, Niagara boasted a microclimate that allowed for forests of a sort not normally seen above the American Carolinas, although certainly Jeremy was unaware of such facts. But he did know these woods supported a wide range of flora, with a mixture of hardwood and softwood of both deciduous and evergreen varieties. The greenery of the area created a breathing carpet which swept from atop the escarpment, down the slopes, and on to the very lake known as Lake Ontario, broken only occasionally by the growing clearings of the settlements below.

These impressive forests boasted towering larger trees such as the acorn-laden oaks, sugar-producing maples, and whispering aspen. Many other varieties provided a leafy canopy in the summer and a vibrant display of brilliant colours in the autumn. The numerous varieties of evergreen, on the other hand, which were generously interspersed throughout, provided homes for wildlife and shelter from the winds year-round.

Many species of plant lower to the ground also thrived in these conditions. Shrubs, some that flower and many that did not, berries of many colour and descriptions, vines that grew between the ground and the towering branches of the trees overhead. Tiny white, pink and violet flowers occupied the same soil taken in early spring by trilliums and other bulbs. And matter that no longer served its function among the living became fodder for a seemingly infinite variety of moulds and fungi, to eventually be turned back into the seed-nourishing soil that would begin the entire process anew.

Jeremy would, during times more gentle and relaxed, sit on the edge of a cliff and watch for the wildlife that abounded here. Woodpeckers, gulls, wrens, robins, and countless other feathered creatures lived here by day, some in the warmer months only, while bats inhabited the flying space by night, feeding on the annoyingly endless supply of insects. He had watched in wonder on the point of the escarpment above the settlement known as The Forty as it became the flight path for all manner of hawks, eagles and other raptors on their migrations in spring and fall and, in winter, the noisy and brilliantly plumed blue jays, cardinals and waxwings seemed greatly more evident.

As to the earth-bound creatures, there seemed plenty of raccoons, skunks, rats, muskrats and beavers in the associated marshes, white-tailed deer, mice, squirrels and chipmunks...the list seemed endless, even to someone like Jeremy, who made his living of sorts hunting many of these animals. If one searched more closely to the ground, one would find several species of salamander, tree frogs, toads, bullfrogs and turtles in the streams and marshes, however seemingly small.

One thing that required no searching to be noticed was the insect population. Probably as wide a variety as existed anywhere within temperate regions, from the pests such as the ravenous mosquitoes to the ubiquitous fly to the bees and wasps that brought both pain and pleasure. Though the farmers no doubt cursed them daily, and perhaps nightly as well, they all served their purposes in the grander scheme of things, keeping things functioning in the way that Jeremy understood they should.

Even with all these wonders to see and ponder, the reason that Jeremy rarely felt put out by the ravines along the Mountainside was that they often provided him with the attractions that most inspired his imagination. Where the water from the creeks and streams left the safety of the rocks through which they had rushed, they formed wondrous waterfalls of all descriptions, from the wide, thundering, misting torrents of the Niagara Falls, to the more common falls from Beaverdams or Twenty Mile Creeks. From dribbles to rushes, from cascades to sheer drops from overhangs, they all represented a beauty that, at least to Jeremy, held no equal.

At least, that was, until this very day.

On this day, his mind wandered often to the attractive widow who had shared her meal and some water with him that morning, and he nearly stumbled at times when his head was not clearly on the task at hand. In the purest of physical of terms, she was not the most beautiful woman he had met since Sarah's death, but there were aspects of both her appearance and her manner that had captured Jeremy's heart, although he would, at that time, yet deny a romantic connection. But the memories of the few hours spent that morning in her company filled the long hours of travel rather pleasantly.

Even when he sat to catch his wind at the edge of one his beloved waterfalls, his thoughts ran not to the sparkle of the sunlight as it reflected upon the droplets escaping from the rush, but to the sparkle of Elizabeth's eyes. It was not the silky flow of the water as it caught in the wind of the cliffs that he saw, but her hair as she removed her hat to momentarily set the tresses free. He was smitten, of that there could be no doubt to any but him, but love is blind, and often what it does not recognize is love itself.

A Question of Loyalty

Jeremy arrived at DeCou's house in the early evening, and was surprised to find evidence of much activity at the site. A number of horses were hobbled out back, grazing quietly in the field behind the house and barely paid him any attention as he approached the building. As he reached to knock on the door, he was surprised by the sound of a voice coming from his immediate right.

"What business have you here, sir?" the voice asked, and Jeremy looked closer to see a sentry at the corner of the house. He was dressed all in a type of grey-green coverall, although his bearing was quite military.

"My name is Jeremy van Hijser", Jeremy replied. "A friend of Captain DeCou. Could you kindly not wave that gun in my face, sir? I fear it may go off, and would sorely ruin my day." Seeing the man was about to reply, he added, "I had come to tell the captain that I had been unable to make the contact he requested, but it seems, by the cut of your clothing, that the point is now moot in any case."

"The cut of my clothing, sir?" the man asked.

Jeremy chuckled. "Well, sir, I was looking for Lieutenant Fitzgibbon but, if I don't miss my guess, I have a Bloody Boy standing before me this moment."

"I probably shouldn't admit it, but you are correct, sir", the guard answered with more than a hint of pride in his voice. "James Traynor, late of the Brock's forty-ninth and presently of the Bloody Boys at your service. I should like to announce you to the officers within, but I might be shot for leaving my post", he added, a smile suggesting the probability of such a punishment wasn't great.

Jeremy touched his hat in salute and, after a short rap at the door, let himself inside, wishing almost immediately that he had not. He did not recognize all who were present, but there were several that he did know from his travels. His first thought was that he had walked in on something that, perhaps, was none of his business. It seemed obvious to Jeremy that this was some type of planning session and he was anything but military. He turned on his heels and headed back toward the door, but stopped when he heard the sound of his name being addressed.

"I'm sorry, did someone call my name?" he asked. "I apologize for arriving unannounced. If you like, I've seen none of you here this night."

"Nonsense, Jeremy", John DeCou said, and took the younger man's arm, leading him into the salon, where he had noticed the officers were meeting. He looked about the room, attempting surreptitiously to determine whom he had previously met, trying hard to attach names to some he recognized but did not know.

The person who most stood out as Jeremy entered was a man in his middle age, who was standing near the fireplace, leaning casually on the mantle. He had never met the man in his life, but the man's mixture of European and native dress left no doubt in his mind that this must be Captain Dominique Ducharme, the man who led the Caughnawagas from the Montreal area. His task was to make frequent raids upon enemy troops that dared to venture from Fort George, the goal being to keep them nervous and off-balance.

The man beside Ducharme, whom Jeremy recognized as Captain William Hamilton Merritt, whose base of operations was primarily at Shipman's Corners, had much the same task, but without the benefit of Indian warriors to strike terror into enemy hearts. The Captain stood quietly observing the scene, occasionally saying something in French to his interpreter.

The third man that Jeremy recognized was the commander of the troops stationed at the mouth of the Twelve Mile Creek, Major Peter De Haren. The officer had tried earlier in the year to confiscate the carcass of the two deer Jeremy had shot that day, and had also informed the hunter that he was to serve in His Majesty's Army, all without a by your leave! Jeremy had ended up selling the meat to him, although he had not yet been paid and half expected that he never would be. Jeremy nodded politely to the major, an acknowledgement returned in kind.

At the centre of the room, indeed seemingly at the centre of the attention was the man Jeremy had been seeking since leaving Beaverdams. Even in the presence of these other fine officers, all technically his superiors, Fitzgibbon shone. A strong-looking man, sinewy and graceful, Fitzgibbon was very popular with almost all in the British camp, men and officers alike. He was bright, articulate, courageous, and thought quick on his feet, an attribute that saved his neck on more than one occasion, if even half the stories of him could be taken at face value.

Fitzgibbon was a rarity among British officers in that he had not buy his commission, as was the custom. He had started as a regular soldier, worked his way up to sergeant, and then was given a field promotion by General Isaac Brock, recognizing the younger man's abilities and even going so far as to teach him to read and write. And still he distinguished himself to the point where General Brock promoted him to lieutenant prior to the general's death at Queenston Heights the previous year.

If anyone harboured any resentment at Fitzgibbon's meteoric and unorthodox rise, there was no evidence of it. The fact that they would travel to meet with a man of subordinate rank spoke volumes in that respect. Strangely enough, there seemed little acknowledgement of rank among these men here tonight at all.

There were also four other men in the room who Jeremy did not know. By their bearing, there was no doubt they were soldiers, but in what service or capacity, he could not guess, for they bore no regimental identity. In all likelihood the reason for that was to avoid all indication of their importance should they be captured, for it turned out that these men were in the business of conducting an unheard of brand of warfare.

"Ah, Jeremy, I hear that DeCou had sent you out to find me", Fitzgibbon greeted him, putting his arm warmly about the woodsman's shoulders. "And, if I'm not mistaken, it seems that you have found me at last!" This latter comment brought on a raucous burst of laughter from the others. One would not have suspected, upon experiencing the relaxed atmosphere here this night, that this was a gathering of British military officers.

Jeremy took the ribbing easily. "It would have made the quest ever so much easier had you been where you were supposed to be", he chimed in with mock indignation. "But you will notice that, even as you eluded me, I still tracked you down. One can only hope that the Americans are less accomplished in wood lore than I, or they should be here at any moment." Now it was the lieutenant's turn to suffer the good-natured ribbing, and he did so handily as he handed Jeremy as glass of brandy. "By the way, James, where are your men?" asked Jeremy. "Other than the three standing guard, of course."

"Just down below the hill at John's mill", Fitzgibbon replied, gesturing toward DeCou. "I'm afraid it was just too snug for all of them in the few beds upstairs", he added with a smirk. He then became quite serious as he next addressed Jeremy. "Perhaps you can yet be of service to us", he said. "We have heard that Willcocks has retired to Newark, possibly with information of some kind. Do you know anything of this?" he asked.

"I've seen nothing of Joseph Willcocks since yesterday, when his men tried to attack me at the Twenty Mile Creek", Jeremy replied. "Fortunately, they were too drunk to fight, or I might have been taken", he added with a smile.

"The Twenty", Fitzgibbon considered with some concern. "You don't suppose he might have gone to the Ball Mill, do you?"

"No, I know for a fact that they did not, for I spent the night in the mill and helped John Ball with his repairs in the morning. Later that day, a local who lives at the base of the Mountain..." he hesitated, fearful he might almost be blushing at the though of Elizabeth Rhodes. "A local told me that Willcocks was down the road at the Jenkins place. I can tell you what I saw when I climbed up on my way, though."

"Please do, sir", invited one of the officers Jeremy didn't know. Noting Jeremy's curiosity with his identity, he introduced himself and the others with him. "Three of us were sent here from temporary regimental headquarters in Burlington. I'm Lieutenant Dixon, the man by the door is Ensign Zimbauer and that man there by the window is Sergeant DeForce. We've been sent here to assess the situation as regards the American troops in the region. The fourth of us, that gentleman sitting on the stairs, is Second Lieutenant Carstairs, and he joined up with us on the way."

"Can you tell us how ready the troops are to take back Niagara from the Americans?" asked De Haren. "We've been left quite in the dark by our superiors."

"I'm afraid I cannot give any details concerning our orders or information concerning the troops' strengths or battle plans, although I assure you we know little enough ourselves. I fully understand your desire to know how much support you can count on. Command, however, has ordered us mum for fear that the information may be loosened from one of your tongues should you be captured."

"One of us, captured?" Fitzgibbon questioned incredulously. "And, as for our tongues, they are loose only when exposed to this fine brandy." The praise of DeCou's private stock brought on another peal of laughter and some ribald humour at Fitzgibbon's expense while DeCou poured another round, all the while feigning that he was mourning the loss. "Truth be told", Fitzgibbon added, once glasses were full one more time. "We don't really expect much support. There's been dreadfully little to date." This comment met with general agreement from those of the Peninsula units.

"I'm sorry, Jeremy", Fitzgibbon apologized, remembering that the young trapper had been speaking when the meeting had gone off track. "What did you wish to tell us?"

Jeremy pretended to try to remember. "Ah, yes", he grinned. "I didn't see Willcocks leave. But I did see a party set out on its own from the Jenkins farm, and there were no other signs of life there afterward."

"Perhaps Willcocks had already left", one of the newcomers suggested.

"Yes, quite possibly", Jeremy answered. "But what intrigued me was where the group I saw was headed." He drained his glass carefully, allowing the curiosity of the others in the room to build before proceeding. "They seemed to be riding straight down the road toward Shipman's Corners. Now, correct me if I'm wrong, but don't the Americans tend to avoid the kind of direct confrontation with your forces that this would entail?" he asked, looking directly at Merritt.

Major De Haren knit his eyebrows in thought. "That does seem rather odd. Do they not realize that our men are stationed on that road?" he thought aloud.

"Whatever the reason, I think perhaps someone should go down to have a look about", suggested Fitzgibbon thoughtfully, not quite able to fathom the purpose of such a move. "Lieutenant Dixon, what do you think? Do you and your men wish to ride down and have a look? It wouldn't hurt to give the men posted in Shipman's Corners a bit of a heads-up, while you're at it. There's always the possibility that the others of Willcocks' crew are headed there as well, by a more roundabout route."

Dixon looked at his travelling companions, who nodded their assent. "Very well, Lieutenant. And perhaps Mr. van Hijser would care to join us, in case we need to find an alternate approach. Do you ride, sir?" he asked of Jeremy.

"Only if I have a horse", Jeremy answered, with a grin.

"We'll get you one", Fitzgibbon replied. Sticking his head out of the window nearest him, he gave the order for one to be brought to the fore. "I wish I could go as well, but there's always the possibility that this is a feint of some fashion, meant to draw us off from the supplies here. Take good care, gentlemen."

"Meanwhile, sirs", he said, turning now to the other military men in the room. "Perhaps we should send out some scouts to determine the likelihood that we're being had. It wouldn't do to have the Americans or their lot sneak up here while we see to Shipman's Corners, would it?" The other officers agreed and, draining the last of their brandy, headed out, each to join his men to move on that advice.

Jeremy and the four men from Burlington checked their weapons and headed out into the rapidly waning light of the early evening. Mounting up, they rode off down the road that would take them the back way down the Mountain. Once at the bottom, they forded the Twelve Mile Creek and Jeremy led them down a trail that followed the creek toward Shipman's Corners.

Chapter Eleven

Williamson and his men had by now established a camp across the Twelve Mile Creek from the settlement named after its most prominent feature. At the point of the rise that marked the intersection of two creeks, where the road ran through town, Paul Shipman's Tavern took the position of prominence, easily spotted from either direction on the road. In fact, it was easy for Williamson's men to watch the comings and goings at the establishment, which served extra duty as the stagecoach station, where the horses were changed out and then rested and fed awaiting the next coach.

They could see nothing untoward at the tavern, as they breathed in the cool night air while they sat in near total darkness, for no fires were allowed that night, not wishing to alert the British of their presence. It was extremely difficult to determine whether they had been told true concerning its true purpose, given the busy nature of the establishment. Several times they had witnessed soldiers entering and soldiers leaving, but they could not tell whether they were the same ones.

"What do you think?" Williamson asked Geoffrey Smith, his voice uncharacteristically low. "Do you think our spy was telling the truth?"

Smith looked once again through the cheap spyglass they had been using to watch the tavern. "I really don't know…" he started.

"Well, give me your best guess!" Williamson barked, his voice carrying in the evening air across the creek's gorge. Smith could see several people in front of the tavern look up to see where the sound might be coming from but, seeing nothing, continued on about their business.

"You really must keep your voice down", Smith warned, receiving a cuff across the back of his head for his troubles.

"Never you mind", grumbled Williamson. "Just tell me, should we go for it, or not?"

Smith hesitated, knowing that an opinion on the matter would be little more than a guess. If he said that they should go forward with the plan, he risked disaster, but he knew also that, if he showed an excess of caution, Williamson would brand him a coward, and he would suffer a personal disaster of his own. In the end, he decided that the safest option for him was to suggest that they attack as planned. He would just be sure to keep his head down and be prepared to cut and run should the situation call for it. After all, Williamson will do no less, he thought wryly.

As the last rays of the sun sank below the horizon, Smith began the final preparations for the attack. From the supply wagon that they hauled about with them wherever they travelled, he began to distribute powder, ball, and flints to the men who rode with them. Each was also given a cup of rum to fortify them for battle. Then they settled down to await the wee hours of the morning, when the night would be darkest and no soldier would likely be prepared for an attack.

Jeremy stopped short of Shipman's Corners, down below in the bend of the creek, immediately below the settlement. Something on the opposite side of the ravine from the tavern had caught his eye, although he was not exactly sure why. He waited, not sure if he had been imagining things but, moments later, he saw it again. In the waning rays of the sun, some stray bit of light flashed softly from an object up there, and Jeremy asked the soldiers with him if any had a spyglass on their person. Handed one, he trained the powerful little glass on the top of the hill where the movement had attracted his attention. There was someone atop there, watching the tavern through a glass of his own!

Jeremy handed the soldier back his spyglass. "Someone's watching the settlement", he told his companions. "I think that if it's the group I saw today, they're waiting for something. Perhaps they hope the inhabitants will fall asleep, hoping to gain an element of surprise."

The four men muttered their agreement with Jeremy's assessment. What none of them could understand is why these men of the hilltop would wish to risk their lives against a fair-sized contingent of soldiers in order to attack a tavern. Whatever could Paul Shipman have at his establishment that could engender such a desperate measure?

"Well", said Dixon. "No point in sitting down here, waiting to find out why. Although it might be marvellously entertaining to watch from here, what say we go up top and prepare our side for the performance as well?"

The five men remounted and urged their horses quietly up the trail toward the front of the settlement. Once at the top, they passed the tavern and rode for a several minutes to the British camp, which sat back among the trees, invisible to Williamson and his men. They presented the byword to the guards and were immediately escorted to the lodgings of Lieutenant-Colonel Cecil Bisshop, commander of this small brigade of light infantry.

Bisshop, in all ways the British officer, welcomed the men. "My forward scouts have seen some sort of activity there", he pronounced. "But we've not yet had the opportunity to determine their strength. Have you gentlemen any information as to their strength, who they are, or what their purpose might be?"

Lieutenant Dixon stepped forward and introduced Jeremy. "This man knows something of it, Sir", he informed the senior officer.

Bisshop had always been somewhat sceptical of the involvement of undisciplined locals in the war, as were most British officers. However, he had become fairly accustomed to the filtering of information from the numerous citizens who travelled the area, as they were often the only way to acquire enemy positions and troop movements.

"Do you know this man, Lieutenant?" Bisshop asked, addressing Dixon.

"Not personally, Sir", the junior man answered. "But I have just ridden with him from Fitzgibbon's post, and he is very well-known there. A regular, if civilian, scout for the Lieutenant I understand."

Bisshop still seemed doubtful, his regular military training keeping his guard up. "Very well, sir. Tell me what you know of those men across the creek."

"Well, Sir", Jeremy began, slightly amused with the officer's bearing, and trying hard not to let it show. "I was in the area of the Twelve Mile Creek this morning and I saw a small band of brigands from Joseph Willcocks' group leave their encampment on their own. Although I could not specifically recognize any, I stayed to see if any followed, but none did."

"Are you certain they did not do so later?" Bisshop asked.

"There didn't appear to be anyone left on the farm they were using for their camp last night", Jeremy answered. "But there are any number of other possibilities. Perhaps they met up again somewhere closer to here."

Bisshop appeared momentarily thoughtful, seeming almost to look right through Jeremy. "I wish we knew for certain", he said at last. "It would be much easier to develop a defence if we knew the strengths of the those opposing us."

Against Jeremy's own better judgment, he heard himself speak up. "I'm quite familiar with this area", he began. "I'll make my way across and try to determine how many there are."

"And I'll accompany him", Dixon blurted out. He too was shocked with himself, for his was a military family, and he had often heard his father speak on the dangers of volunteering. It was one's duty as a British officer to follow orders regardless of the risk but only a fool, he was told, would stick out his neck unbidden. This was especially so when one did not know precisely the nature of what one was volunteering for.

"Very well then", the Lieutenant-Colonel muttered, almost tiredly. "Mr. van Hijser, you may scout the enemy, then. But I will not be risking the pair of you. Lieutenant Dixon, you will remain here. We may need every musket we can muster."

Bisshop turned to Jeremy. "You be on your way, then. And when you determine their strength, I want no heroics", he added, although he did not truly care what became of this farmer. The colonel fully expected that, even if he did not turn and run in the face of battle, the untrained man would be of little use to him when it came down to a firefight. His only real concern was to retrieve the intelligence he required before he was shot.

Jeremy checked his weapons and headed out to perform his task. Initially, he headed in a westerly direction, wishing to cross the Twelve around the bend and out of sight of the enemy outpost. He felt that he could safely ford the creek without being seen from that point. Once he was out of sight of the promontory that was topped by Shipman's Tavern, he climbed down the steep slope, using the trees to slow his descent in the dark, barely illuminated by the quarter moon. The creek at this point was also much shallower, and he made good use of the rocks, which stuck slightly above the lower summer water level, to make his way across. Once he was standing dry upon the far bank, he clambered up the other side to the forested heights.

Travelling along the top of the ridge, he made his way to a point almost opposite the tavern. From here on, Jeremy began to move much more cautiously, having little idea what he would find there, how many guards he would find posted, or what level of wakefulness could be expected of their main body of men. He paid careful attention to the sounds all about him as he moved, aware that the presence of people could be detected by either unusual sounds or, conversely, the unusual lack thereof.

He decided to circle well around, away from the gorge. Since these men obviously believed they owned the element of surprise, they were little likely to post much of a guard to the rear. After he had travelled only a few hundred feet, however, he thought he heard something directly behind him. Had he been detected so quickly, he thought, feeling a rising anxiety in his breast? Jeremy slipped quietly into the space between a boulder and some shrubs, waiting to determine who might be the author of the sounds. He heard it again, more closely this time, and now there could be no doubt. Someone wearing boots was attempting to follow along the same route he had been taking.

Jeremy fairly held his breath as the sound edged ever closer, betrayed by such clues as the rustling of leaves as a body passes by, the occasional snap as a twig broke beneath leather soles. His pursuer's attempt at stealth left much to be desired, as Jeremy could now even hear some belaboured breathing.

Silently, Jeremy slid his bayonet from its scabbard and positioned it at his side, at a point roughly level with his hip. He readied himself for the attack as he could sense rather than see that the person tracking him was almost within arm's reach. Jeremy's entire body steeled for the attack, his legs slightly bent to give him spring if necessary, and his muscles taut with the stress of the unknown. Of one thing, he was reasonably certain. There was only one, and he obviously had the element of surprise on this person.

As the stalker moved within a few feet of him, Jeremy leapt out of his hiding place, throwing his left arm around the man's neck and pulling him up against a tree. He brought the bayonet up and pressed it pointed upward toward the surprised man's sternum, bending him backwards to keep him off balance.

"Don't move or you die where you stand!" he hissed menacingly. "Answer me quickly and softly for it would be all too easy and enjoyable to plunge this bayonet upward into your heart. Why are you following me?"

The man stood stock still, his heart pounding, caught totally unawares. "If you'll ease off, I'll tell you", he rasped. Then, when the pressure on his throat eased slightly, he added, "Good show, Jeremy. I certainly wasn't expecting that."

Jeremy released the man, immediately recognizing the voice of Robert Dixon. "What are you doing here?" he demanded angrily, the adrenaline still coursing through his body. "I thought Bisshop forbade you from accompanying me. Do you realize I might have killed you had I not decided to question you first?"

Dixon's reply was somewhat sheepish, and he was quite glad that Jeremy couldn't see his face. That an Upper Canadian farmer could thus subdue a British officer was a disgrace indeed! "Well, we decided that you should be told that those on this side were on the move. I couldn't yet tell what they were up to, but a few of them had started down the grade toward our position."

Jeremy mulled over this latest bit of news. There was no way they would be able to report on the enemy's strength now, even had they known what that strength was. "Come on!" he said, setting off at a trot to the area where the men had been spotted that evening.

"My orders were to retrieve you and bring you back to the camp." Dixon offered his explanation hesitantly, hoping that Jeremy would disobey the orders Bisshop had sent along. For this soldier, the posting was relatively new, and he found his job so far more than a little boring.

Jeremy called back softly, over his shoulder, "Best you follow orders then, Robert. But I intend to see what the situation might be. I came to scout and scout I will."

"But, my orders…" Dixon started weakly, trailing off as he spoke. Best to let it lie, if he wished for some adventure, else Jeremy might just give in and spoil the fun for the both of them.

"Well, your orders don't apply to me", Jeremy said, stopping to face the soldier. "But, if it makes you feel more comfortable, tell Bisshop that you couldn't find me and, after an exhaustive search, finally turned back without me."

If Jeremy could have seen Dixon's face more clearly, he would have seen the hint of a smile on the lips of this man, who had come to save him after all. "Sir, are you suggesting that I lie to a senior officer?" he demanded as though honestly shocked by the suggestion. "Better yet", he suggested, the grin almost evident in his voice, "perhaps I couldn't find you and had to keep looking in keeping with my orders."

Jeremy laughed softly. "Welcome aboard, Lieutenant", he said slapping Dixon across the back lightly, so as not to alert any guards that might be in the area. "But do try to move a little more quietly. Like a bull in a china shop, you were. I'm surprised you didn't alert the enemy's entire encampment."

"Surely", Dixon answered. "But do try to call me Robert. If Bisshop finds out what transpired here tonight, my rank will be a matter of history, and perhaps I too."

As Dixon had reported, Williamson's men had started to move. As quietly as could be expected of a body of men, they climbed and slid down the slope toward the creek, stopping behind cover at the bottom to regroup. Since they were to ford the stream at a point where the water was more than waist deep in places, they had no charges in their muskets. They also had been ordered to remove their flints to assure that no one would fire their weapon inadvertently. The raid was to be carried out in total surprise.

Williamson motioned to his men to join him before crossing, and his men gathered close, the air electric with tension and anticipation. "It's yet a bit early", he said softly. "Just get yourselves into your assigned positions and hold until I say it's time to attack. Now, get to the other side, climb up there quietly, then move on across and spread out at the top."

The men entered the water with a fair amount of splashing, the vision of an easy raid dampening their concern for secrecy. The noise made Williamson and Smith cringe and they personally hung back, waiting to see if their men, crossing like a herd of crazed cattle, would draw unwelcome attention from the tavern. It would matter little just how few Brits were to be found at this establishment. If they discovered Williamson's men, professional soldiers could mow down most of them before they could reach the summit.

Seeing that nothing was amiss, however, the two men followed the others across the water, albeit much more quietly than the others had. They watched carefully from the bottom to make sure that each man took his assigned position as the two made their ways up the steep hill. Once assured that they were would be well covered by their men, Williamson and Smith followed.

What both men had failed to notice as they focused all of their attention on their troops' advance was that the very shadows behind them were moving as well. Robert and Jeremy were following at a safe distance and, once they saw that the two men in charge had begun to climb, they stealthily forded the creek and stalked the assailants up the hill.

"There don't seem to be any more than the few you saw heading out", Dixon whispered. "What would you say? Perhaps twenty men?"

"Mm-hmm", Jeremy replied. "Do you know how the soldiers up top are deployed?"

"I'm not quite sure", came the answer. "But I think they were expecting the camp itself to be attacked. These men, however,

A Question of Loyalty

seem to be heading for the tavern itself." Robert's voice betrayed the bafflement caused by this strange behaviour.

Jeremy was at a loss to explain any of this. "Why would they attack a tavern?" he wondered, mostly to himself, but loudly enough that Robert could hear. The lieutenant had no answer, but it was obvious they would need to make plans quickly. If all the Brits were set to repel a direct attack, these men would certainly be able to take Paul Shipman's Tavern easily. And, once in, it would take a great deal of bloodshed to remove them.

"Can you circle about and warn Bisshop?" Jeremy asked, his voice coming across much louder than he'd intended.

"I'd never get around those men and to the camp in time", answered Robert.

"There's only one thing we can do then", Jeremy sighed. "Let's try to stay with the two men who are obviously in charge", he suggested, adding, "Since they're obviously leading from the rear." Jeremy couldn't help but snicker softly at his own facetious remark. "Maybe we can take them and stop the attack in that way."

Dixon didn't sound convinced as he replied resignedly, "It's the only recourse we have. Let's just follow and see what opportunity presents itself."

Following the invaders up the last bit of the promontory was more difficult than it seemed, in their zeal to get to the top, as the thugs continuously slid part way back down in the loose soil. Jeremy and Robert found they often had to duck behind cover as one or more slid down in a shower of dirt and stones, sometimes right past the two men who were following them. If the situation had not been so dangerous, Jeremy thought he would burst out laughing at these fools.

"With the noise they're making, you'd think the entire settlement and the soldiers in camp could hear them coming", Robert commented once, in obvious exasperation.

Unfortunately, this was not the case, although the attackers' own leaders visibly cringed at every sound. Due to the lay of the land where Dick Creek and the Twelve met, the acoustics were not favourable to those up top. Although each tumbling pebble sounded like a landslide to the men on the hillside, the sound carried not much higher than the source. The noise would be of no assistance to the British soldiers waiting and wondering behind and around the settlement.

After what seemed like an eternity, merely fifteen minutes or so in actuality, the last of Williamson's men crested the ravine's side and took up positions on two sides of the tavern. There they waited, and their two shadows waited in their very midst, still wondering what would possess these people to attack a tavern. The minutes dragged into an hour and beyond. What were they waiting for, and why were they formed up in the way they were? It made little sense, but there was no way Robert or Jeremy could safely sneak around them to summon the soldiers in time to stop it, whatever it might be.

Chapter Twelve

Finally, at almost two o'clock in the morning, when the moon had disappeared behind the clouds that formed overhead, Geoffrey Smith gave his men the signal. Almost as one, they arose from their hiding places to close in on the tavern, which sat dark and lifeless.

"Odd", Smith muttered to Williamson. "Where are the guards? There were supposed to be two or three guards at the tavern."

Williamson studied the matter for a moment. "Well, our informant did tell us that discipline was quite slack here." He chuckled at a sudden thought. "They're probably asleep. Had some of the product on the job and decided to take a rest."

"I don't know..." Smith responded, feeling this was all a little too easy. Williamson's optimistic assessment sounded very much too good to be true, and he did not believe it for a moment. "Maybe we should reconsider", he said.

Williamson's anger flashed to the surface, as it so easily did. "Are you a fool? We'll never again have a chance like this to show our worth to Dearborn. This is no time for cowardice to make our decisions. Let's get on with it!"

Bristling at the suggestion that he was a coward but against his better judgment nonetheless, Smith gave the signal to attack, and their men surged forward in two groups. One of these groups made for the main door at the front, while the others crept along the side of the building to the entrance there. That was where the plan fell apart, for there was no entrance on this side of the tavern.

While the first group forced open the front door, the men at the side milled about, trying to find the elusive entrance.

As they burst through the door, ready to do battle, the group at the front of the tavern realized something was wrong. There seemed to be no one here. Nobody at all. What the attackers could not know was that the soldiers had evacuated all the buildings in the settlement and sent them to the protection of the rear. All these men knew was that they had broken into this establishment and it was empty. Now, these men too began to mill about. They had met no resistance and now did not know what they should be doing next.

Smith noticed the men milling about the side and made his way over to see what the matter was. In the meantime, Williamson entered the front door to determine why there had been no shooting.

And, right behind Williamson, two men with their faces obscured followed along.

Robert and Jeremy were at as much of a loss as their enemies, but there was no time to wonder about what was going on. As they stepped in the door, Williamson began yelling insanely to search for the military stores that they had been told were here. Bedlam reigned supreme in the small building, with men smashing things and opening and slamming doors. The two infiltrators saw this as their chance to contain the enemy, both inside and out, and so they bolted the front door as quietly as they could.

They followed those who ventured into other areas, still looking for the supplies supposedly intended for the men who had so often worried the American scouting parties. Like the others, they swore and kicked at things, hoping they would not stand out. There was but one thing they knew for certain, and that was that they would need to reduce the opposition numbers as much as possible if they were to have any chance of success.

Dixon entered one of the tavern's guest rooms with a man almost twice his size, a brute who would be more than a match for the lieutenant should they be engaged in a fair fight. But a fair fight was the farthest thing from Robert's mind in this extremely explosive situation. As the larger man approached the wardrobe in

A Question of Loyalty

the corner of the room, Robert pulled a dagger from his boot and, pulling the man's head back sharply, so as to give no chance for reaction, sliced cleanly across the exposed jugular. Then he pushed the giant of a man into the wardrobe, hitting him sharply behind the ear with the butt of his knife so there would be no chance of any sounds emitting from the dying man.

In the meantime, Jeremy had entered the rear storeroom with another of Williamson's men. The small room held enough stores for the day-to-day business of a tavern, but clearly insufficient for outfitting three or four raiding parties. While pretending to search around, for what he had no idea since everything was quite obvious, he accidentally came face to face with the other man. It was a face Jeremy recognized and, worse still, the other seemed to recognize him as well.

"So", the man growled. "The man from the Twenty. And what would you be doing here?" Jeremy was surprised, because he didn't think either of the men had actually seen him in the creek bed. "No answer for me? Well, let's have at it, then. I think you'll find I'm not quite as easy when I'm sober."

"Well, well", Jeremy said, attempting to sound light-hearted and facetious, all the while looking for a quick opening that would keep this man from calling for backup. "The name's Will, isn't it?" he asked conversationally. "So, I heard some commotion back behind me as I walked away from you two gentlemen back there. I hope I didn't cause you any problems."

Will's dirty, unshaven visage broke into a vicious sneer. "Damn' near got us hung, you did. And for that you'll pay dearly." Instead of shooting or otherwise directly attacking Jeremy, the raider set his gun carefully against a stack of crates. "I won't be needing a gun for this", he growled. "I'm going to enjoy taking you apart with my bare hands."

Jeremy was glad that the other man was at least vain enough to decide he wouldn't need any help, and wasn't going to alert the others, at least not yet. Seeing that Will was watching for a movement toward the bayonet hanging in plain sight, Jeremy decided to take advantage of the other man's moral weakness. Stepping toward Will, he suddenly pulled free the tomahawk that was secured behind his head. Before Will could react to this change in focus, Jeremy drove the steel blade of the tomahawk deep into the other's frontal lobe.

Momentarily, Will seemed to stare in surprise, his eyes wide open and his jaw working without uttering any sound. Then he staggered backwards, trying to reach for his gun, which he could not seem to find. In a final burst of desperation, and as the darkness setting over his eyes blotted out the pain in his skull, he tried to yell for help. But it was much too late. His voice no longer received commands from his brain. He crashed wordlessly into the crates and dropped heavily to the floor. With a brief convulsion, the man was still.

Jeremy recovered his tomahawk and, after wiping the gore on the man's shirt, he pulled the body of his adversary behind a stack of liquor barrels. He stopped, took a deep breath to recover from the battle as much as he could, and walked to the door. He looked about and spotted two men with Robert, about to enter a room down the hall.

Being sure to hide his face without appearing suspicious, he growled. "Can one of you come here and help me with these sacks? Something doesn't seem quite right here."

The men turned around, apparently both intending to see what had attracted this other's attention in the storeroom. Thinking quickly, Dixon pulled on one man's arm. "Better stick with me", he growled, hoping that his unfamiliar voice would not attract unwanted attention. "I think this is the tavern keeper's office. Knowing those cowardly Brits, this is the place they'd most likely be hiding." The argument was weak at best, but the man seemed to accept it and followed Dixon inside.

To Robert's mild surprise, this was actually the tavern office. In the corner by the window stood a small writing desk, complete with all the requisite implements, including pens, nibs, inkbottle, and blotter. There was an unfinished letter on the desk, and a ledger sat on a spare seat beside the desk. Other than this, there was little to the room. A small bookshelf held several tomes and a pile of paper, and larger papers – plans, perhaps – were rolled out on a table opposite the desk.

"There's nothing here", Robert's companion grumbled, turning to go. "Let's go see what the others are up to in the stockroom."

Allowing the other to go first, Robert then followed him to the door. Then, with a coordinated movement, he simultaneously kicked the partially opened door shut and pulled his dagger free once again. "Oh, to be able to just shoot him", Robert thought to himself. That, of course, was not an option. One shot, and he would have the honour of meeting the entire band at once.

But this foe was much quicker than Robert had expected. As soon as the door was kicked shut, he spun about, his fist flying, and caught Robert square in the right shoulder. The numbing pain flashed through his arm, causing him to drop his dagger to the floor. By now, his adversary had turned around, and was quickly sizing up the situation.

Williamson's man opened his mouth to sound the alarm but Robert's left hand, which had automatically flown to hold his right shoulder, now came flying back across the short interval between the two men. The hand, which was only partially closed into a fist when it connected, slammed into the defender's throat, bruising his larynx and temporarily cut off his breathing. Robert took advantage of the momentary paralysis brought on by the damage and followed up quickly with a flurry of blows to the man's face and body. With a groan, the man dropped as though all strength had suddenly been released from his legs.

Dixon looked down at this man, not sure what he should do next. Expediency ruled that he should incapacitate him in a more permanent manner, and he picked his dagger up from the floor. But, as he was about to perform his coup-de-grace, the door opened and came face to face with two more of these men.

Jeremy pretended to rummage around in the pile of sacks in the storeroom, keeping an eye on his most recent companion by way of his peripheral vision. His heart nearly stopped cold when the man, more fascinated by the contents of the liquor barrels, headed over to investigate.

"Never mind the whiskey, you drunk", Jeremy snapped. "Get over here and help me with these. There'll be plenty of that for all of us when we're through."

The man docilely complied with the order and began to help Jeremy move the stacked pile of sacks. When Jeremy felt the man was completely occupied, he pulled out his bayonet. Clamping his hand firmly over the surprised man's mouth, he quickly drove the bayonet under his ribs, the long blade easily puncturing a lung and sliding on into his heart. The man's eyes darted wildly about while he tried weakly to remove the hand from his face, but the struggle only increased the speed at which he died.

Once again, Jeremy dragged a body behind the barrels. What a use of good whiskey, he thought to himself - a morgue for traitors.

Robert straightened up and sized up the two men facing him, both still standing in the hallway. He could imagine no way in which he could fight both of them, much less silence them before they could sound an alarm. All he could do was wait for them to make the first move.

Then he noticed that the window to the office was open.

Almost without a thought, Robert pointed at the window and shouted, "They got him, and then they went out the window! I couldn't stop them, but I think I stuck one of them in the leg!"

The larger of the two men rushed right in and ran to the window, looking out to see where the assailants may have gone, while the smaller, more wiry man checked on Robert's latest casualty. What the larger man saw was the balance of Williamson's men at the side of the building with Geoffrey Smith. "Did you see two soldiers come out this way?" he asked as the second man joined him at the window.

"No one's come out this way", one of the men yelled. "Most of us have been here all along, since there was no side entrance."

Smith stepped forward and looked up, hands on his hips, at the two men staring down from the window with confusion written on their faces. "Just what is Williamson about, bolting the front door so we can't get in? Something in there he wants to keep for himself?" He would not have dared saying such a thing to Williamson's face, for the consequences would be dire, but suggesting it to these men was no hazard. They knew as well as he did that those bearing bad tidings were as much at risk as the offender.

"The door was bolted?" the thinner man asked.

He began to turn around to question Robert just as the latter slammed into the upper bodies of both men with the writing desk. Leaning out, off-balance, neither could recover from the blow. The larger of the two flew clear of the window, scattering the men below. The other twisted out sideways and hung onto the window frame with one hand, trying desperately to pull his pistol from his waistband with the other.

Robert stepped up to the man, holding on for dear life in the window. "Let go!" he ordered, sticking the point of his dagger to the man's throat.

His foe had other thoughts on the matter, however, and had managed to pull the pistol free. He cocked it expertly and was bringing it about toward Robert, leaving the British officer with no choice. Robert pushed his blade deep into the man's throat. The man made a gurgling sound of protest, let loose the window frame, and dropped down among Smith's group below.

Robert quickly withdrew, for the men outside the window were training their weapons on him. He ran for the hallway, reaching it just as a hail of ball flew through the open window. As he ran, he nearly collided with Jeremy, who had come looking for him.

"Trouble?" Jeremy asked ironically.

"What is going on up there?" Williamson's voice boomed up the stairs, rife with annoyance at the volley of gunfire he had heard from outside, and the subsequent sound of the balls smashing woodwork on the second floor.

Now, with three men left to back up Williamson, Jeremy and his newfound friend, Robert, were forced to make their move. Stepping out into the main room simultaneously, they levelled their guns at the Williamson and his men.

"Your men took offence at being tossed from the upstairs window", Robert commented.

"I hope you're prepared to die", growled Williamson. "I don't know where you came from, but I know where you're going." He paused for a couple of seconds, for effect. "To Hell!" he screamed, unexpectedly shoving one of his men toward the two would-be spoilers.

Robert fired his musket, more an act of reflex than anything, and the man that had come flying toward him let out a loud groan, dropping to the floor, blood seeping slowly across his chest. Jeremy automatically stepped back to clear his line of fire, just as Williamson pulled another of his henchmen in front of him.

They were temporarily at a stalemate. Until Robert could reload, Jeremy was hesitant to fire, for he had only one shot as well. He had to save it for an attack. For what seemed like an eternity, Jeremy waited while Robert reloaded his musket. He seemed overly aware of the time it took his comrade-in-arms to perform the task, as time seemed to stand still in the tension of the moment.

Robert pulled a paper cartridge from the bag at his side and, biting off the top and holding the ball in his teeth, pulled the hammer, flipped up the frizzen and poured a pinch of powder into the pan. He then poured the balance of the powder into the barrel and spat the musket ball in after it, followed by the cartridge's paper, to serve as wadding. This was followed by rapid, solid strokes of the ramrod to push all into the bottom of the gun's barrel.

For the entire eighteen seconds that the process took, their defence was solely in Jeremy's hands, and he was glad that at least he had loaded the gun with shot, rather than the rifle with a ball. If he had to shoot, he could probably incapacitate more than one. But still the uncomfortable truth remained that then both he and Robert would be effectively unarmed. Any survivor would be able to take them unopposed, or at least one of them.

For those few seconds, nobody seemed to move, or even to breathe. They eyed each other carefully, watching for signs that they might make a move, or an opportunity to do so themselves. Each glanced now and then at the body on the floor, now soaked in blood, the lips pulled back in a horrible rictus.

Finally, Robert finished loading and trained his gun back on Williamson and his cohorts. But this type of standoff only worked as long as their opponents had a sense of humanity. Whatever else could be said of Williamson, however, that particular accusation could never be accurately levelled at him. He now had two men to shield him from his enemies' guns and that would be enough, he figured, especially since the second had now moved back closer to him, not wishing to be out in the open alone.

A Question of Loyalty

Without any warning of his intentions, Williamson suddenly shoved both of his men forward toward Robert and Jeremy. Robert was forced to fire again, for the man stumbling toward him had pulled out his knife as his momentum carried him helplessly on. Having seemingly run into an invisible wall, the man crumpled onto the floor between them. The ruse didn't work with Jeremy however, for he merely raised his gun and slammed the stock into the face of the man windmilling wildly as he came toward him.

During all this, Williamson had raised the pistol he had been holding at his side, bringing his arm up level with his shoulder. Since Jeremy had not yet felled the man coming at him, Williamson picked Robert and pulled the trigger. Although pistols were not considered to be terribly accurate weapons, in his hands they were deadly. Williamson, like his commander Willcocks, was an accomplished duellist and the ball flew true, striking Robert just below the throat.

By this time, Jeremy was clear and, seeing his partner fall to this traitor, raised his gun to shoot Williamson. Any thought of taking the man prisoner now vanished from his enraged mind. Taking careful aim at his target, who now had no cover and nowhere to run, Jeremy looked coldly down the barrel at his adversary.

"I hope Hell will take you!" he practically spat, as his finger tightened on the trigger.

And then Jeremy's head exploded in a burst of pain and his entire world vanished before his now sightless eyes.

Chapter Thirteen

"It's about time you got here", Williamson growled at Smith, who stood in a position that would have been directly behind Jeremy only moments ago.

Smith lowered his musket, which he had used to club the Canadian scout. "We needed to get into the building through the second-floor window", he muttered. "But, as for the thanks for saving your life, you're welcome."

Williamson sneered menacingly at his second-in-command. "Watch yourself", he hissed. "My pistol may be empty, but I can still kill you with my bare hands."

The exchange between these two men was interrupted by a commotion upstairs. One of the men who had been with Smith appeared at the top of the stairs. "I'm afraid your men up here are dead, Dorian", he announced.

"All of them?" Williamson asked, incredulous. "Some of my best men? All taken out by just two Brits?"

"Well, one is still alive", the man answered. "He's been beaten rather badly, though. It appears he may have had his throat crushed."

Williamson climbed wearily up the stairs to have a look. It was unbelievable to him that the two men downstairs had reduced his force almost to half strength all by themselves. His perennially foul temper had been building rapidly, and had reached its zenith by the time he entered the room that his men upstairs were indicating. There sat the man with the crushed windpipe, retching and coughing, attempting to regain his air passage. Williamson could feel no pity for the fellow. After all, he had almost let those two Brits kill him!

As he stared coldly down at the man on the floor, a voice sounded the alarm from outside the window. "Soldiers! And plenty of them!" Damn, thought Williamson. *That spy lied to us about everything! If the bastard were only still alive, that he might kill him again, but more slowly this time!*

"Alright!" he yelled at his men. "Everyone back to the camp, at once!"

"What of him, Dorian?" one of the men asked him, indicating the partially recovered man at his feet.

Without a second thought, Williamson snatched the gun from the hand of the man beside him and fired point-blank into the face of the injured fighter. "Leave him here", he muttered, as he turned and stamped heavily from the room.

Back downstairs once more, he noticed that Jeremy had regained consciousness and was being held near the door by two of his men. Williamson strode over to the offending man and punched him in the gut. When Jeremy doubled over in pain, the big man barked in derision "Straighten up!" He paced just inches before his prisoner's face and sneered, "You'll live plenty long enough to rue the day you met me." Then he turned to the men who held Jeremy. "Bring him along", he commanded. "If there's anything left of him when we get to Newark, we'll turn him over to Dearborn, as a spy."

They sped out of the door, almost dragging Jeremy as they made for the promontory, where most of the others had already disappeared. At the last moment, he turned to his remaining man and ordered him to hold off the soldiers.

"By myself?" the man questioned, incredulous. "That's suicide!"

Williamson stopped and turned on the man. "Tell you what", he growled, menace fairly oozing from his throat. "You can take your chances with the redcoats, or you can die at my hands right now!" He brandished his pistol, not yet reloaded, under the man's chin. "What'll it be? Choose quickly."

The man swallowed hard, not aware that there was no charge in the weapon. He ducked behind a large stone, which had been cleared in the improvement of the roadway for the stagecoach line, and waited for the British to show themselves. Such was the power of fear that Dorian Williamson held over the men in his command. Better the whole British Army, which it might have been for all he knew, than to take on that madman.

The British troops under Lieutenant-Colonel Bisshop felt no more secure in their position than did Williamson's lone man holding up the rear. They had heard shooting coming from the direction of Shipman's Tavern but Robert and Jeremy had not yet returned from their scouting foray, so they had no idea of the enemy strengths with which they were dealing. For this reason, the line advanced slowly and cautiously, keeping a sharp eye on the building as they approached.

The men at the forefront had reported seeing men running from the tavern, but they could not be sure that there were no more inside, waiting to carve up the British rear should they give chase to those who had escaped down the hill. So caution was the order of the day, and by the time they arrived at the front door of the establishment and set up a defensive perimeter while they searched inside, the band of traitors had long since retired.

The soldiers sent into the tavern to determine its status were back outside shortly to report to Bisshop. "Two men dead in the storeroom, one in a wardrobe, one in the office, and three downstairs", he looked down momentarily. "I'm afraid one of them is Lieutenant Dixon", he added softly. "Add to that the man we found on the ground outside the window, that makes six enemy dead and one of ours, sir. That farmer you sent out on reconnaissance wasn't among the civilians killed."

Once again, the forward rank pressed on, carefully approaching the edge of the gully. As they were passing a rock beside the road, they came upon one frightened young man there, afraid to open fire on the soldiers, but more afraid to take off down the hill after his comrades. They found no sign of anyone else save the scuffmarks caused by a number of feet as they changed direction to carefully take the hill.

Jeremy fell several times as Williamson's men pushed him along down the steep embankment toward the creek. Bruised, scraped and covered in numerous small cuts, he finally reached the top with the others. None too gently, he was thrown to the ground by the two who had been given the task of minding him, upon penalty of discipline too tough to ponder. He lay there marshalling his strength and recovering his wind as Williamson himself crested the rise and marched directly over to him.

"Stand up!" Williamson ordered in a level but menacing voice.

Jeremy made no move to rise to his feet. Instead, he just remained where he was, glaring at the coward that killed Lieutenant Dixon.

"I said, stand up!" Williamson again, this time with a maniacal scream that echoed back from the other side, aiming a kick at Jeremy's head and barely missing. Even this elicited no movement from Jeremy. Instead, the prisoner just grinned humourlessly and spat at the man's feet.

Williamson lost all semblance of control. He leaned over, took Jeremy by the shirt collar and, with one great jerking motion, pulled him to his feet. "You will learn that when I speak you will listen!" he bellowed at Jeremy, who could feel the spittle on his face and the man's foul breath assailing his nostrils. Williamson's face was contorted with rage, causing his men to back away, knowing the depths of their leader's depravity when his ire was pushed to its limits. And that ire need not be released all upon the one who triggered it. Anyone within sight would do. "I am God here among these men!"

"You mean you're Satan among these cowards", Jeremy shot back insolently, quite aware that he could die by his next word.

All of a sudden, Williamson's rage broke, but not in a violent manner, as one might expect. His contorted visage softened and then an evil grin broke out on his face. "Yes", he said, apparently considering a new idea. "Satan? I like that. I'm Satan to these cowards." He turned around and yelled at his men, "Hear that, you pack of rats? I'm Satan to you cowards." His men shuddered, many feeling that this new identity Williamson was the one they had always believed.

Williamson smiled at Jeremy, a smile that could freeze blood. "I'll say this for you, lad. You've more guts than all of these", he indicated with his thumb, over his shoulder. He pushed Jeremy away. "Tie his hands!" he ordered. "We've a long way to go."

It took only two hours to reach Fort George at Newark that morning, but it seemed an eternity to Jeremy, who was pulled behind Smith's horse as they rode. His throat was parched and his stomach rumbled with hunger as he stumbled along, falling often as he tried to keep pace over the rough, rutted road. When he could not rise quickly enough, he would be dragged along the ground until he managed somehow to regain his feet, for they showed him no quarter. Twice they stopped and made a huge production of drinking their water and eating whatever they had handy, but fed him nothing, and no liquid dampened his cracked lips. But Jeremy was determined that he would show them no weakness. He merely fed the one thing that he could, the one thing that they were providing him with. His determination for revenge.

As they paraded their catch through the town toward the fort, people came out of their houses to watch quietly. By this time, Jeremy was being dragged, more than led down the main street, but none lifted a hand or a voice in pity, for they lived a precarious lifestyle here in Newark. Their town had changed hands several times already, and any display of favouritism to one side or the other could result in punishment now, or in revenge when the town should change hands once again.

Finally, the journey ended outside the front gates of the fort, and Jeremy slumped to the ground, relieved just to be off his feet. As Williamson entered the fort, no doubt to boast of his conquest, Smith began to order the stand-down of the men. Horses were tied at water troughs outside the gates and the packs and saddlebags removed.

Jeremy asked various members of the band for water, expecting rude remarks and even the occasional swipe of the foot but, although some looked as if they might comply with his request, they passed him by without a word. Indeed, some almost appeared frightened to so much as speak to him. Jeremy could not believe the level to which the fear of Williamson pervaded these men's minds.

After a time, Williamson appeared back at the gate, now accompanied by Joseph Willcocks, Benajah Mallory and an

A Question of Loyalty

American Captain, one Seymour Smythe. Williamson pointed at Jeremy, who sat in the dust, hands tied and looking like death itself.

"Give this man some water", Smythe ordered immediately upon looking at Williamson. Williamson grumbled at the slight of having to serve this prisoner, but did as he was ordered, hoping his greatly embellished story would yet earn him some manner of reward.

Smythe studied the man, obviously a local farmer by the cut of his clothes, as he drank the water greedily. Smythe himself was not a military man by trade and made his living from his farm near Albany. He only wore this uniform as a service to his relatively new country as a reserve officer, and was often overlooked for commands other than guard duty because he was not a full time soldier. With irregulars such as Williamson and Willcocks, however, he held true military sway, and the Lord knew there were none more irregular!

"This is the spy you have dragged here from Shipman's Corners?" Smythe asked, a tone of incredulity in his voice.

"Aye, Sir!" Williamson answered, affecting a military bearing. "He and his squad ambushed us, killing half my unit. I say we should hang the spy!" he said, at the same time throwing Jeremy a glare that dared him to challenge what he had reported.

He should have known, however, that Jeremy could not be so easily cowed. "Indeed, Sir, he said, addressing the American officer. "My squad, the both of us, that is…" Before he could finish the sentence, Williamson lashed out with a boot, sending Jeremy sprawling in the dust.

Smythe was not amused by this sadistic display. "Williamson, pick him back up and let him finish his story!"

"But, Sir!" Williamson protested, desperate that the true story not get out. "You don't wish to hear the words of this spy."

"And why would that be?" the captain asked, one eyebrow raised, more at the anxiety in the man's voice than at the argument.

"Why, it's obvious, Sir!" Williamson sputtered. His mind thrashed about wildly, searching for a plausible answer to the question. Suddenly, he grasped at one that might suffice. "He's obviously been told that, in the case of capture, he should sow misinformation and dissention among the enemy's ranks."

Captain Smythe seemed almost to consider the argument, but then unexpectedly asked with a smile, "If that were the case, don't you think that he would have been instructed to do so only after some form of duress?" He could see that he was making Williamson quite uncomfortable, and he was enjoying every moment of it.

"Yes, they may well have told him that, but the man's obviously a coward", Willcocks offered, trying to bail out his man. As much as he disliked Williamson himself, this was beginning to reflect poorly on his own command.

Smythe now laughed out loud. "I hardly think that this man is a coward", he opined. "I saw the look you gave him, Mr. Williamson, and I should think that, if he were a coward, he would have kept his mouth shut and accepted whatever you had to say. Now, if you two are finished, I should like to hear the balance of your spy's version of what happened at the Twelve."

Jeremy forced himself to his feet and stood, though somewhat unsteadily, facing the enemy, for he wished to look the captain in the eye as he spoke.

"There were only the two of us, Captain", he began, "and the ambush was in Shipman's Tavern, where he and his thugs broke in for a reason I'm still hard pressed to understand." Williamson was once again being restrained by his own superiors. "Robert and I had followed these men into the tavern to try and stop them the best we knew how, and we managed to rid ourselves of six of Williamson's men upstairs. Then, when we went downstairs, he," Jeremy indicated Williamson, "finally managed to get Robert by throwing two of his men at my companion, sacrificing them to the cause, I believe it would be put?" he added ironically. He thought it best not to mention that Robert was a British officer.

"And how were you captured, then?" Smythe asked.

Jeremy smiled. "I'm not quite sure", he replied, not sure how much he should tell this enemy officer. In truth, he was still trying to sort things out in his mind. "When a man came at me, I managed to save my ammunition by laying the man low with the butt of my gun. I saw Robert go down from Williamson's shot, but before I could react, the world vanished from before my eyes."

Smythe turned to Williamson, who appeared about ready to burst in an explosion of anger. "Well, Dorian, this story seems somewhat different than the one you were in the course of telling me." He turned toward Jeremy. "And who are you, sir? Your name and livelihood, if you please."

"Jeremy van Hijser, sir, from near the Beaverdams. I am technically a farmer, but spend most of my time hunting and trading the game to whoever would pay for it."

"Much as I thought", Smythe announced, turning back to Williamson. "He looked me directly in the eye as he spoke, which is more than I have ever experienced when you speak. I, for one, have no doubt of his version of the tale. Mr. Williamson, this man was likely just defending someone's property from thieves but, at most, he's a militiaman. You know the rules of war. If he were an officer, we would take him prisoner until we could trade him. Militiamen are paroled and sent home until an equal number of paroles have been reached on both sides, whereupon they may once again serve. Feed this man, have him make his mark on the articles of parole, and set him free." Smythe turned smartly and, without another glance at these men, started back toward the gate.

"But, Captain, what about the bad information we were fed to bring us to this ambush? Don't you think it was all part of a plot?" Williamson continued to protest.

The captain stopped and half turned his body. "I think that, had this been a British plot, there would have been a great number more men at the tavern. They would have been regulars and they would not have let any of you reach the building. Mr. Williamson, you dealt for false information. Likely someone who recognized a likely fool when he saw one, seeking some quick coin." A grin formed on his lips. "I don't know what you paid him, or even why you might, but I'm afraid you'd bought a pig in a poke. This matter is finished. Now, set the prisoner free as I ordered. Good day, gentlemen." Smythe disappeared through the gate, adding in muted breath, "If there be any gentleman in either of the two of you."

As the captain walked past the gatepost, he muttered to the sergeant-at-arms, "If there were any justice, that man would be one of ours. I'll wager he's worth more than the whole lot of those disreputable bandits known as the Canadian Volunteers, claiming to defend our cause."

The sergeant glanced out the gate at Willcocks and Williamson. "I'd want a piece of that wager, sir. In fact, I'd be willing to pay for your piece of it."

Outside, in front of the gate, Williamson was furious. He turned to one of his men, who had been trying to remain discrete while laughing into his hand at Dorian's discomfort and dressing-down. "Well, you heard the order!" he snapped. "Feed him. But not well. And the matter of the timing of his release is open to interpretation, so wait until I have returned." Turning back to Willcocks, he added, "This matter is not yet resolved, Joseph. Not by a long shot." With that, he stalked angrily into the fort, with Willcocks following behind him, amused with his man's incredible arrogance.

Chapter Fourteen

Willcocks and Mallory, along with Williamson, were led into the office of the commander, Major-General Henry Dearborn, a former Secretary of War. A man who had begun the campaign a political appointee with more enthusiasm than ability, he was now just a shell of his former self. Looking much older than he actually was, he appeared defeated, surprised by the frequent military setbacks of the campaign and the inability of his troops to just "roll over the British", as the politicians who started this war had promised. He was also constantly bed-ridden, with an undetermined ailment that seemed to sap the very life from him.

Now the general appeared pale and haggard, dark circles beneath his eyes, and a physical shadow of the proud soldier that had left Washington, he hid in this fort with his army. He was angry with his counterpart in the U.S. Navy for refusing him cover from the lake and he was afraid to attack the British for fear they would use their navy to cut off his supply lines from home. His officers laughed behind his back and there were already whispers back in Washington of recalling him, or even ordering a court-martial for apparent cowardice.

Also in attendance, seated at the table were Brigadier General John Boyd, who had effective command of Dearborn's forces, Colonel Winfield Scott, Dearborn's adjutant-general, Captain Smythe, and Dr. Cyrenius Chapin, leader of the raiders from Buffalo, ever-so-slightly more respectable than the Canadian Volunteers. Pointing to an empty seat, Willcocks was invited to sit, while Williamson was expected to join the junior officers that lined the walls of the office. As the latter moved begrudgingly to his place between a navy ensign and a lieutenant, he could have sworn they parted to distance themselves from him.

"Gentlemen", Dearborn started, his voice weak with the fever that seemed to consume him on an ongoing basis. He didn't have the energy to distinguish between his officers and the civilians in the room, as military protocol would dictate. "It's high time we did something about the upstarts that plague our scouts and forward forces incessantly." He coughed roughly before continuing. "You know of whom I speak: Merritt, Fitzgibbon, Ducharme and his damnable Indians from Montreal. All those of their ilk that terrorize this peninsula and keep us from the destiny for which we were designed." Again, Dearborn issued forth with a long, unproductive fit of coughing.

"Well, we may have been handed an answer", Dearborn finally continued. "We have word that Fitzgibbon's headquarters, and the supply depot for all these groups, are situated at the DeCou residence just the other side of Beaverdams."

"Where have I heard that before?" Williamson muttered, mostly to himself.

Dearborn looked up at the man who had interrupted his briefing. "Ah, yes, Mr. Williamson", he said, drawing out the words to denote his disapproval. "If you were one of my men, you would be immediately reduced in rank for speaking out of turn in such a manner. But, knowing something of you, I will allow it to pass, but just this once. As for your comment, I have heard of your adventures – or should I say, misadventures - from Captain Smythe, and I assure you that my sources are somewhat more reputable than yours." He glared at the ruffian, who merely looked down at the floor.

"Not that I owe you any such assurances, sir!" Dearborn snapped, bringing on another fit of coughing. "Now, if you don't mind, I shall continue. And, if you do mind", he added, seeing that the man had not the wisdom to keep his mouth shut and was, at that moment, about to reply, "I'll have my men take you outside the fort and have you shot!"

This last burst of anger was simply too much for the General, and he slipped into a violent round of coughing that nearly finished him. By the time he had the spasms under control once again, he had kept the room waiting for several minutes, and he saw that everyone in the room was eyeing him, each with their own personal reaction displayed on his face or betrayed by his body's attitude.

For the next two hours, the officers at the table argued about how the depot should be attacked, with each wanting the glory of what they all considered to be an easy victory. They bickered over command, they bickered over tactics, and they even bickered over the details of how the expedition should be supplied. It was obvious that none liked or trusted any other, for a variety of reasons, and the session ended without resolution when Dearborn could go on no longer.

There were only two things they agreed upon. The first was that they would await the perfect chance, that being when Lieutenant Fitzgibbon was known to be at his base of operations. The second was that every other man in the room was a fool. The target was too vital to pass up – it would definitely be a feather in this division's cap and a public relations coup in the U.S., which could certainly use one at this point of the war – so the matter would be revisited, but not on this day.

The Canadian Volunteer camp was situated outside of town, about a mile toward Queenston from the Fort George, and well clear of Newark. Willcocks had ordered this isolation of his men for basically two reasons. First, the former newspaper editor and politician personally knew almost everyone in town, and all loathed him for the traitor he had become to Upper Canada but more locally, to the former capital itself.

The second reason was that Willcocks knew his men were wild and undisciplined. They followed orders, in most cases, only as long as there was some personal advantage to them. While he cared not a wit for the effect these men and their antics might have upon the townspeople, whom he despised, he was concerned that the military command not think any less of him than they already did. He still had aspirations of military recognition by these men and was determined that he should be given an officer's rank for his efforts on behalf of the United States of America.

Hidden within each reason, however, was the common thread that Willcocks refused to be judged either by people who he believed to be his inferiors, such as the citizens of Newark, or those he considered his equals. He was a proud man and the decision to pitch his camp some distance from both the town and the fort prevented any overt blows to that pride.

He and Mallory rode into this camp together in early evening, with Williamson in tow, muttering angrily to himself. The three men immediately retired to the farmhouse that had been "commandeered". While eating a late meal in the salon, they spoke little, each man sizing the other up for the confrontation they knew must eventually come. Finally, as the man who had been cowed into serving as steward that day cleared the dishes and other appurtenances of the meal, Willcocks nodded at Mallory, who accepted the silent signal and excused himself from the room.

Willcocks sighed and looked at Williamson across the table. "Do you realize how bad you made me look in front of the Americans today?" he asked in an even voice.

Williamson was much like his leader, although neither would ever have admitted to any similarity between them. In fact, the only significant difference was the higher level of education and social experience Willcocks could boast. But Williamson was not about to brook any criticism, even if this man was his boss.

"How bad you looked?" he replied, his voice heavily laden with false incredulity. "Why, you just stood there and said nothing while that popinjay of a captain all but called me a liar! Where was your support, Joseph?"

Willcocks began to laugh, a sound filled with venom. "Support what, Dorian? That you bribed a man you thought to be a U.S. agent to part with his secrets?" Williamson looked down, having no answer to that charge, for he had foolishly told the facts to the captain when challenged on the source of the information. But Willcocks wasn't yet finished with him. "Or would you have me defend your stupidity at taking the man's word for it all, without confirmation? Or, rather", Willcocks was up to his full oratorical politician's form now, "would you have me defend your lack of judgment in having present the one man who could put the lie to your tale?"

Willcocks had risen to his feet and had begun to pace about, and now stood behind his subordinate with wrists clasped behind his back. "What was your thinking in buying the man's information, anyway?" he demanded, his voice soft, but his tone leaving no doubt of the level of his anger, of the volcano that lay waiting to erupt just below the surface. "Did you think to come back here in triumph, outdoing your leader? Perhaps to steal my thunder?" He stood quietly behind Williamson's head, his mouth but inches from the man's ear, waiting for the reply that was so long in coming. "Well?" he shouted suddenly with enough violence in his tone to make his henchman leap almost completely from his seat.

Williamson sat speechless in the chair, his entire body trembling with a mixture of rage, fear and confusion. He would have given answer, but he had no answers to give. Somehow, his commander had laid the facts out exactly as they were. And somehow, he had divined Williamson's true motives behind today's debacle. How would he know, the man wondered? For the moment he even managed to ignore the fact that his interrogator still stood behind him, awaiting an answer, while he pondered the injustice of it all. First a lying spy whose false information nearly decimated his force, and now a traitor in his midst. For how else would Willcocks have known his heart so?

Willcocks now shifted slightly to Williamson's side, positioning his body in such a manner that allowed him to look into the man's face while yet standing behind him. "Would an explanation be forthcoming, Mr. Williamson?" he asked, his voice deceptively pleasant. It was not for nothing that this man was considered to be an excellent interrogator, at least in political circles. "Or, would you, perhaps, like more time to dream up a lie that I might possibly believe?" His voice rose again as he spoke, signalling an expectation that Williamson should keep his mouth shut.

"I..." Williamson began, but had not yet formulated a reply, and his mouth snapped closed, his anger quickly coming to a boiling point at the indignation of this incriminating – not to mention embarrassingly accurate – inquisition.

"Oh, shut up!" Willcocks shouted, now directly in front of, and only inches from, Williamson's face. "Don't even bother to lie again. I already know the facts! So, let me give you fair warning for the future", he said, pacing around the table, his arms clasped once again behind him. "If you ever try to undermine me, to make me look such the fool again in such a manner, your body will be found floating in the Niagara. Do you understand?" Seeing a weak nod from his subordinate, he continued. "From this point on, you and your men will remain with the main body of my Volunteers. That should make sense, even to one as dense as you seem to be, since you have so few men remaining", he added with a smirk. "However, should that not be to your liking, let me give you fair warning never to show your face near this fort again, for it will not show itself long with a musket ball embedded in it. Do you understand?" He waited only long enough for Williamson's head to bob once again. "Good!" he shouted. "Now get out of my sight and stay away from me until I should have the opportunity to calm down!"

With the finality of that command, Willcocks turned his back on his man, and Williamson rose quickly to leave. In truth, the former politician rather wished that the man would gather up his few remaining men and leave his sight forever, never to foul up his chances at prestige with the military again. But such was not to be, he knew. Williamson stood to gain from this association and therefore would chafe and rage, but he would not leave. Willcocks sighed deeply as he heard the flaps of his tent fall closed. At least, perhaps, the man would stay from underfoot for a few days.

Jeremy sat against a post in the small barn that was located some distance back from the house where Willcocks and his lackey were having their discussion. The injuries that had been inflicted on him in the course of his journey at the end of Williamson's rope were aggravated by the rough wood of the timber. His eyes cast about for a possible means of escape, but none was readily apparent at this moment.

When he and the remnants of Williamson's platoon had arrived at the commandeered farm, he had been hustled directly back to this structure. Here, they had shackled his legs with military leg irons to this corner post, which was quite securely a part of the building. They had carefully searched the area within reach for anything that might be used as a weapon or as a tool with which to either sever the shackles or to work at cutting apart the post. Then they had given him a tin cup of water and some stale, dry bread, leaving him alone with his thoughts for the balance of the afternoon.

Although, Jeremy was exhausted and he knew it was imperative that he get some rest, sleep would not come easily, his mind roiling with the events of the day. The sight of Robert dying at the hands of the man who had become his sworn enemy repeated steadily when he closed his eyes. His head swam with thoughts of escape, of killing Williamson with his bare hands and, in moments of melancholy, of Elizabeth Rhodes. He had heard Williamson's words and seen the expression on his face, and knew that he might never see her face again, a thought that disturbed him to a surprising degree considering the short time he had known her. All of these thoughts, in aggregate, redoubled his determination to break free of these bonds.

As the last light of day vanished from the spaces between the rough boards of Jeremy's prison, he heard the voice he recognized as belonging to Williamson. The sound of the scraping of the door on the hard-packed ground as it was dragged open soon followed. Jeremy's nemesis swaggered toward him, and he struggled to fight back the urge to scream obscenities in the villain's direction, obscenities that formed of their own volition at he back of his tongue and fairly screamed to be released upon this man who so richly deserved them.

Jeremy rose to his feet, not willing to be seen to cower before this brute. Looking into the other man's eyes, he saw hatred smouldering there, hatred to match his own. If there was any consolation, it was in the sudden dawning of realization that the hatred was wed to a strong sense of insecurity. That realization might not provide much succour in the hours ahead, however, as he also recognized in that glare that this visit was to be far from pleasant. But it might be something to remember for the future.

"So, you would make a fool of me in front of the Americans, would you?" Williamson growled. His open hand flew across the small space between them and struck Jeremy so hard that, in his weakened condition, his legs gave out and he sank to one knee.

Jeremy straightened himself back up and forced an insolent grin onto his now bleeding lips. "You did the making yourself", he replied. "I merely pointed your foolishness out to them." He immediately braced himself for the blow he knew would follow, and he was not to be disappointed, for Williamson struck him again, this time with the other hand, now opening a small cut across the bridge of Jeremy's nose. He was well aware that it would be suicide to strike back at this bully, for the man would merely have his henchmen hold him and beat him mercilessly. His verbal baiting was dangerous enough.

"What do you want of me?" Jeremy asked, shaking off the effects of the latest blow.

Williamson smiled a smile totally devoid of warmth. "All I want of you is revenge", he answered, so low that only Jeremy could hear. Then, in a louder voice, "I want these men with me to see what happens to those who oppose me. Especially those who do damage to my reputation, such as it is", with this, he broke out into a raucous laugh, joined in by the men that had accompanied him. Just as suddenly, his laughter ended, as a hand lashed out unexpectedly, this time knocking Jeremy into the dirt and straw of the barn floor.

Jeremy had enough for one day, and he decided to stay down this time, the hatred yet glaring from his eyes, one of which was rapidly swelling. Biting his tongue against any further sarcastic comments, he waited until the rogue and his companions left before sitting up against the post once again. He gingerly touched the wounded areas on his face, wincing sharply with each contact, then softly and sparingly applied water directly to the wounds to keep them clean.

This contact had done nothing for Jeremy's spirits. He could see no way to escape, and he knew Williamson would be back to exact more of his revenge. He couldn't help but wonder how long this would go on before the cowardly brute would finish it, a prospect that, in the light of Jeremy's assessment of the situation, almost seemed appealing at that point in time.

Chapter Fifteen

As Jeremy had expected, the treatment followed again the next day. He was fed a simple breakfast of stale bread and fresh water and, soon thereafter, Williamson appeared once again. He beat his defenceless prisoner, this time punching him several times so hard that he vomited the bread and water into the dust. And so it continued, in varying degrees of cruelty and effect for the next two days.

Jeremy whiled away the hours listening to the sounds of the camp, to the barked commands, the fights, the news coming in with new arrivals. The night of the second day, he heard two men who were apparently sitting up against the wall of the barn, for there was a bump at the wall each time one audibly shifted position. They spoke in muted tones about a spy that was said to be riding with the Bloody Boys, who seemed to be feeding information to the Volunteers. That was all Jeremy heard of the discussion, for one of the men suddenly shushed the other, followed closely by the unmistakable bellowing of Williamson ordering the men away from the barn.

On the third day, the door creaked open as usual at midday and, as Jeremy steeled himself to receive his visitor, he was surprised to discover that it was Willcocks, and that he had not brought Williamson with him. The leader of the Canadian Volunteers walked from the light toward the dark corner in which Jeremy cowered. The trapper was no longer able to withstand the demoralizing effects of the beatings, his sharp tongue silenced, his only hope that this time the beatings would be of short duration. The ex-politician looked down at the man and offered him a hand up, which Jeremy cautiously accepted, not knowing what to expect of this gesture.

"So this is where Dorian's been hiding you", Willcocks said conversationally, looking about as if admiring a man's parlour for the first time. "I really had expected that the devil had killed you on the way here that first day. But then I heard his men talk about what great fun they were having here in the barn, and I decided to investigate."

Jeremy said nothing, and just eyed the traitor leader suspiciously from the one eye that had been beaten only half closed. He shifted to a more comfortable position, now that it seemed there might not be a beating on this visit, at least not immediately. This cast a bit of light upon his face, and Willcocks moved in more closely to examine Jeremy's injuries.

"Well", he sighed. "It certainly appears that Mr. Williamson has had at you these several days", he commented, clearly perplexed. "That will be the end of that, though", he promised, rising to his feet, sending a bolt of hope coursing through Jeremy. Turning toward the door, he shouted out, "Jefferson! Get in here, right smartly!"

One of the men who had always accompanied Williamson for the beatings, stuck his head inside the door and looked about into the gloom of the barn, squinting to see who had called. He had left his post to relieve himself, and he feared that his boss had discovered his lapse. The poor fellow now feared a beating of his own - or worse. After a moment, however, he recognized the figure of Willcocks and not Williamson, and the sigh of relief that escaped him was nearly audible before he replied to the summons.

"Yes, sir!" he cried at last, affecting a military posture, knowing that such affectations pleased his commander.

Willcocks smirked, wondering what type of fool these men took him for. "Do you have the key to these shackles?"

"That I do", the guard replied shakily, now wondering if he would be in trouble with this man instead. "Sir", he gulped as an afterthought.

"Well, come in here and unlock them", Willcocks ordered. "And then bring this man into the house. He is sorely in need of some medical attention. Just what have you idiots been doing in here?"

he asked. Seeing Jefferson turn to leave, he called him back. "Just where do you think you're going, man? Didn't I just give you a direct order?"

Jefferson looked confused. "Well, sir...that is, I thought, sir... that is..."

"Come on, out with it!" Willcocks barked, losing his patience rapidly.

"I thought I should go get Jonesy", the guard finally spit out. "Wouldn't want the prisoner to overpower me and escape, sir."

"Get in here and do as you were commanded, Jefferson! Look at this man! Look at what you and Williamson have done to him! Do you really think this man poses you, or anyone else for that matter, any threat whatsoever?" Willcocks' voice dripped with sarcasm. 'If you feel yourself not man enough to handle him, however, just toss me the keys and I'll do it myself!"

The guard, now completely chastened and utterly shamed by his commander, almost ran into the barn and proceeded to remove the prisoner's chains. Just as Willcocks had said, this man posed no danger to anyone and certainly was no flight risk. The two men found they both had to support Jeremy to move him to the house. They sat the injured man down in a chair at the table, and Willcocks proceeded to place some leftover food and a cup of whiskey, the universal cure-all, before him.

"Now go and bring Williamson here!" Willcocks barked at the guard, who nearly tripped over his own feet in his haste to leave the room while he still could.

Jefferson returned, though, only moments, later. He ran into the room, and stood at attention just inside, as if he were awaiting permission to speak.

"What is it?" Willcocks sighed.

"I'm afraid Mr. Williamson isn't here, sir", the man replied, visibly flinching as though expecting a beating for bearing bad tidings.

"Where is he then?"

"Jonesy told me that the boss went off to town by himself."

"By himself, eh?" Willcocks mused. "I wonder what mischief he might be up to now?" he said, mostly to himself. He looked up and saw that Jeremy was looking at him, and laughed. "I threatened to shoot him if he left camp without the rest of the Volunteers." He chuckled softly. "Perhaps I should give that particular option more consideration."

Willcocks dismissed Jefferson and turned back to Jeremy, who was still struggling to eat the food he had been given through cracked and split lips, cut mouth and broken gums, which created a definite impediment, and all brought about by the beatings he had received. The whiskey with which he'd been thoughtfully provided burned in the partially open wounds, dribbling down his stubbled chin and onto his torn and dirty clothing. Willcocks was no stranger to brawling, or even outright acts of cruelty toward those he felt deserved it. But he was somewhat uncomfortable with the treatment of this prisoner who did nothing but defend a man's property, as far as he could tell. It was, after all, an establishment frequented by both sides in this accursed war, depending upon who had the upper hand that day, or that hour. More important, he saw in this situation an excuse to demean that fool Williamson one more time, and perhaps be rid of him once and for all.

"Tell me", Willcocks began, pulling up a chair across the table from Jeremy. "What possessed you to attack an entire platoon of cutthroats?"

"If you'll tell me why you became a traitor to your own", Jeremy replied, his strength, and therefore his courage, beginning to return once again. Too smart for my own good by half, he thought to himself, fully expecting an attack by this man as well.

Willcocks eyed him angrily at first, but his sense of humour and fair play won out, turning his ire to laughter. "Well put, sir", he said. "Fair enough. I'll go first if you like, since my question was more out of curiosity than a matter of great import. The truth is, I don't see myself as a traitor."

Jeremy looked up from his food, which was now nearly all consumed. "How can you not, sir?" he asked bewildered. "You served as a member of the legislature and acted as an emissary to the Mohawks on Brock's behalf. Since you are now acting on behalf of the Americans, I would suggest that there is nothing to label you but traitor."

"Very well. I understand your point", the Volunteers' commander started, leaning back in his chair. "I consider my action on Brock's behalf to be a departure from the things I have held dear. My formation of the Canadian Volunteers was an act that righted the transgression I committed toward myself."

"What do you mean, a departure?" Jeremy demanded, breaking into Willcocks' narrative. "You've served the crown practically since your youth."

Willcocks bristled with indignation, both at the interruption and at the premise put forth by this younger man. "I'll have you know that, if you study the record of my life, you'll find that I have been battling the Crown all of my adult life", he asserted. While in the Legislature, I fought to remove that cabal of elitists that override the decisions we made, in order that we might replace them with a proper democracy. You may not be aware, Mr. van Hijser – that is your name, right?" When Jeremy nodded, he continued, "but I was arrested on more than one occasion on the trumped-up charge of sedition because I demanded the power of the people come first." He sat back again, somewhat satisfied with his defence.

"While running my newspaper here in town", Willcocks continued after taking a sip from the glass of whiskey that sat before him also, "I was a constant champion for the type of democracy that exists on the other side of the Niagara, a position that did not sit well with the townspeople. In fact", he added conspiratorially, "they tried more than once to have me arrested for my thoughts."

Willcocks drained his glass and watched the farmer before him. "That is my tale, sir. Now do you understand my position?" he asked, obviously looking for validation.

"Yes, I see", Jeremy replied, now finished with the dinner this man had provided. As far as he was concerned, no argument would convince him. The man had started the war on one side and then switched to the other. That was surely the definition of a traitor.

Should he provoke the man any further? He decided that, against his own best interest, he would, for he felt an overwhelming desire to determine what made this man what he was. "But none of that explains why you have gone about terrorizing the countryside, your own neighbours? To justify a political cause?"

Once again Jeremy could see Willcocks flare with rage before settling into a jovial persona. "I believe you're baiting me", he said, talking as if to a schoolboy. "They are but receiving their just desserts for turning on me when they had the upper hand. Surely you wouldn't deny me some simple, if base, revenge for the things done to me for years?"

Jeremy knew that there was little point in arguing with the man any further, so without further comment, he carefully drained what little was left of the whiskey and set the tin cup on the table. "Well, thank you for that enlightening opinion, Mr. Willcocks", he said. "Am I to return to the barn now?"

"In due time, sir", the other man chuckled. "But, for now, you haven't yet honoured your part of the bargain."

"My part…" Jeremy began, and then stopped in mid-sentence as he realized what was meant by the remark. "My apologies, sir. I had quite forgotten that you had inquired as to my display of foolishness at Shipman's Tavern. For that's the best way to describe it, although it turned out not nearly the task that I thought it would be. You see", he said, playing absentmindedly with the whiskey cup, "once inside, my friend and I bolted the door, leaving fully half of the enemy outside the tavern, at first apparently unable to summon the originality required to think of climbing in through the window." Jeremy laughed at the thought, and then continued. "That done, we merely followed your men around…"

Willcocks broke in. "Not my men, be sure of that!" he proclaimed. "Those were Williamson's men. A special breed they are", he added, a smile forming once again on his lips. He would make good use of this information in dealing with that cur. "I'm sorry", the man said, breaking his reverie. "Please continue with your tale."

Jeremy had been watching the other man and realized that the differences between Willcocks and Williamson went much deeper than a mere matter of discipline. What he had been witnessing all along, although he did not recognize it until now, was a power struggle. Perhaps he would be able to take advantage of the situation, if he played it right.

"Are those men not under your eventual command?" he asked archly.

Willcocks did not deign to respond to this, for Jeremy was right to a point. But attempting to explain his lack of control over Williamson's buffoons would only complicate the discussion. He did find, however, that he was deriving immense enjoyment from the thrust and parry with this man, as much as it seemed to infuriate him at times. It was not often that he could enjoy an honest exchange with another human being, cast out as he was by his neighbours and unaccepted by the Americans. He believed that the men who served under him lacked either the nerve or the intellect or both.

"As I was saying before you corrected me", he continued, "We merely followed Williamson's men around from room to room, eliminating them as they isolated themselves."

"And as you walked among them, none realized you weren't one of them?" Willcocks asked, obviously puzzled.

"Only one that I know of", Jeremy replied. "A gentleman who claimed you tried to hang him for allowing me to escape at the Twenty."

Willcocks thought on this a moment, and then burst out laughing. "Oh, yes, one of those idiots we caught drunk and unconscious in the creek bed", he said. "They hadn't told us you were there. In fact, they weren't even certain how they'd come to be there. We pretended to hang them for dereliction of duty and being drunk on guard duty", he explained. "Leave it to those fools to not even understand for what they were being punished!"

His laughter calmed to grin as he continued with his questioning. "So, to the tavern once again, you and your friend managed to eliminate, as you say, six men upstairs without a serious challenge", Willcocks mused, rubbing his chin, a glint in his eye.

"Well, not exactly", Jeremy explained. "We pushed two men out of the window onto the others who were milling about at the side, apparently confused. Unfortunately, we were forced to shoot one when he wouldn't let go of the window frame. And the one man had merely been knocked unconscious by Robert."

"I thought there were four bodies upstairs", the other remarked, puzzled.

"There were. The man Robert had flattened was shot by Williamson himself in a fit of rage after the battle downstairs had finished", came the explanation. "You travel with a dreadful coward, sir. I'd mind my back if I were you."

"Hmm, I do believe you're right on that count, anyway",

Willcocks mused. "He's certainly not a man you'd want behind you in battle."

"At least, not unless you don't mind a push from behind, like those three men downstairs."

Jeremy felt Willcocks' dark looks, not focused anywhere in particular as the man digested this information about his supposed subordinate. He could not read the leader's thoughts, but at least he had given this jailer something to think about. And now, when Jeremy was returned to the barn, he himself would have something to occupy his time. He had some planning to do, as he determined how to drive in the wedge even further.

Willcocks withdrew from his reverie and suddenly rose to his feet. "Well I'm sorry, Mr. van Hijser, but I can't be entertaining you in this manner all the day long. I'm afraid I must return you to the barn, and I'm equally sorry that the chains will go back on, until I decide what is to be done with you. And, finally, I'm sorry I couldn't convince you of the righteousness of my cause."

"Well, sir, you could always release me, as the captain at the fort ordered", Jeremy offered hopefully, knowing that was no longer an option.

"I'm afraid that ship has sailed", Willcocks, with what appeared to be honest regret, although it was difficult to determine with this man. "Things are no longer quite that simple, as you know too much about this camp."

"I'm not quite sure what it is that I supposedly know. If it's your camp's existence, I'm quite sure that will change anyway. Regardless, what if I were to promise to keep my mouth shut? I guarantee you, my word is my bond."

Willcocks smiled an almost sad smile. "You've been privy to much, through the thin walls of the barn, I'm sure. My men know nothing of secrecy and talk freely of all they know. And I should like very much to be able to take you upon your word. I'm afraid, however, that I have travelled in the company of scoundrels too long and can no longer accept anyone's word as truth." With that, he sauntered to the door and called for Jefferson.

"Aye, sir", Jefferson replied, and saluted smartly, with the same forced affectation he had used at the barn earlier.

"Take this man back to the barn and lock him back up. But

be sure that more harm comes to him", came the order. "Tell Williamson I now know of this abomination and will be more than displeased if he should carry on in this same manner again."

"If it's all the same to you, perhaps you could tell him, sir?" The man was obviously too frightened of Williamson even to pass on an order from the commander.

Chapter Sixteen

Williamson was in one of his usual stormy moods when he returned from town that evening, for Jonesy had displayed the incredibly poor judgment of confiding in his boss the details of what had transpired with the prisoner that day. Now Dorian was forced to fabricate a tale explaining the lapse in protocol that had occurred when he had kept the information from his commander. The worse part of that exercise was that, try as he might, he could come up with nothing. His alternative and, in fact only, plan was to attempt to avoid Willcocks altogether.

In that he was no more successful than he had been in thinking of an excuse.

"Dorian", Willcocks called out pleasantly enough, from across the yard. As pleasant as the hiss of a snake, Williamson thought. "Where have you been, man? We've some planning to do before we set out again. Get Smith and I'll get some of the others. Meet me back at the house in ten minutes."

Williamson was immediately suspicious. Although there had been no rancour in his superior's voice, it was quite unlike him to speak kindly to him. Usually all of his communication with him was in the form of commands and this polite, almost friendly treatment unnerved him. Nonetheless, he did as Willcocks bid him do, and sent for Geoffrey Smith, meeting him outside the barn. There he told his subordinate of their boss's unusual behaviour.

"What shall we do, then?" Smith asked, more than a bit nervous.

A Question of Loyalty

"Exactly what we've been told", came the reply. "We go to the planning session and hope that the subject of our pet spy in the barn, here, doesn't come up. In fact, I think it's best if we stay close to the door and try to be the first ones out when we're through."

The two walked nervously to the house and entered with great trepidation. There they found the other men of their "ranks" already in attendance, and seated or standing in such a way as to make it necessary for the latecomers to work their ways to the middle of the room. Apparently they were not the only ones to want to make a quick exit, Williamson thought hopefully. But hope was not his strong suit and he felt very uncomfortable with the way this was shaping up.

To make matters worse, the moment they walked through the door, Willcocks, whose voice they had heard as they crossed to the house, suddenly stopped talking. As if on cue, the whole room fell silent with him. Smith, who was by far the more skittish of the two, was ready to bolt, but his fear of what might happen if he did so was much greater than what they faced for keeping their secret.

When the two men were seated at the two chairs that were too conveniently vacant at the centre of the table, Willcocks hammered for silence with the butt of his hunting knife, for the lapse in time taken as the two men seated themselves had brought on a renewed round of general din. "Gentlemen", he said, looking about the room as if addressing the Legislature. "We had a bit of a problem this day." He noticed Smith visibly blanche and smiled directly at him.

He waited for dramatic effect, increasing the tension in the room, especially for the two poor fools who had no idea what was coming. "We have among us this evening two men who feel they can act independently of the rest of us, even while in our midst." He stood up and paced to the wall, his back to the table. "They seem to think they can disobey a direct order from a U.S. officer, and then keep a prisoner here under our noses against specific instruction to the contrary."

Willcocks turned around suddenly and looked directly at the two men. Smith, never a confident man to begin, was nauseous to the point of vomiting the meal he had recently eaten. Even Williamson, who thrived on bravado and liked to challenge any man who should question him, was trembling, and hoping desperately that it did not show before all these men.

"Williamson and Smith!" the voice thundered in the small room, causing them both to jump. "Stand and face the room!" he commanded. When the pair hesitantly complied, he continued. "Do either of you sorry lot deny that you were ordered to parole the beaten and tortured man I found in the barn today?"

Both men were speechless, dumbfounded by the formality of the proceedings. This was much more serious than either had expected. Finally, Williamson managed to pull himself together enough to answer. "No, sir", he muttered at a level barely audible to the others.

Smith just shook his head, too terrified to speak.

"What was that?" Willcocks screamed at the two men. "Speak up you two! Williamson, I've never seen you at a loss for words before. Now I want an answer that every man in this room can hear and remember!"

"No, sir!" they answered in unison, and then Smith added, his voice quivering, "We don't deny it, sir."

Willcocks' lips curled into a sneer. "And do you admit that you've kept that man prisoner in the barn since then, beating him regularly?"

"Yes, sir", they both answered, Smith first and then, less eagerly, Williamson, but both practically shouting so that they would not be required to answer again.

"You two are guilty of disobeying a direct order and endangering the security of this camp by holding that man here. We could all have been in trouble should the Captain of the Guard have discovered it before I did."

The two guilty men stood as still as their variously quaking bodies would allow, not knowing what they could expect now. They knew the punishment for disobeying a direct order in wartime could be anything, from jail to death, and they both kept silent, waiting for the sentence to be pronounced.

Willcocks paced about some more, using the hiatus to maximum dramatic effect, and then leaned with his knuckles on the table's surface. "You are fortunate there are more important matters than you two for me to deal with. Just let this be a warning, and not an idle one, that next time you do something such as this you will be shot!"

Williamson and Smith turned their heads ever so slightly and looked cautiously at each other, barely believing their ears. Was Joseph going to let them off this easy? Was it over? There was to be no punishment? The two bent to seat themselves once again at the table.

"Did I tell you to sit?" Willcocks questioned in a dreadful roar. "Remain standing until I tell you to sit! Did either of you work so hard today as to require a rest?" He expected no answer to this question, for he'd never seen either man work, ever. But now a cruel smile was forming on his lips. "Now we deal with one of those more important matters."

The two men looked at each other once more, their puzzlement this time evident in their expression. Williamson appeared slightly annoyed, but it was evident to Willcocks that Smith harboured grave reservations about what was to come next. They had thought the matter done with, that they would now move on to planning their next move.

"Mr. Dorian Williamson", Willcocks said, quite formally. When the accused man started at the formality of the mode of address, shock evident in his expression, the commander continued. "You are hereby charged with the crime of murdering a fellow Canadian Volunteer. And you, Mr. Geoffrey Smith, are hereby charged as an accessory to the fact."

Smith and Williamson looked at each other disbelieving, as if to seek verification of what they had just heard. "What the hell do you mean murder?" The larger man demanded. "How can we murder anyone? This is a war."

Willcocks smiled that secretive grin once more. "Not when you kill someone on your own side", he answered evenly.

"On our own side?" Williamson shouted in disbelief. "Just who in damnation are we supposed to have killed?"

"I'll get to that in due time", Willcocks replied, clearly enjoying this game of cat and mouse. "In the meantime, you gentlemen may now sit." When neither man took a seat, remaining rooted to the floor with fear and surprise, he suddenly erupted. "I said sit! If nothing else, you two will learn to follow orders before you take the noose!" he roared.

"Noose?" Smith said, almost in a whisper. He was noticeably trembling as that word reverberated in his mind.

Willcocks ignored the slight man. "What we have here, gentlemen", he began, injecting judicial airs into the proceedings, "is a case of unmitigated cruelty against a fellow Volunteer, shooting his own man, who had been injured in the line of duty, while he lay helpless on the floor, unable even to defend himself." As he continued, he was quite beginning to enjoy this role as prosecutor. He began to pace about in the little space he had at his end of the table with hands behind his back, attempting to appear like a lawyer.

"And this man", he said, pointing suddenly at Smith, who required all the courage in him to keep from bursting out in tears, "did nothing to stop him! He just stood there and watched!" he cried in mock disbelief.

Smith appeared as though he might break into tears at any moment. "But, Sir, I wasn't..."

"Silence!" Willcocks cut in. "You'll have your opportunity to answer the charges, as will your co-accused", he said, and then continued with his case. He sailed into an emotional tableau, setting the scene for the alleged murder, embellishing freely to improve the telling. He went into great detail telling his audience how the cowardly Williamson had pushed his other men forward, fairly feeding them into the muskets of the enemy! Then with voice rising and falling in his best oratorical fashion, arms waving, and pointing and gesturing to drive home his points, he described the horrible crime committed by these men in much greater detail than he could possibly have known.

Finally, with the perspiration borne of his performance, he stood silently before the others. He sported an anguished look upon his face and what some would later claim was a tear upon his cheek. "So, gentlemen, you've heard the story as told to me by the witnesses, not all of whom could be here today." With that final pronouncement, he effectively silenced any question of the veracity of the testimony. Not that any man in this room would have dared do so even had any of them cared to do so. To many, this evening's

A Question of Loyalty

diversion was great sport, and none held any love in their hearts for Williamson.

"Now, Mr. Smith, I believe you had something to say in answer to these charges?" Willcocks asked, his tone betraying his complete lack of interest in anything the man might have to say.

Smith rose shakily to his feet. "Yes sir!" he managed to blurt out through dried tongue and lips. "The truth is, I was downstairs at the time of the shooting, er, alleged shooting. If that's the right way to say it." He realized it must sound as if he were babbling, so he wisely said no more.

"Is that right?" Willcocks asked, with one eyebrow raised. "Well, let's see about that, shall we?" Turning to the man who had been shoved toward Jeremy and knocked unconscious, he asked for verification.

The man glanced at Smith and then nervously at the man he truly hoped would from here on be his former leader. "Yes, Sir!" he said tentatively, not knowing whether he would end up paying for his testimony with something objectionable. "Mr. Smith was downstairs helping me up after Mr. Williamson pushed me into that farmer fellow." He looked around the room at the others. "That's because the farmer laid me low with the butt of his gun", he added, by way of explanation.

Willcocks looked at the witness while he pondered this unexpected piece of evidence. Without doing so directly, he looked about at the faces of those gathered about the table, coming to the rapid conclusion that it would be in his own best interest to at least appear to be fair.

"Very well", he said with a sigh. "Mr. Smith, by the strength of the witness' testimony, I find you innocent of all charges. You may stay for the rest of these proceedings or go, whichever you desire", he pronounced.

Smith jumped up from his seat, almost falling onto the floor as he did so, for his fear had risen to such a fever that he had little blood left in his head and his legs were almost numb and completely lacking in strength. But it was essential to him that he leave this room with all haste, if he could do so at all. He needed fresh air, but more important still, his bowels felt as though they might cause him an immense amount of shame at any moment.

Willcocks turned his attention back to the remaining accused man. If only he could manage to wrap this up without letting the man speak! That would be most desirable, since he was not completely certain how much sway the brute might hold over these others. However, he needed to maintain a certain amount of respect from these men, or they would cease to follow him. And there was so much that he still desired to attain! "Go ahead, Mr. Williamson, if you feel you can defend yourself against these facts. It's your turn to speak."

Williamson sat silently for almost a minute and then, just as Willcocks feared the man might actually present a cohesive defence, the big man played right into his hands. "I don't need to answer these charges!" he exploded, vaulting out of his chair. "You have no authority to try me like this! This entire affair is a farce and I demand you let me go this minute!"

Willcocks smiled. The man could not have handed the case to him in a better manner. "Well, Mr. Williamson, since you say you have no defence to offer, it's time for me to pronounce your sentence."

The appearance that settled over the accused's face made it evident that he seemed suddenly to realize the position he was in. While it was indeed true that Willcocks had no legitimate judicial authority, as Williamson himself had stated earlier, this was a war. Many things were done without proper authority, the activities of this entire organization a perfect example. "Wait!" he cried out. "I do have something to say!"

"You had your opportunity", Willcocks replied, in a voice almost too even, devoid of emotion. His eyes were as cold, reptilian, as he made his pronouncement. "Mr. Williamson, stand and face your peers", he announced, for the benefit of all in the room, although he knew that some would not appreciate the suggestion that Williamson might be their peer. "You have been found guilty by this court and have offered no defence. Therefore it is the ruling of this court that you be taken from here and locked in the barn until sunup, at which time you will be taken to the tallest tree and hung by the neck until you are dead."

Williamson was completely speechless for what might quite probably be the first time in his life. This was partly out of the shock arising from this unexpected trial, but partly also because he knew by Willcocks' expression that it would not go well for him if he raised a fuss. In part, it was also because his mind was already churning, grasping for a way out of this ordeal.

Before anyone in the room could react, he bolted from his seat and dove through the open window onto the hard ground. All in the room could hear a sickening impact as he struck, but he temporarily ignored the pain, getting back to his feet and stumbling toward the lane. One of the volunteers, returning on horseback from some unknown locale, received a shock as his whiskey-sodden mind suddenly realized that someone had grabbed hold of him and was now pulling him unceremoniously from his mount. Williamson ignored the man's weak, slurred protestations, pulled himself up into his saddle and, with a hard kick to the horse's flanks, tore off down the lane, disappearing from view at the road.

One of Willcocks' men ran to the door and shouted for guards, but there was no one sober anywhere near to give chase. In any case, it had all happened so suddenly that Williamson was now well gone into the night.

"Never mind, Carl", Willcocks said tiredly to the man. "We won't find him tonight. With the fright he received tonight, he won't stop riding 'til morning." A weary smile worked its way onto his face. "How far can he get, anyway?" he asked. "The man has no one to do his bidding, he's riding around enemy-infested territory without any protection, and no one in the civilized world wants anything to do with him, especially the American soldiers." He looked out the window absently, adding, "I think tomorrow we'll let Captain Smythe know what transpired here, including Williamson's direct disobedience of his orders. Then, if he ever shows his face around here again, either we'll hang him, or the Captain will. It makes no difference to me."

Willcocks placed both hands palm down on the table, pushing himself erect. "Well, gentlemen, I thank you for your attention this evening. Be sure to tell your men how justice was dispensed here this night. We can't condone cold-blooded murder in this camp. Especially when it concerns one of our own." With that, he turned and walked from the room, climbing the stairs to the sleeping areas above.

The "officers" of the Canadian Volunteers looked about at each other, a little sceptical of the events here this evening, but none wanting to voice it for fear that word would get back to Willcocks. No one wished to be the next to be targeted for the man's "justice".

With only the odd "good-night" traded among them, they filed out to join their men for whatever drinking time may be left of the evening. If they yet had men, that is, for many Volunteers had been leaving in the night, tired of this game. One never knew for certain how many there would be in the morning's light. Indeed, some of them began to wonder if it was not time for them, too, to take their leave of this hideous charade that was producing more casualties than rewards.

Chapter Seventeen

Jeremy had heard all the fuss coming from the house at the end of the trial, although he had no way of knowing its significance. All he knew of this night was that he would likely be going to sleep without a beating from Williamson, thanks to his discussion with Willcocks. Although he had little use for the traitor, he felt that he could trust the man to a point, and he lay back into the little straw he had gathered for a mattress. Within minutes, he had fallen sound asleep.

He was not asleep long, however, when he heard the barn door open, notwithstanding an obvious attempt to do so quietly. Panic coursed through Jeremy's body. Had Williamson decided to defy his commander and come for revenge against him? He could see only a vague silhouette as the figure moved stealthily toward him, and he considered crying out, hopefully to attract help before his enemy beat him again or, worse yet killed him.

As the shape coalesced in the poor light provided by the flickering of flames from campfires filtering through the barn's planking, he saw that it was the man known as Smith. Jeremy was puzzled, for Smith had never taken any part in his beatings before this.

"Shhh!" Smith signalled, his finger to lips. "I've not come to beat you."

"What is it, then?" Jeremy asked, the anxiety falling like weights from his heart, but puzzled all the more at the little man's presence.

"I've had quite enough", the man said softly, regret hanging heavily in his voice. "And I'll wager you have too. We're getting out of here." He pulled a key from his pouch and proceeded to unlock the chains.

"Why would you be helping me?" Jeremy asked, suspicious of some plot, perhaps a musket ball as he left, the wage of attempted escape even then. "You could be long gone by now and you probably wouldn't be missed for some time. And what of your boss?"

"My boss is of no more concern to me", Smith muttered, impatience evident in his voice. "And I'm not at all sure why, but I feel a certain responsibility for your predicament. Are you coming or not?" Smith punctuated his intent by handing him back his weapons, which had of necessity been confiscated when he had been captured. "You'll want these", he muttered.

Jeremy wondered at the true motives behind this man's actions, wondering if he would be jumping from the frying pan into the fire. In the end, however, he thought it over only briefly. Willcocks had not said anything about setting him free. In fact, he had said that was no longer an option. He shrugged to himself, and rose wearily to his feet, and followed Smith out of the barn and then slipping carefully along the wall. A musket ball would be greatly preferable to sitting out the duration of the war chained to that post, if that was indeed Willcocks' intention.

The two men slipped quietly through the camp. Those yet awake at this hour were not sober enough to care who these men were or what they were doing. In spite of the fear and accompanying tension both men felt, they moved as casually as they could manage, avoiding drawing attention to themselves. As they approached the far side of the camp, they heard a great hew and cry behind them. Looking back over their shoulders, they could see torches being lit near the barn.

"Damn! They've noticed you're missing", Smith muttered, his throat constricting with fear. "I didn't think you'd be missed until dawn at least."

Suddenly, a cry went up behind them, "Look! Over there! At the edge of the field near the woods!" Had the disappearance been detected a moment sooner, they would not have stood out, for they would have yet been among the tents and, if it had been a moment later, they would been safely among the trees. The two men were, it seems, to become victims of bad timing.

The sounds of general confusion arose in the camp. As the Volunteers awoke from the din that came from the barn, they began to mill about around their tents, not knowing what was happening. The men who had noticed Jeremy's absence were trying to run through this confusion, shoving aside those who, understandably, wished to be informed as to what great emergency had wakened them from a sound sleep. Their progress was greatly impeded by the crush of humanity that had appeared, completely confused, and who had begun to push back, not appreciating this treatment they were receiving from their own.

"Run for it!" Smith cried. "They've spotted us! But maybe the confusion will hold them long enough for us to escape."

Jeremy required no prodding from this man who had been, only this morning, a part of the group he classed as his enemies. He set off into the bush, buoyed by the prospect of freedom and reinforced by the adrenalin coursing through him, brought about by the fear of losing that very freedom once again. He had quite enough of the shackles that had bound him to barn's post, and the uncertain existence that would result from his recapture.

Only a couple of hundred yards into the trees, they were both startled by the thunderous report of muskets. Their pursuers must have reached a point where they could shoot blindly into the trees with minimal risk of hitting their own men. Perhaps they were ordered not to be concerned whether they did or not. They were able to crash wildly through the woods for another fifty yards, when the air was rent with the roar of a second volley. This time they could hear the smash of musket balls as they tore after where the shooters calculated the runners to be, with no visible target. Unfortunately, they were not far wrong.

Jeremy called to Smith, who was ahead and becoming separated from him, "Over here! Sharp left! Maybe they'll keep going straight!" he suggested hopefully.

But their luck was not improving. Expecting that their quarry would change tack in the woods, the hunters now were ordered to fire in a wider pattern, and the next volley shredded the undergrowth in a much wider arc. It was obvious that taking evasive action would not help them. There was nothing for it but to run as far and as fast as they could without wasting time or distance on a zigzag course. At least they would gain some distance each time their pursuers stopped to reload.

Once again, Jeremy heard the order to fire through the trees, and he could no longer determine even where the sound was coming from. Had it not been for the moon, clearly visible through the branches, they would have been in danger of circling back toward their pursuers. Suddenly, Jeremy thought to himself, that this perhaps was not such a bad idea. He let out a low whistle and, when Smith looked in his direction, signalled his intent.

Smith appeared dubious, but turned to follow. At that moment, another volley sent both men diving for the ground, as musket balls thudded and bounced against tree trunks, tore leaves, and generally devastated the area. When the noise cleared, Jeremy figured this would be their best chance, while the Volunteers were reloading. But, as he sprang to his feet, he noticed that Smith was not following. He let out a low whistle like he had before, but Smith did not respond. Jeremy made his way over, crouching low in case they should reload and fire quickly.

As he shook Geoffrey Smith's shoulder, there was no response, so Jeremy pushed the man more forcefully, causing Smith to roll over onto his side. To Jeremy's horror, much of his saviour's jaw had been torn away from his face, leaving a gaping mass of bone, muscle and blood hanging obscenely from the part that was left. Jeremy was sickened, and he felt a strong urge to vomit, but he knew he must get moving or he would be discovered. He felt that there somehow was little chance that he would be taken alive now.

He did not need to wait long before the next volley struck, more widely dispersed now, the men obviously being spread out to cover a greater area. Before the echo of the volley had died down, he jumped up and ran in a wide arc, heading back in the general direction from which he had come. Twice he almost ran headlong into one of his pursuers, the first time managing to change course before he was noticed, the second time using a sturdy piece of deadwood to fell his antagonist.

It was not long before he heard a shout from behind him in the direction of Smith's body. "Over here!" someone called, and then there was nothing until he heard a voice calling out to him specifically.

"Mr. van Hijser", the voice said, seemingly filling the night woods with sound. Jeremy immediately recognized it to be the voice of Joseph Willcocks. "Mr. van Hijser, you don't really expect to escape, do you?" When there was no reply, "I have some of the best trackers around, and we'll hunt you down. And if you put me through that much trouble", the voice paused for effect. "Then, believe me, you will never see home again."

All the while Willcocks was speaking, Jeremy moved quietly through the undergrowth, now even more careful to avoid leaving a trail that could be followed at night. Being an accomplished tracker himself, he knew it would be extremely difficult, if not impossible, to find much but the most obvious of signs in the dark woods by torchlight. And, if he could put enough distance between himself and these men, it would matter little if they found his sign in the morning. Once he reached the road, it would be nearly impossible to follow him.

To avoid leaving overt marks of his passage, Jeremy stayed as much as possible to the way the men had come into the woods. They had had no reason to be careful, and their trail was marked by crushed ground cover and broken branches. As long as he took pains not to do any damage himself, the signs would all indicate someone heavily travelling in the direction from which he was coming now.

After several more minutes of practicing this deception, he came near the edge of the brush, not far from the Volunteer camp. It was obvious to Jeremy that he could not exit at this point, for he was within sight of the camp should he insinuate himself accidentally between the moonlight and some watching hunter. But he was sure that he had lost his pursuers by now, so he moved stealthily just within the tree line, still trying his best not to leave obvious evidence of his passing.

Even when he felt he was well clear of the farm where he had been imprisoned, Jeremy feared to leave the relative safety of the woods. Exhausted from running, still depleted from his beatings while in captivity, torn and scratched by tree branches and thorns, and hungry and dehydrated, he finally stumbled onto the road not long after dawn, near the settlement of St. Davids.

Jeremy knew a man here who might give him a place to hide and rest until he could marshal his strength for the balance of the journey, and he was not disappointed. All the rest of that day, after being fed a modest but most welcome meal by his host and drinking his fill of water from the man's well, he fell sound asleep in the root cellar, not a place of utmost comfort, but relatively safe all the same.

In the evening, Jeremy awoke and cautiously climbed from the root cellar, his clothes dirty and in tatters. He was told that Willcocks' men had been riding up and down the road all day, asking questions about strangers. Of course, since he had not travelled during the day, no one had seen anything, a good thing since, in these times, it was difficult to know whom one could trust. He accepted another quick meal from his host, drank more water, thanked the man profusely, and hastened on his way. Jeremy did not wish to endanger anyone who might be connected to him, so he headed along the road from St. Davids and to the Mountain Road, which would take him, finally, back home.

When Jeremy was but a short distance from his farm, it was well after midnight. He had given the matter little thought in his haste to return home, but he really had no idea how much Willcocks and his men might know about him. However, he was about to find out in a most unpleasant manner.

As the trees parted ahead of him in the forest at the back of his east fields, he was treated to a shock that made his heart go cold. Flames shot into the still night air from the very place his home should be, and the sounds of shouting and laughing and gunfire rolled across the fields, these things simultaneously assaulting his eyes and ears. He crossed the field to a small thicket not far from the main homestead plot and then crept cautiously closer. He stayed to shadows wherever possible, but there was little cause for concern. The men celebrating the demise of all he held dear were so loud, so preoccupied, and so drunk that he would scarcely have been noticed had he stood in their midst and loudly announced himself.

Jeremy assumed that these were Willcocks' men, for he had told the U.S. captain at the fort that he was from near Beaverdams, and the traitor had been present at the time. He could feel his blood course heatedly through his body, his mind occupied by nothing but the desire for revenge. After all he had been through in the past week, he felt he certainly did not deserve this. Only a last minute breeze of wisdom caused him to refrain from walking into the drunken reverie and start shooting and clubbing every man in sight. His jaw twitched angrily as he swore quietly to himself that Willcocks must surely die to pay for this.

He surveyed the scene, the flames of his anger growing by the second. His small barn, which had obviously been torched later than the house, had tendrils of flame escaping from the cracks between the planks and licking up along the outside wall. As he watched, there came a light crashing sound as the door, made of lighter material and burning fiercely, fell away to meet the ground with a sound inaudible amidst the revelry, throwing off a shower of sparks. The flames, which consumed the door, roared higher now as fresh oxygen from the night air rushed to the fuel.

The barn exploded into a fresh frenzy of burning, also from the sudden intake of oxygen, and a chicken – only one – burst almost miraculously from the flames, like a phoenix, but this poor animal was not springing to life like that mythical bird. The feathers on the edges of its wings, already smouldering when it shot from the out building, now burst into full flame, and the chicken, not familiar with the physics of fires, ran about giving off a piteous screech as its fanning fed the flames even more. Its cries were cut off only when one of the drunken men staggered up with a pail and doused it. Before it could enjoy this relief from its torment, however, the same man picked it up and, grasped its neck with both hands, silencing the animal's suffering permanently. With an expression of disgust, he then tossed the hapless bird back into the conflagration from whence it had escaped.

"Hey!" someone shouted, although no one seemed to hear. "That could've been tomorrow's breakfast!"

Jeremy watched to see if any other of his animals would escape the flames. He did not have many, just a few chickens, some rabbits, a goat, and an old cow that no longer gave milk. But nothing else emerged from the building pyre.

Jeremy's house itself was fully involved when he arrived on this scene, and now it began to sag. With a great crash and an explosion of sparks high into the night sky, the roof dropped in amongst the walls, providing both more fuel and more air to the flames that raged inside. Then the walls surrendered to their weakened condition, the very substance of the wood no longer able to sustain the adhesion of its molecules, and the entire building imploded, more with an exaggerated sigh than a crash. The flames still reached for the sky, sending sparks from their fiery fingertips soaring into the night air to disappear until they, too, dissipated.

It was then that a man who was certainly the ringleader of these men staggered drunkenly into the almost daylight-like glow of the fire that had been Jeremy's house, and his jaw dropped although he had suspected it all along. So, it was that animal Williamson! Not satisfied to imprison him to inflict torture upon him, the man was now destroying his home! Was this man sent by Willcocks to repay him for escaping?

"Hey, Williamson!" someone yelled, breaking through the haze of Jeremy's hatred for this man. "Don't you think we should be moving along? Willcocks might figure out where we are, and you certainly don't want to run into him."

What had the man said? Jeremy was confused, not knowing of what had transpired the previous evening while he was locked in the barn. Had there been a falling out in the traitors' camp? That would certainly explain why Smith had decided to help him, but had it been only to take him to this madman?

As the questions swirled about in Jeremy's head, another voice, laughing drunkenly, added, "If he catches you, you'll surely hang this time, Dorian."

"Ah, let him try", Williamson replied, barely pushing out the words past an uncooperative tongue. "Then he proceeded to unbutton the fly of his trousers, and let loose a stream of urine, golden in the firelight, directly at the grave markers of Jeremy's family!

It was too much for Jeremy to take. All common sense deserted him, and he primed his gun and fired it in the general direction of the offensive man. He fully expected that he would pay dearly for his foolishness, but hoped he would be able to fell the devil before the others put an end to his now seemingly meaningless existence. The manoeuvre, however, bore unexpected fruit, denying Jeremy his revenge but likely saving his life as well.

"Mount up!" Williamson yelled at his now small group of men, who'd left Willcocks' compound while the Volunteers were hunting for Jeremy in the woods, meeting up with him near the Queenston. Apparently Willcocks had been wrong in assuming that the man would have no one to ride with him.

One of the other drunks now shouted out in terror. "It's Willcocks!"

Before Jeremy could consider his next move, the brigands jumped onto their horses with a level of agility entirely unexpected, considering their level of insobriety, and tore off into the night, whooping and shouting and firing off their guns. Jeremy stood at the edge of the bushes where he had been hiding, slack-jawed, not able to think clearly as the adrenalin ebbed and a semblance of sanity returned. How close he had just come to dying on this very spot!

Chapter Eighteen

Jeremy sat as close to the burning house as the heat would allow, still as the log he sat upon, looking deeply into the flames that consumed the few things that remained of his previous life. In the white inner flames of the blaze, he could see his late wife and imagine his stillborn child, their memory not softened by the desecration of the graves or the destruction of his property. As he stared longer, he could imagine seeing the sneering face of Dorian Williamson as he shot Robert, as he tied Jeremy to be dragged by the horse to captivity, as he tortured him in the barn to the laughter of his fellow thugs, and finally, as he drunkenly pissed on his family's graves in the light of the conflagration that was recently Jeremy's house and barn.

At the outset, he was too numb to feel anything but a great loss, as if every last thing in his life had finally been taken from him. But then he realized that this wasn't exactly true. Williamson may have taken all that he'd held dear, but he'd also left him with the one thing that burned ever stronger in his breast. What remained was something that was consuming him as the fire did his farm – an unabiding hatred of the man who had done this to him. And as that fire within him burned ever more darkly within him, it pushed out all other feelings, until there was but one thought left in him. Hunt down and kill Dorian Williamson!

Lost in concentration on the flames, both external and internal, Jeremy was oblivious to all other stimuli. That solitude was disturbed, however, by the sound of a voice, persistent and growing ever louder. "Jeremy! Jeremy! Do you hear me?"

Jeremy turned and looked over in the direction of the sound that invaded his dark thoughts, but he could see nothing, the persistent brightness of the fire's innermost flame blinding him to anything in the darkness outside of its corolla of light. But eventually, as his eyes became accustomed to the dark once again, a figure materialized nearby. It was Jim Dorsett from about a mile down the road, a neighbour all Jeremy's life.

"Jeremy?" Jim ventured tentatively, approaching carefully, hesitant about sneaking up on the obviously distraught young man and eyeing his musket as though it might swing in his direction at any moment. "Are you alright, boy?" The man, who was older than Jeremy's father had been when he died, had referred to him as "Boy" for as long as he could remember.

"Hello, Jim", Jeremy replied wearily. "I'm just fine, but thank you for asking." He stood up to shake the neighbour's hand as though every movement caused him pain. "There's nothing left, though. Nothing left at all." Jeremy's tone was as one utterly defeated, the energy brought on by his overwhelming hatred of Williamson now almost, though not quite, dissipated by the surprisingly welcome distraction.

"You can always build another house", Jim said, trying to lift the younger man's spirits. "You know all your neighbours around here will help."

"Is that right?" Jeremy snapped at his well-meaning neighbour. "Well where were they this night when my house was being destroyed?" he demanded.

"Now, Jeremy, you know that's hardly fair", Jim chided. "These folks are scared these days at the best of times, with men riding all over, and we not knowing their hearts. You know these men would have killed all your neighbours if they had showed up. I know you have anger in your heart at these men that did this, but that's no reason to think badly of your neighbours."

"Yes, sir, I know", replied Jeremy somewhat wistfully, appropriately chastised for his remarks. The old man was right. Williamson and his men might well have burned down all of their farms as well for their trouble. He let out a long slow sigh. "And you know I appreciate the offer. But I'm not sure at the moment that I even want to rebuild."

He looked away from his neighbour and down the road in the direction the arsonists had taken. "But I don't intend to make any decisions one way or another right now. I have something I need to do." He turned back to face the old man, but still seemed to gaze right past and through Jim. "If I come back from that, I'll consider it. Thanks all the same."

Jim studied Jeremy in silence for a moment, fearing for his young neighbour's state of mind. "Well, for now you just come back to my place", he offered firmly. "Dorothy will be glad to see you. It's been awhile since you've been to our house."

"Once again, thank you, but no, sir", Jeremy answered. "It's a very tempting offer, but I think I'm just going to sleep here beside the fire for awhile. When I wake up, I have to leave. I've a man to find. But, say hello to Dorothy for me and tell her I'll come and say hello when I get back."

Jim could read his intentions as if they were printed on his face. "Now, you don't need to go after those fellows", he advised. "If they're who I think they were, they're vicious men. No sense of honour whatsoever." His face showed genuine concern. "They'll kill you, boy, without a second thought."

Jeremy's jaw quivered and his neck muscles became tight as cords. "I already know who they are, Jim. And I already know about their lack of honour." His face hardened and the flames reflected in his eyes seemed almost to issue straight from the depths of his soul. "But they'll not kill me if I kill them first."

"All of them?" Jim asked, incredulous, not mention more than a little frightened by the younger man's intensity.

"I only want the one", Jeremy said, his voice cold as he stared into the embers of the burning remains of his house once more. "I want the leader, that's all." Then he looked suddenly up at Jim once more, and said with a razor edge to his voice, "But if the others get in my way, then they'll have to die too."

Jim did not know what to say to the stranger before him. The young man he had known as Jeremy seemed to have been replaced by this seething ball of hatred, and the realization frightened him. "I know there'll be no talking you out of it", he said, his voice a husky whisper. "But if you ever become Jeremy van Hijser again, stop by at the house, son." With that, the old farmer sadly turned and vanished back into the dark of the night, leaving Jeremy once again alone to deal privately with his anger and his hatred.

The sun had just barely broken the horizon in the morning, but Jeremy was already up and about. With nothing around for him to eat, he dusted himself off and decked himself out with the weapons that had served him so well in the past, for both hunting and fighting. He threw a last wistful glance at his former home, which was now nothing but a huge, smouldering collection of embers, here and there interspersed with the odd unburned log end. He sighed heavily, swallowed hard, and set off to find the man he owed so much revenge.

From a hill atop the escarpment, from where he could see most of this end of Niagara, he watched carefully for anything that betrayed signs of either Williamson, whom he was hunting, or Willcocks, who was hunting him. Seeing no sign of either, he headed off in a general westerly direction, calculating that, by what he had heard the previous night, it was no safer for Williamson and his men to go east than it was for him.

For several days, Jeremy travelled the central part of the Peninsula, questioning everyone he met along the way. Some had seen men fitting the description of Williamson and his men, but did not know where they had gone, some had seen no sign of them, and still others seemed guarded in their replies, as if afraid that those men would come back to exact revenge if they should speak to him. There were even a few who were evasive in their replies, leading Jeremy to believe that these people might be Volunteers themselves, gone home to tend to farm matters before once more striking out in the name of their brand of justice.

Often Jeremy found himself hiding by the roadside as Willcocks and his men tore by on their way to torment some poor farmer who did not see his right to free speech his way. Sometimes he evaded American soldiers, on an advance patrol and watching carefully for ambush from one of the groups of British raiders such as the Bloody Boys. But he seemed to make little headway in finding his nemesis.

Three days along on his quest, Jeremy found that, in the course of his search, he'd been shadowing the road that ran along the base of the escarpment. He was approaching Elizabeth Rhodes' home, and her image flooded his mind with pleasant memories, nearly crowding out thoughts of revenge against Williamson. The more he thought of her, the better he could see the lovely eyes from under the farmer's hat, twinkling in amusement at his confusion.

By the time he stepped from the trees onto her side yard, his purpose in being on this road had been driven to the back of his consciousness. Elizabeth made his heart, and his step, feel much lighter, and he had not yet even seen her.

He walked purposefully to the front door of the cabin and knocked. There was no reply, so he tried once again, this time with more authority. Still there was no reply. Thinking she must be working in her vegetable gardens at the rear of the house, he went around back, but there was no sign of her there, either. Could she have gone to a neighbour's house, he thought to himself? But he thought that unlikely, for Elizabeth had said that she didn't feel particularly welcome among her neighbours, mostly due to her unusual independence.

Jeremy had been keeping his voice low to this point, hoping in some way to surprise her. Now, seeing that there was yet no reply, he had decided to call out her name, in case she was in the woods nearby collecting firewood. However, just as he was about to do so, he thought he heard a sound and stood stock-still, waiting to hear it once more. But he could hear nothing out of the ordinary, nothing but the sounds of birds and the breeze rustling the leaves overhead.

Shaking his head, he decided that it must have been a figment of his imagination, wishful thinking brought on by the hope she would be home. In the shadow of the Mountain, sounds were amplified, distorted and echoed, often making it difficult to identify everyday sounds. So, with a shrug, he turned to leave, when he heard something again, only this time it was much closer, and there could be no mistaking its nature or content.

A woman's voice, and there was no doubt in Jeremy's mind that this was Elizabeth's voice, seemed to be drawing nearer and cried out angrily from the trees. "Get away from me, you filthy pigs!" Jeremy could make out these words, but not the sounds that followed it.

Then he heard that second sound again. Another voice, and this no doubt the reason for the woman's distress. "Get back here, wench!" The source of this voice was definitely male, and was quickly joined by another, accompanied by breathless laughter. "Can't you hold on to your woman?" it mocked.

The sound came closer yet, and Jeremy hid at the corner of the Elizabeth's house, priming his pan for the load of scattershot in his gun. It had been loaded for bird, for he was planning to hunt for his supper before deciding to come here. It really was not ideal, for the men would probably be close behind, if not by then holding onto Elizabeth, and he would be able to shoot this load only if he could separate them. It would not do at all for him to shoot the lady.

As they crashed through the brush into Elizabeth's yard, she slipped, falling heavily into the yard. The two men who were chasing her pounced with great glee, for obviously she had demonstrated some skill in eluding them. Now they had caught her at last and they were certain that the lady was now quite helpless.

Jeremy moved to step from cover, but Elizabeth unexpectedly lashed out with her left foot, catching one of the men hard in the groin. As often seems the case in such a situation, Jeremy nearly groaned aloud, sharing universally in the man's pain as he watched him fall to ground, holding onto his injured parts and shouting obscenities at the world. The other pursuer stopped in his tracks, apparently also affected by the other's discomfort.

Elizabeth took advantage of the momentary break to roll over and jump to her feet, running toward the well with all the speed her exhausted and frightened body could muster. Thus the chase had begun anew, one man tearing off after her, his injured partner staggering in the full extent of pursuit he could manage while still breathless from his injury and holding onto his suffering parts.

Jeremy could not help but wonder what the injured pursuer thought he could accomplish should he catch up to his quarry with the necessary equipment so damaged, but it was soon obvious that he now sought naught but revenge. It was more than his scrotum that had suffered at this woman's hands, or feet in this case. His pride had also been greatly damaged with that one devastating kick.

Putting the well between her and her pursuers, Elizabeth reached across it and hurriedly pulled across the bucket that hung suspended there. She reached in, a mild look of satisfaction upon her face, but it quickly turned to puzzlement, then to fear.

"Looking for this, Dearie?" the uninjured man asked, his voice triumphant as he held out a pistol for her to see, grinning and showing her his yellow and black teeth, those that remained. Obviously Elizabeth had been hiding her pistol in the well, and somehow this animal had discovered it.

Jeremy knew this was his best opportunity to act, for Elizabeth's attackers would momentarily move in opposite directions around the well to capture her. Stepping out from the shelter of the house, he pulled the trigger, sending a cluster of tiny lead balls airborne. The pellets covered the ground between him and his targets in the bat of an eyelash, but they struck only the man with the pistol, felling him in a bloody mass. The other man began to reach for a weapon, but Jeremy never had the chance to see it.

Elizabeth leaped around from her side of the well as she saw the standing man fumble in his belt, and snatched her pistol from the wounded man's hand. Without aiming, she pulled the trigger. There was a loud report, and her target's eyes widened in surprise. The pistol ball had lodged deep in his chest and the blood from the damaged tissue quickly soaked his shirt. He looked down, grasping the injured area with both hands, the ache in his groin now forgotten. Then, with a spasm that shook his entire body, he slumped to the ground.

The man that Jeremy had shot lay on the ground, soaked in blood from the many balls of shot that had violated his body. He was not yet dead, and he looked up at the pair with a plea for assistance written upon his face.

Jeremy turned to Elizabeth. "What shall we do with this one?" he asked her, noticing she was almost finished reloading her pistol.

With a calm Jeremy would not have expected of anyone in this position, much less a beautiful woman, Elizabeth pointed the weapon at the injured man. "Send him to Hell", she answered, her voice seemingly devoid of emotion in spite of the anger she must have been harbouring inside. With that simple phrase, she squeezed the trigger and sent the pistol ball into the man's skull, smashing away the front of it, just above the brow ridge.

Jeremy said nothing. He just stood and stared in shock of what had just occurred, looking first at Elizabeth and then the executed man. He looked back at Elizabeth and watched as she calmly reloaded her pistol once again and placed it back into the well bucket. That chore completed, she turned to him, tears now welling up in her eyes.

Jeremy stepped forward and took her awkwardly into his arms. He had not held a woman since Sarah's death, and the feeling no longer seemed natural to him. However, Elizabeth seemed to surrender quite naturally to his offer of solace, moving into his arms and burying her face in his chest. Then she finally allowed herself to give in to the stresses that tore at her mind, letting the tears develop into great wracking sobs and a flow of tears that threatened to soak Jeremy's shirt as he held her, still uncertain, still not knowing what to say. So he said nothing and just allowed her to delve into the emotions of fear, anger and horror that caught up to her now that it was, at least physically, over.

After several minutes, Jeremy ever so gently pushed Elizabeth away, but for only the few inches that he needed to see her face. "I think that we should go inside, away from this", he suggested softly but firmly, guiding her from the site of the carnage. Elizabeth offered him no resistance, so he led her inside her house, still clinging tightly to him. He eased her back onto her bed and covered her with the blanket that lay there. She did not wish to release him, though, even when she agreed that he should set a kettle to boil for tea, and he had to finally pry her hands loose. She turned over on her side, face turned away from him, and entered into a new round of sobbing.

Jeremy knew there was nothing for it but to let her cry it out, so he set about drawing water and stoking the fireplace to boil the kettle. When he finally had the water roiling, he went over to her bed and asked her softly how she preferred her tea. There was no reply from Elizabeth. The fatigue brought on by events had finally overtaken the remainder of her resolve to fight it, so Jeremy quietly pulled up a chair and sat beside her bed, watching her sleep.

After a time, Jeremy went out to the tiny shed in the back and found himself a shovel. To work off his own stresses, which threatened to overtake him as well, he set about finding himself ways to keep busy. Laboriously dragging the bodies of Elizabeth's attackers well into the woods and away from Elizabeth's house, he placed their bodies into a crevice and proceeded to fill it, first with rocks and then dirt to fill in the last few inches of the depression. That done, Jeremy dragged himself back to the house, exhausted, and sat himself in the chair beside Elizabeth's bed once more, quietly holding her hand. Soon, he too was sound asleep.

They awoke sometime later, neither knew how long, but it was getting dark outside the small log cabin. Elizabeth was the first to awaken, at first disoriented, and then remembering as the day's events came flooding back. She nearly began to cry again, but then she noticed Jeremy asleep in the chair beside her, covered in dirt, his hand hanging roughly where hers had been. In spite of all that had occurred, she found that she had to smile. A true gentleman had come to her rescue, it seemed.

She took his hand and squeezed it, in an unspoken act of intimacy, and the light pressure awakened Jeremy as well. He looked about in confusion and then finally settled his gaze on Elizabeth, a smile coming to his lips the instant he realized where he was. He had been thinking about this woman since the day he had left here and finally he was back with her. Granted, the circumstances were hardly ideal, and he would gladly have traded her ordeal away even if it meant he would not be here now. But that was an impossible wish, and he selfishly contented himself with being here now, holding her hand.

Elizabeth stretched languidly and then rolled from the bed on the other side. "It seems to be very late, Mr. van Hijser", she said with strange formality. "I think you must be hungry by now. I know that I am." And she set about with the busy work of preparing supper, apparently not wishing to discuss the day's events, which didn't disappoint Jeremy in the least. He would not have known how to deal with it himself.

They ate in complete silence, neither quite sure what to say to the other. They had shared a most intimate moment that day in the killing of those men, and there were not enough words to express what it meant to either of them, either before or after the event. They stole furtive glances at each other while they slowly downed their food, smiling shyly when caught, but still no words passed between them.

With supper done, they sat for a while before the fire, still speaking little but for the occasional small talk. The crackle of the of the wood as it succumbed to the flames and the impressions of dancing given by the ignited wood gases as they ebbed and flowed soon made them both drowsy. In time, they reluctantly decided it was time to retire, she to her bed, he to a blanket on the hand hooked rug in front of the now-cooling fireplace.

It was now that the only words exchanged that night were spoken. "Goodnight", whispered Elizabeth. "Goodnight", the soft reply.

Chapter Nineteen

Jeremy woke up in the morning as the first rays of light filtered through the oilpaper that served as a windowpane on that side of the cabin. As he stretched and began to roll over, he was surprised by an almost-forgotten sensation – he was no longer alone here before the fireplace. It was not an objectionable sensation by any means, and he feared to move any more lest it was all in his mind and the feeling would vanish with further investigation.

Then Elizabeth's voice came to him softly from just behind his head, a singing lilt wishing him good morning, and he turned ever so slowly to find himself face to face with the woman he had dreamt about for weeks. Even in the morning light, face unscrubbed, she was as beautiful a woman as he could remember having seen, and he felt himself blush at the thoughts crossing his mind.

"I found I couldn't sleep, jumping at every sound and fearing that those men had friends that may have found me, so I came and joined you so I wouldn't be alone", Elizabeth said still softly, and Jeremy could almost swear that she was blushing, although it was difficult to determine in the morning's early light.

"It was quite nice, waking up to company", Jeremy replied, his mouth dry and not able to think of anything more poetic. "Especially to company as charming as you."

Elizabeth threw back the blanket and climbed to her feet, almost losing her balance in the process. Jeremy saw that she was wearing what must have been her late husband's woollen underwear, the shapeless garment covering her from throat to ankles, and yet

Jeremy could feel his desire rising as though she were wearing nothing. To avoid embarrassment, he rolled quickly over to face the fire, pretending to allow Elizabeth her modesty when, in fact, he was hoping to protect his own modesty from the body part that would betray him.

When he finally did get up, Elizabeth had already dressed in the masculine farmer's clothes that she used to disguise herself, and was preparing porridge on the table. She busied herself with her task, exchanging small talk with Jeremy so as to avoid any uncomfortable discussion of feelings that might lead to repudiation of her, for she too had noticed a rising desire. Such thoughts were simply not acceptable for a respected widow, especially since she feared that Jeremy might reject such forwardness. Still, she found it difficult not to watch him in secret as he put his shirt back on.

They ate their porridge cheerfully discussing the possible weather for the day, the likelihood that the war might end soon and the details of the chores to be done that day. Not a word passed between them of hopes and fears, their desires or the events of the previous day. Elizabeth had allowed herself to display her vulnerability, something with which she was not entirely comfortable in light of the reputation she had developed locally as a fiercely independent woman who needed no man. Especially now, when she felt herself softening toward this man who had once again appeared from nowhere, and at just the right moment at that.

When the breakfast was done, they set about performing the chores that life in the country demanded of all at the start of a new day. In addition to these mundane tasks, Elizabeth had asked Jeremy to repair the cold cellar, since the wall was collapsing from continuous frost heaving, and he seemed more than anxious to throw his back into some heavy work.

Jeremy found he could not simply force the walls back into place from the inside, so he decided the only thing to do was to dig along the spot where the bulging occurred. It took him until mid-afternoon to finish, resetting the stone that made up the wall and then backfilling the hole. By the time he was finished, he was covered in sweaty dirt from head to toe.

Elizabeth waited for him at the door, a stern expression on her face as she surveyed his appearance. "Oh, no. You're not coming into my house like that", she admonished. "Take off those filthy clothes and hand them to me. You can wash up over by the well while I wash these things out. Here. Wear these until yours have dried", she ordered, throwing him what he assumed must have been some of her late husband's clothes.

They made their way to the backyard where Elizabeth drew him a pail of water to wash in and handed him a bar of strong soap she had made herself. Then she drew out more water and partially filled the washtub, adding water from the pot she had heated inside. While she washed, she surreptitiously watched Jeremy.

He had removed his undershirt now and was washing up naked from the waist. His muscles, toned from the years of farming and hunting, rippled softly as he washed himself, shuddering occasionally as a light breeze chilled his glistening wet torso. And, as he washed, he stole glances at Elizabeth.

Elizabeth's own clothing was, by this time, wet from her chore, almost to the waist. Soaking wet, the woollens no longer completely hid the form of her body, and Jeremy could see that she was quite shapely. Her round breasts pushed against the wet fabric and as the cool breeze wafted across her, her nipples hardened visibly through the layers. And if she noticed the effect at all, there was no sign of it.

Jeremy hurriedly finished washing, hoping Elizabeth would not notice his body's reaction to her form, and approached her, his still-wet skin emphasizing his physique. "Do you perhaps have towel?" he asked, the closer proximity arousing him still further.

Elizabeth, for her part, sucked in her breath and looked away, not wishing to betray her shameful lust for this man she barely knew. In the process, her hard-nippled breasts pushed still tighter against the wet fabric. "I'm afraid I don't", she said weakly. "But you look a bit chilled. Come on inside before you catch your death."

"You too look like you could use some drier clothing", Jeremy replied, trying hard not to get caught looking at her, sure that his lust would be obvious.

Jeremy opened up the door for Elizabeth and the two walked inside. "Come sit by the fire while I stoke it", Elizabeth offered. "We can both take the chill off."

A Question of Loyalty

They sat down on the rug that Jeremy had used as a bed the previous night and huddled before the embers of the fire. While it surely could not have been that cold on a June day, both shivered from an excitement neither wished to display or even acknowledge. Once again, small talk filled the silent void.

Jeremy was telling Elizabeth about the DeCou house, when he noticed her staring at his chest. Excitement coursed through him like a bolt of lightning, excitement that would not subside despite his best efforts. Finally, not able to fight it any longer, Jeremy put his fingers gently under Elizabeth's face and pushed it up so that they were looking into each other's eyes. They stared in this manner for only a moment, and then Elizabeth did the unexpected. She tilted her head slightly and kissed him on the lips.

This was all the urging Jeremy needed. He pulled her slowly to the floor, kissing her harder and receiving the same in return. Though she gasped that they surely mustn't, she'd completely given in to the urges herself and they began to pull desperately at each other's clothing, cursing the buttons of both.

Elizabeth stopped to take in his body, admiring the muscles, and gasping at Jeremy's obviously throbbing desire that she knew was for her. She ran her hands gently across his chest and down his stomach and stopped. Then she ran a hand up Jeremy's thigh until she held him firmly in her hand, eliciting a sharp intake of breath from Jeremy.

Now, with renewed fervour, Jeremy stripped the undershirt from her body. With a bit of help from Elizabeth she lifted herself toward him, he pulled off the trousers and woollen undergarments from her legs. In between the now fierce and hungry kisses, he caught glimpses of her own naked form. He revelled in the sight of her naked breasts, the nipples still erect, but now from desire instead of cold. Her hips, whose actual shape he saw for the first time, came into view, and his eyes travelled in toward the place where her legs met, the place where their bodies would finally be joined together. His mouth moved from her lips down to her nipples and sucked hungrily as his hand moved softly up her thigh, finding the spot that made her let out a soft moan.

Elizabeth could scarcely believe the feelings that coursed through her. The lovemaking she had experienced during the short time of her marriage had been nothing like this. She thought the passion - the feverish passion - and the unbelievable sensations would drive her mad, and she desperately wanted Jeremy inside her.

Jeremy responded to Elizabeth's encouragement, moving over her and began slowly to enter her. She arced her hips up to meet him and both moaned, almost in unison, as he now plunged into her the rest of the way. She enveloped him warmly, wetly, tightly, and he began to move, slowly at first and then, at her urging, harder and harder. Their bodies joined in a feverish sweat, and Elizabeth kissed and nipped at whatever part of Jeremy's body came within reach of her mouth. Faster and faster, harder and harder, he drove into her, with her hips answering each movement.

And then Jeremy shuddered as he finished, bringing on a sensation unlike any Elizabeth had before experienced. As Jeremy finished, she felt a spasm build, deep within her, growing and growing until it exploded with power that made her whimper in delight. Jeremy, although spent, continued to move inside her, moving slower and slower, and she clamped her legs together, trying to hold him, wanting him never to leave or the feeling to stop. As one, they rolled onto their sides, still together, and lay there in each other's arms, not wanting to let go. In fairly little time, both were asleep, holding each other, fearing that the first good thing in their lives in a long time might end.

Shortly before midnight, Jeremy awoke, and lay there, studying Elizabeth's face while she slept. Shortly, she too awoke, and the two talked in hushed tones, like lifelong lovers, as if they had known each other forever.

"How long do you think we slept?" Jeremy asked, not really caring.

"All through the evening, at least", Elizabeth answered. She became suddenly silent, a troubled expression taking over her countenance.

Jeremy could sense the change, better than see, the change in her mood. "Is something the matter?" he asked. "You're not thinking about those men again are you? I promise they'll not bother you again."

"No", Elizabeth sighed. "I just feel so wanton, carrying on like this with a man I barely know. I should hope my neighbours don't find out about this." She moved slightly away from him, but he would not let her go so easily.

"Are you sorry that we've done this?" he asked, feeling the whisper of an impending loss. He certainly hoped that this day's sexual episode wasn't about to lose him the only good thing in his recent life.

"Yes, I mean…no", she sputtered. "I mean, I don't know. What do we now? You can't stay here, for it's but a matter of time before someone should notice, and I would never be able to show my face in church again." She continued on, more as an exercise to sort it out in her own mind than as an explanation for him. "It's not that I'm a terribly religious person. But the church and those people are my only contact with the outside world. They're my family in a way, my community."

Jeremy lay back, still for the moment, wondering how he could best answer these concerns. He could suggest that he would become her community and her family, but he fully realized how egotistical such a suggestion would sound. It would never be enough, nor should it be. And it certainly would not be sufficient for him, either, not in the long run. Family is one thing, but to hide forever from your neighbours with only one person in his life would not be practical. Everyone needs more than that.

"Well, what do you suggest?" he asked at last, not wishing to offer the only answer that came to mind.

"Maybe you should leave in the morning", she answered sadly, feeling a tear on her cheek.

Jeremy felt lost, but he knew it was probably the only answer. "Very well. But, before I go, answer just one question for me."

"And what is that?" Elizabeth murmured warily.

"Before I go, would you kindly consent to be my wife?" The question, spoken aloud, surprised him as much as it did her. But he was not about to retract his offer. He needed this woman more than he had needed anyone or anything in quite some time. He found that he needed her to balance his life and the darkness that otherwise occupied it.

Elizabeth lay quiet in the dark, simultaneously shocked and happy. "But we hardly know one another", she argued tentatively.

Jeremy lifted the blanket they shared, looked underneath, and laughed softly. "I dare believe that we shall never know each other better than we do this night, Mrs. Rhodes."

Elizabeth giggled back, in spite of herself. As inappropriate as the comment might be, the thought of marrying Jeremy brought a warm glow to her heart. It would be good to share her bed with him every night, to be able to be a woman again and not need to hide behind men's clothing, maybe even to admit she didn't wish to be as independent as she told everyone.

"In that case, Mr. van Hijser", she replied, with mock formality. "I find I must accept your kind proposal."

With that, the two lovers fell into each other's arms with hearts feeling as if they might explode with the joy of the moment. They held each other tightly, murmuring endearments and making plans for the future for hours.

"I suppose that we should get some more sleep before the dawn breaks", Jeremy said finally. "But I'm wide awake now. I fear I won't be able to sleep again."

"Oh, I don't know", purred Elizabeth, her right hand tracing the muscles on Jeremy's chest, that motion being all the stimulus he needed.

"Aren't you afraid that you'll feel wanton once more?" Jeremy asked the question half joking, and more than half hoping he was not killing the mood.

"I may", Elizabeth replied thoughtfully. "But there's no use in closing the barn door now. The horse is out, and can never be put back."

"And what if this isn't enough to put us to sleep for the balance of the night?" Jeremy asked archly, his fingers gently kneading her nipple.

Elizabeth feigned thoughtfulness, fighting the desire that threatened to overtake her, and then a grin grew on her face. "Then, sir, I'm afraid that, like it or not, we shall have to do it again. After all", she added. "You'll be gone for a week, so we'll need to make the most of this one night."

It was late morning before Jeremy found himself back on the road and he walked quickly along, a spring in his step, certainly much lighter than it was before he arrived. It had been decided, mostly by Elizabeth, that she would make the arrangements with her church for the Saturday two weeks away. He had offered his assistance, but she feared that his presence would create too many uncomfortable questions, and shooed him out of the door. He left under protest, but agreed to use some of the time to tie up loose ends back home. He told her he would be back on Friday, so that he could find out from her what the arrangements were to be, and with which neighbour she had determined he would be staying with the night before the day of the nuptials.

The thought of going back to what remained of his home gradually brought on a revival of the dark thoughts that had brought him here. Alone with himself, the anger and hatred that he had vanquished from his breast in the euphoria of his rediscovery of Elizabeth slowly began to clamp down on his heart once more. There was no avoiding the reality that he was going home to a place where there was no longer a home, and that Williamson was responsible for that. And the very recollection of the man's name unavoidably migrated Jeremy's thoughts to the treatment he had received at the bastard's hands.

He was not sure exactly what it was that he would wrap up when he got back to the old farmstead. It was worth little enough to begin with and now, without a barn or cabin, was practically worthless. He was truly beginning to regret his decision to head in this direction. Better he had gone on to the Forty, or even Stoney Creek to continue his search for that devil Williamson than to put himself through the pain of once more confronting his emotions at home.

Jeremy decided that was exactly what he would do. There was nothing at what once was his old home, so he would travel down to the mouth of the Twenty Mile Creek and then on to the settlement at the Forty along the lake road. He would try once again to find the man whose very image tortured his soul and perhaps, in the bargain, give himself a wedding present in the form of a freed mind. That question finally decided in his mind, he set off across fields and used whatever paths through woods that he could find to pick up on his quest once again.

Chapter Twenty

With Jeremy gone and but a lightness in her heart, Elizabeth prepared herself to speak to her pastor about the impending wedding, but two weeks away. She hoped only that she could keep from blushing, with the salacious memories of last night so fresh in her mind. And, once the pastor was dealt with, she'd need to keep herself composed while she went to speak to the neighbours and invite them all to the event.

She bathed slowly, the water caressing her skin like Jeremy's fingertips had just this morning, and providing her with sensations that water and soap never had before. It took all of her resolve, and a cooling bath, to get out of the old steel tub and get dressed, donning petticoats and a dress for the visit to the church, and feeling like she had been reborn as a woman once more. Hopefully, the days of men's clothing would soon be a vague memory, and she would be able to dress like this more often.

At the small church, Elizabeth found it would not be a simple as the plans she and Jeremy had made. When she tried to make the necessary arrangements, both the pastor and his wife congratulated her heartily on their decision, but protested the timing.

"It takes time to get a wedding set", the pastor admonished. "People must be notified and the bans must be published and read to the congregation and, well, you know how it works. You've gone to this church long enough to know better."

Elizabeth thought she might burst into tears at these words. She had not really given the process much thought, overcome by the romantic fervour behind the errand. "Yes, pastor", she acquiesced glumly, her voice barely above a whisper.

The pastor's wife now pushed forward and stepped in to face her husband down, hands on her hips. "Come, Henry. These times are anything like what they should be", she scolded, "and there's no reason you can't be a little flexible about this. Help the poor girl out. By the time we follow these stupid rules of yours, her beau could end up being shot." Her hand clasped her mouth, as she realized the insensitivity of the latter comment to someone that they all knew had already lost a husband to the war. "I – I didn't mean it like that", she stammered lamely.

The pastor ignored the last comment. "These aren't my rules", he snapped. "These are the rules of this church, and there's nothing to say there can be flexibility for a war or any other reason."

"Is there anything that says there can't be?" his wife asked softly, "like compassion?"

The pastor looked at his wife, and then he looked over at Elizabeth, who seemed about to cry, and he found that he could not keep up the righteous anger. "Very well", he whispered. "But you'd better do some extra praying for my soul, not to mention my job."

Elizabeth fairly launched herself at the pastor and gave him a loud kiss on the cheek, startling both the man and his wife, who did not expect such an open display of emotion. Before they could react, however, Elizabeth had thanked them heartily and vanished through the door.

Each of the neighbours that she visited to bring them the glad tidings and an invitation to the happy event similarly wished her well, although some harboured thoughts similar to those of the pastor's wife. Such was life in rural Upper Canada, for there was precious little news to be had here. These people did not often hear even word of the war, nor would many of them have cared, but for the occasional travesty performed by such as Willcocks and his gang of cutthroats. The British and their Loyalist friends had mainly fought the conflict from the start. Most Niagarans gave little thought to what government played with their lives. They farmed their land and raised their children, leaving the rest to those in power who had the time and energy to devote to such nonsense.

It was true that a few more had taken the notion to fight against the Americans once the raids by those such as Willcocks began, for they reduced the war to a personal matter. But even in those cases, many answered the clarion call for militia for only a short time, often for but a single battle. When that battle was lost or the weather turned bad, or it was time to sow or harvest the crops, they merely left the field of battle to return to their fields of corn at home, their martial ardour dissipated.

But goings-on in the community were an entirely different matter. Every member of this parish, when they had a moment's time felt it was their God-given duty to keep watch over their neighbours and safeguard their souls. The Bible told them, did it not, that each man was his brother's keeper, and that meant straightening out the errant ways of those in their community, even if not to their face. This heavy responsibility was taken very seriously here as in most other rural God-fearing communities around the world, and it would be most sinful not to point out people's shortcomings to the world.

Elizabeth had known that there would be talk but, not having any details, it would die out soon enough. It would be only a matter of time before some other poor soul's more obvious transgression would draw their attention away, and nothing would dull people's barbs so well as a church wedding.

Now, as she walked up the laneway to the Schmidt homestead, she found it strangely quiet. Absent were the usual sounds of the working farm. No animal calls, no hammering, no ring of the axe - nothing. This strangeness should have made her wary, but she was far too happy to give it serious consideration. She stepped up onto the porch of the house and knocked loudly, knowing that both residents were old and hard of hearing and their children dead, one of war, but most of the various diseases that occasionally spread throughout the region.

There was no answer to the knock, so she walked around to the back of the house. This was a reasonable reaction, since this was the middle of the afternoon and the couple might well be working in the field at this time of day. Seeing no one, she looked about for some sign of life and that was when she saw movement in the barn. She set off toward it, assuming she had found the Schmidts.

Just feet from the door, she called out to announce herself and the reason she was here. But the person who came to the door was neither Mr. nor Mrs. Schmidt.

The man who stood leering at her in the doorway was filthy, and flashed her a grin that displayed very few healthy teeth. He reminded her of one of the men who had accosted her at her own home. "So you're getting married, are ye now?" he asked in a course voice.

"Where are the Schmidts?" Elizabeth demanded. She could feel fear rising in her, but was loath to show it to this animal.

"Who?" the man asked, looking genuinely confused. Then, suddenly, "Oh, you mean the folks that used to live here?"

Elizabeth swallowed her heart, which was rapidly rising to her throat. "What do you mean 'used to'?" she demanded. "Where is that lovely old couple? What have you done with them, you animal?"

"Me?" the man asked with mock innocence. "I didn't do anything with them ma'am. It was them", he said pointing over his shoulder with his thumb.

At that moment, the door opened the rest of the way, revealing two more men, both grinning lasciviously at her. She could almost have sworn that one was drooling!

"Or maybe it was one of them", the first man suggested, indicating either front corner of the barn, from which had stepped half a dozen more men. They all looked at her with interest, although not all as warmly as the initial three.

One of the men, obviously the leader of this group, pushed the two men with him out of the way. "Who did you say you were marrying?" he asked with genuine curiosity.

Elizabeth fought the instinct to turn on her heels and run. There would be no chance of escaping all these men on foot anyways, at least not in this dress. What a time she had picked to become feminine, the thought immediately seeming ludicrous, even to her.

"I'm marrying Jeremy van Hijser two weeks, if you must know", she pronounced defiantly. "And if you harm me in any way you'll need to deal with him."

"And would that be the same Jeremy van Hijser that once lived in Beaverdams?" the man asked. It was evident by his tone that he had no doubt what the answer would be. He was obviously toying with her.

"What do you know of him?" Elizabeth responded, confused. How would this ruffian know of her Jeremy? "What do you mean he used to live there?"

The man stepped a little closer and looked her over, admiring her femininity. "You sure demand a lot of answers", he growled. "And not a please or thank you from you." He put his hand to his chin and turned away. "But, if you must know, I heard that his farm was burned down over a week ago." Then, with a wicked smile, he added, "And it seems those that did it also did rude things to his late wife's grave."

"How would you know of…?" Elizabeth started, and then the horrible truth slowly crept into her mind, sending panic through to her very soul. "You…are you…would you be Dorian Williamson?" she asked, praying the answer would be no.

"At your service, Ma'am", Williamson replied, turning back around and doffing his grimy hat in her direction. "Though now you have me wondering how you would know that. Or how he'd know that himself."

"He was there, you animal!" spat Elizabeth, momentarily forgetting her fear at the thought of the outrages performed by this creature.

Williamson thought about that explanation for a few seconds. Then he laughed at the image of Jeremy hiding in the dark, watching him dance around the fire and piss on the grave. Shaking it off, a leer formed and he stepped toward her menacingly as he murmured, "Now, let's see what we can do to make the most of his wedding day, shall we?"

Williamson closed in on the trembling woman and put his hand under her chin, wiggling his fingers lightly. Then, with an utter lack of finesse, the offending digits dropped down and began to tug on the collar, the intent originally having been to rip open the front of the dress in one quick motion. But the collar held, and Williamson was obviously frustrated by the way he must look in front of his men.

"It's clear that your dress is well made", he muttered, anger and embarrassment coming together in a dangerous brew. "So why don't you take it off for me?" He pulled his knife from his belt and played with it in an intimidating manner.

"Keep your hands off me, you pig!" Elizabeth commanded, fairly spitting the words. "You aren't even man enough to open the dress. What makes you think I'd have anything to do with you? And, do you think that you can frighten this poor helpless woman with your knife?" Her voice became increasingly mocking in tone as she continued. "Is that what it takes for an animal such as you to have your way with a lady?"

She saw that her challenge was having the effect she had desired, and Williamson put the knife back into his belt. What she little expected, however, was the hand that lashed out suddenly. Her head exploded in pain and she nearly blacked out, catching herself just as her knees began to give out.

"Don't you ever talk to me like that again!" Williamson bellowed, his rage nearly out of control. "No woman speaks to me in that manner!" His eyes flashed darkly with the fury that she had stoked within him.

Elizabeth wondered if baiting him had been a good idea after all. But she could not submit. Her pride would not allow her to be used by this creature that had caused so much pain – emotional and physical – to Jeremy, who had already suffered so much at his hands. She drew herself up, stared him in the eyes...and slapped him back, not nearly to the physical effect he had, but enough to wound his pride before his men even further. She continued to stare him down, watching his eyes to attempt to determine what his next move would be.

With a roar, the powerful man lunged toward her, fully intending to throw her to the ground, using his bulk to subdue her. At the last possible moment, Elizabeth sidestepped, reached to his belt, and pulled the pistol from its place in his belt. Williamson, unable to immediately stop himself, continued past far enough for Elizabeth to spin around before he could recover. When he turned to face her, he heard a click as the hammer was drawn, and he found himself staring into the business end of his own firearm.

Still blustering, although he did so now with a tremor of fear in his voice, he challenged Elizabeth. "And just what do you intend to do with that?" he asked, feigning sarcasm, trying to keep his composure.

"Move but an inch, and you'll find out what I intend, sir", she answered, adding, "And I use the term 'sir' very loosely."

Williamson stood stock-still. It was obvious she knew how to use the weapon, and he did not know how to respond next. Suddenly, a grin broke out on his face, first just a hint and then growing wider as he seemed to look right past her. But Elizabeth was not about to fall for that ruse. She knew that, if she turned to look, Williamson would overpower her, so she listened carefully instead for the telltale sounds of someone attempting to creep up behind her.

"If I so much as hear a blade of grass move behind me in the breeze, this bastard's head will be found at the end of the laneway!" she barked at Williamson's men, not at all sure they would not be happy to see it happen. Men such as these rarely were bound by any great loyalties to each other.

Williamson was still grinning, though, and it was all she could do to keep from turning around. She decided she would need to get the leader between her and his men, so that she could keep an eye on them. "Very, well. Slowly and easily, turn with me", she commanded, and the two began to turn, almost as if the pistol were a tether.

Half way into the arc, Williamson suddenly dropped to the ground. Elizabeth fired the pistol out of reflex and struggled to think of what she should do next. Surely she should run, before that brute Williamson regained his feet. Reloading was out of the question, for she had no powder or ball, so run it would be.

She was halfway into her first step when she heard the explosion behind her, and she realized too late, that someone had discharged a weapon at her. Before she could complete the step, the musket ball struck her solidly in the back of the head, smashing through the soft spot at the base of the skull and continuing on through the brain, to the front of the skull, where it hit with just enough force to create a bump on her forehead. Elizabeth dropped to the ground, dead before she could feel any pain.

Williamson, rose to his haunches and stared at the dead woman. He felt a measure of remorse for, while he had little compunction about striking women, he was not generally predisposed to murdering them, especially beautiful ones. Such a waste, he thought, looking at the attractive face, the light already long extinguished from the eyes.

"You idiot!" he shouted at the man who had fired the fatal shot. "Why did you kill her?"

"I didn't intend to, Dorian. Honestly", he replied in a tone bordering on a plea, developing a sudden fear for his own life. "I intended to scare her into stopping. But you know how devilishly inaccurate this damned Brown Bess is."

Williamson stood and began to walk away, stopping several feet from the body. Without turning back to look, he told his men, "What's done is done", he said sadly. Then, recovering fully to his normal demeanour, he ordered, "Pick her up and throw her on a horse. We'll drop her off with the pastor as a message to van Hijser. And just in case he doesn't easily understand, I'll send along an explanation." He walked heavily into the house through the front door and set about writing a letter, using the former occupant's stationery and ink.

Chapter Twenty-One

Jeremy trekked on through the Niagara peninsula for the balance of the week, looking for clues as to the whereabouts of Williamson and his men. Both above the brow of the Mountain and below on the plain, he passed through tiny settlements that had sprung up virtually overnight, based on nothing more than a mill or a quarry. Tiny settlements that could just as well soon vanish as the tides of commerce turned against them.

As before, he was finding nothing of value for all those whom he approached either knew nothing, was afraid to speak, or plain refused to divulge any information. Finally, exhausted and dejected from his failure to discover anything useful concerning his archenemy, he headed back toward the Twenty and his future bride. That, at least, lifted his spirits, for he could feel his life was about to change.

He trudged heavily for the last few miles, tempted to lie down at the side of the road and sleep, but knowing that Elizabeth would be expecting him to go to the church tonight to tell him of the arrangements for him as well as for the wedding. The thought crossed his mind that he might have been expected to harbour second thoughts concerning the upcoming nuptials, but he had been able to summon none. He could barely wait the intervening time until the wedding, when he and Elizabeth would be joined, and his life would be complete once again.

He reached the small church near Elizabeth's home in the early evening on the Friday, and knocked gently upon the door

A Question of Loyalty

of the pastor's cabin next door. He hoped it was not too late in the evening for this call, for he wished not to disturb anyone. He wished everything to be absolutely perfect, and a it simply would not do to make an enemy of the minister.

The door creaked open slowly and a face peered carefully from the dark space beyond. Recognizing the young man by the description that Elizabeth had given him, the pastor pulled open the door and pulled him inside, hastily shutting the door behind him.

"Is something the matter?" Jeremy asked. "You act as though there might be bandits about."

The pastor looked up at Jeremy, who was several inches taller. "Jeremy", he started, and then stopped. He took a deep breath, gathered his resolve, and then started again. "Jeremy, there's something..."

"What is it, pastor?" Jeremy snapped, a rising panic quickly gaining hold. "Elizabeth?" he asked. Seeing a flicker in the minister's eyes, he continued. "Is something wrong with Elizabeth? Has she taken ill?" he demanded.

"Jeremy", the pastor said firmly. "Sit down here." The man steered him to a chair near the shuttered window, where an oil lamp on a small table provided just enough illumination to see each other's faces.

Jeremy remained standing, feeling his world crashing down around him, not even knowing what the problem was. He felt faint, his hands trembled, his mouth was dry, but he didn't wish to sit.

"I said sit", the pastor said kindly but firmly, standing to push Jeremy into the waiting chair. Once they were both seated, he looked the young man in the eyes, seeking the words that would attempt to explain what had happened. The words that would cushion the blow of bad news without destroying the man's faith in God, as often happened in cases such as this. He could not know that Jeremy's faith had left him several years earlier. But he could see that his chore would be no easy one, for the man was growing impatient.

"I would normally try to break bad news to a person gently", he started.

"Bad news?" Jeremy could feel the bile rising in his throat. He knew now that Elizabeth was not merely ill. "What bad news? Just tell me and stop trying to make it easy, please."

"If you'll stop interrupting me, I'll tell you." The pastor was loath to admonish the young man so sternly, but he felt he needed to take some manner of control over the situation. This was much too difficult for him already without these outbursts interrupting his explanation. "Jeremy, Elizabeth was murdered the day she came to me to make the wedding plans."

"Oh, my God!" Jeremy had by now suspected the worse, but actually hearing the words still came as a heavy blow. He felt his world dissolve before his eyes, their love, their happiness, their new beginnings together. He looked hard into the minister's eyes. "Tell me, Pastor, do you know who did it?"

"Yes", the pastor answered, looking down at his hands. "I do. It was one of those land pirates, a son of the Devil named Dorian Williamson, and he seemed to indicate that it had something to do with you." He looked back up into Jeremy's face questioningly, searching for what, neither knew.

"How do you know that?" Jeremy asked numbly.

The pastor pulled a sealed sheet of writing paper from a corner of the desk. His sleeve must have been concealing it, for Jeremy had not noticed it earlier. Although the wax seal on the stationery obviously belonged to someone other than Williamson, a fact which came as no surprise to the younger man, he stared at the writing on the outside of the folds. In neat cursive script, Jeremy read his own name. Nothing more than that, just his name.

Jeremy held the stationery in his hand, unable to open it. He stared at his name, at the seal, and looked up into the clergyman's face, pleading for advice.

"I'm afraid you'll have to open it eventually", the pastor said softly. "Whether it be here and now, or somewhere else at some other time, you can't leave the question unanswered. I'll make us some tea. If you wish to read it in private, feel free to do so. If you wish to share it, wait until I bring us the tea." With that, he arose from his chair and pushed the kettle onto the fire's still live embers. He looked up and saw his wife looking at them from the other room of the two that made up this house. He merely shook his head and, without a sound, she disappeared back into the other room.

Jeremy slowly cracked the wax seal on the paper, wanting to throw the offending document into the fireplace, but knowing that he could not. With tears blurring his vision, he slowly, ever so slowly, unfolded the paper and looked at the words, uncomprehending. It was not that he was illiterate, for he was taught to read by his father. It was simply that his mind would not focus upon the task at hand.

As the time passed as if without dimension, he realized suddenly that the pastor had seated himself back at the small table, and had placed a tea before Jeremy. He had not even noticed.

"What does it say?" the older man asked quietly. "Do you wish to tell me?"

Jeremy looked from the letter to the pastor and back at the letter again, confused. He finally just shook his head. The pastor gently removed the paper from his hand, putting on his spectacles and, holding it up to the lamp's poor light, he began to read aloud:

"Dear Mr. van Hijser", it reads. "I regret I am returning this to you, for I have no further use for it, much as I had finished with your house and barn. I regret that you will not get to know her better, for she was a spirited woman, but she insulted me, a shortcoming that seems to run in your circle of acquaintances: first that soldier, then you, and then your fiancée. I simply cannot countenance such rude behaviour as regards my person and sincerely hope that our future encounters will be much more cordial and respectful. With regards, your perhaps not so humble servant." The pastor looked up from the letter at the shell-shocked young man. "And he signs it, Dorian Williamson. P.S. I'll be the death of you yet."

The pastor folded the letter back into its original configuration and, saying nothing, handed it back to Jeremy. There was nothing he could say to this affront to decency. He said a silent prayer that the man who would commit such a crime and then write this, obviously to gloat, would be punished, if not in this life, then surely in the next. Preferably both, he thought, then silently chastised himself for entertaining such vengeful thoughts.

Jeremy sat silently also, tears making tracks in the dust, which yet covered his face from the many days on the road. Numbness pervaded his being, his body shutting out the insufferable agony as he tried desperately not to think of the possible circumstances surrounding her final moments. But it was not long before the anger, and the hatred that the anger engendered, mixed with unspeakable grief, pushed its way back to the surface.

He looked once again at the pastor, who obviously sat praying, presumably on Elizabeth's behalf, and perhaps on Jeremy's as well. The wild mixture of emotions roiled within him and, finally, burst forth. "I hope you're praying for vengeance", he said, getting up from his chair. "Because that's exactly what I intend."

The minister stood up also, and rounded the table, putting his hand on the younger man's shoulder in an effort to calm him down. He gently but firmly applied pressure, hoping to guide Jeremy back to his seat, but the rage would not allow it. Jeremy pulled free of the pastor's hand, and spun to the side.

"Vengeance is mine, saith the Lord", the holy man intoned, quoting from scripture. "It's not your place to seek revenge upon this man. It will only lead to more death and destruction. The Lord will take care of it in His own way and in His own time."

Jeremy glowered at the pastor. "I've been waiting a long time for the Lord to take care of the injustices that have plagued me", he muttered coldly. "And He's abandoned me to the Other. It's time I took care of this myself." With that, he pulled his hat tightly down on his head and stalked to the door, where he collected his weapons. Opening the door, he stopped and looked back at the shocked minister. "Besides, Pastor", he said with a dead smile, "Who's to say that I'm not merely the Lord's instrument?"

He stood and looked out the door at the evening sky. "Not that it, or anything else matters any more. At least, not until the moment that I see that animal laid in his grave, and I can stand at the gravesite and spit into it." With that, he stepped out of the house, pulling it roughly shut behind him.

"My, my", the pastor heard his wife say, and saw her staring from the other room, a shocked expression upon her face. "That young man is much too angry for his own good."

The pastor stared at the closed door, and then turned to his wife. "He has every good reason to be, dear."

Jeremy walked on down the road toward the east, not knowing exactly where he was going, or what it was he would do. He'd had

A Question of Loyalty

no luck thus far trying to track down Williamson, and he was not sure how he would find him any easier now. He just trudged mindlessly on, ignoring the dark, ignoring the fatigue that had crept back into his body and mind now that the burst of adrenaline had dissipated. But after a time he thought that the memories and the anger would drive him mad, and he broke into an all-out run, dashing furiously along the deeply shadowed road, until his lungs cried out for oxygen and his legs cramped mercilessly.

He kept on in this manner for almost two hours, running, cramping, walking until he could run again. Then he suddenly stopped, and looked all about him in confusion, the speechless forest seemingly stretching on to eternity. He had no idea where he might be, for he'd paid no attention to his surroundings or his changes of direction, not when he was walking, and certainly not when he was dashing madly along the road. The very air about him seemed to have become too thick to draw into his lungs, as he began to feel as if the trees were closing in on him, suffocating him. His world was spiralling out of control, as recent misfortunes took on greater-than-life proportions and threatened to overwhelm him with their enormity.

All attempts at concentration failed him and the very thought of encountering others while in this state sent waves of panic coursing through his being. Perspiration soaked his body entirely, leaving him clothed in damp, cloying apparel in a matter of minutes. His breath came on in ragged gulps, and he could feel what he knew with certainty to be his broken heart fluttering in his chest like a wounded butterfly.

The combination of panic and depression interfered severely with his ability to make decisions. Tiring of the effort to do so, he simply stopped trying to make choices, and merely sat down where he was, in the middle of the dirt on this unknown stretch of road. He found that he had even lost the ability to care that he was lost, exposed and uncertain what, if anything, he might do to remedy the situation. He shut out the very rustle in the trees and the cries of nocturnal creatures.

Nothing mattered any longer, not the past, not the present, and certainly not the future. Jeremy curled up in a protective ball and eventually surrendered to the sweet oblivion of deep, dreamless sleep right on the spot where he had stopped, unconcerned with his exposed position.

The sun's first dim rays found Jeremy still in this same position, and in the same place. He was startled awake by the loud snorting sound of a horse, which seemed very close to his head. An indignant voice rang out sharply, cutting through the haze of Jeremy's sleep, disturbed as it was by the unwanted sensory input.

"My good man. What on earth are you doing sleeping in the very middle of a public thoroughfare?" the voice demanded. "Are you quite addled, sir?"

Jeremy sat up slowly and stared at the man who had vocally accosted him in such a contemptuous manner. His mouth opened and closed as if to speak, attempting to formulate the explanation he did not have, but no sound issued forth. The panic he had felt the previous night returned once again, almost instantly taking over his entire being, and he took the only course of action he could identify as being readily open to him.

Like a frightened hare, Jeremy dashed off into the woods, allowing his panic to rule him. He ran for the better part of a half-hour, crashing carelessly through the undergrowth, brambles and thorns tearing at his clothing and exposed skin, trampling plants underfoot, and splashing wetly through a small stream. He finally slowed only when he found himself winded by the ever-steepening grade of the terrain. It was obvious to even his addled mind that he had reached the Mountain.

Gradually his pace slowed to nothing and Jeremy sat down hard on the damp, dew-laden forest floor, looked all about at the unchanging terrain, and immediately began to cry. Great wracking sobs rent the stillness of the forest, frightening wildlife. Tears flowed heavily from between the fingers covering his eyes and ran down the backs of his hands, dripping at last from his wrists to splash soundlessly onto the rich black loam of the escarpment.

After what seemed hours to the emotionally wounded man, his emotions spent, he stopped crying, seemingly as spontaneously as he had begun. He remained rooted to his spot, however, content in his solitude, physically drained by his crying. Slowly he surveyed his surroundings and, through his depression and despair, the woodland took on a different light - as a friend that could hide him and protect him from life's pain. It seemed a sign, an epiphany, that this was the way for him to survive the horrors of the world. He would stay here forever, safely hidden away from humans, away from the evil they caused.

Jeremy climbed slowly to his feet and began to climb the ever-sharpening angle of the escarpment's slope, keeping a sharp eye out for what he might consider to be the ideal base from which to start this new existence he had decided upon. One possible site after another was explored, scouted, tested, and finally rejected. The slope was wrong, there was too much or too little room, not enough cover or the cover obstructed his view of the surroundings. There was no water or it was never dry, there was no platform to build a shelter on. Some were discarded as indefensible, some as lacking an escape route.

One not familiar with Jeremy's situation would have regarded his decision-making process as picky in the extreme. However, this obsessive behaviour was cathartic, helping his mind to, at least temporarily, deal with the pain of his loss. Physically, it allowed Jeremy to work off the nervous energy he had amassed, which in turn helped to relieve the panic that had so totally taken hold of him.

When Jeremy reached a point approximately forty feet from the top, at the bottom of the cliff line, he came across the barest trace of a path, probably made by animals, running between a stand of cedars. He followed along it carefully as the ground narrowed to a mere foot of width, still hidden from the surrounding countryside by the hearty evergreens. At a distance of about thirty feet, the ledge widened out, not only sticking farther out from the cliff, but also running under a rock overhang.

From where he stood, Jeremy could see down a long stream valley, and movement to the left found his gaze drawn all the way to Lake Ontario. And yet it was unlikely anyone could see him here, for an effective screen had been formed from the cedars that grew up from the ground below and even, seemingly, from the very cliffs. Continuing off the opposite side of the shelf, he found the path continued on, climbing up through the cliff rocks to the very top. The clincher for this location, however, was the spring he discovered seeping from the rock wall into a tiny pool not a quarter-mile distant.

The site having been chosen, Jeremy set about constructing his hermit's shelter. With poles and cedar boughs, he built a front wall of sorts for the overhang, a screen from wind and rain and sun. For now, he made his bed of more cedar branches, but made plans to improve upon this when the opportunity arose.

His home such as it was having been completed, Jeremy went foraging for food. There would be no time to hunt today, as the day had slipped by him almost without notice. Instead, he set about collecting such nuts, berries, and greens as he recognized. Having been through this exercise many times in the past while on non-productive hunting trips in isolated locales, he was confident that he would not poison himself.

Back at his fortress against the world, but not himself, Jeremy sat cross-legged on the shelf in front of his shelter, contemplating the vista below and ahead as he devoured his meagre meal. The sun was beginning to set and, although the sun itself was not visible from his vantage point, he could see pink traces in the wisps of cloud that streaked across from the northwest. There was a slight chill in the air and Jeremy shivered, feeling the cold much more than he had the previous night because of his exposed position. All things about this new life taken into consideration, he was confident that he had found the answer to his problems in this newfound solitude.

The following days passed at a lazy pace, and Jeremy spent much of his time nursing his depression, readily giving in to it and allowing it to draw him into new depths. The initial euphoria of the discovery of this new life had faded in direct proportion to his level of activity, and there was nothing but the darkness in his mind now to keep him company.

Chapter Twenty-Two

Time was meaningless to a mind slowed almost to a standstill and, by the third day, so too was his appetite. Jeremy ate nothing for the next three days and had even stopped drinking water, and his being had been reduced to mere existence. He no longer felt any pain, nor any joy, nor any emotion at all, and there was nothing left for him but to die. And, in this enterprise, he was well on his was to attaining complete success.

As the fortunes of the world would have it, though, his brain and Mother Nature would not allow it. As he lay wallowing in his own filth and self-pity, a violent early summer storm struck the peninsula. Rain fell in massive sheets of water, blown about by winds that howled in from the east and picked up speed when squeezed by the air currents between the lake and the escarpment. Lightning flashed in such quick succession that the sky, which had become almost as dark as night in the moments before the storm hit, now lit up in an almost constant, blinding light. The thunder rolled in a steady rhythm, with insufficient time during the intervals to hear it as crashes.

Jeremy was awakened by the rain soaking him as it angled in through the wilting cedar branches that were to have sheltered him. As the winds blasted at the cliff face, the loosely tied boughs finally surrendered and separated, leaving the man inside exposed to the balance of the storm's fury. Adding to his misery, water began to flow from the cracks and crevices in the cliff itself as the water worked its way down from fissures in the rock overhead.

Jeremy struggled not to care, trying desperately to convince himself that the discomfort was immaterial, that this would just hasten his death, which was what he wanted. But the torment of the soaking was unbearable and the water that dribbled into his mouth each time he opened it to breathe was reviving him from his self-induced catatonia, however unwillingly. His animal instincts made him startle at every new roll of thunder and every new sheet of lightning. This constant bombardment of incessant and calamitous stimuli was his depression's undoing. It was simply impossible for him to just lie here and wait for death after all. He was cursed with that most animal of all instincts – that of survival.

In Jeremy's weakened state, he had difficulty rising, and found he had to crawl along the ledge to the main path that would take him below and out of the direct blast of the storm. From there, he eased himself down the incline on the seat of his trousers, pulling himself down and forward with his feet. Water rushed down this path as well in a steady stream, using the lack of vegetation as a path of least resistance. Several times he tumbled over, as the water sloshed over the edges at curves in the trail, once almost being washed over a straight twelve-foot drop. He had little strength to resist, but resist he did and managed to get to the bottom in one piece.

Jeremy found sufficient strength now to rise to his feet by leaning up against a tree and slowly straightening out his legs, sliding his back up along the tree's trunk until he was upright, the pain of the rough bark's abrasion awakening him further. He staggered unsurely along, falling often and using the same painful method as before to get back up each time.

Finally, after what seemed an eternity, Jeremy reached a small copse of trees on a slight rise. He had reached a measure of shelter at last! Jeremy positioned himself in such a way that his head and shoulders where inside the umbrella of a tree in the middle, and there he stayed, half hanging, half propped, his arms draped over low branches so that he would not drop to the sodden ground, there to wait out the storm.

Although it seemed like forever to the young man, his reprieve from the weather came but twenty minutes later. As quickly as the storm had roared down upon the area, it seemed to just vanish, and sunlight once again flooded through the sodden leaves of the trees.

Jeremy allowed himself to slide down out of the tree and settled wetly at the base. He turned his back to the trunk and sat quietly, exhausted by the effort in his depleted state. The brilliance of the sunlight was thankfully shielded from his eyes by the leaves of an old maple a dozen yards away, but was painful all the same. With his eyes closed tightly against the light, he soon slipped back into a deep slumber, soaked through and through, water still dripping onto his head from the branches above.

He slept the balance of that day, and well into the morning of the next. When finally he did awake, he forced himself to his feet and, without realizing that he was resuming his life, began to gather edible materials. He devoured these foodstuffs immediately, and his completely empty stomach cramped several times from the sudden onslaught of food, but he ate until he became nauseous. Once sated, he stopped and looked up at the perch that had been his home for the past week or so.

Jeremy had no desire to revisit the ledge, fearing almost that the hold it had over him would return, hurling him back into the state he had suffered while there. But he needed to go back and retrieve his belongings, which he hoped would still be there. With some strength returning, he made the climb back up the trail, slipping on the wet clay and having to break often. With great relief, he saw that his gear had survived the deluge.

It had not all survived unaffected, however. As he picked up his gun by the stock, water poured out of both barrels, and it was obvious that there would no longer be any powder in the pan. Jeremy's cartridge case had been lying on a small ledge in the overhang's wall and it had fallen off, the flap opening upon impact with the shelf, dumping most of the contents out and dissolving the paper of the cartridges in the rain. Those few cartridges that remained were soaked and would likely not be of any future value.

He would be forced to survive without it, he thought, an about-face in attitude that was not entirely lost on Jeremy. Just one day previous he had planned to kill himself through apathy, and now he was disappointed that he would have to survive without gunpowder!

If he had been in a position to relish the irony properly, he would have laughed aloud.

Early that same evening, Jeremy set about laying traps for several types of game, hoping meat would more quickly return him to his former strength. The depression that had almost killed him still lurked in the recesses of his mind, but it had been forced into the background by the feral need to survive that had been reawakened by the storm. He wasn't ready by any means to return to the society of man just yet, but Jeremy now felt that he would be able to regain some semblance of control over himself, and eating would be the first item on the agenda.

Jeremy remained awake most of that night, napping only when he could keep his head up no longer. He had wasted enough of his life lying about waiting for the end, he thought, and he found that he just wanted to sit and watch the moon and stars as they traversed the night sky toward the dawn.

In the morning, he went out to check his primitive traps. The rabbit snares had yielded nothing, and neither had the deadfall snare he had built for deer, a source of more than just food, and that for more than one day. Almost ready to give up and prepared to rely on forage for another meal, Jeremy discovered that he had been successful with a squirrel snare. With meat to begin the day, he felt strangely uplifted, and he picked some berries down near the stream to accompany the feast.

With his morning repast inside him, he sat back against a rock and tipped his head back until the sun bathed his face with warmth. He opened his eyes and looked up at the clear blue sky, and smiled. There apparently was yet a glimmer of life left in him, and it was forcing its way to the surface, past the anger and depression and pain, not subduing it, but breaking free enough to live again.

Jeremy had decided that he would first strengthen himself physically and emotionally, and then head back into a semblance of the life he had known. In order to do that, he'd need to acquire some supplies, and that in turn meant he would require at least a rudimentary income, or at least produce some good for barter. As a result, the noonday sun found him resting and improving the traps he had set the day before, and adding several more.

He checked what was left of his cartridges to see if he might be able to restore some to a useable state but once they dried, he knew it to be a lost cause by the colour of the gunpowder inside the paper. Attempting to use them would produce unpredictable and perhaps dangerous results. In all likelihood, nothing would happen, leaving him standing dumbly watching his game scamper away, but there was always a possibility that he might blast his gun apart, injuring himself in the process. He set them aside with a sigh. The traps would have to do for now. Instead, Jeremy picked up the gun, inspected it for damage, and began to swab it out to ready it for the next time he might lay his hands on fresh cartridges.

Two days passed and Jeremy had not trapped anything substantial. While he had snared some rabbits, they were most valuable to him as food. Their pelts, while not worthless, would have little purchase power. Frustration ate away at him and he realized that the only way he would catch larger game would be to hunt them, and that required the use of his rifle. Picking up the few rabbit and squirrel pelts that he had collected, he decided that a wait at he the road might bring him some passer-by who would trade him for a couple of cartridges.

Over the short time since the storm, he had regained much of his strength, in every sense. His ease of motion and his physical confidence had returned, which in turn also improved his emotional state. His anger with the world still simmered just beneath the surface but for the time being at least, he didn't allow it to rule him. There was much to do to prepare for his return to the world of man, to continue his quest and, until such time as he was ready, there was nothing he could do to avenge Elizabeth, Robert, Sarah and himself. But he knew with deadly certainty that the time would indeed come.

Jeremy reached the road early in the day, although he did not yet know exactly which road it might be. As he sat down to wait, the trees along the road yet cast long shadows toward the west as the sun still hung low on the horizon. He had chosen as his seat the log of an old oak that would grow no older, a victim of the march of civilization when this old Indian trail was widened to accommodate the white man's wagons.

There he sat, with little to do but whittle away with his father's old hunting knife on a dry piece of cedar he had brought along. What it was he was whittling, even he did not know, but it passed the time, for he knew that it could be some time before someone came along. He had considered going on to civilization, for Niagara was well populated, especially along the King's roads. He did not feel quite ready to face anyone just yet, to have to explain what he was doing here, or why, or to explain what had happened to him. Here he would wait for civilization to come to him.

After two or three hours - just how long he did not know exactly - he heard the sound of shod hooves and voices. As the sounds drew nearer, something about the sound unnerved him. On a subconscious level, the fact that there was more than one horse and more than one voice had triggered the concern. On this stretch of road, it could be anyone – soldiers of either army, raiders, highwaymen, or just locals out for a ride. Deciding at the last moment to play it safe, Jeremy lay low until he could determine the identity of the authors of these sounds.

Jeremy watched as four men rode into view, and the sight of one made his blood run cold. The second man in the group was none other than the hoodlum that had stood guard with the one called Will along the Twenty Mile Creek, and also fought for Williamson at the tavern, the one named Seth! Jeremy sank deeper into the woods, almost holding his breath for fear of being discovered. Hopefully, the men would continue on their merry way down the road, for he did not feel ready to take on four of these ruthless men, especially with no gun.

He watched as they filed by, talking of little, seemingly half asleep as they rode on. The first man passed, the one that Jeremy had recognized passed, and then the third man rode obliviously past Jeremy's hiding place. The fourth man was nearly passed when something caught his attention. He stopped, suddenly appearing alert, and stood up in his stirrups, searching the woods around him.

"What is it?" one of the others called back, noticing the absence of a hoof cadence directly behind him.

"I don't know", the man answered, still searching. "But look at this." He climbed down from his horse and headed straight for the log on which Jeremy had been sitting.

"What?" the first man called back, a mocking tone to his voice. "You found a log? Plenty of those along this road." He started laughing uproariously, finding his comment extremely humorous.

"Shut up! I'm talking about this", the man on foot explained, holding up two fingers in which were pinched shavings from Jeremy's whittling. "Someone was here a very short time ago. These are still fresh."

The second man in line alit from his mount as well and joined the man at the log. "Jameson, I think you're right", he said thoughtfully. "Chances are, that person's still around. Maybe watching us right now." He began to scan the undergrowth slowly, and Jeremy thought momentarily that he had been spotted, but the man continued to look about.

The man named Jameson walked back to his horse and pulled a fowling piece from its place on the animal's flank. He pulled back the hammer, checked to see that the pan was primed, and raised it to his shoulder. "What do you think, Seth? Shall I open up the bushes a little and see what's skulking there?"

Jeremy watched as the man with the gun aimed directly into the trees only several yards to Jeremy's right. The gun went off with a dreadful roar, shattering the still of the morning, and the shot scattered widely, shredding leaves, snapping twigs and generally creating mayhem along a wide swath of flora. He then quickly and efficiently reloaded his piece and once again took aim, this time in Jeremy's general direction.

Jeremy had few options now. He rose quietly to a crouch and then quickly took off through the trees and bushes, wishing he were more stealthy, but realizing that speed was much more important in this case. He heard a shouted, "I think he's running!" and then there was another loud blast. Jeremy flattened himself on the ground immediately, and he heard the devastation being caused all around him, as Jameson fired blindly into the trees once more.

Jeremy stayed down, not daring to move. There was no sound from the roadway, and he guessed that the men were listening for the sound of their quarry fleeing. He discovered that his fear was slowly being forced to share space with indignation at being shot at once again by some of Williamson's men. And the worst of it was that these men did not know what they were shooting blindly at. It could well be a woman or some child, since he had little idea of how far he might be from a house.

When the four men began to talk again, it was obvious that they had moved into the woods, as evidenced by the snapping and rustling sounds that accompanied their voices. Jeremy rose to a crouch once again and headed away from the trouble, circling around to get behind it, the safest position he could think of. Hopefully, they would tire of the game and mount their horses, never to be seen by Jeremy again.

But it was not to be. What the four men thought was a chase continued well into the afternoon, with Jeremy still following behind at a safe distance. He thought seriously of heading back toward the road and heading east, the direction these men had come from. But he became concerned that the rest of Williamson's group might be anywhere along, in either direction, or at any house he might approach for assistance.

Instead, he decided on a course of action that another might consider ill conceived, perhaps even stupid. He would try to eliminate these men. If they thought that this stalking of a fellow human being was a game, then he could play as well.

As the four men reached rougher terrain, they decided to spread out. They knew their quarry could be hiding anywhere and they did not want to lose it. They felt quite confident that the person they were chasing had no gun or it would have been used by now, so they felt little fear in separating to maximize their search area.

Chapter Twenty-Three

Jeremy began to creep up closer behind them and watched to see who would most isolate himself from the rest of the group. The man who had been first in passing Jeremy on the road unknowingly elected to become that person, circling around a large rocky outcropping covered in vines and surrounded by trees. Jeremy closed in on the man who thought he was the hunter and readied his tomahawk.

The man heard something move softly behind him, and he started to turn. "Is that you, Jameson?" he asked. "I thought we were going to spread out. Wait. Who are you?" he demanded, as he noticed that it was Jeremy and not his companion who had been behind him. The realization that this must be the one they were hunting finally appeared to dawn upon the man, for he started to raise his gun, simultaneously opening his mouth to call for the others.

But he was too late in realizing his error. Jeremy was within arm's reach of the man and swung the tomahawk with all his might. The blade caught the surprised man across the throat, and he fell to the ground, blood gushing from the severed blood vessels, unable to speak as the air escaped soundlessly, blood rapidly filling his throat and his lungs as he gulped for air. He writhed momentarily on the ground, trying desperately to breath, and then lay still.

Jeremy looked down at the man, a measure of horror seeping slowly into him as the full realization of what he had done filtered through the heart-pounding adrenalin rush. This business of killing men still was not easy, although the remorse was much less than last time. He was struck with a sudden fear, most inappropriate under the circumstances, of becoming accustomed to it if this damned war did not end soon.

He shook off these thoughts and dragged the earthly remains of the hapless man into the bushes, leaving him there. Jeremy then picked up the man's musket and his cartridge case, checking the gun's load. It was ready, although Jeremy hoped not to use it, for the sound would surely end the element of surprise that would be necessary to survive this ordeal.

Tracking back around the rock, Jeremy picked up another trail, this time the third rider. This man's name was a mystery to him also, and it momentarily seemed to bother him in some strange way that he would not know the identities of the men he was killing. This war had become personal for the trapper, and he wanted to know upon whom he whetted his appetite for revenge.

He marvelled at the ease with which he followed the man's path, and his foe did not exercise any care to practice woodcraft, no doubt feeling quite secure that he was the hunter. Jeremy caught up with this one at the base of the trail heading up to the ledge that had become his prison only a week before. As he reached the bottom, he found that the man had already spotted the pathway leading behind the trees and had started to follow it toward the overhang. Jeremy followed quietly, climbing the hill quickly to stay in cover.

As he came to the point where the two paths converged, he was surprised to meet the man he had been following face to face, apparently having decided that he was wasting his time here and had turned about to head back. It would have been difficult to determine which of the two was more startled, for initially neither moved. They stood staring at each other for what seemed an eternity, and then both moved at once.

The man who had thought that he had been tracking Jeremy tried to bring his musket to bear, but Jeremy was much too close to him to level the barrel. For the same reason, Jeremy found he could not effectively use his tomahawk, leaving them with a standoff. The man backed away down the path, hoping to gain enough room to shoot, and Jeremy followed right along, step for step, to prevent it.

A Question of Loyalty

Jeremy would not be able to get a shot off at the other man either, for the gun he had taken from the other stalker was still on his back, and he could not possibly take it off and shoot before the other man had shot him. Instead, Jeremy worked his bayonet from his belt, causing his foe to back away more quickly yet, and now Jeremy found he was fairly chasing him along the narrow path.

Just before the two men reached the place where the path widened out into the shelf, Williamson's man missed his step. With his arms windmilling wildly, he lost his balance and pitched over backward into the space between the cedar trees that formed the screen Jeremy had so prized, falling the distance to the ground without hitting anything at all. But when he hit bottom without even the time to scream, he landed with bone-jarring impact upon a pile of rocks, breaking his back. His final act on this earth was to retract his trigger finger, firing off the musket into the air.

Jeremy believed he could feel the ball whiz past his face as the roar of the musket reverberated from the cliffs of the Mountain. Forgetting his situation momentarily, he stood exposed as he looked down at the shattered body below. He was sternly reminded, however, when he heard a shout from below and saw the man named Seth point his finger up the cliff toward where Jeremy was standing. Any advantage of surprise he had enjoyed was now gone.

Jeremy quickly pulled back from the edge, and skirted the wall of the overhang until he reached the spot where the path continued to the top of the Mountain. He could hear cursing as the two men climbed up toward the spot where Jeremy had been last seen, obviously having a hard time of it. He did not wait to see if they made it and clambered up over the rocks.

Once at the top, he had to come up with a plan. There was little cover up here to make a run for it, so he would have to either make a stand or take another path that he had found farther along the cliff. Unfortunately, this way led back down, risking the possibility that one would circle back around and wait for him. Jeremy decided upon the back door.

Jeremy slowly made his way down a steep crevice cleft in the rock by unknown forces of nature, lowering himself carefully from foothold to foothold. When he emerged at the escarpment face, he peered carefully out from the rock, to see if he could spot his pursuers. Over on the ledge, he could see just Seth, inching along the path, just about to the ledge. The man was obviously moving with great caution, although whether it was because of the width of ledge or because of the possibility that Jeremy might be waiting up ahead, Jeremy didn't know. There was no sign, however of the other man. Where had Jameson gone?

Jeremy waited, nerves taut as a pocket watch spring, until Seth moved out of sight along the ledge. Then the trapper continued his climb down. Reaching the bottom, he positioned himself behind a fallen tree to get a clear shot at anyone who might follow him down this way. He did not need to wait long before he heard, and then saw, Seth coming down through the crevice. He slipped often and swore loudly each time, hardly concerned about silence or stealth and more about his comfort. But there was no sign of Jameson, and not knowing where the second man had gone put Jeremy even more on edge.

He placed Seth squarely in the sights of the old Brown Bess that he had confiscated, waiting for his target to come close enough to ensure the best possible chance of a hit. This type of musket was notoriously inaccurate at any reasonable range, and was used in battle by infantry soldiers because firing on a line did not require any great degree of accuracy. With enough balls flying from enough guns, surely something would be hit in that general direction.

By the time Seth stumbled to the bottom from the last of the rocks jumbled about the base of the crevice, he was much the worse for wear. His shirt and trousers were torn and filthy, his hands and one knee were bleeding, his face was beet-red from the exertion, and the strap had been torn loose at one end of the man's gun. He was puffing vigorously and perspiration poured down his neck and onto his sodden shirt. It was a wonder to Jeremy that the man had any energy remaining to continue hurling offensive epithets at the Mountain, the rocks, the trees, Jeremy, and anything else that crossed his mind.

Still no sign of Jameson, Jeremy thought. Had the other man given up, to return to his horse? Had he abandoned his companion to the vagaries of fighting the enemy by himself? Anything was possible with the types that rode with Williamson, he thought, but it seemed highly unlikely, and the insecurity was driving him to distraction.

Seth had straightened up now and stood scanning the forest carefully, but seeing nothing other than trees and bushes. "Where the hell are you?" he finally screamed in frustration. "Come on out here and fight like a man!"

Jeremy was considering doing just that when he caught a slight movement out of the corner of his eye. Ducking down further into his natural screen, he kept an eye on the location, finally seeing motion once again. So that had been Jameson's plan. He had left Seth to chase after Jeremy, while Jameson waited below. He had obviously been fully expecting that, either as victor or escapee, Jeremy would reappear here below, offering Jameson an opportunity to shoot him in the back.

A fair fight with Seth was now abandoned as an option, and Jeremy repositioned himself so that he could acquire his target and yet remain hidden from the second man. It would be necessary to take his shot and then try to vanish into the undergrowth, hopefully using the smoke and noise of the shot to mask his exit.

As Seth moved cautiously closer, repeatedly screaming out the same challenge, Jeremy pulled the trigger of the captured weapon. There was an explosion as the powder lit and the ball crashed through the few leaves in the way, finding its way straight and true to Seth's chest. As the man went down, obviously surprised, the echo of the gun report bounced back from the rock wall beyond, and smoke enveloped the whole area in which Jeremy had been hiding.

Jeremy did not wait to see if the shot was fatal. It had hit and, regardless of the severity of the damage, it would be quite incapacitating. If it didn't kill the man right away, it would before long. He threw down the weapon, hoping from here on to use his own weapon and dashed off through the brush, hoping to distance himself well by the time the other man could pinpoint the source of the shot.

He dashed through the trees, avoiding the heavier undergrowth as much as possible. Dense growth would only contribute greatly to the noise he could not completely avoid, and it might slow him down as well. He zigzagged as he ran, lest Jameson already be on his trail, hopefully making himself a more difficult target, even with the spread of a scattergun. Just ahead, he saw a familiar rock formation, two groupings of rock that formed a narrow passage between them. Jeremy had often spotted deer tracks here when laying his traps. He ran directly for the gap and dashed through, just as Jameson's voice boomed from behind him.

"You can't run forever", the hoodlum taunted Jeremy, slightly breathlessly. "I'll hunt you down eventually."

Jeremy did not answer, hoping that Jameson had seen him duck in here without the ruse appearing obvious. Luck was on Jeremy's side on this particular occasion, as Jameson had spotted him just as the tail of his shirt disappeared between the rocks.

Now it appeared to the last of Jeremy's tormenters that his quarry would be his in short order. By the lay of the passage, it was obvious that there was limited egress from this place, consisting of only the other end of this narrow passage. He calculated that all he would need to do is to fire his scattergun in among these rocks, and he had a good chance of hitting Jeremy, if not directly then probably with ricocheting shot.

As if Jeremy could read his opponent's mind, he began to scale the left side of the rock pile, intending to stay out of the direct line of fire should Jameson fire blindly inside. He had climbed nearly to the top when he heard the man's voice from behind and below him, in the gap not quite at the point where it widened out. And Jeremy smiled.

Jameson stepped out into the wider section of the passage, kicking aside a branch that stuck halfway out into the passage, creating a tripping hazard. He noticed an odd sound and looked up just as a large log came straight down upon him, snapping his head backward so violently that it broke his neck. Jameson would never know it, but he had unwittingly kicked away the trigger stick to Jeremy's deadfall deer snare, a propped up section of log with a notched stick that would release the former tree when hit. The device was used to break the back of any deer that might disturb the protruding branch, but the deer had been too smart, their prints showing that they continued to travel this way without ever triggering the snare. However, it had worked like a charm with Jeremy's unsuspecting stalker.

Jeremy climbed back down the rocks from his perch and checked to make certain Jameson was dead. Then he picked up the man's scattergun and proceeded to take the weapons, cartridges and anything else of value from the others, taking a special interest in an ornately engraved pistol from Seth's belt. None of these men would have any further use for these items.

Chapter Twenty-Four

Jeremy sat at the roadside once again, deep in thought, idly feeding oats to the four horses from a bag on one of the saddles. There was no point any longer in hiding out here among the trees. It was plain that there could be no sanctuary from the world, he thought. The world will just come looking for you. The main thing he had to decide was where he would go from here. His house was destroyed and Elizabeth's was too full of memories right now.

Not coming to any satisfying conclusion, Jeremy packed up his newfound arsenal onto one of the horses and began to lead all four along the road. He'd never been much of a horseman and besides, when one doesn't know one's destination, it's best to take one's time about it.

Jeremy soon broke clear of the forest. He was about to step from the shelter of the trees than he noticed a small farm down a narrow, rutted laneway on the escarpment side of the road. Jeremy stopped at the edge of the cover and watched the property carefully, looking for signs of anything amiss, especially since the four men who had attacked him had come from this direction.

He could see nothing wrong, however. A lone man toiled at the side of the house, splitting wood, while a woman scrubbed vigorously at laundry in a tub at the back. There was no indication of the presence of any others, so Jeremy decided to risk approaching the couple.

As he rode up, string of horses in tow, the man straightened up and looked intently at him, not certain what to make of this stranger. He calmly but firmly shouted something toward the back of the house and the woman abandoned her laundry to run inside. Jeremy supposed that this was now normal behaviour at the sight of strangers, behaviour that could not be faulted, considering his own experiences, but he continued on up the lane, casually hailing the man.

"Good day to you", the man replied suspiciously. He'd no doubt noted that one of the four horses fairly bristled with weapons.

"Oh, don't be alarmed by these", Jeremy said, trying to reassure the man. "I took these from some men who tried to waylay me down the road."

The man looked more closely at the loaded horse and squinted at Jeremy. "Looks like it was an army", he commented sarcastically. "Took them on by yourself, did you?"

Jeremy smiled. "I know it's hard to believe, sir, but I outsmarted them more than fought them. They weren't hard to fool, either."

Just as he finished speaking, Jeremy heard a loud click from the corner of the house. Looking in the direction of the sound, he saw the woman that had been washing earlier using the building both to shield her and to steady the musket she had trained on him. "Just get on your horse and keep riding", she said evenly.

The man just smiled, although his eyes didn't join in. "Better do as she says, sir", he suggested. "She's quite a crack shot with that, even with her size."

"I just wanted to ask for a drink of water, and to learn of what news there may be", Jeremy explained. "I'd be willing to pay you handsomely for those services."

The man looked at Jeremy with renewed interest. "How handsomely?" he demanded curiously. "You don't look like a rich man."

"I'm not, at that", Jeremy laughed heartily. "But you can have all four of these horses for your hospitality. And all but a few of these guns", he offered as a clincher to the deal.

The farmer looked over the mounts. They were not the finest animals he had seen, but they would fetch a few pounds if he could find a customer. As for the guns, he rather fancied the scattergun he could see poking from the four-legged armoury's pack. He signalled his wife to lower the gun and invited Jeremy inside, suggesting his wife put the horses away.

Jeremy didn't spend long with these people, for they never relinquished the aura of suspicion that pervaded the conversation as they discussed the recent news from around the Peninsula. He was not certain what it was that he had expected, for he had only been out of circulation for a short time, but it gave them something to talk about while he sipped clean, cool water drawn on their well and tore into a welcome slice of bread offered by the wife.

When he left, Jeremy was good to his word, leaving all four horses behind. It was no hardship upon him, for he had never grown fond of travelling by horseback. He'd discovered long ago that the animals were useless for hunting in the Canadian wilderness, not sure enough of foot to easily negotiating the obstacles of the forest, and the noise they produced would frighten game. Then there was the trouble of keeping the creatures, shoeing them, feeding them, watching them for parasites and skin disorders. He felt much less encumbered traveling on foot.

He also left the farmer the scattergun he had confiscated from Jameson. While it could be a handy tool to have around, his over/under could fulfil that function admirably. He wished to carry an extra musket for a situation where he might not be to be able to reload quickly, and the engraved pistol was a thing of beauty. Added to his regular weapons, he was formidably armed, and he left the rest behind with the couple as he resumed his journey.

At least now he knew where he was, the farmer having drawn him a rough map. Merely a few miles from Shipman's corners, Jeremy decided instead to take the old back trail up the escarpment toward DeCou's house. He hoped to find Fitzgibbon there, to ask if he could join up with his Bloody Boys, perhaps as a regular scout, finally ready to commit to the war, but only on his own terms.

Jeremy strolled almost casually through meadows and woodlands on his way to his new destination. His depression had been relegated to the dustier regions of his mind, at least for now, and he was finding it much easier to take enjoyment from the simple aspects of life once more. He watched carefully as a red-tailed hawk soared over the field in which he was walking, and he could not help but wonder what he might look like from the raptor's viewpoint, and what the silliness of man must seem to a creature that soared so high above it all.

He started slightly when a rustling sound near his feet turned out to be garter snake, just one of the numerous types of snake that inhabited the area. This one was at least no threat, he thought as he watched the animal escape almost sideways into the tall grasses. Jeremy continued walking through the meadow, taking in the many sights of those environs.

But it wasn't until he had almost reached the edge of the grassland that he chanced to look back, checking over his shoulder, as was his habit. And as he did so, there was a flash of brown as the hawk he had seen earlier dove soundlessly from the sky toward the ground. Just when anyone watching would surely expect that the bird would bury itself deep in the earth, it suddenly pulled back sharply into the air once more, but now grasping a vole that had the misfortune of coming into the bird's line of vision.

Resuming on his way, he reached the bottom of the escarpment once more. As he crossed a small opening, a goldfinch suddenly shot across his path, the brilliant yellow with black markings seemingly a warning sign to Jeremy. Stopping cold at the unexpected flash of colour, he sensed that something was out of place, though he could not determine exactly what it was. He stopped and listened carefully, and he was not entirely certain at first, but he thought he had heard low voices coming from the southwest, out of the valley that fed the Twelve Mile Creek. Now barely breathing so as not to interfere with any sounds, he soon discerned the soft padding of moccasined feet off to his right. He stepped aside from the trail, out of plain sight, watching and listening until soon he could determine the exact source of the sound. Breaking into the open from a faint path that crossed Jeremy's trail, a half-dozen Caughnawaga warriors appeared at an easy lope.

The Caughnawagas were the Indians that served with Captain Ducharme. Known to some as the "Praying Indians" because of their conversion to Christianity, they were also referred to as "tame Indians" because of their, at least partial, acceptance of civilization. Mostly Mohawk, but also with a smattering of other tribes from the Montreal area, they had come to Niagara to fight their sworn enemies, the Americans. So far, they had been generally disappointed, because the U.S. soldiers were hiding in Fort George and other fortified American enclaves. This gave them opportunity to fight only proxy Americans, such as Willcocks and his Canadian Volunteers, and Dr. Chapin's vigilantes.

As they came abreast of Jeremy, the lead runner noticed Jeremy beside the trail. He let out what sounded to Jeremy like a grunt of sorts, and he and the others seemed to melt into the surrounding forest. Their sudden disappearance made Jeremy laugh aloud.

"You can come out", he chuckled. "I'm all by myself and I'm obviously not an American, else I would have screamed like an old woman and run away through the woods."

After a moment's hesitation, there was a short burst of nervous laughter and the Caughnawagas stepped back into Jeremy's sight, approaching him carefully, still glancing warily about, in case it should be a ruse. The man who had been in front of the file of Indians studied Jeremy for a few seconds, then smiled and held out his hand.

Jeremy proffered his hand as well, and the two shook. "Weren't you at DeCou's with Ducharme when I was there?" he asked.

"Truly, I was", the Indian replied. Jeremy was somewhat surprised with the man's command of English. Although he spoke in French cadence, and an accent was barely discernable, he pronounced the words quite well, unlike their nominal commander, Captain Ducharme, who could speak no English whatsoever. "What you are doing in the trees here, eh?" He pointed off along the escarpment base in an eastward direction. "All the fighting is there, at what you call the Beaverdams."

"What fighting?" Jeremy asked, wondering immediately if he should have inquired.

"The Americans, they think they're going to surprise the Bloody Boys", the Indian replied. "But they are still down below. We're going right now to try to stop them."

"Has anyone gone to warn Fitzgibbon?" Jeremy asked, ready to volunteer.

"I don't know. No time for that", was the reply over the Indian's shoulder, already running again. "Come. We can use the help."

Jeremy looked up at the escarpment, in his intended direction, and then with a shrug, he set off after the Indians, finding their pace bearable enough. Although he felt winded at times, the pace always seemed to allow it to pass and on he went, lagging a bit behind and then catching back up. He was no stranger to covering moderate distances at this pace because he would sometimes need to chase a wounded deer until the bleeding allowed him to catch up, but this was different. He was not at all sure he wished to get into another battle so soon, for his strength was not yet completely recovered since his self-imposed fast.

Chapter Twenty-Five

As they approached the base of the Mountain well below Beaverdams, Jeremy saw numerous other Caughnawagas already there, along with the Captain and a handful of other woodsmen such as he. There was yet no sight of the American force that was rumoured to be heading in this direction, but he was assured that they had been seen in St. Davids, where one of Ducharme's men was shot. A handful of Caughnawagas had gone down the road to wait and then shadow the enemy when they arrived.

It was not long before the U.S. troops appeared far down the St. Davids Road, and the Caughnawagas, deciding they could not hold off all these troops on the narrow Mountain Road leading to the top, had decided to head upward, to await the battle in the place and conditions of their own choosing. Jeremy scampered up the side of the Mountain with the others, struggling to keep up with his load of extra weapons. They reached the top and quickly worked out a plan that would help them overcome the numerical superiority of the Americans. They spread out along the road in the trees, where the Indians had the advantage, and the Americans would be most easily spooked.

As the enemy came into full view, they could see that the column was being commanded by Boerstler, obviously having talked Dearborn into giving him command of the expedition. He likely had no doubt at all that this would be an easy victory, something to be added to his record and possibly gain him the promotion he felt was so long overdue. And, at the head of the column, rode the advance party of approximately fifty men under Dr. Chapin who, Jeremy thought, were probably along for the anticipated plunder.

The U.S. column stopped short of the woods, as their commanders eyed the trees suspiciously, looking for a trap. They knew that the forest stretched far into the distance, with no end on the right until the escarpment edge itself, and beyond the sparser trees on the left, the marshes of the Beaverdams. Ducharme's men gave no sign of their presence, holding their positions admirably so that the Americans could see nothing obvious. Forward the enemy's advance party rode once more, and Jeremy could feel a sinking sensation in the pit of his stomach, as the line of soldiers seemed to stretch on to infinity. How could this handful of men possibly defeat such an overwhelming force?

At a signal from Ducharme, his Caughnawaga skirmishers opened fire from the trees along the road, accompanied by blood-curdling war cries. The forward column in the U.S. ranks, Chapin's men, found themselves facing a wall of lead musket balls. Like dominoes, they fell before the deadly hail, their cries muffled by the sheer volume of noise that accompanied the smoky blasts. They fought back desperately but the only thing they managed to accomplish was to screen the main body of Boerstler's men from the unforgiving fire. A few who survived the initial onslaught dove into a small coulee that ran along the south side of the road, but succeed only in giving their enemies a concentrated position to fire upon. In little time they were felled, almost to a man, but Chapin himself was not among them. He had vanished at some point during the firefight.

The American soldiers found they no longer had an advance guard, and the perpetrators of the massacre were not the hated Bloody Boys or even British troops, but the enemy they feared most. They blindly returned fire into the trees, uncertain of their targets, who stepped from cover only to discharge their own weapons. Boerstler could be seen desperately signalling to his men, trying valiantly to rally them in the face of the withering fire, attempting in vain to get them to form up. Fortunately for him, his men could not obey, for a European battlefield-type stand at this point would likely have wiped them out.

Boerstler ordered his wagons and supplies kept to the rear, in the open, and ordered his three cannon set up in the open area just before the woods. He then advanced his troops, trying to mount a counterattack, his men finally performing as bid, surging toward the Indians and shooting in their general direction as they came. The attack was met by unbelievably heavy fire from the Caughnawaga warriors pouring death and destruction into the American ranks, men collapsing in all manner of poses, some dead, some alive, some uncertain. Parts of men's bodies were torn from them as the large lead of iron blasted into them, too slow to create clean wounds. All about were the sight, and occasionally, the sound of musket balls shredding leaves and bouncing harmlessly from trunks and branches onto the ground, while the remains of burning cartridge papers drifted, still burning, through the air.

Boerstler tried in vain to fall back, but the battle was now fully joined, and there was nowhere to turn. He had allowed himself and his men to be drawn much too far into this uncontrollable battleground and there was little they could do but fight.

Jeremy could hear the roar of the Americans' cannons, and screams followed even before the echoes had died. The smoke, the men and the trees all conspired to block his view of that part of the battlefield. He couldn't see what happened next, but the artillery was heard no more.

Following the first fatal volleys, the battle seemed to slow to a steady but much less intense rhythm. The initial storm of musket balls as thick as black flies in early spring, settled down to more controlled firing. While most of the Americans were fighting from formation as much as the situation would allow, many had made the trees now. Although they still could not see the enemy, they at least felt more secure in the coverage afforded by the trunks.

Boerstler's move to send the wagons to the rear to protect them from sudden ambush, since they could easily be reached from the trees, had left him another problem. The move required him to set up a detail of men to constantly bring up ammunition to the soldiers, who they then needed to find among the trees without themselves being shot. These men bravely ran the gauntlet to the rear, skittering from tree to tree, trying to determine whether that person before them was friend or foe. Fortunately, there were times when the enemy was just as confused, and some made it to the supplies without a major skirmish. Some did not.

The Mountain Road was quickly being turned into a charnel ground, the dead and wounded lying in the road and in the gully. The trees had found a new purpose, as they propped up those who could no longer support themselves, their blood soaking darkly into the bark. Visibility was fading quickly, with the smoke of hundreds of guns drifting sluggishly along the road and through the woods, making the selection of targets a matter of guesswork. The noise created by the myriad individual musket blasts was deafening. Officers' mouths opened regularly and occasionally a fraction of a word could be discerned but, for the most part, commands had become an exercise in futility.

Chapter Twenty-Six

Jeremy crept slowly forward with several Indians, trying to get a shot at the leader, hoping that would lead to American capitulation. They crept up slowly through the woods, using a small defile to cover their movements. No U.S. soldier noticed their advance, and they moved in close enough for Jeremy to hear Boerstler giving commands to his troops, some of who had frozen in place, afraid to move. He also heard the officer shout at one of his subordinates that he thought Cyrus Chapin had led them into a trap, and where was that scoundrel anyways?

There was no clear shot at the commanding officer for Jeremy and his band, however. The man had obviously been injured. The blood on his leg testified to that, but he worked hard at hiding the wound from his men to keep up morale, and he seemed successful so far, for none had drawn attention to it. It was impossible to determine how bad the injury might be because of this, but he seemed otherwise charmed, as he dashed about ordering his men into new positions, limping only occasionally.

To Jeremy, the battle seemed almost organic, as it expanded and contracted much like the movement of a gigantic, poisonous snake, the line drawing itself out and collapsing in on itself according to the fortunes of battle. The Caughnawagas were practicing warfare in their own terms, and they came and went as they pleased, a maddening prospect to the British officers no doubt. The American officers shouted orders which, when not lost in the general din of battle, were being generally ignored by their men. They often fought on only because they were threatened with being shot, or because they saw the enemy draw a bead on them. The chaos was conspicuous, and the only things that seemed to remain constant were that the Americans remained pinned down, and their ammunition was dwindling.

The hot summer sun was taking its toll on the U.S. troops, having been confined mainly to the fort for some time now without drilling. In addition, with numerous ailments circulating throughout the fort unchecked due to the close proximity of the soldiers, they were not at the peak of their health. They had been marching since dawn without stopping, and their strength had been sorely tried before they had arrived. The woollen uniforms were ill suited to fighting under these conditions, and some men collapsed entirely from dehydration.

On the British side, however, the odd tactics of the Indians seemed to be producing results. As they disappeared for periods of time, they always seemed to come back refreshed and ready for more battle. Although they were greatly outnumbered, they held off this greatly superior force, and only partly because of their greater experience at fighting in close quarters such as this.

As the fighting raged on, Jeremy, a small group of Caughnawagas and two local skirmishers worked their way to the back of the American line. From here, they made the maximum noise their few bodies could manage and firing, sometimes without picking a target. Their aim was to keep the American ammunition detail from bringing up more supplies, and it was working admirably. Rail and threaten as they might, the American officers could not get the soldiers to pass the noisy Indians that blocked their way.

Casualties were not confined to the Americans, although they were surely receiving the worst of it. The woodsman who was shooting from beside Jeremy suddenly made a strangling sound so loud that he could be heard above the general din of battle. He made no other sound as, clutching at a hole where his throat previously joined his shoulder, he twisted slowly to the ground. Not far away, Jeremy watched as an Indian lay on the ground beside an American soldier, both covered in blood, the Indians lips still moving, assumably in prayer, although to which God or gods Jeremy could only guess. Not that it mattered, Jeremy thought. It certainly did not appear as though any gods were watching today, for this day obviously belonged to the Devil. All physical space in the field of battle was fast being filled with bodies, and the groans and cries of the dying vied with guns at times for the ears of all.

For three hours this battle had raged, and the Americans were generally feeling the fatigue much more than Ducharme's Caughnawagas. As noon arrived, Boerstler watched desperately for the reinforcements he had sent for, not knowing the messenger had been intercepted and killed. His troops were trapped, surrounded by the trees and the Indians that knew so well how to take advantage of them. He wished now more than ever that he could have brought the sharpshooters that were deemed too important for the protection of the fort to be allowed to go along. It was obvious that he had advanced too far at the start of the battle, but there was nothing for it now. And he was much too proud to surrender.

To Jeremy's great surprise, the fighting seemed to die off suddenly. As curious as any other on the field, he looked in the same direction that all eyes seemed fixed upon, and saw Lieutenant Fitzgibbon marching out into the open holding a white flag. Jeremy moved closer to find out what was happening as he saw Boerstler, now also under a white flag, come out to meet the lieutenant. Were they surrendering to the Americans?

Jeremy watched and listened to the exchange the best he could. Not all of the sound carried clearly, but it was understood to all that Fitzgibbon had gone out to offer to accept the Americans' surrender. The British officer described in great detail his vastly superior force and offered to save his enemy from the bloodlust of the Indians fighting for him.

Boerstler listened and then looked all around, trying to find the evidence of the British superiority. Seeing no sign of all these soldiers, he loudly proclaimed that he was not in the habit of surrendering to a phantom army and wished to see these soldiers before he could agree. Jeremy was unsure of what happened in the next few minutes, but a junior U.S. officer walked off with Fitzgibbon, to return moments later. Looking over in the direction from which they had come, Jeremy saw dragoons, De Haren's men, standing at the edge of the clearing, obviously fresh and unrumpled.

Jeremy felt his heart lighten as he allowed himself to think that maybe fresh troops had arrived to relieve Ducharme's men.

Boerstler still seemed reluctant to surrender, either out of disbelief or pride, or perhaps a bit of both. As Fitzgibbon saw the reluctance, he proclaimed, at the top of his lungs so that the American rank and file could hear, that he could not hold the Indians back much longer.

That was enough for Boerstler. Giving into the American fear of Indians, he surrendered without further consideration. Normally, enemy soldiers were allowed the honour of carrying their weapons to the internment location, but Fitzgibbon obviously feared that the Americans might change their minds if they saw the actual numbers on the British side. Therefore, the U.S. soldiers were told to ground their arms, for the excuse that marching with their weapons past the Indians might infuriate them, resulting in a massacre.

Jeremy and the surviving men who had fought with him stood looking down along the road in the direction the American soldiers were being taken. All along the length and breadth of the recent battleground, men helped each other to their feet and placed others on makeshift litters to be removed for treatment or burial, as the situation dictated. There was nothing glorious in the victory from this angle. Just men from both sides who would never see their families again or faced an uncertain future without the full abilities necessary to farm or perform a trade. Shattered bodies and shattered minds, as some would find sleep difficult for some time to come, playing over and over the sight of a friend or comrade, or even a complete stranger, becoming so much shattered flesh before their eyes.

As Jeremy and the handful of survivors of his little force followed up the stragglers, egging them on, he noticed something moving among the trees on the north side of the road, near where he and these men had guarded the rear. It wasn't likely to be wildlife, for the noise of this battle may have scared away all wild animals permanently, he thought. He decided to go and investigate.

Running quietly in his moccasins, Jeremy took a shortcut he knew of, that would allow him to cut off any person who might be following the road. As he came to the edge of the trees, he saw a large man running after two others toward the point where Mountain Road seemed to drop off the edge of the escarpment. Jeremy put on a burst of speed, rapidly gaining ground on the hind man, who still had no idea that he hadn't made good his escape without being seen.

At the last second, the man heard a noise behind him over the sound of his own pounding feet and gasping breath. He turned his head to look behind him, slowing him down. Just as he recognized the danger, Jeremy launched himself at the man, catching him solidly in the back, knocking him to the ground. He aimed a few well-delivered blows at the man's head and kidneys before his heavier opponent managed to throw him off.

Just before he hit the ground, Jeremy saw the other two men disappear over the Mountain's edge, but he threw off any consideration of that fact. He sprang lightly back to his feet and launched himself once again, this time to the man's midriff. But instead of knocking the man to the ground, he managed only to wind him slightly. Now the two men stood measuring each other on the stretch of open road above St. Davids. They each looked for weaknesses in the other that they might exploit to their advantage. It looked like this might turn into quite the fight, and they both seemed a match.

As Jeremy sized the man up, he suddenly realized that he knew this man. He had seen him often in his travels, although he had never had any personal contact with him. This was the man that Boerstler was cursing earlier. The man who had disappeared from the fighting while his men died at the front of the battle. Dr. Cyrenius Chapin.

At long last, the large man sighed. Jeremy steeled himself for an attack – an attack that didn't materialize. Instead of taking a swing at Jeremy, the man pulled a pistol from his waistband, beneath his waistcoat, and pointed it directly at the smaller man's head.

"I don't know who you are, little man", the physician began. "But I don't have time to spend on common fisticuffs with you right now." He cocked the hammer. "So I suppose I'll just have to shoot you in the interest of saving time."

Chapin smiled broadly, his obvious pleasure at shooting this unarmed man before him seemingly at odds with his profession.

A Question of Loyalty

Jeremy took a deep breath while he desperately searched for a way out of this predicament. He certainly could not pull his own pistol in time, and reaching for his tomahawk or his bayonet would just hasten his death. His pride and joy, the over/under, lay in the dust a few yards away, for he had thrown it free to avoid injuring himself when he tackled Chapin. Finding no recourse available to him, he closed his eyes, awaiting the inevitable.

Jeremy heard a loud report, a fact that seemed odd to him, since he was not yet dead. Could Chapin have missed at this range? But the shot seemed to have come from off to his right somewhere. He opened his eyes just in time to see Chapin drop his pistol to the ground.

Following Chapin's glare, but not wishing to take his eyes from the man, Jeremy moved eyes only a little, to see by peripheral vision one of the Caughnawagas that he had been fighting alongside. He was standing only twenty feet away with one musket on the ground, smoke still pouring from its muzzle. In his hands, aimed directly for Chapin's midsection, he held another, apparently ready to fire.

Chapin scowled as he surrendered to his fate. Indians had massacred his men and now it was his turn, he thought. Well, there was no way he would allow the savage to see his fear. But no shot came. He thought that the Indian had missed with the first, but now he realized that the aim had been to disarm him all along.

Jeremy picked up his gun from the ground and told Chapin to start walking. "I am certainly glad to see you", he said to the Indian. "Did you have to wait so long, though?" he joked.

The Caughnawaga looked sternly at him and then his face broke into a broad smile. "I just wished to see what you do to fight with your eyes closed", he chuckled with his slight French inflection.

Jeremy returned the grin and then turned to Chapin. "Very well, Doctor", he said. "I think it's time you met James Fitzgibbon." He waggled his gun to indicate that Chapin should start walking up ahead, and the three headed back towards the DeCou homestead.

The American soldiers were herded on toward DeCou's house, and when they finally came out into the open, Boerstler realized that he had been duped. However, there was now no longer any recourse, for the American weapons all lay on the road back in the forest, and they could hardly fight hand to musket, tomahawk and bayonet, against even as small a force as this.

The American soldiers were marched off for sorting into which were to be prisoners or to be paroled and the scene behind them broke down in utter bedlam. The Indians were allowed to fall ravenously onto the discarded weapons, some staggering off with their arms loaded down by their booty. As proof that life is rarely fair, though, the Caughnawagas did not end up with the lion's share of the haul. That fortune befell the Mohawk Indians, who had arrived late with the De Haren's troops and had fought little in the course of this battle.

Jeremy trod heavily to Fitzgibbon's headquarters, dehydrated, exhausted, and the adrenaline which had kept him going through the stress of battle was now gone. As he chanced to look down at his arm, he could see that he had been shot at some point. His sleeve was torn and blood had already dried, gluing the fabric to his arm. Still not feeling any pain, he sat down heavily at the back of DeCou's house, soon forgetting his own injury, and gulped water from the dippers that were being passed around to those not required for sorting the prisoners. The wounded and the dead of both sides were dropped unceremoniously onto the lawn until they covered every inch of churned grass and mud, indiscernible one from the other but for the screams that issued forth from those who still had the strength and the will to do so. Occasionally, some hapless soldier would be loaded onto a stretcher and brought into one of the surgeries set up in the tent that had been erected at the back of the yard, and an entirely new course of screams and moans could be heard.

Some would die that day, and some would wish they had, as the wages of battle for them would consist of missing limbs or other body parts, some immediately but some only after intense suffering brought on by gangrene. Jeremy could not tell which men had died in there and which had merely succumbed gratefully to unconsciousness during the procedures, for they all appeared the same to him; limp vestiges of humanity, drenched in blood, pale as the winter snows.

He lay in the shade with another woodsman, a man he had

previously known by reputation only, and two Caughnawagas, including the one who had saved him from Chapin. They could hear raucous laughter coming from inside the house as the officers compared war stories, each man trying loudly to claim a portion of the credit for himself. In a loud voice, Fitzgibbon explained to De Haren's latecomers about the bluff he had to perpetrate on Boerstler to get him to surrender.

"He thought we were going to lose, so the only answer he could think of was to get the enemy to surrender", someone commented to loud guffaws. This analysis was followed closely by toasts to the hero of the day, Lieutenant James Fitzgibbon.

Jeremy, even through his haze of physical and emotional exhaustion, could not help but think wryly that there seemed to be no toasts to the Indians and the locals who fought so hard in this battle. Never mind the fact that the Caughnawagas fought the Americans to exhaustion. And there was no mention at all coming from the house, not even from Ducharme through his interpreter, pointing out that it was the Americans' mortal fear of Indians that allowed Fitzgibbon's ruse to work.

British officers would never change, he thought. It was all about the regular army, and the locals be damned, whatever their race or contribution. Granted, they had not been well served by the locals in the regular battles of this war, but this fight had been unusual, one more in keeping with the nature of the North American wilderness. A little credit where it was due, Jeremy thought. But it did not sit long upon his mind, for he was soon fast asleep beneath the boughs of DeCou's shade tree.

Jeremy slept all that night and well into the next morning, not feeling the hard ground or the heavy dew that night that soaked them all or the pain from indeterminate wound he had suffered. In time, his mind was able to cut out all the screaming and moaning of the injured and dying that continued well into the night, although his mind translated some of it subconsciously to his dreams in various forms. He moved without waking when someone tripped over him or rolled up against him. The exhaustion was total.

When consciousness finally did return to the newly minted warrior, he sat up confused, looking about for several seconds before the full horror of the previous day once more hit home. He stumbled unsurely to a bucket of water that had dipper handles sticking from it and drank his fill. Obviously, someone had been refilling it during the night or earlier this morning.

Jeremy began to take stock of himself and found that, aside from a great deal of dust and dried sweat and the musky odour that the combination produced, he was in fairly good shape. The blood that had receded to his body core due to his uncomfortable sleeping position, which he had not even noticed, was beginning to return to his limbs. It created an uncomfortable tingling sensation in his arms and legs and, quite suddenly, that was when he felt it. The pain began as discomfort but quickly rose to a burning, excruciating pain that almost seemed to incapacitate him until he became accustomed to it.

Sitting on a stool near him, a man sat watching Jeremy's face go through contortions as his body realized the pain. "I think maybe we'd better have a look at that", the man suggested.

It was then that Jeremy realized that the other man was wearing a bloody smock. Obviously this was one of the camp surgeons, and panic immediately flooded into him. No, he thought, grasping his arm defensively, I'll not let him cut off my arm!

The surgeon had come over by Jeremy's side and was squatting beside him. He removed a pair of bloody scissors from a pocket in his smock and, roughly grabbing Jeremy's arm to keep it still, began to cut away the fabric of the damaged shirtsleeve. The blood was completely dried by now and refused to relinquish its hold on the homespun, but the surgeon still tried to pull it free. The pain shot through Jeremy's arm and into his shoulder, while he shouted his protestations to this sadist who he was sure wished to tear off his arm without benefit of a saw. As he looked at the wound, he could see fresh blood once again seeping from under the scab and through the material of his shirt.

"It looks like the scab has a fair hold on your shirt", the surgeon muttered matter-of-factly. He stood up, ordering Jeremy to come with him to the tent.

Jeremy resisted. He had seen the men that went in there come out with parts of their anatomy missing, no longer able to walk of their own power. He pulled his arm way from this man that he was certain wished to torture him.

"Come along, then", the surgeon urged him, his voice acquiring an edge of impatience. "I've been up all night while you've been sleeping and I'd like some rest myself. We haven't all day."

Jeremy hesitated a few seconds longer, but then followed meekly, in the end succumbing to the man's officer status. As he walked into the tent, he almost fainted from the assault of unfamiliar sensory stimuli inside. Everywhere he looked was bloody cloth. A box in the corner had severed limbs visible; no one had yet removed them for burial, and Jeremy could feel his head spin at the sight. There was a strong odour of poultices and medicines that Jeremy could not even begin to identify, and the coppery smell of blood was sickening.

"Sit here", the surgeon ordered.

Jeremy did as he was told, too woozy to resist. The surgeon poured fresh water into a pan from a kettle that sat simmering on a brazier in the corner of the tent and added some cold from a pitcher. He guided Jeremy's arm into the pan and told him to let it soak for a bit. He then set about looking for a fresh cloth with which to clean the wound so it could be inspected. When he returned, he firmly but gently pulled the cloth away from the wound. The scab still fought to hold on, causing Jeremy great pain, but the soaking had softened it sufficiently that the surgeon could finally pull it free.

The surgeon inspected the wound carefully. "Doesn't seem to be anything serious", he said, using a bloody knife, which had been used as a scalpel to pull back the edge of the wound for a better look. He mumbled more to himself than to his patient when he spoke, perhaps out of exhaustion, the result being that Jeremy could scarcely hear him. "Looks like a ball just grazed your arm." Then he proceeded to bind the wound with another fresh cloth, making Jeremy grimace as he tied the knot directly over the wound.

"It seems to be a little red, though", the surgeon said, looking up at Jeremy's pale face. "I want you to open this up every now and then and keep an eye on it. If it gets gangrene, that'll be the end of your arm." With that encouraging prognosis, he washed up his hands and walked out of the tent, leaving Jeremy sitting on the chair, staring at him in disbelief.

Chapter Twenty-Seven

Jeremy wandered slowly back out into the light from what he thought of as the "death tent", lost in thought as to what he would do next. He no longer had any intention of joining up with the Bloody Boys; the disenchantment over the officers' lack of respect for the non-military fighters in yesterday's battle was still fresh in his mind. Perhaps he should just continue to look for Williamson and get that part of his life cleared up.

He heard two officers, likely De Haren's men, since Jeremy did not recognize them, speaking in muted voices near the house. "Do we know what the final tally was?" one asked.

The other looked around the yard at the men that still covered the ground. "Yes, sir", he replied. "At rough count, the Americans have lost about eighty men, dead and wounded. We also have over four hundred and fifty prisoners."

The officer who was obviously senior whistled. "Over five hundred Americans taken out of the war", he said thoughtfully. "And our side? How did we fare?"

The junior man shrugged. "It's hard to tell, sir", he replied. "We think there were only about twenty-five dead and wounded, but one never knows."

"How's that?" the other asked.

The junior man, who had fought with natives in the past, looked about the yard one more time, and replied, almost distractedly, "Well, sir, the Indians are known sometimes to remove their dead and wounded from the battlefield and, with all their comings and goings, we're not quite sure what their final tally might be." He looked around at the men on the ground, many now missing arms and limbs that had fallen to the surgeon's saw in the tradition of battleground surgery. "And I'm not sure I blame them for not wanting our form of medicine, at that", he muttered.

"How many officers among the prisoners?"

"Not many, sir. I believe there were only three or four left, and only one can walk. I'm afraid the officers took heavy loses early on in the fight." The junior officer looked over at Jeremy and then continued as if he wasn't there. "A pity, really. They were officers, after all."

Jeremy made his way to the door of DeCou's house and knocked weakly. A voice could be heard inside, but he couldn't make out what was being said. Once more he knocked, this time louder. The door swung suddenly open and there stood Lieutenant Fitzgibbon, still in his bloody uniform, looking somewhat hung over.

"Bloody hell!" the lieutenant blasted at Jeremy. "What in blazes do you want at this hour?" He looked more closely at Jeremy and blinked. "Ah, Mr. van Hijser." His voice became at once somewhat conciliatory in its tone. "And what can I do for you today?"

Jeremy cleared his throat as he looked at Fitzgibbon. "I just wanted to let you know that there may be a spy among your men", he said, matter-of-factly. "I heard some of Willcocks' men talk about it while I was his prisoner."

"Among my own men, eh?" The officer looked thoughtful or a moment. "That would explain how the Americans knew when I'd be here, or at least I assume they did. Did you hear any hint as to who this man might be?"

"No, that's all I heard. They just said the man was riding with you."

Fitzgibbon nodded slowly. "As you know, Jeremy, we've known there was a spy somewhere, but it's the first I've heard that he rides with me. I'll need to think long and hard about who would sell me out."

Jeremy lost interest in the conversation. He bid the lieutenant farewell and headed off across the property toward the road. He had no wish to be connected to this war any longer. Not to suggest that he would support the Americans. Not by any means! He did not totally understand their concept of democracy, for politics had never been of great interest to him, and he had found during his travels that the average U.S. farmer had little interest as well. Most people had too many everyday problems to contend with for such abstractions, he thought.

But the Americans had allowed the likes of Willcocks, Williamson and Chapin to run roughshod over Jeremy's neighbours, terrorizing them and stealing from them. He could not abide the invaders for that alone. For those things and the things they had done to him, they would receive no support from him.

Jeremy had just tasted of his first battle, and the taste was not good. The young men he watched die that day, whether American or British subjects, or Indians like the Caughnawaga and Mohawks, deserved better than to lie in a roadway, screaming from the injuries. He could not imagine a political gain important enough for the misery he had witnessed yesterday.

His hatred for Williams, however, was another matter. That animal deserved to die, to be shot down like a rabid dog before he could harm anyone else. If Jeremy had any say in the matter, he would be the man to perform this service to humanity. Shouldering his gun, he started off down the road toward the marshes and the property that was all he had left of a home. Perhaps, when this madness was all over, he could consider rebuilding on the land, but for now, there seemed little point.

Jeremy had not gone far, however, before he heard the sound of someone running up behind him. Still edgy, he turned automatically to defend himself, swinging his gun from his shoulder as he did so. But there was no menace here. The footsteps he had heard belonged to the Caughnawaga warrior who had saved his life the day before. The native stopped beside him, saying nothing.

"Where you are going?" he asked finally.

"Back to my land", Jeremy replied. "I need to get myself organized before I take care of some unfinished business."

"This business, has it to do with the army?" he asked.

"No, this is quite personal." Jeremy explained about his vendetta and the reasons for it in as few words as possible.

"Then I think I'll go with you", the Indian stated quite naturally.

"I am not so happy with the war, you know? I think I will not fight with the soldiers again."

Jeremy opened his mouth as if to argue, then thought better of it. "But what will you do coming along with me? Certainly you don't wish to fight my war?"

"Better your war than theirs", he said. "Show me where this home of yours is. Maybe we'll make plans for catching this Williamson, eh?"

Jeremy thought about it for a moment, and then offered his hand to the Indian. As they shook, he said, "Well, if we're to fight together, you may as well know, my name is Jeremy."

"I won't try to break your tongue with my Indian name", the other answered with a smile. "My Christian name is Josef. Like the father of Jesus, yes? Josef DuLac."

"Well, Josef", Jeremy said, slapping his new partner on the back. "Welcome aboard. I'm quite sure you'll regret this, and probably sooner than later."

To his great chagrin, Joseph Willcocks had been summoned to Fort George, and ordered to report directly to Dearborn's second in command, Brigadier General John Boyd. He grumbled all the way, feeling slighted at having been so ignominiously ordered to appear. Upon his arrival at the gates, he announced himself curtly to the guard on duty, impatient when the enlisted man did not jump to at his appearance. The guard, having been alerted to Willcocks' impending visit, wordlessly ushered him to the same room where Willcocks had previously attended the meeting to speak of a possible attack on Beaverdams.

He waited there impatiently, sitting alone at the table, drumming his fingers incessantly, and cursing these American soldiers under his breath for their impudence. After almost fifteen minutes of killing time in this manner, General Boyd finally walked into the room. Willcocks rose to shake his hand.

"Please sit, Mr. Willcocks", Boyd said flatly, snubbing the man's civilian greeting, and indicated the chair from which Willcocks had risen.

Willcocks could not help but feel insulted yet again. Now he apparently was not even good enough to shake hands with! He had a mind to tell this self-important popinjay exactly what he thought of him.

"What is it I can do for you?" he meekly asked instead.

Boyd began speaking without looking up at Willcocks. Instead, he rummaged through some papers he had brought into the room with him. "Mr. Willcocks, it has come to our attention that there has been some sort of falling out between you and some of your men."

It was a statement, and not a question, so Willcocks realized that someone had been keeping the fort apprised of the state of affairs at his camp. He merely nodded.

"Would you mind explaining the nature of this problem you have with your men?" Boyd asked, already knowing the answer, but wanting to nettle this man anyway.

Willcocks sat straighter in his chair, fuming at the implication that it was his command that was the problem. "Williamson disobeyed a direct order and kept a prisoner who he was ordered by your Captain Smythe to release. In addition, contrary to all the rules of civilized warfare, he was torturing the man."

"I see", the general replied, beginning to pace about the room. "And what did you decide would be appropriate punishment for this crime?"

"It wasn't just that crime", Willcocks shot back. "Although one would think that obeying a direct order during wartime would merit the death penalty. No, this man also murdered one of his own men while incapacitated by wounds suffered in battle." Willcocks sat back again in his chair, feeling quite vindicated in his judgment concerning Williamson. "So I did the obvious and sentenced him to hang."

Willcocks' words hung over the table like a cloud while Boyd seemed to take this in and mull it over.

"You realize, don't you, Mr. Willcocks, that you haven't the authority to pronounce a sentence of death, or any other punishment other than simple lashes or temporary imprisonment?" Boyd was now looking directly at the civilian, his eyes displaying a range of emotion that lay somewhere between anger and satisfaction. "If you had charges of this gravity to bring to bear against any man, you should have bound him over to us and we, as the government

A Question of Loyalty

of occupation and your military commanders, would deal with it." His eyes flashed. "Do you understand?"

Willcocks swallowed heavily. "Yes. Yes I do."

"Yes, who?" Boyd roared, beginning to enjoy this game immensely.

"Yes, sir!" Willcocks shouted, filled with trepidation and anger, wondering what this interview was leading to.

Boyd had begun pacing again, his hands clasped behind him. "You know that, had you succeeded in hanging your man, you yourself would have been liable for charges?"

Willcocks said nothing. Under the circumstances, perhaps he had already said too much, so he held his counsel, allowing the general to continue.

Boyd sat down on the chair opposite Willcocks and leaned toward him. "Here's the reason you were summoned here", he said. "General Dearborn is concerned that we may need every man with loyalties to the U.S., especially since the fiasco at Beaverdams. The exact numbers aren't important, but we lost many men there, and Dearborn is concerned that the British might attempt to push their advantage while we're down."

"And what has that to do with Williamson and myself?" Willcocks asked, not quite sure where this was leading.

"Quite simply this", the officer started, not feeling entirely comfortable meddling in what was surely a civilian affair, and between thieves at that! "You're to pardon Mr. Williamson and place him back under your command." He pronounced the word 'command' in a cynical manner, letting Willcocks know how he felt about civilian groups that pretended to a military structure.

"What?" Willcocks shouted, bolting from his chair.

"Sit down, Mr. Willcocks!" the general shouted, even louder than the outraged utterance. "Let me remind you that you are supplied and backed only by the indulgence of the general. If you feel you can't carry out orders, perhaps you'd like to take on the British without logistics or support? That can, and I say quite enthusiastically, will be arranged unless I hear a yes sir coming from your mouth immediately."

Willcocks was trapped. The consequences of maintaining his pride would be too dire, so he swallowed hard and muttered, "Yes, sir."

Chapter Twenty-Eight

On the second night, the two men sat together under the lean-to shelter they had constructed from boards salvaged from one of the sheds, the process hampered somewhat by the increasingly painful burning sensation in Jeremy's arm. Although the shed too had been set afire by Williamson's men, it had only partially burned, leaving enough lumber for this crude shelter. They had intended to sleep out under the stars that night, but they'd seen the dark clouds forming to the northwest and decided that, in this case, preparation would be the better part of valour.

They watched the fire sputter as it fought courageously against the latest downpour, but apparently was about to lose the battle. All evening these showers had passed over them, not long in duration but more than making up for it in intensity.

"Why is it you speak English so well?" Jeremy asked finally, giving in to his curiosity. "Don't you come from the same area as Ducharme?"

"Generally", Josef answered with a wry grin. "But he is from the city. Montreal, you know? He only comes to the reserve at Kanesewake often enough to justify his pay." The Indian threw another piece of wood on the fire, watching it sputter, crackle, and then finally catching a small flame.

"So where did you learn to speak English?" Jeremy repeated.

"We learn partly from the missionaries", Josef explained. "Some speak English very well. We also learn much from the people we come into contact with to the south. It's in our best interest to learn because our reserve is in both Lower Canada and the United States." He cast a sly glance at his new friend. "We need to know for doing business."

The night was developing a cold edge as the dampness worked its way into them, and they considered the possible loss of the fire a disaster. In the end they surrendered to the inevitable, as the wood no longer caught flame, too wet to burn. Pulling their clothes about them, they tried their best to get some sleep.

In the early hours of the morning, Jeremy awoke, feeling parched and ill. He put his hand to his forehead to find he was burning up with fever and reached for some water to cool himself. As he did so, he rolled onto his injured arm, only to discover that he had not the strength to hold himself up, pain shooting to his shoulder. Repositioning himself, he managed to reach the bottle and bring it to his lips, drinking greedily.

Nausea washed over him as the cool water hit his stomach, and he had to roll over quickly to avoid vomiting on himself, perhaps choking in the process. He had eaten little that day, but what there was soon projected weakly onto the ground.

Josef woke up, hearing the retching coming from his friend. "Have you caught some illness?" he asked, half awake.

"No", Jeremy replied breathlessly and then vomited again. "No, I think my wound's become infected.

The rain had stopped by now and Josef set about rebuilding the fire with what dry wood he could break from the inside branches of a pair of pine trees. As the flames began to reach above the fuel, he placed some of the damp wood on top, careful not to extinguish the tiny blaze. Once that was accomplished, he took a small burning piece of wood to use as a torch.

"Let me see the wound", he ordered Jeremy, who had neither the strength to comply nor to resist.

Josef looked carefully at the wound and pushed gently at the edges, confirming his fears. The area all around the wound had gone bright red and the wound itself was oozing a sickly yellowish discharge. If something wasn't done soon, gangrene would set into the whole arm, and amputation would be the only answer.

So far, the arm did not exude the telltale odour of corruption that signalled that most feared of battle wound reactions.

Josef knew he dared not wait until morning to deal with this. Searching about the trees and the field with a new torch, he began to pick certain herbs that he had learned would help. He had watched as the healer in his village had used these same plants for dealing with symptoms like Jeremy's to mixed results. But the result of not trying would be to almost certainly watch his new friend die.

First off, he boiled a mixture in some water and set it aside to cool, while he started pounding up the leaves of several other plants, mixing in water as he went. Slowly, a pasty substance took shape from this last concoction and he plastered it liberally on Jeremy's wound. Then he retrieved the now-cooled potion he had made first and, propping up his patient, proceeded to coax him to drink.

Jeremy had no idea what his companion was doing, or why. What he did know was that his stomach was beginning to settle, still mildly nauseous but no longer feeling the urge to vomit, an exercise that had become a series of non-productive dry heaves. Now more able to appreciate other sensations, he noticed that some of the fire had gone out of the wound on his arm. He smiled weakly at Josef and thanked him in a shaky voice. He wasn't quite sure what his friend had done, but he relaxed enough to slip into a deep, dreamless sleep.

Josef stayed up for the balance of the night, keeping an eye on Jeremy to see if anything more dangerous developed. He would look at the wound more closely in the light of morning. In the meantime, however, he bathed the patient's head with cool water from Jeremy's old well and fed the fire to keep away the chills of the night.

Halfway through the next morning, Jeremy woke up, not quite certain what had happened. As his senses slowly returned, the memory came seeping back in. He had been quite ill, and whatever it was that Josef had done made him feel better. He looked around for his friend and found him lying on the ground beside the burned-out fire, sound asleep. Not wishing to disturb him, Jeremy tried to get up, but found he was too weak, and the effort brought on a renewed wave of nausea. He lay down again, not wishing to experience the vomiting of the previous night.

It was only a few minutes before Josef woke up himself and sat up. "How's my sick friend's doing today?" he asked.

Jeremy smiled as gamely as he could, wondering if his grin appeared as idiotic as it seemed from his side of his face. "Fine", he croaked, not quite finding his voice.

Josef laughed. "Ready to go fight another battle, eh?"

"Just hand me my gun", Jeremy joked, wincing as he stuck out the injured arm. "And, while you're about it, aim and fire it for me, will you? There's a good man."

Josef came over and crouched beside his patient, feeling his head. He frowned. "Seems like you still have the fever. You lie in the shelter and I will go look for something to eat."

Jeremy lay back and looked up at his physician's face. "Just what is it you did?"

"It's what you call, how do you say it? An old family recipe." Josef's knowledge of English idiomatic expressions almost failed him this time. "If it works, I'll give it to you."

"What do you mean, 'if'", Jeremy countered. "It's already worked wonders."

Josef shook his head slightly. "You still have a fever and, though the red is not so much around the wound now, it's still infected. You rest, and I will try another of the old recipes that I know of."

Jeremy sighed. He still felt quite weak and it made him feel resentful, for he was not accustomed to others taking care of him like this. He should be up and fending for himself, as he had all his adult life. The resentment was short-lived, however, as he soon fell asleep once again, this time experiencing uncomfortable, but ultimately inexplicable dreams.

The next two days continued in the same manner. Jeremy would wake up, Josef would goad him into drinking one or another of his medicinal potions and sometimes tinker with the dressing or clean off the paste so that he could inspect it, and Jeremy would fall back to sleep.

Finally, on the fourth day, Jeremy found he was feeling somewhat better. The nausea was now completely gone and the pain in his arm had receded to the point where he could sit himself up. His appetite had returned, and he tore into his first full meal with enthusiasm, leading Josef to caution him to slow down, for his stomach was not accustomed to the volume.

After eating, Jeremy decided he would try to get up unaided. When Josef left on some errand, he rose shakily to his feet and stood there for almost a minute before he became dizzy, almost falling to the ground. Maybe he got up just a bit too quickly, he thought. So he tried it again, more slowly this time, using the frame of the lean-to to support him in his effort. Once more, he felt his legs begin to buckle under him, and he lowered himself back to his makeshift bed, just as Josef returned.

"I have no Indian cure for a broken neck", he warned, semi-seriously. "If I was you, I'd stay down, you know?"

"I've been lying around for three days already", Jeremy complained. "I can't accomplish a thing lying here all day and all night."

"Ah", Josef said, looking like he was attempting to solve a conundrum. "But you are doing something. You're getting better." He turned and sat down opposite his friend, the edge of the shade of the lean-to catching him across the forehead.

Jeremy studied his benefactor carefully, never before seeing him up close in the daylight. He wondered why they called the Indians "redskins", for Josef's skin was hardly red. He seemed tanned, the colour no different than that of any white man who'd spent time working in the sun. Jeremy was having a hard time trying to determine the man's age, however, because his appearance presented conflicting signs. His hair was mostly black, shot through with streaks of grey, but his skin was smooth, except around the eyes.

Josef seemed in excellent condition and often acted like he had not a care in the world. But his eyes seemed ageless, like they had seen everything, more than anyone should, more than anyone should be capable of absorbing. Jeremy wondered at the experience behind those eyes, but felt he did not know him nearly well enough for questions so personal. Then he noticed a thick, ragged scar just under the man's hairline.

"Where did you get such a scar?" Jeremy caught himself as he said it and felt he was being somewhat rude, so he tried to cover up with a flippant remark. "Fall off a cliff?"

Josef grinned, and then touched the scar, running his index finger along the length. His grin turned to a saddened expression. "No, this is where I was scalped."

Jeremy almost performed a double take at this unexpected remark. "You were scalped?" he said, incredulous. "Was it another tribe? How did you survive?"

Josef did not answer immediately, seemingly considering his reply. Jeremy took this momentary silence to mean that his companion had no wish to speak about a difficult memory. "I'm sorry. I didn't mean to pry into something you likely don't want to talk about."

The native man shook his head slowly and raised his head to look into Jeremy's eyes. "No, I will tell you", he said softly. "This was not done by other Indians", he started. "I was scalped by a white man."

Jeremy looked at his friend in astonishment. "White men tried to scalp you?" he asked, dumbfounded by the thought that one of his own people would perform this abomination on any other man.

Josef nodded. "I was hunting with a friend. While we slept, we were attacked by four white men who accused us of stealing a cow."

"A cow", Jeremy repeated, incredulous. "Which side of the border were you on?"

His friend shrugged. "I don't know. It doesn't matter, because we don't know what side of the border these men came from anyways. They beat us hard, with fists, feet, even butts of guns to get confession. When we didn't confess, they held us down and scalped us." He looked away toward the horizon, not really seeing it. "My friend, he died." A tear appeared in his eye, but he quickly wiped it away. "They thought I was dead too, but I fooled them. Before they could finish the job, I jumped up and ran away. I hid in the forest for several days; afraid the men were still around. The wound became sick, like your arm, and I nearly died. That's how I learned of the medicine I used on you, when one of my tribe found me and brought me back."

His soft focus on the sky remained as he added, mostly to himself, "They never even asked us where the cow was." His voice caught as he said it. "They never asked us if we did it and they didn't ask where the cow was."

Jeremy felt ill at the implication. The men had known they did not steal the cow. In all likelihood, there had been no cow. It was all just a convenient accusation because they wished to beat up on some Indians.

"It's a good thing for me that you survived, friend", Jeremy said, not knowing how else to react, and wondering whether he should have reacted at all.

"It surely is", Josef shot back, his voice stronger and a laugh in his throat.

Jeremy was trying to think of a comeback to his friend's attempted cover-up, but he was becoming rather woozy once again, and his mind refused to focus clearly. In minutes, he had fallen soundly asleep once more.

Josef looked down on his friend and smiled sadly. It was a good thing not all white men were the same, he thought. Every once in a while, there was one who could actually be an Indian's friend. With a shrug to ward off any further sentimentality, he set about grinding up some more plants for Jeremy's arm. He had no idea why, or what they were fighting, or how the medicine worked, only that they would need to continue the treatment for several more days before the danger was past.

By the middle of July, Jeremy and Josef were spending their days hunting game, dressing it and then selling what they could at the various settlements. There were few customers, however. The taverns that once took Jeremy's wild meat had little use for it now, as there were not many travellers on the road these days. And there was always the danger that any food they purchased would be confiscated in the name of whatever army controlled a given area at a given time. In that case, they would be out whatever they may have paid for it. But they were able to raise some modest coin from some townspeople, who needed the pelts for various purposes.

It was on one of these frequent hunting trips that Josef and

Jeremy stumbled upon Joseph Willcocks' and his men, occupying a farm just outside Chippewa.

"I wouldn't have expected to find them here", Jeremy whispered to his partner as they watched from the edge of a coulee. The gully, which had likely been full of running water in the spring, was now completely dry.

"Why is that?"

"This has always been Chapin's territory", Jeremy answered. "The two men have no use for each other, so they stayed out of each other's way most of the time. I guess now that Chapin's safely in the hands of the British, Willcocks is expanding his kingdom."

Being sure to stay low, the two men crept along the inside of the coulee, trying to get as close as safely possible. The growth along the edge was a good screen, but one never knew where they might find a sentry posted. When they reached a point where they were only a dozen yards from the raiders' camp's perimeter, they decided they had gone far enough. Both wished to make sure they had an avenue of escape open to them, should they be discovered.

They saw nothing of note in the camp. Men went about the daily drudgery of basic chores, fetching water and wood, repairing items of clothing, cleaning weapons. There was no note of urgency to any of it, just routine complaints of boredom and the boss, of whom there was no sign. Jeremy assumed that he must be in the house, likely with his "officers".

As they lay there watching, one of the men walked to the edge of the coulee a mere twenty-five feet away and relieved himself, still talking to someone unseen over his opposite shoulder. Josef and Jeremy both tensed, expecting that, at any moment, the man might turn around and spot them hiding there. Josef pulled his knife and positioned himself to spring to his feet should it become necessary, but the necessity never arrived. The man completed his task and, with loud laughter, went away.

The two hunters looked at each other, both realizing how close they had come to being discovered. "Let's go back to our own camp and wait until nightfall", Jeremy suggested. "That was much too close."

Josef agreed readily, and they eased themselves back along the coulee the way they had come, looking back over their shoulders often to see if they had been noticed. Jeremy, bringing up the rear, was so intent on watching their backs, in fact, that he failed to noticed a washed-out section before him.

He stifled a curse as he lost his balance. He tried to save himself from falling by taking hold of a root that hung near his hand, but the plant to which it was attached dangled too precariously at the edge. Jeremy crashed to the bottom of the coulee, a shrub still firmly clenched in his fist. He lay in the bottom, looking up a Josef, who in turn was looking back down at Jeremy, an amused grin on his face. The only time Jeremy could not see the laughter in his companion's eyes was during the quick glances back, to see if anyone had noticed.

Jeremy stood up and dusted himself off, muttering under his breath words that would not be accepted in polite company. The good thing was that the only injury was to his ego. Josef would be reminding him of this for some time to come, he thought.

As he started to climb back up the side of the coulee to where Josef waited, no doubt bursting with a desire to laugh aloud, Jeremy saw movement at the top, near where they had been lying to watch the camp.

"Over here!" a voice rang out. "Over here! There's someone..." The one who had come to investigate noticed Josef. "Indians!" he cried with some urgency. "It's Indians!"

The two who had been spies but moments ago now heard a general alarm being raised in the camp. They could hear cries erupting from what had, until now, been a tranquil if boring camp scene. "Indians!" "To arms!" "Where?" They're trying to surround us!" The matter would have been humorous had it not been so deadly.

Josef and Jeremy crossed to the other side of the coulee and vanished into the woods, just as the sounds of gunfire assailed their ears. Despite the amount of shooting, however, there was no sound of musket balls smashing through the undergrowth or smacking into tree trunks. Willcocks' men seemed to have no idea of what they were shooting at or where. They were probably hoping just to scare the "Indians" off with the general din and confusion. As for the two men, they ran for some distance before they dared to look back.

"Well, I think they'll have a close eye on the perimeters tonight now", Jeremy sighed, angry with himself for his embarrassing plunge. "They'll especially be watching the coulee." He shook his head in exasperation.

Josef was nothing if not an opportunist, and a chance like this to rib his partner was heaven sent. "I'm sure they won't need their eyes if you're coming", he grinned. "All they'll need is their ears." He burst out laughing at the expression on Jeremy's face at this comment.

Jeremy stood looking at his friend for a moment and then launched himself, catching Josef across the chest. Down they fell into the dirt, rolling and laughing so hard, neither man could stay on top and gain the advantage. Finally, they both dropped down and lay gasping.

"Well", started Josef. "At least you know you can pass for an Indian."

Chapter Twenty-Nine

At the raiders' camp, the shooting had stopped. The men all stood about, wondering if they had frightened off the Indians. They talked so noisily among themselves, they certainly would not have heard if there had indeed been an entire tribe of Indians surrounding them. They had all reloaded their muskets, rifles and pistols and stood watching and waiting for the inevitable war screams and a horrible death.

Willcocks, who had been awakened from a noonday nap by the noise, now strode heavily onto the short porch that had been constructed at the back door by the farm's owner. "What's going on out here?" he demanded, in a voice that was surprisingly loud enough to carry over the general din. "Did I hear the cry of Indians?"

One of the men came running up to the porch, still excited by the event. "Yes, sir, you surely did, sir. One of the men caught a couple skulking about in the coulee, so the cry went up, but we think we sacred them away."

"If one of the men caught the Indians, where are they?" Willcocks asked, his voice much more level than his temper.

"Well, he didn't actually catch them", the man explained tentatively, now sorry the he had stepped forward. "He saw them, but they escaped."

Willcocks took full advantage of his physical position, two feet higher from the ground than this man. It allowed him to literally look down upon the fool, although he would certainly have done so figuratively at any rate.

"There was a great deal of shooting and shouting", he started. "How many Indians did you see altogether?"

The man looked back at the others, who seemed almost physically to step back when he turned his head. It was not a good time to be connected with this bearer of bad news. Willcocks' temper had not improved in the past couple of months, since the prisoner escaped, probably tipping off Fitzgibbon at DeCou. It was the man's own fault, though, they all thought. He would not be in this bind if he had not been so anxious to cozy up to the American brass.

If that had not been bad enough, after Beaverdams their boss had travelled to the fort. When he came back, he was more irascible than ever, although he did not ever say why. They only knew that he had tried to send for Williamson for some unknown reason, with the order to tell the renegade the crime had been pardoned.

"I didn't see any, myself", he answered.

"And you!" Willcocks bellowed, pointing to another man in the crowd. "Did you see any Indians?"

"No, sir. I didn't, but we was told they was all around", this new victim replied.

Willcocks said nothing for several minutes, just staring intently at his men, incredulous. The raiders assembled there were feeling increasingly uneasy. There was no way of knowing what the cost of this debacle might be, but they were sure something unpleasant was about to happen.

"You idiots!" Willcocks exploded at last. "One of you thought he saw Indians, so you all started shooting wildly into the trees! Did anyone at all follow these supposed Indians to see?" He looked around, but no man dared raise his hand for fear of being caught in a lie by this man who didn't countenance liars in his presence. "So, once the shooting stopped, has anyone yet gone out to see if you hit anything?" His eyes swept the throng once more but again, no hand rose into the air.

Willcocks waited for effect once more. "I want you men to break up into small groups and go out there to look for Indians, dead ones or live ones. If you find any, bring them here." He glanced about again. "If you don't find any, every last one of you will be standing watch tonight. And I mean all night long!"

Nobody moved, rooted to the ground where they stood. They were not sure which they feared more; Indians that might yet lie in wait for them, or Willcocks himself. At least he had not shot anyone yet, or challenged one to a duel, which he was known to do.

"Move!!" Willcocks bellowed, overcoming each man's inertia. The men scattered off into the trees, down into the coulee and into the trees on the other side.

Willcocks stood on the back porch, watching and waiting. No one had yet found a prisoner or a body, but no one wished either to be the first to return to camp. Finally, however, a few found the nerve to return. And once the few had returned and lived, others materialized from the trees, until all were back except for the few who had decided to return to their own homes rather than face their leader in this mood. No sign of anyone had been found.

Willcocks said nothing; just nodded at the men he referred to as his officers, and marched heavily back into the house. He could hear the group leaders shouting orders to the men to eat and then prepare to spend the night on guard duty, as promised. Then they came in to determine what, if any further orders awaited them.

"Let them stew for a little", Willcocks muttered darkly to his officers, meeting them at the back of the house. "I want them to think about this a bit and maybe they'll remember to think next time." He scowled at the men now before him. "And you had better think about it as well. Why didn't you try to control the situation?" One of them started to open his mouth to offer an explanation, then shut it again, obviously thinking better of the idea.

"Right now, we choose a new location for our camp", Willcocks continued. "Just in case there was someone out there, let's get well away from here before nightfall, in case they come back with reinforcements", he said. "So, in ten minutes, I want you to go out there and tell them they have to pack up the camp and prepare to leave for a new location, where they'll set up and post guards before dark."

"Will they all be standing post all night?" one asked.

Willcocks sighed heavily. "No. I would be cutting my own

throat. I can well picture myself waking up to Indians at my throat while all my men are sleeping soundly on guard detail. Work out a schedule." He turned his back on the men. "Now get out. I want to be by myself, at least until it's time to leave."

He stood and listened until the door closed, and then retired to the house's salon. Standing near the window was his second-in-command, Benajah Mallory, and seated beside him, in the shadows of the corner of the room, well out of sight of the windows, sat the guest he had sent Mallory to escort here earlier that day. As fortune would have it, he was able to bring in the man unnoticed during the confusion over the Indian attack, and it was unlikely anyone had noticed.

"Well, what do you think of my troops?" Willcocks asked ironically. As the man moved to reply, however, he just waved his hand. "No, pay that question no mind. I already know the answer. But they serve a purpose after all."

He walked about the room slowly, looking out the window at nothing and raising his eyebrows questioningly at Mallory before finally swinging a chair to a position in front of his guest. "Well, have you any information I might be able to use? They weren't all that pleased with that last bit you fed me."

There was a chuckle from the shadows, and then a voice replied. "That was hardly my fault", the man answered, his British accent apparent. "The information I gave you was quite sound. I can hardly be blamed for the inability of the fools to capitalize upon it."

"They say the information I gave them, which of course came from you, was already outdated by the time they attacked", came back Willcocks' reply. "Next time, try to give me the latest positions, will you?"

The man snorted with annoyance. If it had not been for the gold that was enriching him every time he passed intelligence on to this fool, he would not deign to waste his breath on the man. "I can hardly just leave the camp every time I learn of a change", he snarled. "It would surely draw the attention of those who I'm betraying, wouldn't you think?"

Willcocks rose from his chair in order that he might look down on the man, hoping to intimidate him. "I pay you in good gold", he snapped. "And so far you've done precious little to deserve it!"

The man sat back in the chair, not willing to rise to Willcocks' bait. "I gave you information on Fitzgibbon and his Bloody Boys, and the only reason it didn't turn out with you receiving your reward from the Americans is that they fouled it all up and then surrendered to a vastly smaller force." Seeing that Willcocks had no answer to this, the man continued. "And when that idiot man of yours, that Williamson bloke, attacked Shipman's Tavern for no apparent reason, I convinced that fop Den Haren to hold back, giving your men a chance to escape."

"I wish you had just allowed Den Haren to kill them all, to a man", Willcocks replied darkly. "It would have saved me a great deal of trouble."

"Well, in future, you'll just have to give me a list of the men you wouldn't mind losing", the man suggested with a chuckle. He rose from his chair and stood face to face with Willcocks. "I'm afraid the news I have for you this time won't make you any happier. The Brits are consolidating their position and are intending to move on Newark before winter comes. If you think those cowards hiding in the fort can use that to their advantage, more power to them."

"Now, if you've nothing else to say, I'll be collecting my last payment."

Willcocks watched as the man took his pay packet from Mallory and walked to the door. With a sigh, he was resigned to wait for something better. And the man was right. It was hardly his concern that the Americans had made no better use of the information.

Willcocks shrugged and took a seat close to the window, where he could watch his men as they prepared to break camp once again. This war was going on much longer than anyone had expected, likely even the British, he thought. He placed his head in his hands tiredly, just as Mallory walked by with the spy, Second Lieutenant Carstairs.

Chapter Thirty

That night, Josef and Jeremy decided to take the risk and approached the farm again, this time from alongside the road. That way, they reasoned, if they were seen, they might easily be mistaken for travellers and left alone. When they arrived, however, they found the farm deserted but for the original owners, who were more than a bit leery of the strangers in light of their recent experience, but especially of the Indian. They were sitting out on the front steps of the house, and the old woman, seemed terribly upset.

"Do you know where they went?" Jeremy asked, referring to Willcocks and his men.

The man who had worked this farm all his life looked at Jeremy tiredly. "No, and I really don't care", he muttered. "All I know is, they're gone, and I'm quite happy to know that. They kept us in our room the whole time they were here, and wouldn't even feed us. Thank God my wife and I weren't hurt in all this."

The woman was crying bitterly on the steps. "They took it all", she wailed. "We didn't have much, but what we had, they took. The things passed down from my grandmother and all."

The man took his wife by the arm and began to lead her into the house. He turned at the last moment and addressed the two men. "If I were you, and if I found out where those men were going, I'd be heading in the opposite direction", he offered. "Those men had a meanness to them you could feel long before they talked to you."

"Thank you, sir", Jeremy answered, "But we already know them and what they can do. But we're not really looking for all of them. Just a group of them that head out on their own quite often. Led by a man named Williamson."

The old man thought for a moment, and then brightened as he seemed to recall something. "Is he a mean-looking, powerfully built man?" When Jeremy nodded, he continued, "And would they have called this man Dorian or something to that effect?"

Jeremy's hopes rose. "Yes, that's his name exactly. Was he here?"

"Only for a few hours. Then he and six or seven others rode away when another man rode in to bring him some news. Didn't even seem to tell Willcocks he was leaving. Heard Willcocks ask around for this Dorian later and nobody seemed to know what happened to him." Having delivered of his memory, the old man finished guiding his wife back into the house.

Jeremy managed to call out just before the door closed on them. "Did you happen to see which way Williamson went when he left?"

The farmer stuck his head out of the door. "Can't tell here. The road only goes two ways from here, you know. But I did hear Niagara Falls mentioned." With that, he withdrew his head and softly closed the door, leaving Josef and Jeremy standing in front of his house, staring at each other.

"What do you think?" Jeremy asked of his friend, sure he already knew the answer to the question before he voiced it.

"Same as you", Josef replied. "It looks like we're going to Niagara Falls."

"Tonight?" Jeremy asked, a bit startled as his friend began walking the road in the general direction of the falls.

"Why not?" came the queried reply. "Nobody will be expecting any visitors at night."

Jeremy stood and watched as the Caughnawaga walked off down the road without him, not at all certain of this particular line of action. Then he shrugged to himself and, pushing his gun's strap farther up onto his shoulder, he pursued the other man. Josef had covered almost a half-mile by the time Jeremy caught up to him, his walking speed impressive.

On they walked in the dark, and Jeremy continued to ask himself if this was such a good idea. They were walking blindly at night, not certain where Williamson had gone, not really sure they had gone to Niagara Falls at all. And, if they managed to catch up to the villains, what would they do then? Certainly they had little hope of taking on the entire group by themselves. Jeremy had experienced that before and was not at all ready to experience it again.

What if Williamson's men had stopped elsewhere along the way? Would they stumble blindly right past them, missing them in the dark, a situation that could perhaps result in an ambush from the rear? There were too many questions involved in taking this tack, and Jeremy raised his doubts to his friend, but Josef merely waved them off as though they were minor details. They would deal with all eventualities if and when they arose, he explained confidently.

Jeremy wished he had Josef's sense of calm and his self-assuredness. As they travelled on, he continually looked over his shoulder, starting at every shadow, imagining each to be one of the enemy. Each time they passed a house, he stopped and studied it carefully, with the result that he found he was forced to run to catch up after each property.

It was shortly before midnight that the two men reached a point above the falls, not far from Goat Island. This was an entirely new experience for Josef, since he had never been to Niagara Falls before, and they stopped to watch the water rush and swirl by the island on both sides. Even from the south of the island and by the light of the moon, one could see the river rush ahead, only to fall with a roar off what seemed the end of the world.

They continued on along the curve until they passed the edge of the falls. Jeremy had seen this marvel a number of times, but it never failed to stir him. It was as though he could actually feel in his breast the power of the enormous volumes of water as they thundered over the cliff, and perhaps he could, for the rumble vibrated throughout his body. Using the available moonlight, he allowed his eyes to follow the crest all the way across in a wide curve, broken only near the American side by a jut of land that marked the second channel, and the separate falls on that side. The bottom of the gorge was not visible at night, at least not from where they stood, but they could see the mists roil back to the top, creating a breathtaking and surreal, almost sheer curtain across the expanse of where the base should be. Even at the distance at which the two men now stood admiring this incredible work of nature, the mist could be felt as the breezes created by the volume of crashing water blew the moisture across them.

"I would like to see this by daylight", Josef shouted, to be heard above the roar. "Whether created by God or the gods of my people, this is truly a divine creation."

Jeremy had no opinion on matters divine, other than he did not believe in them, but he too was taken by the sheer scope of this spectacle. Most people never had the opportunity to witness Niagara Falls, and they never would, distances to almost everywhere being what they were. That was a shame, he thought, but maybe for the best all the same. The vista as it was now, especially by daylight, was still relatively undisturbed and he hoped that it could remain that way.

"If we're still about in the morning, we'll have another look", he assured Josef. "If not, we'll come back when this is over and it's safe to move about, spending great amounts of time watching water fall over a cliff." He tried to sound sarcastic with this final comment, but he knew in his heart that he would like nothing better than to be able to do so. Nothing, that is, once he had settled his score with Dorian Williamson.

Now close, at least to the actual Niagara Falls, they slowed down, taking time to survey each new area they covered. There was no sign of the raiders they were hunting, for there were few homes here near the falls, and no sign that a fair-sized group might be at any of those few. Still they searched on, but began to feel that perhaps the mention of Niagara Falls was unrelated to where they were headed that day. Or perhaps they had been here and had already moved on.

Finally, they came to a stop on the hill overlooking the falls, scanning the lower land before them in case they had missed something. No clues were readily apparent however.

Jeremy turned to his partner. "Josef, I regret to suggest this, but I fear that we'll not find anything in the dark. Perhaps there's nothing to find but, at least in the morning, we can ask around if the villains have been seen here."

Josef nodded slowly, a subtle gesture that Jeremy might have had difficulty discerning even in broad daylight. "I think you're right", he sighed. "Let's find a place to make camp – a cold camp would be best – and we'll start again at first light."

True to Josef's word, the two men arose at the crack of dawn, on no more than three or four hours' sleep. Downing a quick breakfast consisting of various grains, nuts and fruits that they had previously collected and dried for themselves, an ideal mix for hunting, they were again on their way.

Few locals were up and about for the two men to question, but being this close to the border, and in enemy-held territory at that, any intelligence they might receive would be suspect at best. However, the daylight did offer them the opportunity to use this rise they'd been following and upon which they were now perched to look for signs of the enemy. But they could see no concentration of men or horses.

"I think perhaps we should work our way farther down river", Jeremy suggested. "They might be farther along."

"I suppose", Josef answered absently, his eyes locked on the thundering falls now that the sun was up. It wasn't quite as captivating from here, the sound being muted by the rise and the distance dulled the feeling of sheer inadequacy one had standing beside it, but it was a sight to behold just the same. With a last wistful glance at the wondrous view, he snapped his attention back to the matter at hand.

"Isn't Stamford up from the river?" he asked, depending upon his memory of contacts and places from their hunting trips.

"True", Jeremy answered. "But I don't think they'd stay in town. And why would they say Niagara if they were going to Stamford?"

Josef nodded slowly. "But that could then mean all along the Niagara River all the way to Newark", he suggested. "And maybe the old man actually heard 'Niagara' instead of 'Niagara Falls'. In fact", he added, "Maybe he was talking about Fort Niagara."

His friend stopped short at that last suggestion. "You may be right. But let's hope not." Fort Niagara was the American fort at the end of the Niagara River, almost across from Newark. If

Williamson and his men had gone there, Josef and Jeremy would have to abandon their search and come looking again another day. The thought was most disheartening.

It was more than five miles to Queenston, not a great distance to be walking in the course of a day, but made all the longer for two reasons. First off, the two men did not dare use the main road in broad daylight. There were often Americans and American sympathizers travelling this stretch, and they were as likely as not to be members of either Willcocks' crew or one of the military scouting patrols, coming and going from the fort. Many in the U.S. camp knew Jeremy now, and he dare not risk identification by them in this area.

The second reason for their delay was that they would often cross to farms along the way to check for signs of Williamson's men. It was tiresome and frustrating work, but they had no wish to risk passing the enemy by.

For that, Josef and Jeremy stayed close to the gorge much of the way, sheltered by the trees as they followed a course that allowed them to keep a watch on the road most of the time. They often would find themselves staring into the gorge, with its steep, carved walls of rock. The Niagara River had spent millennia carving this geologic wonder from the layers of hard and soft rock so that it was now positioned miles from Queenston, which was actually at the edge of the escarpment.

The two men knew little of the geology, of course, nothing but a hunch that the waters had chewed their way into the rock as they had seen on a much smaller scale in countless other places. But they could not but experience each their own sort of reverence at the chasm of winding cliffs on both sides that towered over the rushing waters below. Here and there a much smaller waterfall or a ravine poured water into the great river, adding to its flow and draining the lands to either side. The mostly barren walls were adorned here and there by stubborn trees and bushes that seemed determined to hang from the rocks and ledges, at times by their very roots it seemed, demonstrating a stubbornness otherwise attributed to humans.

The sun had just recently passed its zenith when the travellers came upon one of the most remarkable of sights along the waterway, short of the falls itself. The river, which twisted and turned to various degrees all along, now made a radical turn to the right through one of its narrowest points. The water, however, was first forced into a round basin carved out of the rock at this corner, creating a violent counter clockwise spin to the water. From the edge of the cliff, looking down into the gorge, they could see a large whirlpool, the bane of any who should dare to attempt to cross at this point. White water swirled dangerously, crashing against the sides as it tried to escape the unnatural push of the tons of speeding water behind it. Beyond, to the north, it regained its centre within the wider banks and slowed to travel on in a more relaxed fashion, its momentum slowed in the tempestuous whirlpool.

These distractions aside, the trackers quite suddenly encountered a pair of men who seemed to be standing guard duty. They were not very alert, probably lulled by the presence of the American post not far away at Queenston Heights, a position they had captured from the unfortunate General Brock, who had died defending it. The two men seemed to be arguing about some young woman they had both met in a tavern, likely a barmaid who had paid little attention to either one. Each appeared to be convinced that they were the young woman's favourite, and the tenor of the disagreement seemed to be rising by the moment.

Josef and Jeremy decided that it would be imprudent to attempt to overpower the two, since they were in the middle of a clearing and their position easily seen. Regardless of their level of stealth, the guards would probably notice them, and they decided it would be much easier to bypass them than to risk alerting whomever they were guarding. Quietly, they circled the two, each still trying to convince the other of his desirability to women.

The two men had no idea what the guards were, in fact, guarding. It was difficult to tell the military from the militia from the desperados such as Willcocks' men during these strange times. There were no obvious sounds coming from up ahead, and they were not quite sure they were moving in the right direction, producing a profoundly unsettling feeling.

At times, Jeremy felt their progress was painfully slow, but he was well aware that both the stealth and the pace were necessary. Although accustomed to hunting for a living, he still was not entirely used to the extra precautions required when tracking people. Care was required in hunting deer but, if one sensed your presence, at least they were not able to shoot at you.

At long last, though probably not nearly as long as they felt it had been, they heard the muted sounds of a camp ahead. Creeping up slowly, they found the main body of the men they had been seeking were on the opposite side of the road from where they were. These men were surprisingly quiet, and not displaying the usual level of boisterousness Jeremy would have expected from the men he had been hunting for some time.

They seemed almost too tired to carry on as expected. This did not seem to be an actual camp - just a rest stop along the road. But who were they? Jeremy saw no one he recognized and feared they had found the wrong group. Signalling to his partner, they crept closer, stopping as near to the road as they could without risking giving themselves away.

"Do you see anyone you know now?" Josef asked in hushed tones.

Jeremy shook his head. "I'm afraid we'll probably have to continue looking. We should have known it was unlikely to be Williamson. They haven't come far since yesterday, and this isn't even a proper camp. Where would they have been all this time? Also, look at their numbers. Williamson left with only a half-dozen men, and there must be close to twenty here."

It was a question neither could answer. These men looked exhausted, like they had been travelling hard for some time, but choosing this as a resting place when they were so near to an American position was even harder to understand, if they were indeed on the U.S. side. They were exposed here, much more than they would be under the American guns, either at Queenston or at Fort George, so why would they stop so close?

As puzzling as these questions were, the two men decided they would continue their hunt, and began to creep away. But, just as they were almost out of sight of the road, they heard a commotion behind them.

"Get up, you sluggards!" a familiar voice boomed into the surrounding woods. "We must be ready to move at a moment's notice!"

"We've got to get some sleep, Williamson", one voice whined from the ranks.

So, it was Williamson after all. But where did he get all the men and why were they so edgy? Jeremy started back toward the post they had occupied near the road, but Josef's hand restrained him.

"What's the matter?" Jeremy whispered. "I've got to get closer and find out what's happening. All of this is very strange indeed."

Josef did not answer, but just put his finger to his lips and pointed in the direction from which they had previously approached the enemy's resting spot. They could see the two guards they had seen arguing earlier coming back through the woods, still arguing. They almost tripped over the place where they had been moments before. The two fools would literally have stumbled upon him, had they still been there!

"Thank you", Jeremy breathed, letting out a sigh of relief. "I'm becoming too anxious to have at that blackguard, Williamson, and not being nearly careful enough about it."

Josef grinned. "Yes, not nearly", he whispered back, as always enjoying his friend's discomfort. "For now, though, I think we'd better withdraw, and think this through. There are very many of them, and only two of us", he suggested, becoming serious again. He began to make his way back toward the gorge, making sure that his partner was following.

Chapter Thirty-One

Williamson looked coldly at the man who had been whining about rest. "You'll have rest aplenty when they bury you in the ground", he growled. "All of you fools listen! It's time we moved along. We're still too close to Queenston to make a long stopover now. If any feel they can't take it, stay here and face the Americans' wrath when they find you." With that, he turned to stalk back to his horse, the poor animal itself appearing exhausted, a lather of sweat covering its body.

"Why'd you have to go and strike that officer, Williamson?" a voice demanded behind him. Dorian spun about to see who dared challenge him when he'd made it obvious that his was the last word.

What he saw was the same John Newsome who had challenged him near Beaverdams after the episode on Lundy's Lane. Newsome had not ridden with Williamson since that night, preferring to stay closer to Willcocks' main body of riders, when he was not off by himself. Dorian had been quite happy to have him ride along when he left Chippewa, however, because the numbers of his "platoon" had been constantly dwindling. Some had been killed or disabled, some simply became sick of the war and had gone home to farm or whatever it was they had been doing before the fighting had started. Newsome, he knew, would be an asset in his ventures, provided he could control the man. It now looked like he could not.

"I asked you a question, Williamson", Newsome growled. "What're we supposed to do now? Run from both sides?"

To his credit, Williamson did not back off from the menace in this man's voice. If he showed any weakness now, he would lose control over all the rest, and would then be left to face all his enemies by himself. He was basically a bully and he needed the strength of numbers to carry out his plans.

Williamson was not about to take Newsome on with a knife this time. He had no time, for one thing, and he was much too tired as well. He walked purposefully back toward Newsome as if to confront him face to face, and the man assumed a defensive position, his hand readying to reach for his knife. But the knife never had a chance to see action. Williamson pulled his pistol, already loaded and cocked and fired it point-blank, into his opponent's face.

The rest of his men immediately stepped back from the scene, their voices suddenly silent, as Newsome's face vanished in a splatter of blood, bone, muscle, and brains. The man's body flew back from the force of the close-quarters blast and landed on the ground, arms akimbo. The men stared for what seemed like an eternity at what had been, only a short time ago, the body of one of their own. Their eyes were held to the gruesome sight in spite of their revulsion, taking in the details of the man's position, his left eye hanging down where his cheek once was, the well-trampled dirt and horse manure, which had become his permanent resting place.

"Anyone else?" Williamson demanded loudly, himself shaken by the sight directly in front of his face. With a shiver of revulsion, he wiped Newsome's remains from his own face, and then barked, "Very well, then. Mount up!"

At Fort George, the Americans were on alert. Their commander was livid and when Dearborn was upset, the entire fort felt it. Ill as the old man was, he fired off orders through his subordinates on a constant basis, often contradicting a command only a few minutes after issuing it. Apparently, there was to be no peace here until the matter was resolved.

For General Dearborn, his posting at the head of this campaign was to have been the crowning glory to his career, which had been built upon his reputation in the War of Independence. This war, however, was turning into a complete rout as far as he was concerned, with disgraceful losses at every turn. It seemed to him that he had nothing but incompetence all around him, as his men were made fools of just about every time they went into battle, including the latest fiasco at Beaverdams.

It would never occur to the old politician to accept any of the blame for the losses, of course. He had been duped by a never-ending parade of fools and scoundrels into handing command to men who couldn't handle the responsibility. He would never have fallen for the old "I can't control the Indians" ruse that had been perpetrated upon his lesser officers at Beaverdams. People back home were calling for his head because of these losses, and he'd had nothing to do with it! It would never occur to him that might be the problem.

Now, however, here was a situation that demanded immediate attention. This Williamson fellow had attempted to murder his captain of the guard the previous day, and he would not stand for it! Yet, somehow, his band of incompetents had fouled up once again, letting the man, who pretended to a military rank, and his entire group of criminals escape!

Soldiers had been combing the countryside for the group although, in truth, they did not comb far for fear of being caught away from the fort by the British. But Dearborn had tired of the haphazard search and ordered Captain Smythe, the very man who had been assaulted, to take a squad and perform a proper search. Dearborn ordered that Williamson be returned to the fort alive, if possible. If that were not possible, then dead would do as well, so long as the body was brought back as an example to any others who might consider challenging his authority or that of his officers.

Smythe took mostly men with whom he was acquainted, and for whom he had some reasonable level of confidence. No militia or volunteers on this hunt; trained and experienced professional soldiers only. And that meant his own men for the most part, except for a pair of sharpshooters with Kentucky long rifles. Travelling with minimal baggage except for extra loads of powder and ball, the patrol of eleven men exited the gates of Fort George just after noon.

The captain, sporting a split lip and a darkened eye from

A Question of Loyalty

Williamson's two-fisted attack, led his men directly up the road along the Niagara River toward Queenston. He guessed that his quarry would head for what he might consider to be the safety of Willcocks and his Canadian Volunteers. He had last heard that the raiders had gone to the area around Chippewa and, before he and his men left, had sent a rider to try to find Willcocks first. It was hoped that a warning about harbouring this fugitive would not be looked upon kindly by the General. Willcocks still clung to his dreams of a U.S. Army commission, after all, and there was known to occasionally be bad blood between the men.

Josef and Jeremy withdrew to the edge of the gorge, trying desperately to think of a way by which they could overcome such overwhelming odds. They soon decided they were coming up dry, however, but perhaps a fresh perspective would help and they went back to look once again. It was then that they heard the crack of a pistol, followed by the indecipherable but unmistakable voice of Dorian Williamson. They ran with all reasonable caution back toward their previous hiding place by the road, just in time to see the entire phalanx of bandits filing out. They seemed to be in quite some hurry, riding hard in the direction from which Jeremy and Josef had come such a short time ago.

They waited until the last of the raiders had passed and then ran to the clearing they had occupied, to see if, by some odd chance, the bandits had left any clues as to where they might be headed. All they found, however, was the faceless body of Newsome, lying upon its back spread-eagled as he had landed, flies and other insects already taking advantage of the situation. Jeremy felt nauseous and looked away quickly, trying hard not vomit in front of his companion.

The two men stared up the road in the direction that the fleeing traitors had taken; their spirits laid low by the realization that there was nothing they could do now. Nothing at all, it seemed, for their quarry had bolted once again, and back in the direction they had spent the better part of two days tracking them. Disheartened and angry all at once, Jeremy walked resolutely, if without rational thought back to the road and, forgetting all thought of the dangers began to plod back toward Chippewa, knowing only that this was the direction he had seen his enemy take.

Josef caught up to his companion and, for a time said nothing, just walked quietly alongside. After a time, though, he turned to Jeremy. "I think we'd best get off the road, eh?" he suggested, leading to a path, which led them back toward the gorge once again. Jeremy followed quietly, lost deep in thought.

The two sat quietly at the edge of the chasm that framed the mighty Niagara, and Jeremy stared intently at the churning water below. His enemy had been so near, yet so far. There was nothing they could have done with a reasonable expectation of success, but Jeremy was not feeling exactly reasonable at the moment. Over and over in his mind, he berated himself for not making an attempt at felling the monster when directly in front of him.

Now there was nothing to do except to start back toward Chippewa and hope that was indeed Williamson's destination. With a sigh, he turned to inform his companion of his decision but, as he looked in the Indian's direction, he saw that the man was looking right past him. Jeremy's eyebrows rose in question, but Josef just nodded slowly in the direction he was looking. There, apparently unheard by either man, stood two men with muskets pointed directly at them. By their uniforms, it was obvious these were Americans.

"Captain!" the taller of the two shouted toward the road. "Over here!"

After a moment a figure appeared, pushing noisily through the undergrowth, two more soldiers at his side. Jeremy groaned inwardly. This was the Captain of the Guard from Fort George who had ordered him fed and watered when Williamson had captured him.

"Well, well!" the captain proclaimed cheerily, immediately recognizing Jeremy. "I hadn't thought we'd meet again. And this time you've brought an Indian." He walked all around the two men, appraising them while the soldiers were disarming them. "Just what brings you to this particular area just while Dorian Williamson was known to be here? You weren't here looking for him, were you?"

Jeremy didn't reply; just stared at the captain, trying to deduce

A Question of Loyalty

his fate. There was no sign of animosity from the man, however. This search and questioning just seemed to be a routine matter to him, as he might any other strays that wandered into his territory.

"We're just hunting", Josef remarked. "We're from Beaverdams and we hunt up around here. Is that a crime?"

"Shut up, Indian!" one of the soldiers snapped.

"Now, now, Corporal", admonished Smythe lightly. "I did ask them a question and it's only fair they be allowed to answer." He walked over to a fallen log and sat down. "Now", he started conversationally, "Why don't you tell me what you're really doing here? If I'm not mistaken, the Indian here is a Caughnawaga. Also, if I'm not mistaken, Caughnawagas don't live in Beaverdams, except for the ones that ride with Lieutenant Fitzgibbon." He stopped talking, allowing the questions to sink in.

Jeremy gave the officer a dirty look. "He got tired of killing. Even Americans. So now he hunts with me."

Smythe rose from the log and paced around once more. "It seems to me that the last time I saw you, you were in chains, accused of being a British spy. Why should I believe you're just hunting, now?"

"For one thing", Jeremy threw out lightly, "There's nothing to spy on out here. For another, you must consider the source of the previous accusation. Now, sir, if you're finished with these questions, we'd be grateful if we could get on our way."

"I think not", Smythe replied, the smile vanishing from his face. "I think you know something I need to know. Perhaps, when you've told me that, you can be on your way."

"What is it you think we know?" Josef asked innocently.

"I think you might know where I can find Dorian Williamson."

Josef and Jeremy exchanged glances, wondering whether to tell this soldier what little they knew. They both wondered at the marks upon the officer's face, and if it could have had anything to do with their search for Williamson. But, they had no opportunity to ask questions or to provide answers at that moment because, just then, a shout came from the far side of the road, where Williamson's troops had rested until very recently.

Smythe started off in the direction of the cry, then turned his head and ordered the soldier he had addressed as Corporal. "Bring those two along. If we can't get our answers, we'll just bring them along with us and sort it out later at the fort." With that, he stalked off in the direction from which he had come, taking long strides as he walked, as if he were on a parade ground with no obstacles to possibly catch him up.

The two soldiers directed Josef and Jeremy forward with their guns while the two who had arrived with the captain collected their weapons and then followed behind as they moved out. In moments they arrived at the raiders' former rest site, and the murder scene of Williamson's man, Newsome.

"What do you two know about this?" Smythe asked, no hint of courtesy now in his voice.

Neither of the two men answered, not knowing what would cause them the most damage, the truth or a fabrication or perhaps a flippant remark. "We found him like that", Jeremy finally answered truthfully. They had seen nothing of the altercation that had led to this killing.

Smythe put one arm across his chest and the other he placed on top, with his hand rubbing his chin. "I think you had better tell me what you do know. Now!" he barked suddenly. "Or else, I may have no choice but to charge you with murder and return you to the jail in Newark to stand trial."

The suggestion sent a shiver along Jeremy's spine. After having previously been accused of spying, there was little chance he could get a fair trial. He looked at Josef, who appeared unruffled, but nonetheless nodded almost imperceptibly.

"We followed Williamson's trail here after finding out he split from Willcocks' main band last night", he began. "We came across them here after following them all day, and they seemed to be resting on their way back from your fort. There were too many of them for us to attack, so there was nothing we could do."

"And what happened to this unfortunate individual?" Smythe asked, nudging the body with the toe of his boot. "Do you know who he is, by the way?"

Jeremy pointed back the way they had come. "We were over there when the shot rang out, trying to figure out what we could do next. Maybe we could manage a way to separate them. As for who he is, we don't know. Williamson was yelling orders at all of them when we turned away."

"And which direction did they take when they left?"

Jeremy pointed again, this time toward the south, down the road. "We saw them ride hard in that direction. Not long ago, maybe twenty minutes before you arrived", he added, anticipating the captain's next question.

Smythe's smile now returned to his face. "And just what were you two going to do before we arrived?"

Josef answered this time. "That's what we were trying to figure out", he said flatly. "We weren't sure whether to try to follow them back again or just give up and head home."

"Well, I think you should follow them back toward the south", Smythe answered, making their decision for them and leaving no room for argument in the tone of his voice. "After all, that's the way we're going and I think you should come along as our guests. Then you can tell me on the way just what this is all about. You chasing Williamson around the peninsula in this manner." With a signal to his men, the prisoners had their hands tied in front of them and they were hoisted to a pair of the spare horses they had brought along.

"And what of our freedom, sir?" Jeremy asked, a demand apparent in his voice.

Smythe looked at him with mock surprise displayed on his face. "I wouldn't think you'd care of such things, Mr. van Hijser. Some of your countrymen are investing a great deal of effort in fighting the freedom that we offer. Instead, they seem to prefer the tyranny of the British Crown over democracy."

Although anger swept through him, Jeremy decided to keep it in check. He remembered a saying he had learned in the course of his meagre education when practicing debating; no debate was ever won in anger. "I think you misunderstand, Captain. What my countrymen are fighting is for the right to be left to their own devices. To be allowed the self-determination to choose how to deal with our government in the manner and time of their choosing. This is our land after all, sir, and not yours. Besides, of what value is your democracy if it is forced upon us? Would that not also be a tyranny?"

Smythe looked thoughtful for a moment and then turned away, obviously having lost the appetite for this discussion. "You will gain your freedom when we've found our man and determined exactly what transpired here today."

Jeremy looked over at his friend, wondering how they would get out of this. Josef shrugged softly and muttered, nodding at the horse he sat astride "At least we'll find your enemy faster this way." The tone of fatalism did nothing to ease Jeremy's mind, but he had to admit that, at least for the time being, there was little that could be done about their situation.

As they rode along, Smythe dropped back from the lead of the American soldiers until he was riding abreast of Jeremy. "Perhaps you can tell me why you seem to wish Williamson's head as much as you do", he asked.

Jeremy glared at the officer sullenly. "It's a personal matter", he snapped.

The captain looked across at the Canadian thoughtfully and then a smile played momentarily across his lips. "Ah, it's a woman then, is it?" he suggested. He saw Jeremy flinch, and felt he had hit a nerve. "That's it, isn't it? This fight is over a woman."

Jeremy shot Smythe a murderous look. "In part it is", he snarled. "But not in a way that you think. And that's but a part of it."

"You may as well tell me", the captain goaded. "I'll find out the story eventually. If no other way, then when I find Williamson and extract the tale from him." He noticed that Jeremy stiffened visibly at that last comment. "And I'll wager his version will be considerably less flattering than yours."

Chapter Thirty-Two

Jeremy thought about this for a moment. He looked over at Josef for guidance, but the Indian seemed to have no opinion in the matter, at least no opinion that he felt inclined to share. "If you must know, my problem with Williamson started when he murdered an unarmed man in cold blood at Shipman's corners", he started. "And it continues with my torture at his hands, and his burning of my farm for the crime of escaping him, ending to this point with the murder of the woman I was to marry and leaving me a letter to taunt me over it."

Jeremy threw a glare in Smythe's direction that seemed to burn directly into him as he finished the explanation and looked away. He had no desire to let the American officer see the tears he felt welling behind his eyes at the thought of his lovely Elizabeth and Williamson's disgusting letter. He saw from the corner of his eye that Smythe was looking away as well, probably shamed now of his previous thoughts, he hoped. He cast about desperately for another topic, wishing to save himself any further embarrassment.

"And how about you, captain?" he asked. "Why are you hunting my sworn enemy?"

Smythe turned back in Jeremy's direction and shot him a wry smile. "It's a military matter", came the curt reply.

It was Jeremy's turn to smile now. "Military secret, eh, commander?" he taunted. "By the looks of your face, I suspect that it's more of a personal matter. And personal matters are fair game here this day, apparently." He saw the weakening of resolve that appeared about the captain's eyes. "Come now, captain, out with it. Turn about is fair play, as I've heard it said."

Now Smythe laughed openly. "Alright, since you've guessed it, I suppose you're right. After all, my tale isn't nearly as tragic as yours. Williamson appeared at the fort last night with some of his men, the whole lot already drunk. Then they proceeded to become even drunker and began insulting and challenging everyone they came into contact with. This behaviour went on all night, until the early hours."

"So you were insulted and fought him?" Jeremy interrupted.

Smythe shot Jeremy an annoyed look. "Please allow me to finish, sir. When General Dearborn passed on one of his infrequent sallies forth from his quarters, he ran into the foul creature and endured quite the obscene dressing-down from him. In my presence! Well, the General ordered the lout arrested but when I moved to do so, the scoundrel struck me two quick blows to the face. The General was quite incensed that one of his officers was treated in such a manner, and ordered him arrested for court martial."

"Well why didn't you arrest him then, on the spot?" Jeremy asked. "Why is it you're chasing the man now?" The captain's face reddened visibly at the question, and Jeremy suddenly realized why the officer had not wished to talk about it. "He'd quite caught you off your guard, didn't he?"

"That's right!" Smythe snapped. "He hit me hard with both fists and I dropped like a sack of wet sorghum! Then he ran for the gate, ordering his men to ride or be left behind. The General shouted at them that if they rode with the man, they would also be hauled before a military court, but they all rode out of the gate, many of them laughing, all of them cursing the General. I was ordered to put together a patrol, and here I am. Are you happy?"

Jeremy had become keenly interested in the story, but he felt no joy at the officer's humiliation, likely before some of his own men. He did not say as much, but he was well aware of the force with which Williamson could throw a punch, especially if one was not expecting it. To say so to the captain at this point, however, would merely seem patronizing and hardly welcome.

They rode along, all in silence, no one having anything else to say for the moment, the soldiers maintaining a basic level of military propriety. Smythe rode on to regain his place in the front of the small column. All were now looking about for any sign that Williamson and his men may have stopped somewhere, but it was an exercise in futility. This was a well-travelled roadway these days and the signs would need to really stand out to be noticeable.

Williamson and his men were by now within a few miles of the site that Willcocks had chosen for his new camp, although Williamson had no way of knowing it had moved again since he had left. The altercation with Newsome had plunged the man into one of his trademark dark moods, and no one had yet dared to speak to him. The nineteen men rode on in complete silence but for the occasional snort or whinny from the horses, or a cough or indistinguishable mutter issued from under the breath of one of the men.

Williamson was struggling to think through all that had occurred. A splitting headache had set in, the result of last night's foolish revelry. It was wreaking havoc with his ability to regain his mental focus, to say nothing of his visual focus. He was not entirely certain that returning to Willcocks' camp was a good idea, for the man was constantly attempting to curry the favour of the American soldiers. There was no telling how he would react once he heard of the arrest ordered for him. He had suspected that his boss had only pardoned him at the suggestion, or worse, of the Americans, for it was most unlike the man. After all, there was certainly no love lost between the two men. Willcocks kept him around only to do the dirty work that no one else would take on.

He knew nowhere else to turn, however. The Americans would probably imprison him at the very least. The British would hang him as a traitor and their various groups of raiders throughout Niagara would not grant him that much; they would shoot him on sight, although they might not do so immediately. Willcocks was an unknown quantity at this point in time and might offer him some degree of protection, up to a point, as long as Williamson got to him before the U.S. Army did.

"Come on, you sluggards!" he shouted, bringing a stab of torment to his throbbing head. "Let's make some time!" With that, he urged his own horse forward into a trot, that being the most he could manage from the poorly fed and rested beast.

As the ragtag column picked up the pace slightly, he heard a cry from the rear. "Rider coming fast!" His men began to give way, as the normal courtesy of the road would have them do, but Williamson turned in his saddle, still positioned in the middle of the thoroughfare, to see what the noise was all about.

Bearing rapidly down upon them was an American soldier, riding at all speed in the same direction that they were going. Through Williamson's pain-addled mind, he vaguely recognized that there was some sort of significance to this event, but the exact nature of that significance was eluding him. He merely sat and stared dumbly and wondered as horse and rider thundered on by him on the dirt road.

At the last moment, however, there was a flicker of recognition in the rider's eyes and a noticeable increase in speed. Williamson could swear that he saw the man's lips move to mouth his name in surprise. Now the significance struck home.

"He's off to tell Willcocks about us!" he shouted as the meaning sank in. "Get after him! Bring him back or kill him! I don't care which!" Williamson repeated the command to chase the rider, seeing that no one was accepting the initiative, perhaps all thinking that some other would do so. "If he gets through, Willcocks will hear the Americans' story before we get there! Now, move! All of you!"

Finally, Williamson's men galvanized as one and took chase as the military rider disappeared around the bend, some quarter-mile down the road. Their tired mounts strained to catch up and, slowly, they began to gain on the soldier. Not all were of the same speed, and there quickly developed a gap between the pursuers as they raced along. Although the ones farther back had no hope of catching up, however, they dared not stop, and the result was a string of riders that stretched well along the road. Their fear of Williamson, especially knowing his level of desperation, was greater than any other consideration.

In a short straightaway, the American courier hazarded to look over his shoulder to determine his level of comfort, only to see he had none. Not thirty feet behind him were two of Williamson's men, and they gained slightly with each passing second. The man spurred his horse on to a speed he knew was reaching the extremes the poor animal could take, but he also realized the consequences should these reputedly unprincipled men catch him. The trees flashed by close to his left leg as he and his mount brushed by the trees that blurred by at the edge of the turn in the roadway. He could feel his heart in his mouth as he never had before, for he'd been told that he could expect no quarter from these men.

One of Williamson's men drew a pistol from his shirt and tried to aim it at the fleeing man. Finally, thinking that he had the range and motion, he fired, but pistols were quite inaccurate at the best of times. The ball flew well clear as both shooter and target bobbed, weaved and bounced along the rough road. The only noticeable effect deriving from the shot was that the courier's horse was pulling away slightly in terror from the noise behind it.

Just as they rounded another curve, at the edge of a farm property, one of Williamson's riders finally caught up to the courier and, with a leap from his stirrups, pulled the military man from his horse. Both men fell hard onto the road, slightly dazed and began to wrestle rather ineffectually in the dirt. Williamson's second man caught up soon after and dismounted. He pulled his companion off the courier, pointing to those they could see coming running, guns at the ready, across the field.

"Let him go, Jake", the second man shouted. "We're too late. Anything we do to him now will only make matters worse." He climbed back onto his lathered and panting horse, grasping the reins of his companion's mount. "Let's get out of here and tell Williamson."

The man on the ground hesitated. "I think I'll just take my chances here, Sam", he said resignedly. "You fellows will have nowhere to go. It's Williamson they want. They'll probably leave us alone."

The man on the horse appeared to mull over this line of thought for a moment, then pulled his own pistol from his belt. "I was going to shoot him, but I have only one ball. I'll reserve it for traitors instead." Without another word, he trained his weapon upon the man he had called Jake and pulled the trigger.

Sam turned his horse sharply and rode back off down the

road, with Jake's horse still in tow. As he rode, he came upon the stragglers and told them to turn around and follow him back to Williamson. They did as they were told, not knowing what had happened up ahead or having heard Jake's reason for deciding to stay behind.

The now seventeen remaining men met up with Williamson a mile along the road. Sam quickly filled him in on what had occurred up ahead, and Williamson ordered them back the way they had come. The horses could barely trot by now, but it was imperative that they find some place to hide until they could divine some way out of this predicament.

The courier hauled himself to his feet and began slapping the dust from his uniform, just as the first of Willcocks' men reached him. He did not hear the initial questions being hurled at him as he stared, first at the body lying in the road's dust, and then down the road at the fleeing man. He had never been outside of Fort George during his active duty in Niagara, joining up after the fort had been taken, and this was the first man he had seen killed. He could barely believe the cold ruthlessness that was required to simply execute an unarmed man actually existed.

Now a man of imposing stature pushed his way through the crowd of men who were all attempting to question him at once. He walked up to the courier and smiled, at the same time raising his hand. There seemed to be immediate silence as the others deferred to the newcomer.

"What's your name, lad?" he asked, not unkindly.

"Jimmy, sir", he replied, then realized how immature it must sound, not like a soldier at all. "Er, actually, James, sir."

Willcocks laughed a fatherly laugh. "Well, James Actually, I think I will call you by the first name you gave. Jimmy, that is. Much shorter to say." He smiled again and there were some laughs from the onlookers.

"What brings you to our camp, Jimmy?" Willcocks continued.

Jimmy pulled himself up into full military bearing. "I was sent by General Dearborn to ask you to keep a lookout for one Dorian Williamson, sir. And to ask you to apprehend same and return him to Fort George if encountered."

Willcocks could not hide his amusement, either at this boy who as playing soldier or at Dearborn asking for his help. This would cost the general dearly. "And, by any chance, was that 'same' or his men that chased you here?"

"I'm afraid I flew down the road like a madman", the courier said. "I didn't expect to pass the man on the road, but he didn't react very quickly and I rushed right by. It wasn't until I was around the next bend that I heard these men pursuing me." The words rushed from his mouth as the relief of still being alive after that close call caught up with him.

"And how many were there, young man?" the chief Volunteer asked.

"I'm not completely sure", the young soldier replied, trying hard to picture the group he passed. "But I'm certain there weren't more than twenty. Yes, yes, I'd say about twenty."

"Did you happen to figure out why this man was shot by his partner?" the leader asked out of pure curiosity.

Jimmy nodded. "Just before he shot this man he called Jake, he said he was intending to shoot me, but he'd rather shoot a traitor." Then, quietly, he added thoughtfully, "Though it seems to me that he's the traitor here."

Willcocks turned to his men, most of who had gathered around by this time. "Well, gentlemen, you heard him. Get your horses. That idiot Williamson finally took his smart mouth and foul disposition too far this time. It's time to go hunting!"

His men went for their mounts with various amounts of enthusiasm, some not as anxious as others to hunt down a colleague. Most of them live locally in the peninsula, and would have to live with the families of these men for a long time afterward. They could live with looting the Loyalists in this community of mixed loyalties, but shooting a comrade for refusing the orders of a foreign officer was another matter entirely.

As soon as the bulk of his men were mounted, Willcocks led them northward on the road to find Williamson. This gave him a large measure of satisfaction since the man had always been a thorn in side, especially when Williamson made him look bad in front of the Americans. But he was a popular man with some of the men. This, however, was a direct order from the men who armed them and supplied them to carry on their campaigns in Niagara. How ironic, for it was these same officers who had ordered him to pardon the vermin. No matter now, however, for this was the excuse he had been waiting for.

Williamson was at a loss. This was quite a predicament, for everything they had, from their ammunition to their authority in dealing with the farmers, came from the Americans. There would be no protection for him or his men from those who sought them out. Their enemies, and they were legion by now, would hunt them down unopposed. By now Willcocks had been informed and they would likely be coming to look for him as well. Williamson had no expectation of loyalty from his boss, as he was always too busy currying favour with the American officers whenever they were around. This could even win Willcocks his commission.

For now, they would have to ride away from Willcocks' camp as quickly as possible. Damn that man for moving his camp again! If he had remained where Williamson had left him, they would have easily eliminated the dispatch rider before he could have passed on his message. As it was now, however, they were much too close to dawdle there in the road, in plain sight of anyone who came riding around that curve. They began to ride back hoping that, if someone had been sent to intercept them from the fort, Williamson could still reach the St. Davids Road first, especially if the search party were moving slowly to check the farms and gullies. Egging on his men, Williamson pushed his already tired horse to cover the ground he needed.

Chapter Thirty-Three

The patrol from Fort George, headed by Captain Smythe, was travelling at a moderate pace, hoping to save their horses. They were only a mile from the St. Davids Road and they had seen no verifiable sign yet that Williamson and his men had been this way, or that they had not. The road up ahead was the only practical way off this road, however, other than the farms and an occasional country lane too rough for a mounted group to make rapid time. There were no guarantees, but Smythe was gambling that Williamson and his men were in too much of a hurry to take questionable detours that might turn out to be cul-de-sacs.

Smythe had once more fallen back to speak with Jeremy. He had quite grown to like the woodsman in spite of the nagging suspicion that he was still in the employ of the British, in spite of his protestations. He had come to identify with the tales told him by the man and he could quite easily imagine how he might feel if a man such as Williamson were to torture him, burn down his farm near Albany, and kill his wife. In fact, his esteem for the man grew with the simple fact that he had not gone completely mad with revenge.

Soon they passed the St. Davids Road and began the climb up the rocky, dusty trail toward Queenston, the road here almost destroyed in places by the previous year's battles for the Heights, as they were known. From up above, first the British and then the Americans, when they had captured the guns, rained death in the form of grape shot, cannon balls and fused, exploding ammunition on whichever side was below or in front at that moment in time as the fortunes of battle changed.

Local scavengers had removed all weapons, shot and anything else that could be reused over the course of the year. But the road itself, which had seen much abuse in the battle, had not been repaired. The Americans, who controlled this road for now, were afraid to expose large details of men to do so, and the British certainly were not about to fix their roads for them.

They finally crested the escarpment and took the turn toward Chippewa, just as Williamson and his men road into view, coming hard at them. The two groups spotted each other almost simultaneously and both stopped dead in their tracks, each attempting to determine what the other would do.

The impasse was broken when Smythe suddenly shouted to his men. "Let's take it to the enemy, men, if they won't bring it to us!" He commanded one of the rear men to stay back to mind the prisoners. Then, with a wave of his sabre, he led a charge down the road after Williamson's group, who finally fled in the face of the onslaught by trained soldiers.

Williamson could be seen looking back, and noticing that he was losing ground to the soldiers' horses, which had been much better handled than his. He was growing more desperate by the minute, but he thought he might have a solution as he headed into a winding stretch of the road. As they rounded a turn, obscuring them from the view of the soldiers chasing them, he instituted his plan.

Smythe's men rounded the same corner at full gallop. He had lost sight of Williamson, but there was another curve not far ahead and the others could easily have made it in time to stay out of sight. On they rode around the next two bends, kicking up dust and stones as they raced by trees of many descriptions, all melded into one blur of variegated green.

Finally, they arrived at a straight piece of road, but the only riders they saw now were Willcocks and the Canadian Volunteers as they raced toward the soldiers from the opposite direction.

Smythe reined in his horse as Willcocks did the same. "They didn't ride past you?" he asked suspiciously.

Willcocks sat high in his saddle and glared at the young officer, his hand now on his pistol. He had been in several duels, and he had no qualms about challenging this pup to one as well. "Just what are you accusing me of, Captain?" he asked with a menacing voice that approximated that of a rattlesnake if it could speak.

"Nothing", Smythe answered dejectedly. He knew of Willcocks' aspirations and his prowess with a duelling pistol too well to continue any line of accusation. "Where could they have gone? There are no other roads and the road has all been forested."

Willcocks sighed as if humouring the younger man. "You must have ridden right past him", he suggested. "Perhaps there's a lane that you missed."

Smythe did not miss the condescending tone in the other man's voice, but chose not to pursue it. If he ever wished to be more than a captain, or even if he merely wished to remain one, he had better find Williamson before he managed to vanish. The personal matters could wait for another day.

"Let's go!" he ordered, waving his sabre back in the direction from which he had come. He was beginning to feel quite the fool, and Williamson would pay dearly for it when he caught up to the vermin.

The moment that Smythe and his men had disappeared around the next corner Williamson and his men urged their horses back out of their hiding place, a narrow path that he had known of and which meandered to the edge of the Niagara gorge. The road entrance to this pathway was not easily noticed, especially by those charging by on horseback, since it was almost completely hidden by a stand of cedars. If they moved quickly, they might make the St. Davids Road before their pursuers discovered the ruse, greatly improving their chances for escaping.

Down the torn mountain road they moved as quickly as the obstacles would allow, probably yet riding their mounts too hard under the circumstances and conditions. Sam's horse, exhausted and going lame, stumbled into a hole and went down hard, throwing its rider almost over the steep embankment that fell away from the northeast side of the road. Leaving the horse lying in the road broken and in pain, Sam climbed onto the unfortunate Jake's horse, and continued on. Good thing he had possessed the foresight to take the nag along when he fled from Willcocks, he now thought, no longer cursing the hapless beast.

As they rounded the last turn in the road, the St. Davids Road was in sight. So too, however, were three men on horseback, the last of which was a uniformed American soldier. Williamson held up his right hand, drawing up his men while he studied the situation, but decided there was nothing for it. They had no choice but to take the time to remove these three men and hope for the best. Going back again would be certain suicide.

Jeremy spotted the riders coming down from Queenston Heights, at once noticing his arch foe, Williamson, in the lead. That son of the Devil obviously had not recognized him, however, as the leader of that riffraff seemed more intent upon determining the strengths of the riders before him than in determining their identities. Jeremy raised his tied hands and pulled the front of his hat brim low over his eyes, hoping to make himself less recognizable.

"Corporal", Jeremy said softly, addressing the soldier behind him. "I think you had better set us free or we'll all three die here together."

The soldier had not yet noticed the other riders as he rode along, bored and resentful that he had been left out of the hunt to keep watch over this farmer and his Indian friend. He looked up now and saw them beginning to move forward once again, still somewhat tentatively. "I can't do that", he muttered. "Do you want to get me court martialled?"

"It looks like you have a choice, Corporal", Jeremy said evenly. "A possible court martial with a safe cell, or a military funeral. You can't fight them all by yourself. Damn, sir!' he barked, seeing that he was not swaying the soldier quickly enough. "We three may not be able to fight them off. But you surely can't do it alone, and we can't outrun them with our hands tied and all the spare horses in tow."

"Perhaps I should just set the horses free then", the corporal suggested.

Jeremy's tone bit sarcastically at the young soldier. "And give them fresh mounts with which to ride and fight? Surely that will sit well with Smythe and his superiors."

The corporal looked and saw the riders had reached the bottom

A Question of Loyalty

of the Mountain, and they had obviously decided to fight for it. Muskets and pistols were pointed at them, although the soldier knew at least as well as anyone that they would be almost useless on horseback except with scatter shot from a close range. He finally stopped vacillating long enough to make a decision, hoping that he would live long enough to regret it. He pulled a knife from his belt and quickly severed the ropes binding the prisoners.

"Our kits!" Jeremy yelled, seeing they were running out of time.

The corporal handed the prisoners the weapons taken from them earlier, and the men laid the horses down across the road just south of the St. Davids Road, inadvertently blocking Williamson's escape. Jeremy could see their error too late, for they had given the enemy no options. Now the raiders were forced to attack, for even the three men waiting nervously behind the horses could hear that the first of the pursuers had reached the edge of the Mountain.

Williamson and his men yelled, shouted and whooped wildly as they started their charge. The distance from the bottom of the Mountain to the defenders' barricade was less than one hundred yards, but they attempted to get up the speed to jump the obstacles. The horses, however, balked at the idea, much too tired.

As the front horse, with Sam riding, reached the barricade, it shied and tried to turn against the reins. Sam fought the horse and tried to turn his head, and the horse stumbled, going down on its right front leg, snapping the bone. Sam flew onto the barrier he had wanted to jump, landing with his musket under him, pointing up. He reflexively held on tighter to his weapon, in order that he not lose it upon impact, and the result was a loud report.

Jeremy pushed Sam over, readying himself to attack the fallen man, but it was unnecessary. The crack they had heard was Sam's musket discharging, sending the ball directly through his chin and into his head. The remains of his jaw seemed to flop almost independently as his corpse roll to the ground.

In the few seconds this took, Josef and the corporal had opened fire on the oncoming attackers. While they had not done any obvious, mortal damage, the horses, which were already leery of taking on the mountains of horseflesh before them, stopped short. Muskets fired harmlessly into the air as their riders fought to rein in their mounts, and there was momentary confusion as horses milled about and men on both sides fought to reload their weapons.

Jeremy found he needed also to reassure their horses. Although they were well trained by the U.S. Army to perform in this manner, the guns and the panicked whinnies of the attackers' horses were making them nervous. Seeing that one of the attackers would be the first to reload, and only ten feet from them, Jeremy stepped up on the horse he was behind and launched himself into the air. The sudden movement seemed a signal to the animal, which then fought to its feet, waiting for its rider.

Jeremy fell short of his target and landed hard against the horse he had leaped at, but grasped the man's arm as he slid down, pulling his adversary over with him. The two crashed to the ground and Jeremy was the first to recover, somewhat prepared for the impact. Before the raider could get up, Jeremy had dispatched him with his tomahawk. Too late, he saw another rider aim at him, but there was nowhere to go. He heard a loud crack and was surprised to feel no pain. Instead, the man who had been aiming at him pitched from his horse, a bright stain goring rapidly across his shirt.

Now Josef needed to reload yet again. As he struggled to do so he felt, rather than saw, the corporal go down. Josef snatched up the man's musket and fired at the first man he saw, hitting him in the arm and breaking it. All three of them now had guns that were useless for the moment and, as Jeremy vaulted back over the horses to land beside him, some of Williamson's men prepared to charge the barricade on foot as they climbed down from their mounts.

Williamson ordered his men back to their horses, and all but three obeyed. They were either too deeply into the heat of the battle or temporarily deafened by the noise of battle, but they attacked the three defenders regardless of their commander's urgings. Williamson, however, had heard a report as one of the soldiers dispatched the injured horse Sam had left on the hillside.

The three men ran madly at Jeremy's position, their muskets across their chests, a natural position for running, but useless for firing. Jeremy and Josef steeled themselves for the contact they knew was coming. With a glance over at the corporal, they realized he would be of little use. The severity of his injury was unknown, but the only sign of life from him was the moan that could be heard now that the main din of battle had entered a bit of a lull.

Josef jumped up in front of the lead man just before he reached the horses, startling the horse he used as a shield. With a shout and a wave of his arms, the horse stood up, catching the attacker completely off guard. With an impact that Josef thought should have been audible, the man rebounded and, off-balance, fell hard onto the ground. The Caughnawaga leaped onto the man and quickly slit his throat before he could recover.

Jeremy waited until the two men coming toward him were almost upon him. Then, with a swipe of his tomahawk, he slashed the thigh of the first man and, bringing his pistol up with the other, discharged it into the man's gut. As the two men lay writhing on the ground, he finished them both off quickly with his tomahawk.

The two men waited, expecting more men to attack, but everything had changed in a moment. They could see now that, while they had been fighting their three attackers, Williamson had led the balance of his party toward the gorge. The American soldiers, now down from the escarpment and accompanied by a number of civilians, had reached the St. Davids Road. They were now stopped, looking in the direction Williamson had gone and planning how they could most safely attack.

One of the soldiers came over to where Josef and Jeremy were now getting the remaining horses on their feet, having to dispatch one that had been hit by a stray ball in the heat of battle. "Is everyone alright here?" he asked, realizing it would be impolitic to ask why the former prisoners were untied and armed.

"We are", answered Josef, "But the corporal's been hit. He's still alive, but we've no idea how badly he's hurt."

The soldier went over and looked at his fallen comrade, looking for the wound. He straightened up at last and, only half addressing the two civilians, muttered, "There doesn't seem to be a great deal of bleeding. Seems to be in a great deal of pain, but I think that's because the ball hit the muscle in his thigh. We'll get him to the fort with some of the Volunteers."

As the soldier rushed off to report and to get help for the injured man, he stopped only momentarily to talk to a civilian who had been heading in their direction in the company of another;

a soldier it seemed by his bearing. The man nodded and he and his companion continued on their way. That was when Jeremy recognized the first man.

"Mr. van Hijser", the man said, doffing his hat. The man who was with him looked extremely uncomfortable as he heard the name and now recognized the man his companion had addressed.

Jeremy returned the gesture, although Josef could see an angry glint in his eye. He wondered why until Jeremy added with forced courtesy, "How are you Mr. Willcocks?" His glare seemed to intensify as he recognized the second man with a slight start. "And you Lieutenant Carstairs? I would suppose that your presence here explains the delay at receiving reinforcement from the British at the Tavern."

Carstairs had stumbled upon Willcocks at his new site later that day when his attempt to return to Shipman's Corners had been interrupted by a rare American army patrol. When they'd opened fire on him, he had headed back whence he came, feeling he might not have the opportunity to provide an explanation he did not really wish to give in any event.

When the courier had arrived to great fanfare, the lieutenant had ridden along with Willcocks for the sport of hunting down Dorian Williamson. Had he entertained any inkling that he had come across someone he knew from the British end of things, he would have demurred, but now there was only one answer he could think of for this dilemma. The soldier reached for his pistol.

"Put that away", Willcocks ordered him.

"But he knows me, Willcocks", protested the lieutenant.

Willcocks eyed the man and smiled. "Aye, and if you shoot him, I fear there'll be much explaining to do, such as why you've been reporting to me instead of the military. You might even be used as a scapegoat for their incompetence at Beaverdams. Now put up your firearm, sir", he said calmly, although everyone in attendance could tell there was no calm in this man at the moment.

"I'll not be able to go back now", Carstairs said dejectedly, as he put away his firearm. He resignedly recognized the truth in what Willcocks had said. "Looks like you have a new man", he said and rode off to the battle that was shaping up behind the village.

"Well", Willcocks said, addressing Jeremy and looking about

as if nonchalantly checking the weather. "As much as I would like to take you to task for escaping from my barn, I'm afraid you've become quite the hero in the good American captain's eyes. So, I'll bid you good day and good luck." With that, one of the peninsula's most hated men, if one discounted his former man Williamson, rode off, leaving Jeremy standing on the road, speechless.

Chapter Thirty-Four

Williamson knew they would be upon him momentarily, and he cast about wildly for an escape route. The only way out that he could see was to continue toward the river, in the shadow of the Mountain and alongside the village of Queenston. Perhaps from some place there he could make his escape if he could hold his enemies off long enough to find a boat to take them across the Niagara to the American side. With a glance toward the sky, he noticed dark clouds forming on the horizon. If only the summer storm that appeared to be coming would move quickly, to interfere with the enemy's vision sufficiently to mask their escape. That had not been their brand of fortune to date, however.

Shouting orders to his men, he headed off along the narrow road that wound down the hills. That route would bring them down to the river, to the scene of last year's battle to land the Americans against the guns and troops of the British. Before they reached the very bottom of the lane, however, he dismounted and ordered his men to follow. He'd seen that the American soldiers and the Volunteers were rapidly closing the distance on them. Once that occurred, they wouldn't have the time or position they needed to mount a defence.

Unlike most of the Niagara River shore to this point, the land here slopes down to the river in cascading hills. This was used to good advantage by the British defenders as they picked off Americans as their armada of small boats crossed the Niagara the previous year. Here, almost at the shore, and but fifty feet from the roadway stood a lone house, with several outbuildings behind. Not one hundred feet back from the house was a hill that dropped off precipitously toward an area that one might otherwise call a beach and which was used to draw up the boats that, in better times, criss-crossed the river.

Williamson decided this property would suffice to attempt a stand against his attackers. He ordered several men into the house to determine if there was anyone home who might object to the use of their home as a fortress or in some other way interfere with the fighting. He and his men then took up positions at the corners of the house and behind any other item that presented a modicum of cover. They were now in reasonable position to fight this battle, hopefully not their final one. There they waited for the arrival of Willcocks and the American soldiers, all of them only the day before considered his allies.

How the world changed, Williamson thought. Well, whatever happened, at least they would get no opportunity to hang him, if he had anything to say about it. As these fatalistic thoughts ran through his head, he could see the first of the enemy and hear the cautious approach of the army amassed against him.

The first of the soldiers broke from the road through the tree line, and Willcocks' men rapidly took positions on their flanks as the mass of fighters expanded into the more open space a hundred yards from the river. At the order, they all dismounted but the captain and Willcocks, the latter apparently feeling himself Smythe's equal. The few professional soldiers formed a rank in the centre; muskets at the ready and prepared to move forward on foot in the classic battle style the American military had inherited from the British.

The Canadian Volunteers were much less disciplined, forming more of a mob to either side of the open space. Some appeared hungry for the battle, some studied the enemy carefully, hoping to find their particular weakness, and yet more seemed extremely reticent to move at all. The latter nervously eyed the dozen or so muskets sticking out from behind the house and wondered if there was a way they could manage to avoid this altogether. If only the gathering storm, which already presented a display of lightning in distance, could arrive and save them the necessity of this battle.

At Smythe's command, all but the most nervous of the Volunteers, who hung back as much as possible, began to move forward toward Williamson's redoubt. To the defenders' leader, it looked like a solid wall of human flesh moving toward them. There were only ten soldiers, but Willcocks' men numbered close to one hundred and fifty, and it mattered little to Williamson whether these men were hard drilled professionals or not.

At a hundred paces from the house, the line stopped. An order rang out from Smythe, who had now dismounted to command his men from the line. Five of the soldiers stepped out in front of the others, forming staggered ranks.

"Gentlemen, ready arms!" the command came, and the muskets went up into position. The Volunteers on either side, watching the soldiers, tried to approximate their movements, resulting in what, under other circumstances, might have seemed quite comical.

Smythe stepped forward of his men and called out. "Williamson, this is your final chance to capitulate. It would be fair to warn you that these volunteers haven't been properly drilled and therefore may not fight according to the rules of civilized warfare. Once the shooting begins, I can no longer guarantee control over all of these men", he said, moving his arm in a broad sweeping gesture, to highlight the combined force, which strained to attack, under his nominal command.

A shot rang out that reverberated across the clearing and back across the river, seemingly repeating itself to a fade as it made its way downstream. "There's your answer, Smythe!" Williamson cried out. As if on cue, his men all opened fire at once doing surprisingly little damage to the other side.

Smythe, who had raised his sabre with his right hand had not flinched in the face of the volley true to his training, now dropped his arm and shouted "Fire!" The soldiers and Volunteers let loose with a volley of their own, and the shots from the captain's men slammed into Williamson's defences. Firing from the slightly higher position was much easier than shooting upward, and two of Williamson's men dropped from sight at the initial volley. Before they could recover, the soldiers reloaded and let loose with another volley of death. In this manner, and due to the sheer numbers of the Americans and Willcocks' men, who fired at will, it seemed as though they were laying down a steady barrage. The soldiers advanced slowly after each loading, forcing Williamson and his men to keep to their cover.

As soon as the shooting began, some of Willcocks' more timid recruits could stand the tension no more. A couple of dozen men broke and ran for their horses, disappearing down the laneway from which they had come before the echoes of the first volley died down. Willcocks, still astride his horse, witnessed the cowardly action, but decided to ignore it. They were likely much better off without these men. Better they bolt now than break during a crucial moment in the battle.

The men behind the house had a few tricks of their own. Although they had not the discipline of the American regulars, Williamson had made sure that each man had brought at least two muskets. While most of his men fired, two scrambled from man to man to reload the discharged weapons, meaning that at least two weapons were firing most of the time. But they now encountered a dilemma less easily solved. They were running short of ammunition, and the men seemed incapable of making what they used truly count, although Williamson did see the occasional Volunteer and one soldier go down.

One of Williamson's men, at a nod from his leader, sneaked off and climbed stealthily up where a stand of raspberry vines covered his movements until he could make the hedgerow. Carefully, taking a wide berth around the fighting, he worked his way in behind Captain Smythe's position. There he knelt with his Kentucky Long Rifle, probably the most accurate sniper's tool of its time. Using the crotch of a small tree to steady his weapon, the man took his time drawing a bead on the American officer. Although Williamson knew that it was perhaps delusion to think so, it was fervently hoped that the death of this man would create enough confusion and destruction of morale to afford his men the opportunity to run.

The shot rang out barely noticed due to the sounds of gunfire everywhere, amplified by the echo from the gorge. The thunder that was now audible between volleys, as well as the moans and cries of the wounded and dying added an otherworldly feel to the cacophony that surrounded them all. The captain went down, but he was not mortally wounded - merely a graze to his shoulder. He had dropped down for fear of being hit again before he could take stock of his position. Smythe looked around to his left for the source of his injury, but could see no one initially, there being too many men in all manner of dress all around.

Williamson's man rapidly reloaded his rifle, with a skill and speed that would be the envy of most military men. When ready, he once again took aim through the crotch of the tree, just as Smythe noticed him. The sniper smiled, for there was nowhere for the captain to go, and it was apparent by the look on the man's face that he was well aware of it.

Smythe realized he had seen the sniper too late for the rifle was already pointed at him, ready for another shot. Being on the ground as he was, his movement was limited and a decent sniper, which this man seemed to be, could easily make allowances for mere body twists, especially at such a short distance. Smythe could imagine the sniper's finger beginning to exert a steady pressure on the trigger as he noticed the shooter, unlike most amateurs, kept both eyes open as he took aim. Staring directly at the man he knew was about to send him to his Maker, he refused to show any fear.

The sniper's eyes shot suddenly wide open and the rifle discharged harmlessly into the air as the man slid slowly down the tree trunk, causing the barrel to point upward. Smythe looked all around to see if anyone near him had made such a miraculous shot, since he had seen only muskets on this flank of the fighting. No answer presented itself here.

When he looked back, a familiar figure had arisen behind the sniper. Walking easily but purposefully toward the downed man was the Caughnawaga who travelled with Jeremy van Hijser. Josef leaned slightly over the body and, putting one foot against his back, jerked free a tomahawk. He wiped the blood on the man's shirt and looked up at Smythe. With a slight nod and a wink toward the captain, he vanished once again into the trees.

If he was still here, chances are that van Hijser was too, Smythe thought. He would have wagered that the two would have used the opportunity to escape. However, it appeared that the hatred the farmer had for Williamson was much more intense than the captain had anticipated. And lucky it was for Smythe. But where was Jeremy, then?

Chapter Thirty-Five

Jeremy had worked his way around the fighting on the other flank and was lying on a rocky outcropping that jutted out over the gorge, possibly the Brock's redan that he had heard so much about, approximately ten feet above and to the back of his enemy's position. Because of his position and the elevation, Williamson's men would have a great deal of difficulty spotting him here, but he had an excellent sight line along the edge. Nobody else had discovered this position, probably for no other reason than the military propensity for fighting battles head-on.

He sighted down the German-made rifle barrel of his over/under, drawing a bead on the man nearest him, at the southeastern corner of the house. Squeezing slowly so as not to jerk the rifle upon firing, he sent a charge from the rifled barrel arcing slightly to the air. Without a noticeable sound, the target's head bounce forward and to the right, splattering blood onto the stone that made up the lower wall of the shelter. With a momentary hesitation, the body slumped and then fell backward onto the ground.

Jeremy reloaded the rifle carefully, trying to make sure that his movement would not give away his position to anyone who looked in this direction. There were now only a handful of Williamson's men left, but they seemed determined not to face the military noose in front of their former friends and neighbours. Still reloading and firing, reloading and firing, they fought like cornered rats, which in essence they were.

Once again he picked out the nearest target in the line and

bore down on the trigger with measured pressure. In one of those unexplainable occurrences, something attracted the man's attention and he turned to look directly toward Jeremy, although apparently without seeing him. The man nearest him asked him what the problem was, and the target answered, obviously not impressing his companion. The second man returned to the pressing problems at hand with a shrug. Then Jeremy's target appeared to give up as well, but turned back once more just as Jeremy pulled the trigger.

It was apparent that the man saw the smoke from the discharge for, immediately before the shot removed his lower jaw, he shouted something to his companion. The other turned around, obviously annoyed, to berate him for the constant distractions, just in time to see his comrade-in-arms fall toward him. He pushed away in a reflex reaction to the grisly sight that met his eyes, and Jeremy's victim flopped down with his head pointed directly toward his comrade.

The second man now raised the alarm. Williamson, at the opposite corner, ordered his flagging troops to keep firing ahead, and stepped over to see what the man was pointing at. He could see nothing except for a vestige of gun smoke drifting languidly away on the air currents, but he knew that something was there.

Jeremy backed off the outcropping, feeling much too exposed now that the enemy knew he was there. He lowered himself to the ground on the other side just as several musket balls bounced from rocks around the position he had occupied moments before. There had been little chance that the men below could see to shoot him directly, but ricocheted musket balls were no laughing matter. In fact, as he backed away, a shard from a chipped piece of rock glanced off his arm, drawing blood.

Williamson could see that there was little hope that they could survive this fight to commandeer a boat. The end was near. They had little ammunition left them, and too few men to use it even if they had more. They had caused more losses than they had taken, but their foes were simply too numerous, with an apparently endless supply of cartridges.

To make matters all the worse, the rain was beginning to fall softly now, in large, cold drops, while flashes of lightning were beginning to provide noticeable levels of light in the darkness brought on by the storm. The rain was not hard enough to screen them from the enemy, but it was making the ground slippery and some of the men had already almost lost their footing while trying to move around in the process of reloading.

As these thoughts swirled madly and confusingly through Williamson's mind, providing him with plenty of problems that had no solutions, he noticed a commotion on his far right side. Someone had just jumped from behind one of the outbuildings and grasped hold the arm of one of his men, swinging him unceremoniously until suddenly he released the man. Williamson's man struggled to balance himself, and almost had managed to do so when he was felled with a single blow of a tomahawk. Now he was reaching into his shirt, for what Williamson could only assume was a pistol.

Josef disappeared around the back of the outbuilding, to reappear from the other side. He stepped out directly in front of two of Williamson's men who seemed to be retreating for the embankment, perhaps hoping to make good their escape by swimming the river. Before anyone could react, the Indian drew one of the men to him and held him, face out, as a shield just as the other fired his musket at the invader. The captive's entire body jerked like a marionette as his body absorbed the scattershot. Josef raised his pistol almost nonchalantly, aiming it directly at the shooter's chest, just as the latter threw his musket and launched himself at the Caughnawaga. The pistol's proximity to the building seemed to make it roar as it went off, and the airborne man seemed to stop in mid-flight as Josef flung the dead weight of the bullet-riddled body away from him. The attacking man seemed to regain his feet for a split second, and then dropped from the embankment to the landing below.

Josef was now unprotected with his pistol discharged as he stood face to face with Dorian Williamson, who held his musket at waist level, aimed at Josef's mid-section. The Caughnawaga pretended to lunge for Williamson's gun and then quickly sidestepped as the musket spewed out its deadly load. Josef fought to find purchase on the slippery, rain-soaked mud and rock for a moment and then made for Williamson for real, just as the American soldiers, along with the Canadian Volunteers, decided to charge the position with what sounded like one long yell.

Williamson pushed Josef away and, before his attacker could regain his forward momentum, ran along the back of the property toward the north. He had an escape route that he had picked out during the fighting, and he pushed one of his own men off his feet in his own bid to get through. After running along for approximately twenty-five feet, he leaped down the embankment, landing on a bit of a ledge in the mud and slipped to another, four feet below, but thankfully staying close to the hillside to maintain his natural cover from the enemy's gunfire. He slid often as he ran, and each time his arms windmilled wildly in the rain as he tried to maintain his balance. More than once he slipped and fell into the mixed media of the ground underfoot, often managing to stay erect only by grasping onto some cedar root or some weed growing precariously from the hillside.

He continued to run along this narrowing ledge, for someone had noticed his escape and some musket balls had begun to fly in his direction, but he had safely reached a point where the level above him rose slightly, removing him from sight before any gunman could find his range. On he ran, fighting for footholds and handholds in the increasingly uncertain terrain as he approached the river's edge, as the ground he ran upon disappeared, the steep embankment seeming to close in on the water

At the outset, he had been shielded against shots from above by the fortunate tendency of the layers of hard and soft rock in the gorge to wear away underneath first and then give way above. This created an overhang in many places, but it probably did not really matter, he thought. No one seemed to be following him now, all the zigzagging along the shoreline and through the trees and the occasional house having apparently done its job, for there was no sign of anyone pursuing him now.

Now the main body of the storm struck the Niagara, and Williamson took cover for a few minutes as hail pelted him from above. Following the ice particles, the real rains came, driven by the gale-force winds that accompanied the storm. Williamson felt that some measure of luck was finally with him, for he was to the lee of the gale, sheltered from the direct blasts. In addition, anyone following him from above would have an extremely difficult time trying to find him now.

He began to edge along the narrow strip of land now left to him, hugging closely to the side of the hill, and he was startled as a wailing man bounced beside him. With a rapid, fluid motion, he dispatched the man with a slice of his knife, before the hapless victim could recover from his slip. Soldier or Volunteer, he couldn't tell because the downpour obscured most vision, but the man was screaming no more. Williamson looked up, aware that someone had been following him after all, but he could see nothing, rain filling his eyes while his fingers grasped the sodden hillside to steady himself. Likely, the man had already been chasing him when the worst of the storm hit.

Jeremy saw how Williamson had escaped as the soldiers and Volunteers overran the property that the raiders had been occupying. He circled back toward the road around the few houses of the village of Queenston, looking for the smuggler's trail that he knew led to the river north of the village. The veteran trader and hunter knew that Williamson would reach the point where this trail reached the river's edge, because there would be no place else for him to go. And that would the spot be where Jeremy would be waiting for him.

As he reached the almost secret top of the path, he was suddenly confronted by someone who seemed to fairly materialize from the heavy downpour. There was a pistol in the man's hand and it was pointed directly at Jeremy's breast.

"Perhaps I won't need to stay with that madman Willcocks after all", a voice shouted into the wind, and his face slowly took on form, with a discernable smile upon it.

"Well, Second Lieutenant Carstairs", Jeremy shouted back, trying to sound confident while screaming through the thunderstorm. "I guess I should have shot you when you were standing before me, and Willcocks be damned."

Carstairs glared and removed the pistol from Jeremy's waist, and then explained, "Willcocks was afraid of the questions if I were to kill you. But that's no longer a concern, is it?" he asked archly. "You were shot in the heat of battle and who would question that?"

Jeremy knew that there was no fault to the man's logic, and he was extremely limited in the avenues open to him in this situation. Perhaps this was his time, then. He raised his arms suddenly as though to beg for mercy. Then, with the accompaniment of a loud crash of thunder, Carstairs seemed to go weak in the knees and fell face first in the mud.

Jeremy looked down at the man who lay at his feet. "Now I guess I won't have anything to explain either, traitor," he shouted to the lifeless ears. He looked at his left hand, which had pulled the ornate handgun he'd previously taken from the man named Seth, who had tried to kill him when he was living on the Mountain's edge. The gun was not smoking at all, not in this downpour. "Let's say that was for Robert."

Turning his attention rapidly back to Williamson, Jeremy climbed down the steep but negotiable path that wound almost secretly down to the Niagara River. Most of the locals knew of this place, but he guessed that few Americans or even non-local Canadian farmers did. It took him but fifteen minutes to reach the water's edge, slipping often, and here he took up his post, covered in mud and soaked to the bone, to watch for his mortal enemy. He had every expectation that the bastard would be forced to climb directly into Jeremy's arms.

He pulled up his collar tight once again, and pushed up his hat brim, which was beginning to droop from the weight of all the water pressing down upon it. He couldn't see more than a few feet in this downpour, making him wonder if Williamson might have passed him already, without either of them knowing.

The waiting was excruciating and Jeremy lost all sense of time, particularly in this storm, where the day had surrendered its essence to the black clouds that blotted out all hints of the sun's existence. The only break from the grey sameness of the driving rain, that confused all sense of direction after a time, was the occasional lightning, multiple flashes that appeared as a flickering sheet and ended with an orchestral roll of thunder that seemed large enough to echo in the open sky. The wind tore at Jeremy, driving the rain into his clothing as if it was not there and threatening to whip his sodden hat into the mighty Niagara.

Chapter Thirty-Six

After what seemed like an eternity, Jeremy thought he could see a shapeless grey apparition, wavering in the curtain of rain like some foul-weather phantom. As he waited further, the apparition gradually took on the form of a man. And indeed it was a man, stumbling over the last of the rocks along the steep shore of the river. That same river, navigable at most times, appeared to have changed from a moderately flowing stream into a raging torrent, seemingly in answer to the currents of the storm and the hatreds that fuelled the battles of this insane war. And Jeremy waited, the anger that awaited release upon the man he expected to see adding to the cosmic fury that seemed to control the recent events in his world.

Williamson stopped cold, as he felt rather than saw the presence of another being. Squinting into the driving rain, the water streaming down and across his face, he slowly began to recognize the form before him. It was that bastard van Hijser again. He seemed to be just about everywhere there was trouble for Williamson – a constant albatross about his neck.

Both men pulled their pistols and aimed at each other's heads, mere feet away. "I believe we have an impossible situation here, Mr. van Hijser", Williamson shouted into the noise of the storm.

"On the contrary, Mr. Williamson", Jeremy replied loudly. "I believe all things are possible and it seems quite possible that you'll surrender rather than die anonymously here by the side of the Niagara River, but I rather hope that's not the case."

Williamson laughed, barely audible above the rain. "You seem not to have noticed", he pointed out. "We both seem to be in the same position of strength, or weakness, however you may choose to look at it."

Jeremy futilely wiped the rain from his face as he might do with annoying perspiration. "Perhaps this shall all come down to who has the best luck, Mr. Williamson. If you'll not surrender to me, then I suggest we shall be forced to pull our triggers and see which of us, if either, is still standing in the aftermath."

Williamson allowed himself a smile that he knew the younger man could not see in any event. "So be it, sir. On the count of three, then. One…two…three!"

Both men pulled the trigger at essentially the same time, in a war of nerves that any sane man would say could produce no winners. They each winced as they imagined, rather than heard, the hammers strike, igniting the powder and driving the ball on its way to its destiny.

But nothing happened. The awaited reports of the pistols simply did not occur, neither one. Apparently the powder in both pans was too wet to ignite, and both balls remained snug in their wadding in their respective barrels.

Jeremy moved first. With a scream that sent a shiver up Williamson's spine, the young man pulled his tomahawk and launched himself toward his enemy, at the same time releasing all the pent-up anger and the tension of the previous several months. Williamson stepped aside and grasped Jeremy's tomahawk arm, pulling his long, razor-sharp hunting knife at the same time. Before he had an opportunity to plunge it into the woodsman's flesh, however, Jeremy spun about, breaking the ex-politician's grip on his arm and repositioning himself.

The two men faced each other again now in the rain, which was finally beginning to taper off. The rolls of thunder seemed to be gaining distance as their still-frequent rumbles moved on to other counties and the world was now reappearing from the dull grey draperies that had obscured it. They could now hear each other moving about as they circled, each man looking for a moment of weakness in the other so he could strike, if not a decisive blow, at least a damaging one. But no such opening seemed to present itself.

That is, until Jeremy slipped on a rain-slicked rock and nearly lost his balance. Williamson, the veteran street fighter, saw his opportunity and moved into the opening created by the stumble and slashed at Jeremy, hoping to inflict a damaging wound upon his opponent. But he slipped as well, and Jeremy once again twisted and squirmed out of the way, the knife catching only the edge of his shirt and opening an eight-inch slice in the fabric. Jeremy seemingly danced away as he regained his balance. Now the two were locked in a standoff once again.

Of the two, Jeremy was the much more impatient fighter, and he moved in without a clear opening. Williamson parried the tomahawk easily, knocking it from Jeremy's hand, sending it skittering across the rocks to the hill's base. Jeremy was forced to take hold of the older man's wrist to keep him from turning the knife to deadly effect. After a brief struggle, he managed to use the other's fatigue from climbing across to this point to his advantage, forcing the man's arm down hard upon his knee. The knife dropped from the bandit's hand and Jeremy, still wrestling with Williamson, managed to kick the wicked blade into the Niagara's current.

Now disarmed, Williamson made a bid to escape, spying the route that he knew Jeremy had taken to beat him down here to this point. Jeremy followed close behind and grabbed the man's shoulders with both hands, turning him around to face him. Without warning the brawler lashed out with both fists, doubling Jeremy over in pain as all the wind left him. Williamson followed the move with a hard knee to the younger man's face, sending him sprawling on the rain-soaked rock and gravel, his nose bleeding heavily.

Now Williamson moved in to finish what he had started. This young pup had been a source of nothing but grief to him at every turn, it now seemed to him. He was convinced that his lot would have been much better if this poor excuse for a British spy hadn't ruined his life, apportioning no blame for himself, of course.

Williamson hoisted a head-sized rock over his head and approached the helpless man lying in wait for the end to finally come. "You must have known all along that it would end with a loss on your part", Williamson growled. "You youngsters never seem to learn the value of the experience that comes with age. And you simply can't win against a more experienced man."

Williamson had moved in range of Jeremy's feet and, seeing his opportunity through a haze of pain, he hooked one foot around the big man's right ankle and kicked at the knee with his other. Jeremy could hear a satisfying cracking sound as the tendons could not hold against the combination of leverage and force, leaving the kneecap unprotected, breaking it.

The large man howled in pain and dropped the rock, which managed to strike Jeremy's left forearm. He could feel one of the two bones break and his eyes saw red once again as pain washed over him for the third time during that fight. He rolled over, holding his arm in pain and sucking air into his body through clenched teeth, momentarily forgetting all about Williamson. There was little to worry about in that respect, however. Although the older man could withstand the pain better, he was not able to marshal the energy for another attack. He tried in vain to stand, or even hobble to where Jeremy lay, but each time he collapsed in excruciating pain as his knee reminded him of the injury.

Jeremy managed to pull himself together and fought to his feet, still holding on to the damaged left arm. He took a deep breath and, with the hatred still burning as hot within him as the fires of Hell itself, he took two steps and aimed a devastating kick at Williamson's head just as he raised it to look up at him. The kick caught him in the throat instead, and he rolled over, coming to rest close to the water, choking and wheezing, attempting in vain to draw a full breathe through the damaged cartilage.

Jeremy stood over him now, a strange feeling of satisfaction overcoming him. He had never felt happy about killing a man before, but his conscience troubled him not a whit on this occasion. However, it was not his conscience that would stop him from inflicting further damage upon his enemy, as another thought sprang into his head.

"I think I'll stop now", he breathed, having hardly enough wind himself to speak any louder. "Turn you over to the Americans and they finish the job on your windpipe with a noose. It's certainly more than you deserve."

A Question of Loyalty

Jeremy turned around and began to pick up his weapons. Hearing voices on the smuggler's path, he shouted out, "Down here! I have Williamson here!" Sitting down to wait, he began to swab out his pistol and loaded it now that the rain had stopped completely, just to be prepared. He put fresh powder in the pan and looked over at Williamson again, who was still unable to get up, still struggling to breathe through his crushed windpipe.

He began to think of all the things this animal had done to his friends, and to him. The anger began to rise once more. He tried to convince himself that justice would be served once Williamson was hanged by the Americans. But it was a long way from this riverbank to the gallows, and many things could happen before the noose might be dropped over his head. He might be freed by comrades, the Americans might show leniency, or he might escape. The thought festered at his soul until he could stand it no more.

Slowly he stood and sauntered, as though casually, to where Williamson lay.

"You know...I'll...never see...the...noose", Williamson wheezed brokenly.

Jeremy nodded. "That's what I'm afraid of", he said evenly, as he sat down upon his haunches and levelled the pistol at Williamson's head. The man's eyes went wide as he realized what was going through Jeremy's mind.

"That's exactly what I'm afraid of", Jeremy repeated, and pulled the trigger.

The report echoed from the walls of the gorge and Jeremy listened with satisfaction as it repeated itself over and over, until it had carried itself off toward Newark to report the news. Williamson was dead at last.

Jeremy stood, an uncertain smile on his lips, as a kind of sadness washed over him at the same time. He knew there was little that could be considered fair play about the way this man's life had ended, but there was nothing for it. He could not risk the chance that this creature might live to torment yet others in the future. It may not have been sporting, as the British upper crust might say, but it was justice in his mind.

There was but one thing left to do. He set the pistol down on the ground and placed his good hand under the hip of the shell that had housed Dorian Williamson. With a concerted effort and a loud grunt, the body rolled over. A second try produced the desired result, and the corpse splashed into the Niagara River. It stayed near shore for a moment, and then washed downstream in the current, picking up speed as it went.

"Good-bye, Dorian."

Jeremy stood and watched as the body of his most hated enemy vanished around the bend of the river, headed for Lake Ontario. As he turned toward the path, he noticed that Captain Smythe had been the first of a group of men to reach the bottom, and he stood at the foot of the trail, the wound on his arm covered with a crude bandage. There was an intense and unreadable look in his eyes, making Jeremy wonder how long the captain was standing there, and how much he had seen.

Smythe cleared his throat as if to speak but at that moment, Willcocks and two of Smythe's surviving soldiers appeared at his elbows, the civilian out of breath and complaining about the climb down. Smythe turned to look at them and then back at Jeremy but said nothing. The young man could see that the American officer had witnessed more than he wished to mention before these others.

"Where's Williamson?" Willcocks demanded between gulps of air, obviously not accustomed to such physical exertion.

"In the water", Jeremy replied softly. He glanced off again in the direction the body had floated. "And he'll not be back again."

Smythe broke in before any more questions could be asked. "I'm afraid Mr. van Hijser was forced to dispatch him", he said in a voice that brooked no further explanation. "I suggest that we make back for the top and have the gentleman's arm seen to." The officer pointed to Jeremy's arm, which had swollen quite noticeably.

As Jeremy and the American soldiers set off to climb back up the smuggler's path however, Willcocks decided to stay. "I believe I'll stay here a moment", he said without further embellishment, although he clearly did not relish the exertion required for the return so soon.

Smythe nodded. "You wish to say your farewells to a former comrade?" he suggested, offering Willcocks an explanation.

Willcocks grinned wryly. "Something like that", he replied, fully aware that these men knew the truth. But what did he care? He was easily the wealthiest of them all and had his age as an excuse. He sat down on a large rock and sat staring at the Niagara's waters.

The Aftermath

When Jeremy and the rest reached the top of the gorge once more, Smythe ordered the broken arm seen to by his men. He sat and watched as they forcefully straightened his arm, setting the tears streaming down the civilian's face but eliciting no cries of pain, just the occasional groan. They then tied splints fashioned from slats the men had commandeered from the local residents to Jeremy's arm and pronounced him ready to travel. Smythe rather doubted the diagnosis, noting Jeremy's pallid features, but said not a word when the man rose to go, wavering and then righting himself to stand before him.

One of Smythe's men stepped forward and addressed him. "Sir, we've found a body just here."

Smythe accompanied his men to where Second Lieutenant Carstairs' body lay face down in the mud and water, half hidden by tall weeds and grasses. "Does anyone have an idea of who this unfortunate soul might be?" asked Smythe, looking directly at Jeremy.

He walked half way around the body as his men turned it over. "Why, isn't this the man that was riding with Willcocks when we arrived?"

"It's hard to say, sir, considering the condition of his face", replied the soldier who had rolled the corpse. "But, if I had my guess, I'd say you were right."

Smythe, never having averted his gaze from Jeremy, developed a quizzical expression. "Now how do you suppose he ended up here, dead?" The question seemed to be directed at the farmer and trapper, as if he expected that Jeremy would have the answer.

Jeremy averted his gaze slightly, finding it oddly difficult to lie to this man, but he could not openly tell him the truth. "I guess he ran into the wrong person", he replied finally, deciding that this was obviously the truth, though not nearly all of it.

Smythe decided to let the matter lie. There was more to this than the Canadian wished to tell, but he had had enough of this and decided it likely was not worth the trouble of pursuing. "Perhaps, some day after this accursed war has ended, we'll run into each other and you can tell me the rest", he sighed, his men now busy searching the body for the identification that Jeremy was certain they would not find. "I'm sure it'll be entertaining if nothing else."

"What of me then, sir?" Jeremy asked, looking the officer directly in the eyes. "Am I to remain your prisoner? And what happened to my Indian friend?"

Smythe smiled. "Your Indian friend vanished in the heat of battle", he said with what Jeremy would swear was a subtle wink. "As for you, Mr. van Hijser – Jeremy – I believe you are a prisoner of war and, as a militiaman, entitled to be paroled for the duration of this war."

Jeremy grinned tiredly, his bloodshot eyes holding the trace of a twinkle. "Or you could just let me go", he suggested. "And what of the charge of espionage?" He knew he should not resurrect that thought, but wanted to know if the charge would follow after him throughout the conflict, leaving him in constant jeopardy.

Smythe almost laughed at the temerity of this man. But he explained with as straight a face as he could muster. "I could hardly charge you with espionage, sir. The man who accused you, and the only witness, is no more." He leaned in slightly toward Jeremy. "As to the suggestion that I just release you, let me say that your word given in a parole would give me a reasonable guarantee that I wouldn't be meeting you on the battlefield as my adversary. I'm quite certain that I shouldn't enjoy that prospect at all." The last was said with a sincere tone that conveyed respect.

"Well, then, a parole it will be", Jeremy agreed. " Have you articles of parole at hand? Besides, perhaps I can persuade your General Dearborn to trade me for Cyrenius Chapin", he joked.

"No, sir, they would be at the fort, and I must be off in another direction for the time being", Smythe replied. "I feel certain that you are a man of your word and that a gentleman's handshake would be your bond. But as for your trade suggestion, I shouldn't lay any great expectation upon that", he added with a smile. "Chapin escaped while being transported to Kingston and is once more at home in Buffalo."

The news struck Jeremy hard, but he shook it off. As he and Smythe clasped hands and the officer leaned forward slightly more yet and, in a voice that he was sure no one would hear, said, "By the way, Jeremy, I would have done the same."

Jeremy asked for no clarification. They both knew well of what Smythe spoke, and the woodsman just smiled tiredly and gave the officer's hand a slightly tighter squeeze. When they stepped apart, there was a new mutual respect between them.

"I think, then, that I shall be on my way", Jeremy said awkwardly slinging his belongings over his shoulder with his one good arm. "I don't believe I'll be wanting to do any more fighting for some time", he added, indicating his broken forearm. "Besides, this war business is best left to the professionals. It leaves rather a bad taste in the mouth for us civilians, and there are times that it's not so easy to tell who should be the enemy."

Without another word, he headed off down the road, too tired to avoid the rain puddles in the muddy passage, but determined to reach home, such as it was, before nightfall. He passed through the almost silent, exhausted ranks of Canadian Volunteers, sprawled haphazardly in various positions along both sides of the roadway, and turned right on the St. Davids Road. In the village of St. Davids, he was fed by an elderly woman who recognized him as the young man who had twice brought her venison in winter, when the snows were too deep for her to venture out for food.

As Jeremy was about to climb the escarpment by way of the Mountain Road, he had the unsettling feeling that he was being followed. He glanced about several times and could see nothing, but the feeling would not leave him. With a quiet, quick step to the right, Jeremy disappeared into the trees, there to wait until he could

A Question of Loyalty

satisfy his senses, one way or the other. He watched and listened carefully, but could see nothing but the road and the vegetation and long afternoon shadows they cast upon the road. Nor was there any untoward sound, just the soft rustling of the leaves in the breeze and the occasional creak of one branch rubbing against another to some tree's sway.

Deciding he had grown paranoid, he stepped back out onto the road, still looking back down the hill, still not completely satisfied that he was alone. Jeremy decided, however, that he could not walk backward the balance of the way, and the day was fading, so he turned around to continue his journey.

And nearly jumped out of his skin! Standing there before him, not three feet away, stood Josef, a huge grin on his face.

"What's the matter with you?!" Jeremy shouted, embarrassed to be caught in such a manner. "Why are you sneaking about like that?"

Josef did not reply, continuing to stand there, his musket hanging by its strap over his shoulder and his arms crossed in front of him. Then, he burst out in full, body-shaking laughter at his friend's mortification.

"I didn't think you'd ever notice you were being followed", he gasped, to Jeremy's even greater discomfort. "I've been following since you turned onto the St. Davids Road and you just now realized that something wasn't right."

Jeremy softened in the face of Josef's good-natured ribbing and swallowed his pride. "Why didn't you just walk along with me?" he asked. "I could have used the company. And someone to carry my gear", he grinned.

"That was one good reason", Josef replied. "That's all you white men think we Indians are good for; fighting and labour." He managed a mock pout for all of two seconds before breaking out laughing once again. Then he turned serious. "Besides, I had to make sure I was well away from the others before I showed myself. I'd been caught for a few minutes, but then Captain Smythe managed to lose me in the heat of battle, as I'm sure he must have told you."

"Why didn't he just parole you?" Jeremy asked, but realized the answer almost as soon as the words left his mouth. "I see", he said slowly, almost hesitating to say it. "Smythe realized the Americans among the men would never let an Indian go."

Josef just nodded, not wishing to enter into a discussion concerning white men's treatment of his people. He jokingly turned the subject back to Jeremy's lack of tracking prowess, letting him sneak up like that.

"How do you manage to shoot any deer?" he laughed. "If I wasn't with you the past while, you wouldn't have been able to find them."

The good-natured joking between friends continued all the way back to Jeremy's land near Beaverdams. Without building a fire, finding the wood too wet to bother, or eating, as they would need to hunt, the exhausted warriors fell deeply asleep as soon as their bodies sank into the semi-comfortable, dried-out cedar boughs. Jeremy did not awaken even when he rolled onto his broken arm, only groaned and turned back to his original position.

The morning found the two with more energy, although Jeremy wasn't in much shape to hunt. Josef managed to kill one of his friend's old chickens, which still occasionally returned to the spot where their coops had been; the few that survived the foxes and other local predators. They built a small fire and ate breakfast before settling back to talk about the future.

"I think I'll give up this property", Jeremy sighed. "There's really nothing left here, and maybe my neighbour will buy it from me for whatever he can manage."

"Then what will you do?" Josef asked. "Live in the woods like an Indian?" He grinned broadly at his friend to nettle him although, in Josef's mind, the idea wasn't that ridiculous. Jeremy certainly had the skills and most of the knowledge necessary to do so. But he did not really think that was what Jeremy had in mind, and he was right.

Jeremy looked off into the sky, which was mostly clear and blue this morning, decorated only occasionally lazily floating wisps of pure white clouds high in the atmosphere. "I think I'll see if I can buy Elizabeth's property near the Twenty", he said wistfully. "If it hasn't already been taken by someone else." He looked over at his companion. "And what about you? Are you required to stay with

Ducharme and the others? If not, you're welcome to come and live with me."

"I owe Ducharme nothing", Josef replied. "As for your offer to come with you, no thanks. I don't mean to seem ungrateful, but I just can't see myself as a white farmer. Besides", he answered, with a grin. "I think my wife and son would like me to come back and be an Indian with them."

Jeremy, surprised by this latest revelation, stared at his friend with an open mouth. "You didn't think Indians had families?" Josef jested. "How do you think there get to be more Indians?"

Jeremy smiled and clapped Josef on the shoulder. "Well, friend, if you don't mind, I'd like you to stay with me for a little while until things are settled. Then you can carry my belongings to my new home." He watched Josef's face as the Caughnawaga absorbed the last remark. "Just having you on", he said, before his friend could strike his broken arm.

For the next month, Jeremy and Josef travelled between Beaverdams and the Twenty. His neighbour could pay him little for the old van Hijser farm. The war was sapping all reserves of everything these days, and it was all a farmer could do to pay for staples after the Army confiscated a large part of their crops to feed the soldiers, paying for the produce in military chits that had practically no use or value.

But, it turned out not to matter. There was also no market for Elizabeth's property, which was of marginal value for farming at best. The locals told Jeremy they had been keeping it for him, since he was practically married to Elizabeth – did Jeremy detect a hint of judgment there? – and he was therefore entitled to it, since there were no heirs. Whatever the reason, Jeremy was happy to have a roof over his head once more, even if it did need some mending, and he and Josef moved his few remaining possessions to the new home.

He finally said his good-byes to his Caughnawaga friend, without a doubt the best friend he had ever had, late in the month of August, as the summer began to fade. It was a quick farewell when the time came, neither man prone to open displays of soft emotion. But the affection was obvious to both as Josef shouldered his small sack of food and his musket and headed off down the road on the beginning of his long trek back to Montreal before winter approached.

Jeremy stood at the roadway and waved one last time, then turned around and looked at his new home. It was to have been shared with the woman who had owned it, but he would have to share it with her ghost instead.

He sighed heavily and headed in to start his new life.